A
PLOT MOST
PERILOUS

BOOKS BY GENEVIEVE ESSIG

THE CASSIE GWYNNE MYSTERY SERIES
A Deception Most Deadly

To all the brilliant theater teachers, dance instructors, vocal coaches, conductors, directors, stage managers, technical directors, property masters, chorus leaders, orchestral musicians, choreographers, supernumerary captains, dramaturgs, costumers, theater administrators, opera singers, and musical theater actors I've had the pleasure and honor of working with over the years... with my apologies.

1

DECEMBER 1883. FERNANDINA – AMELIA ISLAND, FLORIDA

It was a fine winter day on the island, sunny without heat, crisp without a chill, the kind made for an elegant carriage ride on the beach or a quiet stroll along the saltmarsh, bathed in dapples of sunlight filtering through the trees. But Cassie Gwynne, who had her skirts hiked like a showgirl to keep up with a henlike woman clearing a path down Centre Street with a frantic flapping of her arms, was otherwise engaged.

Cassie pressed a hand to her bonnet and glanced behind her. Her Aunt Flora—trailed by neighborhood children Metta and Paddy and an assortment of Flora's pets, all plagued by the generalized panic they had mustered for whatever undefined catastrophe awaited—wasn't faring much better. She was dashing about the carriage traffic trying to corral Danger, her three-legged mastiff, and Luna, a puppy whose moplike locks prevented her from running in a straight line, as Metta repeatedly stumbled into Paddy, causing him to step on Flora's flowing indigo-tinted robes. At least Esy the kitten had caught a ride on Metta's shoulders, though she'd had to wrap all four paws in the girl's bouncy mass of sausage curls to stay on.

"Oh, my, oh, dear. Lady Disaster is upon us!" Their

distraught leader, Charlotte Porter, clapped her hands to her cheeks and shook her head in despair, all while somehow maintaining her inexplicable pace.

"Lottie, my sweet friend—" Flora whistled to Luna, and the puppy somersaulted over a carriage horse's foot back toward her. "Won't you tell us what exactly it is that's happened? I've left my store unattended, and I have three perfume stills boiling."

"And I'm hungry!" said Paddy.

Metta tripped again but caught herself with the wheel of a parked donkey cart. "And these shoes are making me fall down!"

Paddy giggled, his bright eyes crinkling under his large, palmetto-weave boater. "All shoes make you fall down, Metta."

Cassie dodged a merchant carrying a tray of Cuban cigars, then a fruit vendor with a box of oranges, only to bounce off the bustle of an elaborately frocked woman who had bent to examine some coquina souvenirs. She could do with a visit to the privy herself, but this level of agitation in the adamantly amiable Miss Porter was worrying.

"One of the actresses, from the theatrical troupe boarding with me, she—" Overcome, Miss Porter loosed a wail and careened onto the wooden sidewalk, where she startled a goat into a flock of nuns and unleashed an accusatory barrage of sign-of-the-crosses.

Cassie wiped her forehead with her dress sleeve and ducked under the branch of a red-bloomed bottlebrush tree. She should also be working on preparations for her return to New York. When she had come to the island the month before to meet her Aunt Flora, having only learned of her after finding a cache of old letters earlier that summer, she hadn't been sure how long she would stay. But she'd been here a while now, and her late father's law partner, Mr. Renault, had written asking her to come back to address an issue with her father's estate.

The problem was, she didn't want to go back. Both because of what was here and what wasn't there.

She swallowed, waging a practiced battle against the sadness and longing that still clawed up her throat whenever she thought of her father. It had nearly been a year and a half since she lost him, but she was beginning to think time's ability to heal might be overstated.

Finally, they slowed in front of the Lyceum, a handsome community building that at various times served as ballroom, lecture hall, courthouse, or even roller skating rink. There weren't any advertisements pasted up yet, but Cassie understood it was presently configured as a theater to host a traveling theatrical troupe's production of *The Pirates of Penzance*, a wildly successful British comic opera that had premiered in New York a few years before.

A voice called out from across the street. "Lottie! I got your note. What in the bat-blinking blazes is the matter?" Miss Porter's best friend, Alice Keene, a flagpole-figured woman whose typical ensemble consisted of trousers and a vest accessorized with a sea captain's vocabulary and a nonsense-intolerant attitude, was jogging toward them. "It'd better be good. I have a delivery of live—" She glanced at Flora. "I have a regular package arriving at my store any blessed minute."

"It's Mary Rutledge!" Miss Porter cried as she flailed up the Lyceum's shelled footpath. She slapped her way through a stand of banana trees bending over the door. "Her mind has utterly departed, and I'm worried she'll kill herself! And take us all with her!"

Scurrying like chicks after their mother, the group tumbled into the darkened hall, where, beyond a small reception area equipped with a peanut roaster and ticket desk, a sea of chairs flowed toward a brightly lit stage.

Cassie squinted upward as her eyes adjusted to the gaslights. *Is there a—*

"What in coconut-clapping Creation is that loon doing up there?" Mrs. Keene finished the thought on behalf of everyone.

Mere inches from the grid above the stage, from which lighting elements and scenery swung on a network of ropes and pulleys, a matronly woman dressed as an eighteenth-century nursemaid was clinging to the mast of a pirate schooner. The schooner was only a set piece, of course, largely assembled from sheets of painted wood and finished with select materials such as fabric for the sail and real rope rigging, but it rose nearly fifteen feet, and the detail on it, from the brass portholes to the sinister Jolly Roger at the bow, was highly convincing. On either side of the schooner, a variety of other props and set pieces—powder kegs, wooden treasure chests, tables strewn with fake booty—had been arranged to represent a pirates' camp on a rocky shore.

The woman hanging from the mast, whose nursemaid ensemble was incongruently topped by a black bandanna stitched with a skull and crossbones, brandished her cutlass at the group huddled below her in various states of costume dress and undress. "I'll do it. I swear it, I will!"

"Come down from there, Mary, you're holding everything up," said a small man in a red military jacket. He wore a plumed hat and black pants with a stripe down the side and carried himself with an upright official air, so Cassie—tapping into her recollections from the several times she and her father had attended *The Pirates of Penzance* in New York—deduced he must be the actor who would play the patter-singing Major-General Stanley character. And the woman above must be the hearing-challenged nursemaid turned piratical maid-of-all-work, Ruth. "I need the seamstress to finish taking up my sleeves."

A petite woman in a gauzy white sundress and old-fashioned sun bonnet fluttered her fan as she leaned against a policeman in a British custodian helmet. "How did she even get up there?"

"I'm not going anywhere until I've had my say. And if anyone so much as tries to approach, I'll start knocking border lights down. This place will be up in flames in minutes."

She brandished her cutlass once more for emphasis, but accidentally clipped the aforementioned lighting rack above her, sending the whole apparatus swinging.

Metta and Miss Porter grabbed onto Flora, and Paddy whooped with excitement as the actors dove for cover, knocking over benches and scattering goblets and fake treasure. One man leapt over a cave rock and bumped down the stage stairs on his rear, a measuring tape trailing from his pantaloons; another wrapped himself in a proscenium curtain. Yet another squatted by a barrel marked "PIRATE'S RUM" and covered his head with his libretto.

"I said *if*, you ninnies!"

All fell still when a man of considerable height, width, and mustache emerged from the wings. He was dressed as a pirate, as many of the other actors were, but his costume was far grander, signaling an elevated rank. His cape and jacket were made from a deep crimson velvet trimmed with gold brocade, and he wore a plumed buccaneer's hat lined with fur. Diamond studs gleamed from his ears, brilliant in the stage light. The Spanish doubloon hanging from his neck on a thick gold chain looked almost real.

Here was the Pirate King.

As he strode across the stage, each click of his boots echoing through the hall with significance, even Cassie stood straighter.

"It's *him*." Miss Porter was suddenly breathless. "William Gage, the head of the troupe. Isn't he impressive?"

Mr. Gage ran a small comb through his mustache. "All right, Mary"—his deep, rich voice was steeped in a formal

English accent—"what's this all about? We're on a tight schedule with the costume fitting today."

"What's this all about?" Mary jerked her head mockingly. "A curse is what this is all about. A real, live, devil-spitting curse."

"I wonder if she knows that's a toy sword she's waving around." Mrs. Keene produced a handful of peanuts from her tweed Norfolk jacket—Cassie had only ever seen men wearing such jackets before, but it suited her perfectly—and began cracking the shells off with her teeth. Paddy watched her jealously, and the dogs swooped in to patrol the floor for crumbs.

"I've been saying for weeks now that something evil is going on, but no one will listen. Aren't you bothered by the unexplained occurrences that have been plaguing our troupe? Props moved or missing, effects going wrong... And then today, suddenly my costume doesn't fit? The lacing is positively pulling out of the grommets!"

Paddy poked Mrs. Keene's elbow. "Can I have some peanuts?"

"There are other possible explanations for a dress failing to close about your middle," called the actor in military costume.

Paddy poked Mrs. Keene again and dodged a swipe. "Fine, just one. I could eat a stick."

"What of Roland, then?" Mary retorted. "When that table gave out during one of his Frederic monologues and he broke his leg? He was so sure he'd been struck by the curse, he left the troupe for fear of his life. And, just this morning, Mr. Gage's score went missing without explanation... Need I even mention the ghostly singing we've been hearing about the theater all week?"

The actor dressed as a policeman took his companion's fan and gave himself a languid wave. "Perhaps the man Marguerite saw peeping into the ladies' dressing room window the other day was actually an infernal apparition."

Mr. Gage reached into his coat and exchanged the comb for a vial. "What happened to Roland was nothing but an unfortunate accident." He opened the vial and rubbed his mustache with some of the shiny substance inside. "A simple misstep. Poor luck. And I'm sure I've only misplaced my score. As for the singing, we are putting on an operetta, after all." He tucked the vial away. "And, repugnant though it may be, there is nothing supernatural about a voyeur who happens to find a place where he can view scantily clad women."

Mary stomped her foot, but her position hanging from the mast rendered the movement less than effective. "'Unfortunate.' 'Accident.' 'Luck.' Don't you *see*? That's exactly how curses work. And I know for a fact someone named the Scottish play that last night in—"

"You said you heard it through the wall," said Mr. Gage. "It could have been anything. 'In breath,' 'certain death'... There are dozens of words that sound like 'Macb—'"

"Don't!" Mary scrambled to regain her grip. "You'll curse us all over!"

"But what does all this have to do with your scaling a set piece, Miss Rutledge?" A delicately framed man by the footlights shielded his eyes. "And threatening to burn down the hall?" He wore dark clothing rather than a costume, which suggested he worked behind the scenes, and he carried a hefty volume with him, the outer edge of which was neatly marked with tabs cut from different-colored strips of paper. Most tellingly, though, while his overall appearance was collected and purposeful, behind his thick eyeglasses his face was fixed with an expression of perpetual beleaguerment.

That would be the stage manager and his prompt book. In addition to being an avid theatergoer, Cassie had performed in several stage productions herself with her college's dramatic club, so she knew a thing or two about the roles and personalities involved.

Mary tightened her arm around the mast. "Got your attention, didn't I?"

"You just better not be damaging any of my handiwork." An older man with a Stetson hat and a long-nine cigar rolled a cart onto the stage and started unloading what looked like more pieces of rocky shore. Based on his comment and how he was dressed—all in black like the stage manager, but with the addition of paint splatter and wear about the trouser knees—Cassie concluded he was a stagehand.

One of the other actors, perhaps the only one who hadn't panicked before, rested his hands on the ship ladder with a placating nod. He was slim but straight and strong, and he had one of those faces that made a person feel they knew him instantly. "So, now that you have our attention, Mary, what shall we do?"

"Prince Montgomery to the rescue!" crowed the stagehand, punching the air with a hammer. "Yet again!"

Prince. Should we be kneeling? Cassie covered her laugh with a cough, glad that at least she found herself amusing.

"That'll be enough of that, Harland," Mr. Gage said. "And thank you, Prince, but, while *some* may find it hard to believe, I am capable of managing my own troupe." He brushed off the brocading on his jacket. "Besides, I know actresses. You need to apply a firm hand. If you indulge their hysterics once, there'll be no end of it."

Turning with a flourish, he slapped his hands on the hull and called upward. "Miss Rutledge, you come down this instant. There is too much riding on this production, and I'm not going to let your superstitious delusions derail it."

Prince leaned easily against a porthole. "I know actresses, too. I was raised by one." He looked back up. "Mary, please tell us how we can help."

"I told you, that's not going to—"

Mary lowered her cutlass. "I could be open to descending if certain actions were taken."

Amazingly, Prince's face was smooth, with no sign of gloating whatsoever. "And what actions might those be?"

"Um, well, first off, everyone within the theater walls needs to recite Puck's closing lines from *A Midsummer Night's Dream*: 'If we shadows have offended' and so forth, for the reversal. Oh, and the opening couplet from *The Two Gentlemen of Verona*, which is extra good luck. But before that we each have to spin to the right three times while tapping our left shoulders and spitting. And if anyone happens to have some horseshoes we could hang over the doors, all the better."

Mrs. Keene cracked another peanut and looked around at the others, who had begun to spin, tap, and spit, then up at Mary, who was dictating the lines to be recited. "She can't be serious."

"Might as well do as she asks, Alice," Miss Porter said, stepping on Luna as she struggled to get her tapping and spinning organized. The puppy yelped, then resumed trying to lick something off Miss Porter's boot. "It isn't much. Even Mr. Gage is doing it."

Cassie paused her own efforts to look at the stage. So he was. His eyes were rolled back into his skull like an insolent youth's, but he was doing it.

"I agree." Metta moved Paddy's hand from his right to his left shoulder and hopped back as he enthusiastically discharged his obligatory spittle. "It's a charity production, so if the show doesn't go forward, the charity won't get any money, and all those poor children who were going to get fed will go hungry."

"And hunger is a terrible, terrible thing," said Paddy. "Especially when it involves children." He eyed Mrs. Keene's jacket pocket.

A short, confusing while later, the rituals had been completed and the actors began to return to their duties. Mary untangled her legs from the mast roping, which she had used to anchor herself, then, after settling a brief tussle between her skirts and her feet, shimmied down the mast pole and descended the ship ladder with surprising agility. The process was worthy of the theater in and of itself, and at its conclusion, when Mr. Gage gallantly offered Mary his arm to help her onto the stage, Miss Porter erupted into applause.

The stage manager peered into the auditorium. "Pardon me, no press, please! This is a private meeting."

Mr. Gage waved him off. "No, no, Mr. Manning, it's the lovely Miss Porter! And she's brought me more candidates for our contributing chorus, I see!" He handed off Mary, who was now engaged in an encore of swooning motions, to a passing pirate and descended the stage steps. "Welcome, friends! I'm William Gage, proprietor of William Gage's Trip-along Troupe of Altruistic Actors. If I could beg a moment of your time, I'd like to tell you about an exciting opportunity.

"This production is part of a special tour that aims to partner with local communities to raise money for charity. A small donation wins you not only the heart-warming satisfaction of feeding a child in need but also the opportunity to experience the grandeur of the stage, as part of Gilbert and Sullivan's fabulously popular comic opera, *The Pirates of Penzance*! For... *I am a Pirate King!*"—he sang the line, then returned to his booming speaking voice—"and I want *you* in my *pirate crew*! Well, technically, the ladies would play maidens and townspeople, not pirates, and we need some men to play policemen. But you get the idea, ha!"

Miss Porter tittered, which was disconcerting coming from a woman whose chief pleasures in life seemed all to relate to mothering those around her. Mrs. Keene stared at her as though she'd grown a tail.

"See here for firsthand proof of what your generosity will achieve." Mr. Gage unfolded a sheet of paper and held it up.

"This is a letter of thanks from little Johnny Varden, whose parents lost everything, even the home where Johnny had been born, due to the machinations an unscrupulous landlord. He had eaten naught but gruel for weeks before we sent his family a sumptuous Sunday dinner, complete with bloater paste and caviar." Wiping away a tear, he tucked the letter back into his pocket. "What say you? Will you join us? Help us fill the bellies of other hungry little Johnnies around the country?"

"Yes! I love playing pirates!" Metta hopped up and down, clapping her hands.

"Me, too!" Paddy said.

Mr. Gage gave a resonant laugh that was somehow both energizing and soothing. "I'm sorry, children, but this production is for grown-up ladies and gentlemen only. If your adult companions are interested, however—"

"Oh, Mr. Gage." Miss Porter touched her hair. "I only brought them by to see that everything was all right with Miss Rutledge. No one was at the sheriff's office, so I went to Alice's, but she wasn't there, so I went to Flora's, and..." She blushed. "I suppose I was so worried I got carried away."

Mr. Gage smiled and took her hand. "Naturally, you were, dear woman. When you took on my troupe members at your boarding house, you did promise to look after them."

"That's... right." Miss Porter had lost her breath again.

"You have done so very much for the production, for the cause. The rooms you've provided free of charge have been a godsend, as has your angelic voice among the ladies' chorus, but that delightful recruitment tea you organized when we first arrived made all the difference. It resulted in several illustrious individuals joining us, and at quite an impressive contribution level, too! I owe you—the children owe you—many thanks."

He gave a deep bow, which Esy, who had been conducting a one-kitten siege on the hem of Cassie's skirt, acknowledged on Miss Porter's behalf by pouncing on his hat plume. He teetered slightly, then removed the hat and shook the kitten gently into Metta's outstretched arms.

Miss Porter tittered once more, and Mrs. Keene threw a peanut at her.

"I say—" Mr. Gage appraised Cassie's walking dress, one of the several new ensembles she had spent too much money on before coming to the island. The tailor had made it after a recent French trend incorporating an écru nankeen skirt and a basque bodice with polonaise-style panier draping of red-and-blue Chinese silk, which made her appear far more fashionable than she was. "That dress is from Mr. Trudeau's shop on Ladies' Mile in New York, isn't it. I'd recognize his work anywhere." He pursed his lips in approval. "Yes, this young lady definitely looks as though she'd make a fine contributing chorus member. Do you care about the welfare of children, Miss—?"

"Cassie Gwynne." Cassie did in fact enjoy singing, but she wasn't sure how her clothing indicated that, or what it had to do with children. She was still flattered for some reason, though. "Yes, of course I care about the welfare of children. But, unfortunately, I've been called back to New York, so—"

"Come, Cassie," Flora said. "You could delay your departure a little, couldn't you? I'm sure Mr. Renault would understand. That paperwork isn't going anywhere. And I've heard your singing voice. It's lovely, unlike mine. Which is why I'm preparing several cases of marmalade to send along as my contribution instead. Also, the tourist season will be peaking soon, which means I'll have to work day and night to keep my perfume store stocked. Sorry to disappoint, Mr. Gage."

"The children will be pleased to receive contributions of any sort, Miss Hale." Mr. Gage bowed again, though this time he was careful to keep himself more erect.

"So, what do you think?" Flora nudged Cassie. "Stay with us a while longer?"

Cassie folded her hands with a composed smile, though on

the inside she was dancing for joy. She had an excuse to stay on the island, *and* she was going to be in a show. A real one, with costumes and sets and professional performers. "I suppose that could be arranged."

"Very good," Mr. Gage said. "And how about you, s— ma'am? Do you care about children?"

They all turned their collective gaze on Mrs. Keene, who was fending Paddy off with an elbow as she ate her last peanut.

"The roaster's right over there, Paddy. Get your own—" She looked up. "Oh, me? Oh, no, no, no. I mean, yes, but if I say that, you'll—"

"*Wunderbar!*" Mr. Gage clasped his hands together. "Two new cast members! I am touched by your generosity and thrilled to be working with you. We're rather close to opening now, but never fear. Your fellow choristers will make sure you're prepared. You may bring your first pledges to the next rehearsal —Miss Porter will provide you the particulars."

"Pledges?" Cassie asked. "Don't you mean donations?"

"My apologies. I neglected to fully explain. This charity production is structured a bit like a silent auction. You can submit a pledge for how much you'd like to donate at any time, but you can also increase it at any time, up until the start of the performance, at which point you must tender your full, final amount in cash. The highest contributor will then be recognized during the finale with a special feature onstage. For example, if it's a gentleman, I'll 'knight' him with my cutlass. If it's a lady, she'll receive a personal serenade from me."

"Ow!" Mrs. Keene yanked her arm from Miss Porter's grip. "Truly, what is wrong with you, Lottie? The ruffles on your collar too tight?"

"I've found a little friendly competition tends to make it more fun, you see," Mr. Gage went on, "as well as boosting overall donations."

How unusual. But clever. Cassie had participated in a great deal of charity work back in New York, but she had never come across a fundraising structure quite like this. The creativity of it alone was impressive.

Mr. Gage swept his cape over his shoulder. "Well, I must say *au revoir* for now, my friends." He disengaged Esy from his boot laces. "And, uh, precious pets. Prepare yourselves! Adventure lies ahead!"

2

The next afternoon, Cassie embarked on a different sort of adventure at Flora's perfume and scented goods store.

"Gently, now. Only a little at time... Oops!" Flora tried to steady Cassie's hand as she squeezed an entire dropper of jasmine oil into a vial.

"Oh, no, Miss Cassie!" Metta had been watching the proceedings from across the glass-fronted display counter for some time and evidently couldn't contain herself any longer. "Remember, you can always add more, but you can't take back what you've already put in!" Flora's cockatiel, Kleio, bobbed her head in agreement next to her.

Cassie blew a curl of bangs out of her face and reached under the counter for a fresh vial, squeezing her hand past the kitten, who had wedged her tiny mass of white fur among the multicolored bottles and fallen asleep with her face smashed against the glass. Metta was a pinafore-wearing eight-year-old with a professed inability to handle shoes, but she was right. She'd have to start over now. It was either that or make an entire gallon's worth of disappointing *eau de parfum* trying to balance it out.

When Flora had lost her assistant the month before, Cassie had offered to stay on the island and help her with her perfume and scented goods store for a while. She had liked the idea of doing something useful after having spent so much of the past year simply rambling around her father's big, empty brownstone up in New York, alone with her memories. She had also wanted to spend more time with Flora, given that she hadn't known her, or even that she'd had an aunt at all until earlier that summer. Of course, Flora's collection of mischievous but loveable pets was a draw as well.

The only issue was Flora's continuing interpretation of her proposal as a deep-seated desire to learn the perfumery trade. Cassie was always willing to try new things, but, while she'd picked up the financial and organizational aspects of the business quickly, it had become clear after only a handful of instructional perfumery sessions that not all talents run in families.

"My sweet niece." Flora squeezed Cassie's shoulder, seeming to savor the words. "It's all right. There's no shame in starting over when something's gone wrong. Now, I know jasmine's the sort of flower you want to bury your face in, but one of the most important parts of creating an enjoyable scent is balance. Making sure the different components play together well... Say you're a musician. It's like a chord in music. It needs to harmonize."

Metta raised her hand, then abandoned that effort at restraint and slapped the counter, causing the bird to hop up onto her head. "That's why they call the parts of a scent 'notes'!"

"Nose!" Kleio squawked. Catching sight of a fiber sticking out from Flora's belt, a sisal weave studded with large, silk daffodils that matched Flora's amber robes, she dropped back onto to the counter.

"Close, Kleio. And strangely apt." Flora tucked the stray fiber in. "Anyway, Metta's right. Each element, or note, has a part to play so that everything comes together and creates something both beautiful and unique, different from merely the sum of the parts."

"Aristotle must have secretly been a perfumer," Cassie mumbled, her shoulders slumping as she popped a fresh piece of gum in her mouth. Kleio bobbed her head, and Cassie was about to marvel at her grasp of classics humor when she realized the bird had probably just mistaken a pile of perfume test strips for worms.

Kicking her shoes to the side, Metta ran behind the counter and squeezed Cassie's hips with her tiny arms. "Don't worry, Miss Cassie. I know you'll learn soon. You're so very smart!"

"She is, indeed." Flora smiled warmly. "I shudder to think of what might have happened to me if she weren't around during all that horrible business with Peanut." Peanut was Flora's former neighbor, a cantankerous harbor pilot who had finally bullied the wrong person and gotten himself killed shortly after Cassie's arrival on the island. Flora had been accused of his murder, but, thankfully, Cassie had been able to find the real killer and prove Flora's innocence.

Metta gave Cassie another squeeze, and Cassie patted the girl's head.

How lovely it is to be hugged, she thought.

It was one of the things she especially missed about her father. Every child probably thought her own father's hugs were special, but, from stubbing her toe as a toddler to being chased from a National Woman Suffrage Association demonstration as a young woman, Cassie couldn't think of one instance in which his hug hadn't quieted her distress like a snuffer on a candle flame.

She watched Flora lift an armful of roses onto the counter and, after pressing her face into the blooms, begin to separate the petals from the stems. Father wasn't here anymore, but Cassie was grateful that fate had given her back this missing piece of her family to soften the blow. Thanks to Flora, she had felt more at home on the island than she had in a very long time.

Yes. New York, and Mr. Renault and his paperwork, can certainly wait.

The front door opened and Danger and Luna, followed closely by Flora's pet pig, Roger, ran in from the kitchen, barking and *urmff*ing respectively.

The velvet curtain that separated the foyer from the parlor lifted and Miss Porter swayed into the room, arrayed in a shrimp-pink Mother Hubbard gown with a white yoke and buttons shaped like flamingos.

"Good afternoon, all! Isn't it a glorious day?" She ran her hand through the Wardian cases suspended from the ceiling by the window, sending a ripple through the dangling forest of tiny, birdcage-shaped planters, and picked up one of the handkerchiefs Flora had laid out for sale alongside an assortment of scented fans and trunk sachets. She lifted it to her nose, oblivious to the animals nosing and pawing at her. "Ah, that's a lovely fragrance. Is it new?"

Flora lowered the flame on a distiller, where a handful of the rose petals were boiling merrily in a pink liquid. "Why, yes it is. Something I'm trying out. I'm glad you like it." She twisted her lips as Miss Porter sifted through a basket of hosiery, humming to herself. "You seem very well today, Lottie. Any particular reason?"

"It's 'person,' not 'reason.'" Mrs. Keene fought through the parlor curtain behind Miss Porter, her arms around a stack of casserole dishes. "And before you start *that* again, Lottie"—she stared down Miss Porter's blush—"I'd like to be able to stomach some lunch." She lifted a leg to fend off Danger with her knee and Luna with her toe, but Roger ran around and nosed in from the other side. "Thanks for holding the door, by the way. I'm only carrying all the food."

Miss Porter hopped to. "Jam and crackers! I'm sorry!"

She started taking the dishes from Mrs. Keene, unwrapping each one and equipping it with a serving spoon before placing it on the tea table. "Alice, after this, we'll have to set up the chairs and start water boiling for tea. Flora, how many pieces are in your tea set?"

"It serves twelve." Flora opened a jar of dried cloves. "Though, and I don't wish to be obtuse, am I expecting company?"

Metta tugged at Flora's sleeve. "Shall I bring down some more jasmine essence for Miss Cassie's lesson?"

"Oh no, Flora, I forgot to ask you!" Miss Porter said. "I've invited some of the women from the *Pirates* chorus to get together and run through music. We especially wanted to iron out our important first scene—"

"Or maybe she ought to switch to peony."

"—The one where Frederic, the handsome pirate's apprentice who wishes to leave his indentures, comes upon us innocent young maidens frolicking on the beach."

Mrs. Keene snorted. "Mr. Gage really must believe in theater magic."

Miss Porter waved her off absently. "I do apologize. I wanted to host at my boarding house, but I'm having my winter rugs changed in this afternoon. Is it all right?"

"Absolutely," Flora said. "I don't mind at all—"

"But Miss Cassie's in the middle of a lesson!" Metta stomped her foot. Tired of waiting for Flora to respond, she had dragged a stool in front of the wall of silver-spigoted vessels behind the counter. "Here, Miss Cassie." She climbed onto the stool, gripping the seat with her bare toes and bracing an arm against a decorative column. "Why don't you tell me which distillations you want and I'll pour them for you? Then we'll try using a smaller dropper."

"Oh, *Cassie*!" Miss Porter clapped a hand to her mouth. "My dear, where *is* my head? You were meant to be included in the invitation." She located a packet of papers and held them out. "Here are your music parts. You and Mrs. Keene will have to share, though, because there aren't too many copies to go around... We're already operating at three or four ladies per score."

Secretly glad about the turn of events, Cassie accepted the packet and looked up at Metta, who was still standing on her stool with her hands on her hips. "I'm sorry, Metta. I suppose we'll have to find another time."

Someone else knocked at the door, setting off another bout of barking and *urmffing*.

"Good afternoon! May I enter?" came a man's voice.

Miss Porter fluttered. "I also forgot to mention that several of the troupe actors will be joining us as well, to guide us through." She smoothed her dress and hurried over to the parlor curtain. "Yes, please come in!"

The door opened and a young man, pulling off his derby and bending deeply to pass under Miss Porter's arm (since she insisted on holding the curtain for him), stepped into the room.

He grinned when Kleio swooped onto his head, chattering to herself. "Well, good day, my feathered friend. And good day to the rest of you, as well." He bowed, keeping his head up so the bird could stay aboard.

Metta leaned over the counter next to Flora and lifted her arm for the bird. "Come down off the man, Kleio girl."

Kleio, absorbed in scratching around in the mound of fluffy, almost girlish, curls on the man's head, ignored her.

"Do have a seat." Miss Porter nudged Danger off a settee. "And please excuse the animals. Flora opens her big, beautiful heart, and her home, to all of God's creatures in need. She found the big dog injured at the beach, the little dog was maltreated by its owner, she carried the pig off from the butcher's as a piglet, and the bird was left homeless when... You get the idea."

She turned around, knocking one of the casserole dishes with her elbow. "Oops! Uh, everyone, this is Prince Richard Montgomery. He plays Frederic in the play. Prince, meet my friends. This is Miss Flora Hale. She owns this beautiful store. That's Mrs. Alice Keene, who owns the Florida Collectibles and Curiosities Store on Centre Street with her husband, Captain Keene, and this is Miss Cassie Gwynne, Flora's niece visiting us from New York. She's just agreed to join the *Pirates* contributing chorus.

"Let's see... That's little Metta Gordon over there, Officer Jake Gordon's daughter. Have you met him yet? And Kleio's the one on your head. Flora took her in when Mr. Derbigny, the haberdasher, passed on and she had no one to look after her... Did I mention that already? I'm starting to gibber." She fanned her face with her hand. "Goodness. I absolutely abhor public speaking. Anyone who says it's the same as acting is sorely mistaken."

Prince smiled. "Thank you, Miss Porter. That was a perfectly lovely introduction. And I—Yow!" He shifted his gaze upward. "Miss Kleio is, um, very thorough."

Kleio blinked from the top of his head, her yellow crest lifted, then resumed her enthusiastic yanking and tugging.

Metta was again unsuccessful in calling her, so Cassie wiggled one of the perfume test strips enticingly in the air, testing out her worm hypothesis from earlier. Fortunately, the bird, being birdbrained, fell for it. She flew back over, landing on Cassie's outstretched finger, and pecked at the strip with gusto.

Prince chuckled. "Good work, Miss Gwynne."

Cassie curtsied and handed Kleio and her prize to Metta. "Thank you. But you can call me Cassie. Say, you're the one who talked that actress down at the Lyceum yesterday, aren't you?"

"I suppose I am."

"I didn't recognize you at first without your pirate attire."

Prince rubbed his beard. "Is that a good thing or a bad thing?"

"Don't worry. Civilian clothes suit you."

As they laughed, it occurred to Cassie how familiar they were acting with each other, but it didn't feel odd or inappropriate. There wasn't a hint of romantic flirtation about it. Rather, though she'd only just met the man, something about him made her feel casual and at ease, as though they were simply picking up where they had left off.

Prince stretched into the foyer to hang his hat. "In all seriousness, though, it can be surprising to people to meet an actor away from the stage. Even I, having grown up in the theater, still find it astonishing how powerful a costume and a little makeup can be."

"Prince Richard." Mrs. Keene bit into a knot of garlic bread. "Is that a name or a title?"

Prince picked up a bread knot for himself. "It's a name. Given name, Prince, middle name, Richard. When my mother adopted me, she wanted me to have a name that evoked dignity, and to her there wasn't anything more dignified than royalty, so there you have it. A bit theatrical, perhaps, but then that's the family business."

"Right," Cassie said. "I did hear you say you were 'raised by' an actress. But I didn't realize you meant you were adopted."

"Yes, my mother's name is Rosalinda Montgomery. She's known in certain circles for her dramatic roles. Anyway, that's one reason Mr. Gage's troupe appealed to me—I was lucky someone kind took me in and provided well for me, but there are plenty of hungry children out there who aren't so fortunate. As you may have heard, there's no profit involved for this troupe. Anything we raise above the cost of production goes to charities who serve unfortunates... Have you ever heard of such a thing? It's almost unbelievable."

"I was quite surprised, and impressed, when Mr. Gage described it to us."

"And the choice of show is so devastatingly appropriate, with the pirate crew that's unsuccessful because, all being orphans themselves, they allow their prey to go free if they are orphans, too—"

"And, therefore, everyone they capture claims to be an orphan!" Cassie slapped her leg with a laugh. "I had forgotten about that."

Her amusement waned slightly when she smiled over at Flora, expecting one of her playful smiles in return, but Flora wasn't looking at her. She was studying Prince, and while she wasn't frowning, exactly, she was hunched forward, as though deep in thought. Had she not understood the joke?

"Flora's a champion for unfortunates, too," Cassie said, trying to draw Flora out. "I've seen her efforts with injured or abandoned animals firsthand. She not only speaks and writes about the fair treatment of animals, but, as Miss Porter mentioned, she also cares for ones in need in her own home. Some of those she's adopted as pets, but many others she's nursed back to health then released or placed with caring owners. She even keeps a vegetarian diet out of a respect for animal welfare. Isn't that right, Aunt Flora?"

Flora slid her gaze over to meet Cassie's. "That's right."

Cassie chewed her gum, waiting to see if there was more, but Flora simply picked up a pencil and opened her perfume composition notebook.

Cassie tucked her hair behind her ear. "Does your mother still perform, Mr. Montgomery?"

"Not really. She used to own her own theater in Yarmouth, where I was raised. But there was... trouble with her partner a couple of years ago, and she's moved on to other endeavors. And I travel full-time now, so I haven't seen her for a while. I miss her terribly."

Flora flipped a page in her notebook. "Yarmouth?"

"Yes, on Cape Cod, Massachusetts."

"You were born there?"

"No, but I grew up there."

"Where were you born?"

Prince shrugged pleasantly. "I don't know."

"No one told you where you came from?"

"My mother never wanted to talk about it, if she knew."

"And you don't remember anything from before?"

"Not much. Maybe a vague moment here and there, but nothing of a truly identifying nature. Though, I—" He shook his head. "No, believe me, I've racked my brain thousands of times and all I get for my efforts is a headache!"

He laughed, but Flora simply turned another page in her notebook.

What was going on? Did Flora not like Prince? Up until this point, Cassie had only seen Flora be open and warm to everyone she met, so the sudden appearance of this aloof demeanor was confusing. Particularly given how Prince had been so forthcoming in sharing his feelings about missing his mother. Cassie didn't remember her own mother much, since she had been so young when she passed, but she could relate when it came to her father.

She was casting about for another topic when a chorus of chipper soprano voices burst into song outside.

"Climbing over rocky mountain,
Skipping rivulet and fountain,
Passing where the willows quiver,
By the ever-rolling river..."

Just inside Flora's garden gate, several ladies, their doughy, distinctly middle-aged forms swathed in elaborate visiting gowns, were skipping arm in arm up the palm-and-citrus-lined path like girls coming home from the shops.

"Lord, help us," Mrs. Keene said. "The 'young maidens' are here."

"Scaling rough and rugged passes,
Climb the hardy little lasses,
Till the bright sea-shore... they gain!"

The women erupted into high-pitched giggling when they came to the end of the verse then started over from the beginning. A moment later, they reached the porch and, after giving a rhythmic knock at the door, they sang and whirled their way into the parlor. One, upon being rebuffed with a stiff glare from Mrs. Keene, took up Miss Porter's hands, and they hopped in circles together to the music. The dogs howled and pranced by their feet with delight, and Roger, followed by a sleepy Esy, trundled along behind.

"Don't mind us, Miss Hale," said the woman dancing with Miss Porter. Cassie recognized her by her abundance of pearls and moles as the wife of a particular railroad bigwig, and one of Lucy Carnegie's friends. A party had come down from Pittsburgh a few weeks ago for the groundbreaking at a property the Carnegies had acquired nearby for a winter home, and she must have been among them.

"Yes, we're 'in character,'" trilled another woman. Humming to herself, she picked up Luna and snuggled the puppy to her voluminous and elaborately trimmed bosom. She was familiar, too, as were the obscenely large ruby pendants dangling from her ears. After giving it a thought, Cassie realized she was the wife of one of her father's legal clients back up north. Her husband owned an extensive collection of shipyards along the east coast. She owned an extensive collection of lapdogs.

Mrs. Keene watched the woman flip the puppy on her back and cradle her like a baby, murmuring, "Who's a hardy little lass? Yes, you are. Yes, you *are*. Just. Like. Me!"

She took a swig of punch. "That proves it. Idiocy *is* catching."

Continuing to survey the room, Cassie served herself a steaming plate of curried chicken casserole as the ladies busied themselves drinking punch and petting Prince's head. She had to hand it to Mr. Gage: there were some significant fortunes represented here. Pig iron. Matchsticks. Machine tools. She could only imagine the donations this unique, theater-themed benefit could raise with participation from such elite contributors.

Prince, who had been handling his hair-tousling fate with tremendous grace, jumped to his feet when another knock sounded at the door.

"Why, my colleagues have arrived!" He escaped toward the foyer, patting his hair back into place. "I'll show them in. Ladies, why don't you get out your music and take your seats?"

He passed under the curtain and returned with three of the other troupe actors. They weren't in costume anymore either, but Cassie recognized them from the Lyceum the morning before. There was the petite young woman with the sundress and bonnet, now in a sophisticated chartreuse afternoon dress with matching chapeau; the policeman she had been leaning on, who had exchanged his helmet for a glamorous derby made from purple felt; and the little man previously clad in military attire. The last transformation was the most striking, as the man had donned a pinstriped sack suit with a bowtie and straw boater, giving him the outdoorsy air of either a university student or a Venetian gondolier.

Flora and Cassie caught the dogs and pig before they were able to make their usual rush for the new arrivals.

"Thank Heaven we made it," the woman announced,

unaware of the pet onslaught she had narrowly avoided. "It's a miracle I'm still standing."

"Enough with that, Marguerite." The military officer/gondolier plopped onto one of the dining chairs Mrs. Keene had arranged in a circle at the center of the room. "You didn't know where you were going, either."

"How silly of me, Mr. Wilkes, for assuming that those striding along ahead of me had a route in mind."

The third member of the trio, batting his dark lashes sarcastically, pretended to use his derby to dust off another chair. "Here, miss. Please take a rest. Or rather, *give it a rest*." Even with his civilian attire, his eyelids were carefully lined with black makeup, and he had a touch of rouge on his cheeks. It was a becoming, if unusual, look.

"Oh, Arthur." Marguerite lowered herself onto the seat, her chin pointed at the ceiling. "I'm sure I don't know why you've been so mean to me recently."

"Cheers, everyone! Thank you for coming," Prince said, raising the punch glass Miss Porter had foisted into his hand. "For anyone who hasn't been introduced yet, please welcome Miss Marguerite Clifton, who will be playing Mabel in the show; Mr. Arthur Beath, who will be playing the Sergeant of Police; and Mr. Christopher Wilkes, who will be playing the venerable and speedy-mouthed Major-General Stanley."

Murmurs of greeting filled the room.

Prince looked around. "Where's Mary?"

Mr. Wilkes leaned out of his chair, trying to reach one of the casserole dishes without getting up. "Miss Rutledge informed me that she had a critically important appointment with a local spiritualist."

"And the bit players? Vera, Theresa, Ira, Percy?"

"That group never shows up to anything unless Mr. Gage makes them."

"Never mind them." Arthur tossed his hair. "Marguerite can sing Mary's part, and I'll fill in for the others."

"Will Mr. Gage be joining us today?" one of the chorus women asked.

Marguerite and Arthur both started to respond, then stopped and glared at each other.

"No, I'm afraid," Marguerite said. "He's calling on a few more ladies and gentlemen who showed interest in joining the show. I believe Mrs. Reynolds is hosting a tea."

Miss Porter knocked a serving spoon onto the floor. "Mrs. Reynolds is hosting a recruitment tea? She said she was coming here."

"Actually, Marguerite," Arthur said, "Mr. Gage has gone to see a tailor about a matter with his costume."

"No, *Arthur*, he told me he was going to that tea—"

"Well, he told *me* he was going to—"

Mr. Wilkes banged his pipe on the table to get the tobacco out. "Let's just say 'he's busy.'"

They all paused as Esy strolled to the center of the circle of chairs, stretched, then padded off toward the kitchen.

Mr. Wilkes snickered. "Good thing Mary isn't here. She'd be halfway to the next town by now."

"That cat's white, not black," said Marguerite. "And besides, cats are lucky in the theater. Everyone knows that."

Arthur perched on the seat next to Marguerite, as regally as she had, and crossed his legs. "So, if Mr. Gage is at a fundraiser, Marguerite, why aren't you with him, strutting yourself around on his behalf?"

Miss Porter pushed the serving spoon she'd dropped into a casserole, muttering to herself. "Of all the low, backstabbing—"

"What *has* gotten into you, Arthur?" Marguerite pressed a hand to her chest. "Truly, between your fits and Mary's curse talk and everything else that's been going on lately, my nerves—"

"Your nerves have nerves." Mr. Wilkes banged his pipe again.

Marguerite stiffened. "Pardon me, I couldn't hear you from down there. Maybe you should grow a few inches."

"—And her chocolate cake doesn't even hold a candle to my coconut cake—"

"Ah, a joke about my stature. How original. Well, I may be on the shorter side, but I've got more talent in my little finger than you have in your entire oversized nose. I could play Hercules if I wanted to."

"Hercules's left leg, maybe."

"At least I don't have to rely on bedding maestro to advance my career."

Marguerite gasped. "How dare you! Those are unfounded rumors. And I'll have you know..."

Cassie leaned over to Prince as the bickering continued. "Are they always like this?"

"As far as I can gather. But, even though I don't necessarily agree about there being a curse and such, Mary's right. There have been some strange and unsettling things happening around the troupe. That could be causing tension... Who knows, though. This is my first production with them, and each group I join has its own, unique dynamic. Doing what I do, I just have to work with what I get." He gave her a lopsided grin. "You, on the other hand, have involved yourself with these people voluntarily."

Cassie glanced back over at the others. The actors were on their feet now, arguing about the real color of Mr. Wilkes's hair and, it seemed, how many of his shoes could fit inside a child's valise. The chorus women watched with open-mouthed fascination.

"Anything for charity, I suppose."

Prince winked. "Mr. Gage did promise you an adventure, didn't he?"

3

Once the actors had paused their squabbling long enough to sing, the rehearsal lasted for precisely half an hour before it descended into a casserole-fueled debate over the exact ratio of Mr. Gage's mustache length to his shoulder width, followed by a mass buyout of Flora's stock of scented goods, from gloves, handkerchiefs, and scarves to trunk sachets, sacques, neckties, and fans. By the time Cassie finished wrapping up the last parcel, she was exhausted in a way she had never been before. After she'd had only a short rest, however, Flora handed her a package containing an item Mr. Gage had ordered and asked her to deliver it to his suite at the Egmont Hotel.

Cassie shuffled down the garden path and through the wild tangle of purple trumpet flower vines that covered Flora's cast-iron gate, devoting her last drips of energy to plotting the shortest route to her destination, but the moment she stepped into the street, she was met by a fresh, piney breeze that quite restored her. Judging from its coolness and the hint of salt it left on her skin as it passed, it had come off the ocean. Its lofty origins didn't prevent it from being amicable, though, and as it passed through, it tickled the leaves in the trees overhead and tousled the chestnut tendrils that had escaped from the chignon she'd twisted up under her bonnet.

Sneezing heartily into the bright sunlight, Cassie turned down Seventh Street with a light step. Cicadas sawed in the trees above, executing dramatic crescendos and decrescendos as expertly as the world's most practiced orchestras, and the white-and-pink shell gravel that filled the road crunched pleasantly below her boot heels. In every other direction, unseen birds trilled happily as they called on their neighbors, and somewhere nearby, an ornamental fountain tinkled in response.

As tended to happen on the island, the walk ended up flying by without her hardly noticing, and, before she knew it the Egmont's glittering white form soared into view, regal in its tiered skirts of verandas and flower gardens and crown of pennants that flapped proudly in the wind. Skipping the last step onto the airy portico, where several men sat in their afternoon suits on palmetto-weave armchairs sipping drinks and puffing cigars behind newspapers, she entered the lobby and flagged down one of the uniformed clerks for directions to Mr. Gage's room. As it turned it out, it was a good thing she had because his suite was in a wing she'd never been to before, one usually reserved for visiting dignitaries.

Cassie looked around with awe as she padded down the lushly carpeted hallway, though she started slightly every time she passed one of the many gilt-framed mirrors lining the walls and caught sight of her reflection. *These furnishings are truly lovely, but who needs to look at herself this much?*

Finally, she arrived at a large door with a plaque bearing the words "Royal Suite."

She knocked. "Good afternoon! Mr. Gage?"

No one answered, but the door was cracked, so she stepped inside.

She released a low whistle as she entered the front parlor. The Egmont was known for its elegance, so she'd expected the room to be impressive, particularly after seeing the hallway leading up to it, but the suite Mr. Gage had taken was nothing short of magnificent. Aside from a handful of gold accents—on the frames of the diamond-tufted chairs arranged in one corner, the embroidery on the curtain holdbacks, the acanthus leaf motif encircling a heavy oval mirror over the mantel—everything in the room was gleaming white, making the room feel airy and bright and larger than it was. Grand draperies flowed from valances curved like seashells. Flames flickered from a crystal candelabrum on the entry table. Light poured in through the privacy lace over the windows, making the chandelier overhead sparkle like a princess's tiara.

If someone had told her she was standing in the Fifth Avenue Hotel in New York, or possibly a waiting room for Heaven, she might have believed them.

Hearing a voice murmur in the adjoining bedroom, Cassie crossed toward the sound, her boots tapping hesitantly against the floor. She touched a finger to the doorknob. "Mr. Gage? It's Cassie Gwynne."

Something hit the floor with a heavy thump, and Cassie, alarmed, rushed into the room.

Inside she found Mr. Gage, resplendent in a velvet smoking jacket with brass frogging, bent over a flailing heap of fabric and limbs.

"Miss Porter!" Cassie fell forward, but Miss Porter took Mr. Gage's proffered arm instead.

"I'm fine, I'm fine." Miss Porter pulled herself into a sitting position against the bedframe and tried to tuck some hair back into the tight chignon on top of her head. "I, uh, haha—Mr. Gage bet me I couldn't sit on the bed without using my hands, ha, you know, because the bed's tall and I'm not, and I slipped." She laughed as though she were telling Cassie about a book she'd just read, but when their eyes met, she dropped her gaze, her cheeks red.

Cassie took a step back. She wasn't a stickler for decorum herself, but Miss Porter, a woman who covered her ears at the mildest of oaths, absolutely was. What was she doing in a bedroom alone with a man she hardly knew, particularly when there was a perfectly good sitting area in the adjoining parlor a few feet away?

Continuing to work at her hair, Miss Porter let Mr. Gage finish helping her to her feet and followed him into the front room. Cassie trailed behind.

"Please have a seat, ladies." Mr. Gage gestured toward the white-and-gold tufted chairs Cassie had noted when she came in.

He was wearing the diamond studs Cassie had seen him in the day before, and now they were matched by a band of diamonds around his wrist. Were those real? Where would an actor, particularly one in a not-for-profit troupe, get the money for something like that? The same could be said for this luxurious suite, for that matter.

"Now, Miss Gwynne," Mr. Gage said, "so you don't get the wrong idea, let me assure you that Miss Porter is a pillar of propriety. She arrived only a short while ago and wished to tour the suite. I was informed by the clerk that former President General Ulysses S. Grant himself took these rooms when he visited Fernandina a couple of years ago. And the furnishings are rather compelling, aren't they?"

He might as well have asked whether baby rabbits were rather cute and fluffy.

"And never fear. I, the most trustworthy, and most musical, chaperone snacks can buy, am here as well!" Prince danced into the parlor with a plate of cookies, humming a sprightly tune in self-accompaniment. After a few ridiculous spins around the room, he concluded the performance with a bow, presenting the platter under Cassie's nose. "Please help yourself, Cassie Gwynne. How delightful to see you twice in one day!"

The combination of the dancing and the cookies gave Cassie a sudden impulse to tickle him, but she managed to restrain herself.

Mr. Gage fluffed the shawl collar of his smoking jacket. "That's right. Mr. Montgomery escorted her over but stepped out momentarily to fetch some refreshments since the oral annunciator was malfunctioning when we tried to contact the kitchen." He gestured toward the speaking tube jutting out of the wall.

"Thank you, good sir." Cassie took a cookie with a gracious curtsy. "I won't be staying long, though. I've only come to drop this package by for Mr. Gage, from Flora."

Mr. Gage clapped excitedly. "Are those my socks? Brilliant!" He carried the package to the mantel and untied the string. Sure enough, when he folded down the paper, he revealed several pairs of plain-looking black socks. He lifted the fistful of fabric and took a deep inhale. "Ah, yes. These will do nicely. Very nicely." He took them into the other room and started opening and closing the drawers of the secretary against the wall.

Prince turned to Miss Porter. "So, what were you saying before, about a gathering?"

"I know perfumed socks sounds extravagant," Mr. Gage called from the other room. "But you wouldn't believe the difference it makes to the experience of taking one's shoes on and off."

"Oh, I—" Miss Porter leaned to see where Mr. Gage was, then sat back happily as he returned with a few bills in his hand. From the way he kept stopping, turning, and pointing his toes, it was clear he had donned one of his new pairs of socks.

"Yes, that was why I came here to see Mr. Gage, wasn't it. Before I was swept away by these astonishing apartments." Miss Porter tittered, though Cassie hadn't heard any joke. "I wanted to offer to host another fundraising event, perhaps a dinner this time. Something more dignified than a silly old tea."

Cassie took a bite of cookie. More dignified than Mrs. Reynolds's "silly old tea," more like. Had Miss Porter really been thinking about that all afternoon?

"Dinner is a brilliant idea." Mr. Gage handed Cassie the money he'd brought out and leaned against the mantel, tapping a finger to his chin. "We could host it here in the hotel's dining room—"

"Oh, I was thinking I'd cook—"

"And it doesn't even have to be restricted to potential new contributors. If we invite a few existing chorus members as well, it might even inspire more healthy pledge competition. Though we're already doing very well, I think. I need to get an update from Mr. Manning. Maths was never my strong suit."

"Who?" Cassie asked.

"Stuart Manning, my stage manager. And production manager, I suppose. He's the one that makes it all run, anyway. I'll be seeing him later about adding a blocking change to the book and will let him know what we've discussed."

Miss Porter's lips were tight. "By existing chorus members, do you mean even Mrs. Reynolds?"

"Certainly."

"But she's—"

"She's one of our most important contributing chorus members, my dear, and she's very committed to this troupe's work. Believe me, it wouldn't suit to exclude her."

He hadn't spoken harshly, at least to Cassie's ear, but the hurt look on Miss Porter's face was about as subtle as a donkey on a bicycle.

Cassie checked the pocket watch on her chatelaine. "Well, I should leave you all to your planning..."

"Aw, sure you won't stay for another cookie?" Prince's eyes twinkled as he swirled the plate under her nose. "Or a dance?"

He began humming again, but this time he spun in small circles around her, holding the plate over his head like a crown. It was so absurd Cassie laughed out loud.

"Pardon me. If I may interrupt—whatever this is?"

Cassie stopped mid-laugh. Austin Hughes, one of Fernandina's policemen, had stepped through the doorway. He stood with his hands on his waist, pushing back his coat in a casual yet impressive stance that revealed his badge on one side and his firearm on the other.

Cassie hadn't seen Officer Hughes for weeks, aside from the back of his head as he charged by her in the street, absorbed in whatever crime-fighting task he'd assigned himself. His face was as she remembered it, though, with that moody mouth and long but well-conditioned mustache. And square jaw and pensive eyebrows. And smooth, reddish-blond hair, which always fell over his eyes when he was worked up. Eyes that the sunlight shining through the windows, or perhaps the gleam of the white décor, was somehow making a deeper blue—

"Are you all right?" Prince peered at her over the cookies.

Cassie started, almost knocking the tray out of his hands. "Oh, yes, I—yes. Good afternoon, Officer Hughes."

Hughes ran a hand over his hair. "Uh, good afternoon, Miss Gwynne. I didn't expect to see you here."

"Ahoy, Cassie!" came another voice behind him. It was Officer Jake Gordon, little Metta's father and Flora's beau. Though a handful of years older than Hughes, he was about the same height as he was, and was dressed as always in his distinctive combination of formal frock coat and ascot with breeches and paddock boots, but somehow Cassie hadn't seen him standing there. "We're investigating a string of thefts in the hotel and came to interview Mr. Gage."

Hughes patted around his coat for his notebook and pencil. "Yes. Yes, that's right." He glanced at Prince, then Cassie, then back at Prince. "You don't happen to be William Gage, do you?"

"No, sir. Prince Richard Montgomery. At your service."

Hughes watched incredulously as Prince gave him a formal bow, holding the cookie tray high above his head.

"Right." He turned to Mr. Gage. "Then you must be Mr. Gage. I'm Officer Hughes, and, as my colleague Officer Gordon mentioned, we've come on behalf of the sheriff's office to ask if you're missing any personal items from your room—"

"Because we've received several reports of thefts from hotel guests over the last few weeks," Jake said. "Though, so far, only change purses and the like have been taken, so there's no need to—"

"But the thief could make the leap to more significant items at any time." Hughes's mustache twitched with annoyance. "So must be caught as soon as possible."

Mr. Gage smoothed his own mustache. "Oh, no. I don't believe so. Officers. But I'll take a look around and be sure to let the hotel clerk know right away if anything is amiss." He slid behind Miss Porter's chair and placed his hands on her headrest.

"You do that. And tell Miss, uh—" Hughes started to open his notebook, but as he did so, several pink envelopes bound with red ribbon fell out. He hastily stuck the letters in his coat pocket and returned to his notes. "Let Miss Clifton know we're working on tracking down that degenerate who peeped on her in the Lyceum dressing rooms. We don't abide that kind of violation here. No one else in the troupe has mentioned any sightings, have they?"

"Not to my knowledge. Unless you count Mary Rutledge's singing ghost." Mr. Gage smiled.

"I was told there was a curse, not a ghost."

"Who can keep track?"

"Ah." Hughes put his notebook away, glancing at Cassie once more. "Very well, thank you. We'll be off, then."

Prince seized the gilt metal clock on the mantel. "Gracious! Is that the time? Gentlemen, wait. I'll walk out with you."

"Where are you going?" Cassie wobbled as he dropped the cookie tray in her arms and grabbed his hat from the rack.

"I have a—an appointment. You can see Miss Porter home when she's ready, right? You don't have anywhere you need to be?"

"Sure I can, but—"

"Thank you! See everyone at rehearsal tomorrow!" Popping his hat on his head, Prince dashed into the hall.

Jake, who was standing closest to the door, leaned out to look after him.

"He and I must have a different understanding of the word 'with.'"

When Cassie arrived at the Lyceum for rehearsal the next morning, she found a seat at the back of the auditorium before reporting to the stage. Her feet were sore from pacing with her sheet music all night, so she wanted a moment to recuperate after the walk to the theater. She also had a few more things to do before she'd be ready to rehearse.

First, she unhooked the chatelaine at her waist and wrapped it in her shrug with her gloves. There were a few jangly items clipped on there, including a vesta match case, a silver whistle, and her travel-sized sewing scissors, and she didn't want to distract anyone with the noise as she moved about the stage. She placed the pile on the chair next to her, and her hat on top of the pile. Next, she loosened the drawstring closure on the back of her bodice, removed her longest overskirt, and changed out her boots for a pair of soft slippers. Finally, she stretched a wide ribbon atop her hair, careful to leave her curly bangs arranged over her forehead, and secured it at the nape of her neck with a bow.

Moving through these rehearsal preparations felt ritualistic, and memories of the time she'd spent onstage during her time at women's college came flowing back, filling her with a fizzy warmth that spread all over and put a weakness in her knees and a tickle in her toes. She felt like an old soldier suiting up for battle after years at peace.

She had just finished getting situated and was tucking into one of the orange blossom scones she had brought as a snack when Mr. Gage, cloaked in his full Pirate King regalia, took center stage and swept up his arms with a panache that would make Mr. P.T. Barnum take notice.

"Ladies and gentlemen of the chorus, welcome to rehearsal. If you are in the opening pirate scene—that's most of you men and I believe one tall lady—please come up onstage. Use the steps at stage left, which, as a reminder, means my left, your right. Importantly, as you ascend, you will see a box for new or updated contribution pledges. Others with a pledge to submit may also come up to do that, but, afterward, please return to the house and take a seat."

The stage manager bobbed to avoid Mr. Gage's hand as he gestured. "Please be sure your name is on your pledge. And use the box with the slot in the top, people. Not the one filled with costume hats."

At that invitation, an army of ladies, including those who had been at Miss Porter's music rehearsal the previous day, rushed the stage, jostling to be the first to drop a pledge in the box. A handful of gentlemen, less giddy but not as disinterested as one might expect, followed behind.

"I suppose I should make my way up there as well. Once it's safe, that is."

Cassie turned. Prince Montgomery was sitting at the end of her row, his feet up on the chair in front of him and a book in his lap.

"Oh! Mr. Montgomery—"

"Prince."

"Prince. I hadn't realized anyone else was back here."

"There's also your tall, scowly friend over there by the peanut roaster. And your round, motherly one." In the small reception area by the door, Miss Porter was trying to coax Mrs. Keene down the aisle while keeping one arm raised as a shield.

Cassie accidentally snorted instead of laughed, then snorted again when Prince did the same.

"Very dignified," Prince said, snorting.

"You should talk." Snort. "Agh! This is not normal."

Prince put a hand on his chest to catch his breath. "At least my snort isn't as off-putting as my sneeze. It's loud, and it comes on suddenly. It mostly happens when the sun hits my face, though, so—"

"The sun makes me sneeze, too." Cassie rubbed her nose. "And I've been told my sneezes are 'acts of violence.'"

Prince snorted and put his book aside. "Say, do you have any of that Yucatan gum I saw you chewing yesterday? I love the stuff but never remember to buy myself any to keep around."

Cassie lit up. "Oh, yes! I'm never without."

"I knew I liked you for a reason."

Onstage, the pledge line was finally starting to wane, and Mr. Gage shooed off Marguerite, who had been following him around, talking at him animatedly as he moved about the stage arranging cards, dice, gold doubloons, and other items on the tables and benches that had been set out for the pirate's camp scene.

He glanced at Arthur, who was leaning on a powder keg in his stiff Sergeant of Police uniform, glaring at Marguerite over a floral fan, then clapped his hands. "One more announcement. We have a few of the orchestra musicians, a quartet to be exact, joining us today to get a sense of the show"—he gestured toward the dark expanse in front of the stage containing the orchestra pit—"so we will be running each scene as though it were an actual performance, with no stopping. It will be good for you chorus members to hear what the show sounds like with instruments other than the rehearsal piano."

"Mr. Gage—" started the stage manager.

"And it's fine if you don't have your costume together yet—I know some have only recently joined. But there is one rule. If you don't know your music, please don't sing. Just mouth along. There are enough who do know the music to carry things forward." He winked at one of the ladies just stepping onto the stage, nearly sending her reeling back down the stairs.

"If I may—"

"All right, let's have places for Act One, Number Three, the Pirate King song. Once we run that, we'll circle back to the top and see how far we get. Don't worry, lady choristers. You'll have your turn shortly!"

The stage manager hefted his prompt book from one arm to the other. It looked a terribly heavy thing to be carrying around, but Cassie knew it was arguably the most important item in the show. In addition to the full score, annotated with cues for every entrance, exit, lighting effect, and scenery change, it contained most other key information needed to run the show as well, including contact lists, theater layouts, blocking notes, and emergency procedures. One of Cassie's dramatic club classmates even used to refer to it, controversially, as "the Show Bible."

"If I could interrupt, Mr. Gage," the stage manager said, "we didn't budget for orchestral accompaniment today—"

"That's why I only called a quartet."

"But that still costs—"

"Well, they're here now. And I don't have time to discuss it with you. Prince! Where did Prince go?" He peered into the auditorium.

Prince stirred from his book, some old novel called *Moby-*

Dick, and tilted his head, his eyes clinging to the page briefly before he fully looked up. The movement reminded Cassie of her father; he used to do the same thing when interrupted from his work. "Yes, Captain?"

"Don't forget the blocking changes we discussed. I don't want you getting in my way."

"Aye, aye, Captain!"

"Actors! Places!"

Leaving Cassie with a friendly nod, Prince jogged to the stage and leapt over the lip rather than using the stairs. He sat at a table set with a jeweled goblet and a bowl of apples, set his buccaneer's hat on a jaunty angle, and leaned forward with one hand on his knee. Then he fixed his face into a haughty grimace, and, just like that, he transformed into a pirate.

As the rest of the pirates, including Mary Rutledge, hurried into position, Mr. Gage tented his fingers below his chin.

"Now, to set the scene. It has just been revealed that, due to a hearing problem, Frederic—raise your hand, Prince—was mistakenly apprenticed as a boy to a pi-*rate* instead of a pi-*lot* by his nursemaid, Ruth—Mary, raise your hand. And that Frederic, having just come of age at twenty-one years, therefore now wishes to leave his indentures. He loves his pirate family, and has been loyal to them out of his strong sense of duty, but he knows that pirating is wrong and has announced that, once he is no longer honor-bound to them, it will be his duty to exterminate them.

"He urges them to abandon their ways so he doesn't have to pursue them, but, alas, the pirates decline, and I, their leader, the Pirate King, declare: 'No, Frederic, it cannot be. I don't think much of our profession, but, contrasted with respectability, it is comparatively honest. No, Frederic, I shall live and die a Pirate King!'"

He cued the musicians with a nod.

"Oh, better far to live and die
Under the brave black flag I fly,
Than play a sanctimonious part
With a pirate head and a pirate heart.
Away to the cheating world go you,
Where pirates all are well-to-do;
But I'll be true to the song I sing,
And live and die... a Pi-ra-a-ate King."

He milked the verse's closing fermatas, then lifted his cape regally in an even more comically drawn-out caesura before plunging into the next verse.

"For... I... am a Pirate King!
And it is, it is a glorious thing
To be a Pirate King!
For I am a Pirate King!"

The pirate chorus sang back:

"You are!
Hurrah for the Pirate King!"

Mr. Gage repeated:

"And it is, it is a glorious thing
To be a Pirate King."

And the pirate chorus answered again:

"It is!
Hurrah for the Pirate King!
Hurrah for the Pirate King!"

The orchestra played on alone, and Cassie tapped her foot as Mr. Gage parried playful thrusts from Prince then sprang expertly over a stack of crates, eliciting *oohs* and *aahs* from the chorus-member audience.

Another verse followed, then another refrain. As the song neared its climax, the pirate chorus, goblets, cutlasses, and blunderbusses aloft, jigged and hopped into various formations, ultimately fanning out to form two lines extending down the stage, their arms raised in presentation. Mr. Gage promenaded up the middle, and, after turning and flourishing his cutlass toward the audience, began to climb the schooner's rope ladder, pausing every several rungs to turn around and flourish his cutlass again.

"And it is, it is a glorious thing
To be a Pirate King."

He sang along with the chorus in the final verse, continuing up the mast and climbing higher and higher until he'd reached the crow's nest at the top. Then, wrapping his legs up in the rope and holding on to the mast with one hand, he leaned all the way out toward the audience, his cutlass arm outstretched, as the ensemble entered the final refrain.

"It is!
Hurrah for the Pirate King!
Hurrah for the Pirate—"

Mr. Gage screamed, and the music fell off with a cascade of notes and twangs as the front portion of the schooner came away from the rest of the ship and pitched toward the edge of the stage, taking ladder, mast, and Mr. Gage along with it. The motion was at once wrenchingly slow and so fast Cassie could hardly follow it, but what she saw with horrifying clarity was Mr. Gage's enormous body hurtling through the air, cutlass flailing, until the mast hit edge of the stage with a crack, depositing Mr. Gage unceremoniously into the orchestra pit.

Cassie felt the thud before she heard it.

"Everyone, stay back!" Prince waved his arms at the chorus women trying to climb into the pit after Mr. Gage. "Mr. Wilkes, get a doctor! Mr. Manning, bring me a lamp!"

Prince continued to bark orders, and Cassie, trying to keep the sick from rising in her throat, slogged across the auditorium toward the scene, her arms and legs thick with dread. When she finally reached the edge of the pit, she pushed through the crowd using the full weight of her hips and took stock of the stage above—the fallen panel lay flat, with no concerning lumps under it—then of the instrumentalists in the pit, who were huddled to one side around a tuba: *one, two, three, four*. She let out half a breath.

Finally, she looked at Prince, who was kneeling next to Mr. Gage.

She felt her lips move. "Is he—?"

Prince shook his head.

Cassie forced her gaze to settle onto Mr. Gage's massive form. It was as grand as it had been only moments before, with its diamond earrings, gold chains, and brocaded coat, but it was draped in that unmistakable stillness now, the kind that only the absence of life, where life used to be, brings.

The Pirate King was dead.

4

Outside the Lyceum, Miss Porter, supported by Flora on one side and by Mrs. Keene on the other, sank down under a palm tree as Cassie handed her a mug of soup she had procured from a passing vendor. The tree swayed gently overhead, swishing its broad, multi-fingered fronds, and a flock of hooded warblers called *weeta-weeta-weet-tee-o* to one another in the bushes while distant steamships sounded their horns on the harbor.

Inside the Lyceum, William Gage lay lifeless on the floor of the orchestra pit.

"Mr. Gage... He isn't... He can't be..."

"Drink some soup, Lottie." Mrs. Keene spoke quietly, the closest to tender Cassie had ever seen her.

"How could this... I don't understand..."

"We're here for you, dear." Flora stroked Miss Porter's head, and Luna crawled into her lap, sitting on top of the kitten. Danger licked the tears off her chin.

Cassie looked around at the actors, chorus, and crew members milling about in front of the theater, searching for something comforting to say. Arthur was crumpled against the wall by the door, his face in his hands, and Mr. Wilkes stood talking with Mr. Manning by a handful of chairs someone had brought outside. Several of the chorus sat in a circle in the grass, heads bowed and hands linked together.

Beyond them, a man Cassie didn't recognize in an awkwardly large overcoat skittered along the fence, puffing away on a long churchwarden pipe. It seemed the souvenir seekers and gossip gatherers, as Jake Gordon liked to call them, were already beginning to descend.

"He's in a better place now," Cassie offered. When that, predictably, brought a renewed bout of tears, she tried again. "Everything happens for a reason." That was even worse.

As she inhaled for a third attempt, Flora and Mrs. Keene's expressions, and possibly even the animals', suggested she shouldn't.

Cassie rubbed her head. What *was* that? Could she have been any more obtuse? She, of all people, a girl who had been fed every platitude in the book since she lost her father the year before, should know better. That night in the park, she'd sat for hours afterward in the spot where she and her father had been attacked, feeling as though she was being assaulted all over again, but this time by clumsy attempts to comfort her. She'd even lunged at a policeman when he said, "Your father wouldn't have wanted you sitting here all alone in the cold."

Her father was all alone in the cold. Why shouldn't she be?

She looked at Miss Porter. The best course of action would have been to say nothing. To simply have acknowledged, silently, the one thing that all people who suffer true loss know: there is nothing that will ever make it right, because making it not true isn't possible.

Suddenly, Cassie knew what to do. Setting the soup on a stump, she bent and gave Miss Porter the biggest, warmest hug she could muster. Right away, Miss Porter squeezed her back with the earnest forcefulness Cassie was accustomed to from her.

Cassie's shoulders relaxed, though she hadn't realized they were tensed. *I guess we both needed that.*

Finally, Miss Porter sat back, her nose puffy and red. "Shouldn't they have made some sort of announcement by now? It's been hours, and they haven't said a thing. Not even to tell us, officially, that he... that Mr. Gage is..." She waited until she was able draw a breath again. "Gone."

"They'll tell us when they're ready, dear." Flora stroked her head. "It's not the sort of thing that should be rushed."

Miss Porter gulped her soup. "What if it was the curse?"

"Oh, you shouldn't put too much stock in those sorts of things," Cassie said. "What happened here is straightforward: a set piece broke beneath the man and he fell."

"But Mary Rutledge was up there just the other day. You saw her."

"Mr. Gage is—was—a much bigger person."

"Then why is the coroner taking so long?"

"You know"—Mrs. Keene pulled a cracker out of her jacket —"hauntings *are* real."

Flora shot her a look. "Now, Alice, don't go stirring the—"

"But it's true. Like at the building where the Priory girls' school was before it burned all those years ago, taking Captain Avery's bride-to-be with it while she was evacuating the children. Even passing visitors have heard a woman's voice singing sailor songs there late at night." Mrs. Keene shrugged. "I'm just saying."

Miss Porter was quiet for a moment. Then she grabbed Cassie's hand. "Will you go in? To the theater?"

"What? Why?" Cassie tried to stand, but Miss Porter hung on.

"To find out what's going on. I want to know how—why... I need to know what exactly happened to Mr. Gage. It may not be the curse, but I've got this awful feeling in the pit of my stomach, like something's wrong—something *more* is wrong—and it's getting worse by the minute." Miss Porter bit her lip. "Not that I think anyone in the world could possibly have wanted to hurt Mr. Gage. Everyone loved him. He was a thoroughly proper gentleman. Handsome, strong, trustworthy, intelligent... You could tell by the way he pronounced things."

Cassie pressed her lips together. There was nothing to be gained by arguing with a woman in Miss Porter's state.

"Besides, maybe they need help."

Cassie itched her leg through her dress with her free hand (Miss Porter was still clinging to the other). "Oh, I'm sure they have it under control."

"No." Miss Porter shook her head, hard. It made her chignon fall, but she made no move to fix it. "They won't get it right."

"Sometimes, you simply have to trust—"

"No. I don't trust them. I trust you."

Cassie looked to Mrs. Keene and Flora, but they both shrugged.

"She's right," Flora said. "You do have a lot to offer in situations like this."

Mrs. Keene licked her thumb and rubbed a smudge on her boot. "Yeah, and we only need to think as far back as Peanut to know how things can go with this lot."

"But I don't—"

"Please, Cassie? It would be so grateful. He was"—Miss Porter gripped her hand tighter, and her voice dropped to a whisper—"special to me."

Cassie sighed inwardly. She'd been afraid of that. Well, maybe if she did this, Miss Porter would be able to mend her heart and move on.

"All right. I'll go in and ask what they've found, but only if you promise to let Flora and Mrs. Keene take you home the moment the coroner releases everyone."

Miss Porter struggled to her feet, holding onto the palm tree for support. "Thank you, Cassie. I knew I could count on you."

Finding the Lyceum's front door locked, Cassie ventured around the side to see if there was another way in, perhaps a stage door.

"He was special to me." Miss Porter's distraught face hovered before Cassie as she lifted her skirts and picked her way along what appeared to be a path next to the building. She wished she had grabbed her boots before Prince ordered everyone outside to wait for the coroner. There wasn't much grass here, only mud, and she was still in her soft rehearsal slippers.

How could Miss Porter be so gullible?

Cassie chided herself. That was unkind. Perhaps Miss Porter's relationship with Mr. Gage had been a meaningful one. But, based on what Cassie had seen, a number of the other chorus women had felt that way about the man as well. Miss Porter's rivalry with Mrs. Reynolds, the lady who had hosted a tea for Mr. Gage during the music rehearsal the other day, was clear evidence of that. And they couldn't all be right.

She also doubted so many women could have come under such an impression without at least a little intentional encouragement. Unless, perhaps, those women simply saw what they wanted to see. Who wouldn't be flattered by attention from a man like Mr. Gage? And it didn't necessarily mean Mr. Gage was a bad man. Some people just had something about them that drew others to them... Even Cassie herself had felt the pull when she first met him. But she also knew that people who were aware they possessed that kind of power could do some unreasonable things—as could those under their sway.

"Whoops!"

Heeding the admonition (of sorts) that had come from

above, Cassie hopped to the side just in time to avoid being cracked on the head with some sort of metal tin.

"Be a good girl and toss that flask back up here, would you?" The stagehand Cassie had seen in the theater the other day was looking down at her through the branches of a twisted juniper tree. As before, there was a long-nine cigar dangling from his mouth, the clump of ash on the end dangerously close to parting ways with the rest, and from this nearer vantage Cassie could see that he possessed the kind of leathery skin and thick, yet sinewy, arms and legs that tended to come from years spent in physical labor.

Cassie picked up the flask and placed it in the man's outstretched hand. When she met his gaze, she saw that, though his eyes were a handsome shade of gray, they were incredibly bloodshot. His cheeks were pink and patchy as well, and Cassie suspected it wasn't because he had been crying or blushing.

Bracing himself with his opposite arm, the man sat back up unsteadily and straddled the branch, letting a leg hang down on either side, then popped the flask cap and took a thirsty swig. "Glad I remembered I'd hid this extra one up here. Always prepare and have a spare, they say."

An apology for nearly knocking her unconscious, or perhaps a word of thanks for returning his item, would have been more welcome than this homespun aphorism, but Cassie doubted the man was in the habit of indulging in such peripheral niceties.

"Don't you think it's a little early for that, Harland?"

Prince was standing a few feet farther down the path, his arms folded across his chest as he leaned against an open door at the side of the building.

Harland scowled and took another drink. "I dunno, Prince. What time is it?"

"Three in the afternoon."

"Nah. Three's a fine time for drinking. What it's too early for is you minding my business. Again." He swatted the air with his flask, almost slipping off the branch. "Aw, don't give me that innocent face, boy. I know you complained to Mr. Gage about me drinking. It seems a man's personal habits simply aren't personal anymore. Perhaps you'd like to weigh in on how often I wash my drawers next."

"Listen, I wasn't trying to start anything. I was only—"

The man let out a long belch, followed by two short ones, then met Cassie's eye.

"What're you looking at, girlie? See something you like?"

Prince let the door drop and strode over to the tree. "Listen here, that's a lady you're speaking to. What's she done to you?"

"Prince the hero, ladies and gentlemen," Harland grumbled into his flask.

Prince turned to Cassie and bowed his head. "I apologize on behalf of my colleague."

"I don't need anyone apologizing for me, either."

Cassie adjusted her bonnet. "Oh, I'm fine. Really. I, uh—I was looking for a way in over here, since the front's locked."

"Allow me!" Sidling along the edge of Harland's glare, Prince led the way back to the door he'd emerged from and showed Cassie inside.

Prince shut the door behind them. "I really do apologize for the unpleasantness out there. That's Harland McGregor, our head stagehand. He can be a little rough around the edges, particularly when he's—in a certain state. As you may have gathered, he and I have had a little, uh, difference of opinions about that."

Cassie stepped around a rack of costumes but tripped over a treasure chest heaped with fake pirate booty. They were in the backstage area near one of the wings.

"Really, I meant what I said, Prince." She caught herself with the rack and used it to straighten up. "You don't have to worry about me. I'm no delicate young maiden on the seashore."

Prince acknowledged her attempt at a reference to the show

with a polite incline of his head. Or maybe he was trying not to laugh at her clumsiness. Either way, seeing his face relax put her closer to at ease, a considerable accomplishment given the morning's events.

"To be clear," Prince said. "I respect the man, generally. He's incredibly skilled. He used to work with some of the best theater companies out there before his vices got away from him. He designs all the troupe's sets and, for the most part, installs, operates, and breaks them down himself. He usually just hires a couple of sailors in each town to help with the rigging. But I don't understand how anyone can consume spirits the way he does and still attempt to work... I've known others like that, and it never turns out well."

Cassie wrapped her arms around herself and cast another look around. There were several large lamps about, giving off enough light to navigate by, but it was dim nevertheless, and there was a cool stillness to the air that made the whole place feel about as inviting as a crypt. The walls were tall, bare, and black, and their edges blended into each other and into the shadowy grid of pipes and pulleys above. Disembodied set pieces draped in broadcloth hulked in the corners as though ready to pounce. Costumes equipped with everything but a body floated on headless dressmaker's mannequins.

She supposed it wasn't surprising that there were so many superstitions about the supernatural in the theater world.

"It's not exactly cozy back here, is it," she said.

Something chittered, but the echo made it impossible to tell where it had come from.

"I suppose not." Prince looked thoughtfully into the rafters. "For most, that is. To me, it feels like home."

Cassie's foot brushed against something under the props table, and when she looked to see what it was, she realized it was a mean-looking handsaw. If she had kicked it a little harder, it might have cut open her delicate fabric shoe, or her foot.

Mindful of others who might be passing by, she picked it up and placed it on the table.

"So," Prince said, "what was it you needed in here?"

"Oh, right. I wanted to see how things were progressing with Mr. Gage. I've been sent in for a status update."

"They've just finished. I was on my way out when I ran into you. The doctor and the coroner went out the front to make their announcements and release everyone, so you must have just missed them. The undertaker hasn't come for Mr. Gage yet, though, so those policemen from yesterday are waiting for him down in the pit."

"Ah, good. They'll tell me what's going on."

Cassie passed between the leg curtains and padded toward the edge of the stage, skirting the broken set piece, which still lay where it had fallen. As she grew closer, however, voices rose out of the orchestra pit, and they didn't sound particularly chummy. She peered down. Sure enough, there were Officers Jake Gordon and Austin Hughes, standing nose to nose in the midst of one of their typical, often borderline nonsensical, debates.

"It's not even a question," Jake was saying. "Dr. Ames determined that the precise cause of death was a broken neck from hitting the orchestra pit floor."

Hughes flapped his hat against his thigh. "But if that front piece hadn't come away, he wouldn't have entered the pit at that rate. And, therefore, wouldn't have hit the floor and broken his neck. If, then. Cause and effect. It's a simple matter of *res ipsa loquitur—*"

Jakes sputtered. "There you go again. You can't just throw Latin at people and expect them to agree with you because you sound smart."

"So you're saying you think I'm smart."

"No, I said you *sound—*"

"Officer Gordon! Officer Hughes! For shame with that

arguing!" Cassie jammed her fists into her hips. "Have you no respect for the fact there's a *dead man* at your feet?"

Jake and Hughes looked at her, then at the ground between them, where Mr. Gage lay, albeit under a spare curtain panel, waiting for the undertaker to take him away. They each took a step back.

"For what it's worth—" Prince had followed Cassie onto the stage. "I'm not certain *res ipsa loquitur* is relevant to the argument, as that has to do with whether there's been negligence. It means 'the matter speaks for itself,' that is, the fact an accident has occurred at all means someone has not taken proper care. The seminal case, I believe, has to do with a barrel falling out of a window and landing on a fellow—the idea being that barrels aren't particularly prone to falling out of windows, absent mishandling of some kind. Anyway, I believe the legal principle you're thinking of is proximate cause." He shifted when he saw Hughes's stony expression. "In my opinion. Officer."

Cassie blinked at Prince. "You're right. How do you know about *res ipsa* and proximate cause?"

Who was this man? He wasn't what she would have expected for a traveling actor, though maybe it was her expectations that were off. Being on the road, dealing with all kinds of dangers and challenges, probably required one to be pretty tough and clever.

A shadow passed over Prince's face but quickly disappeared. "I like to read. What's your excuse?"

"My father was a lawyer. He taught me, and I used to help him with his work."

"Impressive!"

"Charming." Hughes glowered at Prince, and possibly Cassie, too. He pushed up his sleeves—he'd removed his sack coat at some point—and climbed up to sit with his legs draped over the edge of the stage. "But, for the record, as of this afternoon it's *Pro Tem* Deputy Hughes."

"Co-*Pro Tem* Deputy Hughes," corrected Jake from the pit. "And I'm Co-*Pro Tem* Deputy Gordon."

Prince peered down at him. "Say, nice ensemble you have there, Co-*Pro Tem* Deputy Gordon, with the frock coat and the paddock boots together. Dignified and functional at the same time."

"Why, thank you. I run the Egmont's livery service, so I often need to be both those things."

"You've captured it beautifully, then."

During the course of that exchange, Hughes's annoyance had traveled from his jaw to his shoulders, scrunching them up by his ears. "Fine, Jake. But that's only because you were already on your way here to ask if you could join the playacting around when the incident occurred. The sheriff specifically asked me to come, even though I was deep into other pressing investigations."

"Investigations into a few petty thefts and a peeper—"

"The law's the law."

"—which I'm also investigating."

Prince picked up a prop pirate's hook that had been dropped by one of the other actors during the melee and made a fencing motion with it. "You know, 'playacting around' is an important part of our cultural fabric. To progress as a society, we must be able to dream together, exercise a collective imagination." He jabbed and swooped the hook a few more times, then pointed it at Hughes. "But 'Co-*Pro Tem* Deputy.' What exactly is that?"

Hughes batted the hook away. "It means I—we—are performing the deputy sheriff function, but not permanently."

"Ah."

"It means he's closer to selecting a permanent deputy," Jake explained, "and it makes sense because he's had to take over the county coroner duties since Mr. Shaw left suddenly for a more glamorous position in Tallahassee and a new coroner hasn't been elected yet. As both sheriff and coroner for the moment, he's very busy."

"That's a bit heavy-handed, though, isn't it? 'Co-*Pro Tem* deputy'?" Prince turned the hook over in his hands. "Let's see. *Pro tem*, I assume, is shortened from *pro tempore*, which translates roughly to... 'for the time being.' Why not something like 'provisional deputy'? Or even just 'interim deputy'?"

"Those do roll off the tongue better," Cassie said.

Hughes ran a hand through his messy but smooth, shiny hair and down his long mustache using one connected motion. Cassie watched his fingers as they moved past his mouth. She'd never noticed his fingers before. Or his mouth.

Suddenly realizing she was staring, she busied herself with a coffee stain on her glove.

Prince was probably just trying to poke fun, which Cassie appreciated (no matter how good Hughes looked with his sleeves pushed back like that), but it was true—while Hughes and Jake had been working toward the deputy sheriff promotion since she'd known them, the amount of attention they were paying this somewhat ridiculous temporary title did seem foolish. She understood their taking pride in their work with the sheriff's department, but why this fascination with nominal accolades? Who were they trying to impress?

Hughes in particular had been unusually focused on his policeman duties during the past several weeks. Largely ignoring his clerk duties at Mr. Preston's high-end Cash Boot and Shoe Store on Centre, even though that position typically provided the bulk of his wages, he'd been pursuing one after the other self-generated law enforcement assignments all over town. At one point, he'd been so successful at apprehending minor offenders the sheriff had asked him to slow down because there wasn't enough space in the jail. It was like he was trying to prove something even beyond his fitness for the deputy sheriff position. And, as Cassie had received little more attention from

Hughes in the meantime than an occasional nod in the street, despite any other thoughts she might have had following the experiences they'd shared, it seemed she wasn't all that relevant to whatever that something was. Unfortunately.

"Thank you for the suggestion, Mr. Montgomery," said Hughes. His words were cordial, but his tone, his body, and those devastating eyes of his were not. "And I'm glad you concur, Miss Gwynne."

Cassie cursed her heart for quickening. Could he possibly be jealous? After weeks of acting as though they had barely met?

Annoyingly hopeful, she crossed to where Hughes was sitting and pushed her skirts back so she could bend over the fallen set piece, brushing Hughes's shoulder as she did so.

Had that made him look? No.

"So, Prince—" she said.

Hughes gave an exaggerated scoff, presumably at hearing Prince's unusual name again.

Well, at least he's listening.

"How exactly does it work with these set pieces? Some of them are terribly big, and the troupe travels so often. You said the head stagehand, Harland McGregor, handles it all himself?"

Prince tucked the hook he'd been fiddling with under his arm. "Mostly. Along with a hired hand or two, I understand. Though I assisted him with this load-in. I feel strongly that, in a small troupe like this, those of us who are knowledgeable and physically robust must pitch in where we can."

Hughes scoffed again.

"Let me give you the broad-brush version of the general process. Many actors' troupes do it in a similar way. Basically, the larger pieces are constructed from smaller pieces that come apart so that when we're finished in one location, the sets can be disassembled, transported, and reassembled in the next location.

"Take the schooner, for example. The mast and sail come

off, as does the ladder, and the ship's hull is made up of several other parts. That panel on the floor is the biggest single piece in the whole set. It's kind of like a giant jigsaw puzzle that you're taking apart and putting together over and over. But the pieces are labeled so the assembler can easily see what to do."

Cassie studied the panel at her feet. The back of the wood, the unpainted side, was facing up, and, as Prince had suggested, there were words and symbols painted on it with instructions. However, while some were as straightforward as "this side front," others were as befuddling as "reverse attachment point 3C-ii."

"Easily" might be an overstatement.

"What an ingenious system," she said. "But I expect it comes with some issues of wear and tear, since you have to pull the pieces apart over and over and transport them everywhere." She ran her gloved fingers over the wood as though inspecting it, but her eyes were on Hughes. Still nothing.

Jake tried to jump and pull himself onto the stage next to them but slipped, causing Cassie to stumble and Hughes to drop his gun. "That's what Sheriff Alderman said."

Hughes punched Jake in the arm and slid down to retrieve his gun.

"Yes," Prince said. "That is certainly a concern. And, I'll admit, the finances of a traveling theatrical troupe being what they are, it's not always the case that the highest quality materials are at one's disposal. In fact, according to the stage manager, Mr. Manning, Mr. Gage has a strict policy against buying anything new if suitable materials can be salvaged from a junkyard or purchased at a lesser price from a resale store. I understand the schooner was made from wood Mr. Gage got for free, from a builder who was tearing down houses in an old neighborhood."

"And look where being cheap got him," Hughes said. "Fell right apart during his big moment."

As he spoke, he and Jake tried to jump onto the stage at the same time. They bounced off one another, but still managed to hang on, and a swinging elbow fight ensued.

Prince shook his hook at them. "Gentlemen, be careful! That is a serious drop there, as you know!"

After a few more furious seconds, the two men squeezed themselves up, again at the same time, and bellied onto the stage like circus seals.

Cassie stepped over them and walked across the panel to Prince's side of the set piece. "That's what they think caused the accident, then? The wood was old?"

"Well—"

"Hey, what was that sound?" Jake crawled to his feet.

Hughes did the same. "What sound?"

"It was like, I don't know, a person humming? I think it came from over there." He pointed toward the wings. "Could someone else be in here?"

Prince placed the hook in a crate near the side of the stage. "There shouldn't be. I sent everyone outside right after the accident. And we didn't see anyone when we came in together just now. Right, Cassie?"

That earned Prince some quality Hughes eye-daggers.

"Right." Cassie flicked her own glance toward the wings. She thought she'd heard something herself, but there were a lot of things that could make mysterious noises in a space like this. "So, about Mr. Gage's accident—"

Prince rubbed his temples. "Yes, the theory the coroner has adopted is the piece came off because the wood wasn't sound."

"There's that sound again," Jake said.

Hughes finally tore his glare away from Prince. "I didn't hear anything, Gordon. Maybe it's the ghost—curse. Whatever."

Jake frowned and walked over to peer between the leg curtains.

"I don't suppose it's an unreasonable theory," Cassie said,

"but if the material was so deficient, wouldn't that be something one would notice while assembling the set?"

Hughes muttered to himself as he tugged his sleeves back down. "*Res ipsa loquitur.*"

Closer.

"As a matter of fact"—Prince took off his buccaneer's hat and poked his hand inside the crown, trying to pop out a dent—"the theory the coroner adopted was slightly more nuanced than that. He concluded that not only was the wood old and crumbly, the repeated disassembly and reassembly of the piece over time wore down the holes for the nails that held that front piece onto the base piece. Enough that they became loose and no longer held with a tight fit."

Cassie thought for a moment. "The coroner came up with that theory?"

"No, I believe one of the troupe members suggested it." Hughes checked his pocket watch. "In an interview. I didn't sit through them all, though, so I can't be sure. But that head stage-hand, Harland McGregor, didn't contradict it when asked. In fact, he said he thought it very plausible. And we know the wood was old, or at least obtained secondhand, as mentioned, and the nails did pull free, so there you have it."

Cassie stepped onto the panel for a closer look. As Hughes had said, the wood was worn and had split and splintered in several places. Mr. Gage must really have been trying to adhere to a budget if he was willing to use material like this.

Something clattered in the wings.

"Kicked over a music stand," Jake called.

Cassie examined the nails sticking out of the board. They were long and thick and scary, certainly the kind of fastener one would want for heavy-duty work—or at least one would assume so. She didn't know much about construction practices herself. But their orientation, pointing up like that, did seem as expected for a panel pulling away from another. She touched a finger to one of the sharp points; she ought to have been more careful walking back and forth across the piece. One false step in her thin rehearsal slippers and she would have had a nasty wound.

She straightened up, chewing her lip. Now that she was looking at the board from this angle, the nails seemed distributed haphazardly, like a monster's jagged underbite. It didn't look professionally done. Perhaps the drinking issues Prince had mentioned were making Harland McGregor sloppy. Though, how nicely organized nails looked probably didn't have much to do with their ability to hold two pieces of wood together.

She walked upstage to the upright portion of the schooner and ran her fingers along the exposed beams as high as she could reach.

She turned to look back at the piece on the floor. *This could be a little more problematic.* She obviously wasn't going to be able to go along and compare nail-for-nail, but the holes on this side didn't appear to match up with the nails sticking out of the other side, either in number or in placement.

Jake reappeared from behind the curtain and trotted back over to them. "Couldn't find anything. I thought I heard the door on the other side shut at one point, but when I ran over there and looked outside, I didn't see anyone. Maybe I imagined all of it."

"Well, I could be imagining this, too..." Cassie looked back and forth between the two pieces of the schooner again. "But it seems to me that the nails down there don't go with the holes up here."

Prince walked over and ran his hands over the beams himself. "I see what you're saying. But, as we've discussed, these pieces have been pulled apart and put together a number of times. It's very possible a few nails have gone in different places occasionally and created different holes."

Remembering something from when she was standing in the pit after the accident, Cassie returned to the edge of the stage and bent to look beneath the portion of the panel protruding over the pit. She'd remembered right. There were several nails pointed the wrong way, downward out of the panel.

"And what do you suppose these nails are for?" she asked. "What would they fasten to?"

This was feeling odder and odder. But odd didn't necessarily mean bad, right? Though... Cassie touched a hand to her middle. She was starting to get a feeling in the pit of her stomach, as well. Perhaps whatever Miss Porter had was catching.

Oh, no, Cassie. No, you don't. She rubbed her face. *But, still...*

She set her jaw. "Something isn't right."

"Give it back, Hughes." Jake dropped his notebook and swiped at Hughes, who, it appeared, had stolen his pencil, a little pink stub painted with flowers.

"That is, the old-wood-with-nails-falling-out theory is possible," Cassie continued, "but this nail arrangement really doesn't look—"

Hughes hopped back, the pencil above his head. "Trust me, Gordo, I'm doing you a favor. A grown man shouldn't be seen with a little girl's writing utensil."

"Metta didn't want it anymore, and it still works the same as any other pencil."

"I know. I'll bet Miss Hale gave it to her, and you're carrying it around like some kind of pathetic love token. Everything all right there, by the way? I saw you two having words the other afternoon. Or is that how lovebirds act these days?"

"Shut it, Hughes. And I'm not the one carrying around a pocketful of frilly little pink—"

"Is anyone even listening to me?" She'd had better luck getting the attention of children.

"Uh." Jake lunged at Hughes's hand again. "Sure we are."

"None of this is bothering you in the slightest?"

"Bothering us? What do you—" Jake stopped. "Oh, Cassie. You're not suggesting—"

"I'm not suggesting anything. I'm just asking questions."

Hughes stuck the pencil down his suit trousers, and Jake finally backed off. "Miss Gwynne, you never 'just ask questions.' Everyone knows that."

Cassie couldn't tell whether that was a good or bad thing. He hadn't minded before, when they were investigating Peanut's murder. He had even asked for her help.

"I'm just not sure what you're getting at," Jake said.

Hughes crossed his arms. "Aren't you about to leave and go back home to New York anyway? Why are you wasting your time in here?"

"That's right." Jake picked up his notebook, a little pink thing that was likely part of a matching set with his purloined pencil, and tucked it into his coat. "You should be out enjoying yourself. Take a ride on the beach, maybe. I can get you one of Mr. Littell's trotters, if you like. He's always glad for someone to exercise the horses."

"And," Prince said, "not to nudge in where I haven't been asked—"

"Too late." Hughes re-tucked his shirt, and the pencil slid out of his trouser leg.

"—but isn't this really *their* job? The police officers?"

Cassie's knuckles tightened. What was this? The men stick with the men? "Yes, but they don't seem to be taking the situation very seriously."

Jake put a hand on Cassie's shoulder. "Come now, Cassie. We would if there was anything to be serious about." He glanced at Mr. Gage's body and cleared his throat. "In terms of an investigation, that is. I only wonder whether you might be, well, looking for trouble where there isn't any."

"Not to mention how busy we've been trying to track down that thief making his way around the Egmont, and the peeper who's been disturbing ladies. Not that a bigger crime wouldn't help with my promotion—" Hughes stopped, hopefully hearing his own words and exercising a bit of editorial wisdom. "I mean, we shouldn't be bothering the sheriff unless there's really something to talk about."

"It's good to ask questions," Jake went on. "And I know you're smarter than any of us. But, in this instance, I don't know if there's much to say other than that many different factors came together here and caused a tragic accident. Sometimes bad things just happen."

Cassie glared at the three men, oscillating between hugely irritated and fuming.

Yes, sometimes bad things just happen. But sometimes they get help from bad people. Wasn't anyone else worried about that?

5

Late the next evening, Cassie leaned against a railing at the Centre Street passenger dock, shoulder to shoulder with Esy the kitten. The moon was big, round, and bright, and hung so low in the sky it looked like a piece of fine china perched in a display cabinet, ready to lift out and place with a setting of sparkling silver. Along the horizon below it, a row of palm trees stood dark against the black velvet sky, their outline as clear and sharp as a shadow box cutout, though every so often they gave away their realness with a slight sway, or the release of a single, swiftly winging bird bound for somewhere across the water.

Sighing, Cassie bent to study the riverbed beneath the dock. The tide had gone completely out, leaving hundreds of half-buried mussels to blow bubbles in the mud, and as the irides-cent pockets of air swelled and popped in rapid, chaotic succes-sion, they transformed the gray expanse into another twinkling night sky below her feet. She searched the mussel-stars for a pattern. Perhaps a constellation would appear and help her divine what to do.

She'd been wrestling with herself since the previous after-noon. Should she go to the sheriff with her concerns about the set piece, despite what Jake and Hughes, and Prince, had said? She hadn't mentioned anything to Miss Porter when she stopped by her boarding house, Lottie's Cottage, to tell her about the coroner's conclusions, but that was because she didn't want to disturb her without reason. The official explanation—that the wood was old and overworked and repeated assembly and disassembly had finally become too much—was plausible, even reasonable. And that alone had been devastating enough to cause Miss Porter to take to her room. Mrs. Keene had had to shut down her own store and assume care of Miss Porter's boarders for her.

She watched Esy creep a few feet, her bright eyes trained on a group of pelicans who had perched on the railing with their heads tucked under their wings, leaving one awake to stand watch. The sentry's head jerked as he tried not to nod off.

She also wasn't sure exactly what it was she had to say yet. After all, what *were* her concerns? That she had an "odd feeling" about things? That, in her very informed opinion about the principles of construction, the nails should have been more tidily applied? She knew what her father would have said: *What's the implication, Cassie? Observations are only observations without conclusions. What's the corollary?*

The only answer to that she could think of was one she didn't want to think *about*: What if someone had tampered with the piece so that Mr. Gage would fall?

She stood a penny she had found on the railing and spun it like a top, lifting an arm to keep Esy from batting it off.

If so, the key question would be one of motive, and so far none had presented itself. As far she had seen, Mr. Gage had been an unusually likeable man. It didn't take sophisticated powers of perception to notice the effect he'd had on women like Miss Porter in particular—such as how, with a single smile, he had been able to reduce an independent, levelheaded woman to a tittering girl—or the associated in-fighting for his attention it had inspired. It had made Cassie worry for her friend because of how attached she'd become and how it had made her act, but that sort of thing couldn't have resulted in someone causing Mr. Gage harm, could it?

And then there was Mr. Gage's philanthropic bent. She had never heard of another theatrical troupe that functioned on a not-for-profit basis in the manner that had been described to her. What kind of enemies could such an operation possibly inspire?

Still, though. Whatever the answers to her questions, what business was it of *hers*?

She flicked a leaf off the railing and watched it twist and float toward the watery cosmos below. It wasn't too late to take her planned trip back to New York. She'd messaged Mr. Renault that she would be returning later than planned because of the charity theater production, but that was after she'd already purchased her steamer ticket. That ship wouldn't be leaving for a few more days yet.

No, Miss Porter needs me to stay and look after her, at least for a little while.

The kitten looked at her.

"Fine, yes, Miss Esy. That did sound slightly like an excuse."

Esy headbutted her chin in response, squinting as the breeze ruffled the fur on her face.

The cat was right. Perhaps she was only looking for another reason to stay on the island and avoid returning to New York. First, she had stayed because Flora needed help at her store. Then there was the show and its charity efforts. Now it was for the benefit of Miss Porter... even though she'd done what she'd been asked, and Miss Porter had more than enough support in her other friends.

And, while she was being honest with herself, had the only

reason she had gone back into the theater yesterday really been to appease Miss Porter?

The truth was, the longer she stayed the more selfish she was being. She had spent the year after losing her father hiding behind her grief. Would she spend the next one here on the island, running away from it? She ought to go back, face reality head-on, and show she was worthy of the legacy her father had left her.

She looked down at her feet. They didn't seem particularly inclined to move.

"No, Frederic, I shall live and die a Pirate King!"

Mr. Gage's voice, delivering that spoken line before his final song, sounded in her head, sending tiny shivers down the nape of her neck. The words, originally written to amuse, were macabre now.

Again Cassie saw the terror on Mr. Gage's face as he hurtled through the air, again she heard the sickening sound his body made as he hit the ground. That scene, which had replayed in her head countless times since it happened, had not only kept her from falling asleep for hours the night before, but had also brought back her "sleep migrating" problem (as coined by Flora): Ever since she was a child, in times of stress she would wander from her bed while still fully asleep and take up alternative quarters in locations spanning from the rug beneath her father's desk to the shelves in the pantry. This morning, she had awoken on Flora's back porch with her hands individually wrapped in newspaper.

Mr. Gage flew and fell once more, and the shivers on her neck trickled down to her spine. Something had gone very wrong. What if someone had *made* it go wrong?

She yanked her bonnet down so hard Esy stopped cleaning her rear and looked up at her, her back leg straight up by her head. She was "slapping steak at dozing dogs," as her father would have put it. Jake and Hughes had told her so in no uncertain terms. And doing that had already gotten her involved in one murder investigation since she'd been on the island, which was one more than any normal person should ever have to be involved in.

Why did she always think it was her job to protect everyone else?

Esy snapped to attention, her tail flicking, and rotated her furry white ears toward a figure approaching the dock.

Cassie squinted. *Is that Prince?* He was too far away to be certain at first, but the build was right, and the wreath of curls below the brim of his derby was distinctly familiar. Instead of loping along in his usual easy gait, however, he was hunched forward, his coat collar pulled up. He continued to the far end of the wharf area and sat on a bench with his back to her.

What was he doing out here at this hour? He clearly wasn't out for a casual stroll.

Even though she was still a little irritated about his comment at the theater yesterday, Cassie was about to call out when another man appeared on the end of the dock and headed toward him, scurrying through the circles of lamplight and hugging the shadows as though a winged predator were circling above. He had a slight limp, though, which slowed him down considerably, and if there had truly been a predator overhead, Cassie doubted his overly elaborate maneuvering would have done him much good. Finally, he reached Prince's bench and plopped down next to him.

Cassie craned her neck, but, unfortunately, the moon backdrop had turned the men into cutouts like the palm trees, obscuring any further details.

Prince and the mystery man spoke for several minutes, their heads bowed toward one another. Every so often one of them would pop up, look around, then hunch back down. Finally, they stood, and Prince handed an envelope to the man. The man handed Prince a box in return, then they tipped their hats and parted ways.

Cassie swallowed, her greeting still stuck in her throat. She didn't realize Prince knew anyone in town. Though, that meeting didn't exactly seem like a friendly visit. Who was that man? What were they talking about? What was in that envelope? And that box?

"Miss Cassie! I've been looking for you everywhere." Paddy thundered down the dock with a brown paper parcel under his arm. He swerved to avoid a vendor cart parked by the ticket agent's shelter for the night and panted to a stop in front of her.

"You have?" She didn't realize Mrs. Rydell, the postmistress, kept the post office open this late. Even the pelican sentry had given in to the night—his beak was hovering near his wing, and Cassie hadn't seen him jerk awake for quite some time.

"Mrs. Rydell said to bring this right to you because you'd been expecting it for a while."

"Thank you, Paddy. And Mrs. Rydell, I suppose." Cassie patted his floppy palmetto-weave boater and reached for the parcel. "Hey! What—?"

Paddy had replaced the parcel with an open hand and a grin. As he winked one of his softly tilted brown eyes at her, a lock of his reddish-brown hair fell across his forehead, and Cassie was reminded of how stunning his mixture of eastern and western features were. Paddy's father was Chinese and his mother Irish, making him a living embodiment of Flora's (Aristotle's?) principle about the whole being different from, perhaps even surpassing, the sum of its parts.

"All right, you little imp. You're lucky you're cute." She placed the penny she'd been fiddling with in the child's palm and was presented her parcel with aplomb. "So you're messengering full time now?"

"It pays way more than selling newspapers. And I'm saving

up for something." Paddy climbed the rail to peer over her shoulder as she examined the postal markings, and Esy did the same on her other side. "So, you gonna open it and see what's inside?"

Cassie clapped the parcel to her chest. She knew very well what was inside. Which was exactly why she didn't feel motivated to open it just now.

"Paddy, do you really care, or is there another reason you're asking?"

The boy chewed his lip for a moment, but his honesty won out, as it usually did.

"Mrs. Rydell said she would pay me a bonus tip if I found out for her."

"How much?"

"Fifty cents."

"Gracious. She must really be hurting for gossip. Here." Placing the parcel on the dock by her feet, Cassie reached for her money pouch. "How about I give you a dollar and you leave it alone? Oh no."

As soon as her hand touched her hip, she remembered that the pouch was clipped to her chatelaine—which was still tied up in her wrap on a chair in the Lyceum auditorium, next to that packet of orange blossom scones she had brought to snack on during rehearsal. Not that she was thinking about food at a time like this.

Her stomach growled.

"I'm sorry, but I left my money pouch at the Lyceum."

Paddy hopped down from his perch. "Where that actor fell off the stage yesterday?"

"Uh, yes."

"We could go get it."

"My money pouch? I think it's too late right now."

Paddy stuck out his lip and blinked up at her, his eyes wide and beseeching. He must have learned that from Metta. Or maybe it was the other way around. "But you promised me a tip."

"Mreow." Esy sat on the parcel and looked up at Cassie. Her eyes were a miniature, fur-framed version of Paddy's.

Cassie picked up the kitten and put her on her shoulder. "Fine. But only because you two teamed up against me. And we're not lingering, understand? We get the chatelaine and go. And don't touch anything."

The Lyceum's front door was locked, so Cassie and Paddy, the kitten tight on their heels, proceeded along the side of the building to try one of the stage doors, making their way by the moonlight filtering through the trees.

Paddy pressed his back against the building, sidestepping with exaggerated furtiveness through the shadows. "I'm like Ernest Keen, the Boy Detective from *The Crimes of London*!" He whipped his head left and right, as though checking whether they were being followed, then continued on. "Or one of the Wild Boys."

An owl hooted overhead, and Cassie clutched her parcel.

Paddy giggled. "How deliciously eerie!"

Eerie, yes. Delicious, no.

Disentangling a similarly spooked Esy from the inside of her skirts, Cassie backed against the siding next to him, copying his posture as they inched forward. She wasn't as interested as he in executing a story-perfect covert approach, but, for the moment, keeping the world in front of her felt like a good idea. "Your father doesn't mind you reading those stories? Even I can hardly handle how gory and sensational they are. They call them 'penny dreadfuls' for a reason, you know."

"Aw, Baba says they're nothing compared to the scary stories they used to tell back in China. Did you know we have a whole festival for ghosts whose necks are so skinny they can't swallow any food?"

Cassie grimaced. "Where do you get them, even? The penny dreadfuls? I don't think I've seen them sold in town."

"Mrs. Keene loves them so she has a big collection. She gets them from a sailor on one of the packets that comes through from Liverpool. She lets Metta and me come look at them whenever, and if they're too hard for us, she reads them aloud. That's the best."

"Metta, too? Does Jake know about that?"

"Aha!" Paddy pushed the stage door open with a nonsensical mixture of bravado and stealth. He formed his voice into an important whisper dripping with an unidentifiable accent. "A secret entrance. And it is, how do you say, unlocked!"

"All right, that's enough."

They slipped inside.

Propping the door with her parcel, Cassie used the moonlight coming through the crack to locate a table she knew was a few feet away and light the lamp on it. There was a small light on the stage that had been left lit per theater tradition (superstition) called the ghost light, but the rest of the area was very dark, so she picked up the table lamp and carried it with her.

"Ahoyyyy!" Paddy called, his hands cupped around his mouth. "Eck-ohhh! This place is huge! I came inside while they were holding a court session once, but it looked different then." He was enjoying this a little too much.

"Paddy, I asked you to stop playing around."

"Sorry. Is that the rigging area up there?" He ran over to the spiral staircase next to the door.

Cassie followed behind him, searching her memory from her time in her school's theater. He was probably right. Somewhere at the top of that staircase must be the area where the ropes controlling the grid of suspended lights and backdrops were located.

"Ahoyyyy!" Paddy called again, directing his voice up the staircase.

"Ahoyyyy!" came a response, so soft and distant it sounded otherworldly.

Cassie and Paddy fell against each other.

Paddy grabbed a portion of Cassie's topskirt and pulled it over his head, leaving only his eyes peering out. "That was my echo, right?"

Cassie shook off a chill. "Of course. There's no one in here." She took back her skirt and started toward the wings. "Come on, my things are in the auditorium. Take care crossing the stage, though, because there are—Oof!"

She swung the lamp around accusingly. When she had turned to talk to Paddy, she had walked right into the back of the drop hanging at the rear of the stage, a sunny seaside sky for Act One.

Struck by a sudden curiosity, she stepped around the backdrop and slid along the front of it until she reached the midpoint of the stage. She held up the lamp: before her was the rear portion of the schooner set piece, still hulking on the stage like a giant skeleton. As on the portion lying on the stage, there were words and symbols scrawled across the various beams and other parts indicating how the pieces were to be joined together. Though, for all her other abilities, disciplines involving spatial complexities (along with the art of perfumery, apparently) was not a strength of hers—even children's jigsaw puzzles occasionally confounded her—so those instructions may as well have been written in ancient Egyptian.

"Is that where he fell from?" Paddy appeared next to her, his mouth slightly agape.

"Yes, it is. The back of it, anyway."

He was quiet a moment.

"Do you think it hurt? When he fell?"

Cassie glanced down at him. It was a fair question, if not a pleasant one.

"I don't know, Paddy. Probably some."

"I hope it wasn't too much."

Sweet boy.

They were turning to pass around the set piece onto the stage when Cassie's foot encountered something soft. She angled the lamplight downward as a hat cartwheeled into the back of the schooner.

"Hey, that's Mr. Jake's!" Paddy picked it up and blew what appeared to be sawdust off of it. The kitten sneezed.

When was the last time anyone swept back here? Cassie held out her hand. "Here. I'll take it back to him. He must have dropped it or put it down while he was walking around yesterday, looking for... Never mind."

Paddy handed her the hat and skipped around the set piece onto the stage.

"Careful, Paddy! There are nails on the ground!" Cassie hurried out after him but stopped when she saw him standing still by the ghost light, which had been set on a stool at the center of the stage.

His head was tilted back, his gaze up in the rafters. "What was that?"

"What was what?"

"The singing. It was definitely not my echo this time. It was someone else. Or something else."

Cassie hugged her arms as a chill sliced through her. "Paddy, don't."

Esy mewed in agreement and wrapped herself around Cassie's leg.

"It was like a song the men on Baba's ship sing sometimes, when they're working a halyard."

Cassie peered up into the rafters as well, though neither the ghost light nor the table lamp she was carrying reached that high. "Prince said they hire sailors to work the rigging, but there isn't any reason for someone like that to be in here right now—"

There was a snap like the crack of a whip, followed by the surging whiz of rope on metal, and before they knew where to look, a piece of suspended background scenery, the arch for the doorway of the "ruined chapel" on Major-General Stanley's estate in Act Two, slammed to the floor right behind them.

Esy shot into the wings, and Paddy was close behind. Lifting an arm over her head, Cassie stumbled after them.

Paddy didn't stop after he cleared the stage, however.

"Where are you going?" Cassie called as he leapt onto the spiral staircase by the door.

"To catch a ghost!"

The spirals were small and tight, and the uneven triangle shape of the steps made her trip repeatedly, but Cassie managed to stay mostly upright as they went around and around until finally they reached a suspended landing. Along one side of the platform she spotted the pin rail, a wooden railing with a number of dowels sticking up from it, each tied with a length of rope. Paddy had been right. This was the rigging platform.

One of the dowels was empty, however, and above it, right below a large pulley hub, was a length of rope with a small counterweight attached. That had to be the one connected to the backdrop piece that fell: it was hanging loose. But there was no operator.

Doubling back, they turned onto where the landing continued as a narrow walkway above the stage and raced through the grid to the other side, but when they reached the opposite staircase, they found it empty. There was another stage door down below, so whoever might have been there was likely long gone.

Paddy led the way back to the other platform, where Cassie had dropped Jake's hat.

"Paddy, you can't do that." Cassie puffed by the pin rail as Paddy plopped onto a makeshift seat constructed from a hay bale wrapped in canvas. A smattering of personal items lay by their feet—work gloves, a half-drunk bottle of liquor, empty tobacco tins, a postcard of a scantily clad woman. "I was afraid you'd kill yourself."

"Sorry, Miss Cassie."

Cassie put down the lamp and attempted to sit on the hay bale next to him but ran into some logistical issues with her bustle and tipped onto all fours.

"Besides, it's a curse, not a ghost, that people have been—"

"Everything all right up here?"

Cassie would have gasped if she weren't so out of breath. Standing was also not an immediate option so she settled on swiveling her head emphatically. "Prince?"

Prince took the last two stairs in one stride and stepped onto the platform. "Sorry to startle you. I heard something heavy fall, then running footsteps. What's going on?" He kicked the dirty postcard over the edge. "Filthy sailors."

Cassie smoothed her hair and pushed onto her feet, trying not to kneel on the kitten, who, having followed Prince up the stairs, was now stalking his ankle cuff. She felt a distinct awkwardness with Prince now, though she couldn't tell if it was all on her part, given her lingering irritation at what he had said the previous afternoon, and, perhaps, what she'd seen on the dock.

"We came in to get some belongings I'd left in the auditorium, but when we were on the stage, a piece of background scenery fell right behind us. We ran up to see if we could see what had happened, but no one was up here."

"Because it was the gh—curse." Paddy stuck out his chin.

"I see." Prince walked over to examine the empty dowel, dragging the kitten, who was clinging to his cuff, along with him. "I don't know if it was a curse, young sir, but that piece shouldn't have come down on its own. Riggers use sailor-grade knots. They don't untie themselves."

"That's what I thought." Cassie picked up the kitten and settled her in the crook of her arm.

"Though..." Prince removed the shoes that were hanging from his shoulder by the laces and made his way down the pin rail, leaning back and forth to check the other tie-offs. "A couple of these aren't done up correctly. But whether to the point they would come undone spontaneously, I don't know. I am surprised Harland didn't catch the riggers in their error, though." He scratched his beard. "Come to think of it, the riggers haven't been here since load-in. I heard Mr. Manning tell Harland Mr. Gage didn't want them called back until we ran the show with full scene changes, to save money, so he should manage whatever we needed in the meantime himself. We've definitely used some of these since then... But Harland knows what he's doing."

Cassie looked over the railing, and the kitten, squeezed against her chest, peered down with her.

"So... the curse?" Paddy said.

Cassie turned around. "This is serious, Paddy. Something very strange is going on here. Prince, I'm telling you, those nails really make me wonder whether something intentional may have been involved in Mr. Gage's accident. Can you think of anyone who may have held a grudge against him?"

"You're really fixated on those nails." Prince grabbed a hold of the rope dangling overhead and started reeling the piece that had fallen back into position.

"No, I— Well, all right. But also considering this problem with the rigging tie-offs, and the scenery piece falling... Could someone have something against the production or the troupe in general? Not just Mr. Gage?"

"Now you're really losing me." Prince finished his task and, after giving the rope a confirmatory tug, moved down the line to re-tie the others. "What could someone possibly have against any of us? We're entertainers. It's our sworn duty to make people happy."

Cassie attempted to sit on the hay-bale seat again, and this time she succeeded. "I wasn't trying to insult anyone."

Prince kept his head bent over his work, his mouth fixed in a frown.

"I take it you're on their side, then," Cassie said. "Officers Gordon and Hughes."

"There are no sides here."

"But you think I should leave it alone."

"That's not what I said." Prince sighed. "Look. I understand what you're feeling. I do. When something horrific happens, 'sometimes bad things happen' isn't good enough. You want more of an explanation than that, an actual reason. But let's think this through. So the nails are oddly placed, or whatever you had in mind. Where does that get you?

"What I can tell you is those nails in the boards down there are longest, thickest ones we have. You're not going to get better tensile strength than that, unless you use screws possibly. And those have to be laboriously spiraled in—and, later, out—one at a time... What troupe has the time for that while constantly moving from place to place? My feeling is it all still comes down to the poor quality of the wood, which Mr. Gage himself insisted on, and the repeated assembly and disassembly of the piece."

Cassie shifted the kitten and yanked at a bit of skirt that was bunched underneath her. "But what about the holes not matching the—"

"I thought we talked about this, but fine. Assuming the nails are in fact in the wrong places, what then? Are you saying someone moved them around? Why? To sabotage it? How would that even work? And who would do that? What I mean is, it's a long way from nails to murder."

Why was he being so impatient with her? Had she done something to offend him? He was the one who had made her feel belittled yesterday. Either way, this version of him was hard to square with the upbeat, quick-to-smile one she'd first met.

"But don't you think—" Cassie yanked at her skirt again and finally got it free, but as the fabric unfurled, a flurry of debris flew into the air, raining back down on the platform in a barrage of metallic clinks.

The kitten leapt out of Cassie's arms, batting and pouncing like her life depended on it.

"Esy, stop! Get that out of your mouth." Cassie lunged and worked whatever the kitten had gripped in her jaw into her palm.

She looked up at Prince. "They're nails."

Crawling around the platform on their hands and knees, Cassie, Prince, and Paddy collected the nails that had bounced and rolled every which way, along with a ladies' handkerchief. They deduced that the nails had been tied up in the handkerchief, which had been shoved under the hay bale Cassie was sitting on, and Cassie had grabbed the handkerchief and pulled it out along with her skirt.

"Where do you think they came from?" Cassie asked.

Prince examined the pile. "Well, these are definitely the kind of nails the troupe buys. I can tell by the maker's signature cut on the heads—Mr. Manning says Mr. Gage insists on them because he likes the price point. Anyway, they're the size and length we use for most average connections... I mean, for joining pieces that don't have any special demands. Things that just have to hold together."

"How odd," Cassie said, lifting one up and peering more closely at it. "Why are they all bent at the tip?"

"And why were they up here under a hay-bale seat, tied up in this"—Paddy sniffed the handkerchief—"flower-scented ladies' handkerchief?"

Cassie took the handkerchief from Paddy. It was made from delicate, high-quality fabric, and had an embroidered orange blossom on it. She smelled it. "Violet, I think. And something else, also a little sweet but with more depth. And a lot of power. I think a spice—vanilla, perhaps. But I'm not very good at scent identification... Say, what's this?"

There was a shred of wood sticking to the fabric of the handkerchief. In fact, there were several. She went over the handkerchief carefully and soon she had assembled a pile in her palm.

"They're little pieces of wood," she said. "With paint on them." She sucked in a breath. "Prince, it's the same color as the schooner set piece."

He leaned forward. "Maybe. But—"

"Do you think that means the nails came from the schooner?"

"Oh, now, that's a huge leap. I think we should all take a step back and—"

"Please!" Cassie held out her palm. "Just look at them?"

Sighing, Prince took the pieces into his own hand. As he turned them over in his palm, his expression darkened.

"My thought was," Cassie said, "if you're trying to get a nail out of a piece of wood, you'd probably have to hammer the pointy side a little, so you can have something to grab onto on the other side to pull it out. Which would account for the bent ends. And I would expect some shreds of wood would come off in the process. Whoever collected the nails into the handkerchief probably scooped some of the wood shreds with the nails unintentionally."

Prince continued to stare at the wood shreds in his palm, like a tea leaf reader trying to discern a pattern. Finally, he spoke.

"Are you saying you think someone pulled these out of the schooner piece after it fell and hid them up here?"

Cassie thought about that. "Yes. I believe that's what I'm saying."

"They would have had to sneak back in while we waited outside for the coroner to come. And it would have taken a while to do it."

"The stage doors weren't locked. And we were waiting a long time." Cassie tried to keep her breath steady. "One more question. You said this type of nail is used when there aren't any 'special demands.' Does 'special demands' include a large man hanging off of it?"

Prince dipped his head. "In such a case, longer, thicker nails would be more appropriate."

"Such as the ones currently in the panel. Which, as I mentioned before, seemed pretty hastily applied—going back to your point about there not being much time to do this."

"Someone switched the nails around so Mr. Gage would fall?" Paddy screwed up his face in horror, concentration, or fascination. Or all of the above.

"Then back again to cover it up," Cassie answered. "Possibly." She was certain her face looked about the same as Paddy's.

Inhaling deeply, she carefully swept everything back into the handkerchief and tied it up.

"What are you going to do now?" Prince asked.

"I think it's time to have another conversation with the Co-*Pro Tem* deputy sheriffs about nails."

6

Sheriff Alderman, who had evidently decided that, given the hour, attaching suspenders to his sleeping trousers was dressed enough, regarded Jake and Hughes across the table inside the holding area of the Nassau County Jail that doubled as their office. Through the bars of the small window high on the wall behind him, Cassie could hear the frogs beginning their nightly operetta from among the razor-sharp clusters of saw palmetto outside that served as a secondary deterrent to would-be jail escapees. As usual, however, their melodies were lacking in originality and the orchestration was repetitive.

The sheriff picked up the handkerchief bundle Cassie had brought over from the Lyceum earlier that evening. "So you found—"

"Miss Gwynne found," Jake corrected.

Cassie turned around to look at the facility's lone inmate, a woman with hair like a lightning cloud, who was petting the pearl buttons on the closure of Cassie's dress through the bars. When Cassie met her eye, the woman gave her a bright smile.

Cassie dipped her head in response and took a slight step forward. She let her gaze travel the room. Being back in here, it was hard not to think about that first day on the island, when she'd come to the jail to give a witness statement about a purse-snatching and found Flora behind bars. It had been an unusual first meeting.

The sheriff started again. "So Miss Gwynne found this ladies' handkerchief—"

"Scented ladies' handkerchief," added Hughes.

"Miss Gwynne found this scented ladies' handkerchief hidden under a hay bale on the Lyceum stage—"

"Above the Lyceum stage," Jake corrected.

"Up on the rigging platform," Hughes added.

"On the Lyceum's rigging platform with nails wrapped up in it, and she believes those nails were used in the set piece that fell and injured Mr. Gage—"

"Killed—"

The sheriff's muttonchops puffed like an enraged cat. "Offi-cers—Co-*Pro Tem* Deputies Gordon and Hughes. If you could, for the sake of my sanity and your safety, please save up your corrections and additions until I finish thinking through what you've told me? As you well know, sudden deaths are typically the coroner's jurisdiction, and while you two have been pushing to bring our department more to bear on such matters, I have never harbored such ambitions. Unfortunately, Coroner Shaw's abrupt departure for Tallahassee has left me with no choice.

"So, please be considerate of the fact that, between my normal sheriff's duties and the coroner's duties that have been thrust upon me, along with my wife's insistence on sharing every detail of her new obsession with oriental rug patterns— not to mention the unprecedented run on firewood that is occurring at my wood yard business—my mind has enough trampling over it to rival a herd of wildebeests and I might need a moment to collect myself."

He stuck his thumbs under his suspenders and turned to Cassie.

"Miss Gwynne, to summarize, the theory here is that someone replaced the nails holding the schooner set piece together with inferior nails in order to weaken the connection and ensure Mr. Gage's fall. Then, after the fall, before Dr. Ames and I arrived on the scene, that same person removed them and put the proper nails back in, hastily, and hid the inferior nails in a scented ladies' handkerchief under a hay bale up on the rigging platform, so as to obscure that fact. Did I get that right?"

Cassie nodded, stunned at the sheriff's incisiveness given the mental chaos he had just described.

He continued. "Are you aware that your theory runs contrary to the one I've publicly espoused regarding the incident? That is, that the wood was old and worn and the holes for the nails had simply become too loose after repeated construction and deconstruction? It's a known fact that as wood ages it becomes more brittle and has less resistance to draw-out."

The lady inmate made another reach for Cassie's buttons, and Cassie slid farther away.

"Yes, sir."

The sheriff laced his fingers together on the table in front of him. "I understand a Prince Montgomery was with you when you found the items? And helped you generate your conclusions?"

"That's right."

Jake leaned forward. "You'll remember, Sheriff, from the interviews we conducted at the Lyceum, that Prince Montgomery is one of the main troupe actors. He's a longtime member of the theatrical community and knows a good deal about set construction."

Hughes fought to get his elbow in front of Jake's. "You know, I was planning to search the theater again myself, just as soon as I found some time between hunting down the thief who's been working the Egmont and finding that peeper

Marguerite Clifton reported. I've already completed a dozen interviews and am on the verge of—"

"Do you have something to add to the present discussion, or are you simply going to talk about yourself for the foreseeable?" The sheriff took a sip of his coffee.

Jake's mouth twitched. "Yeah, Hughes. We've got a murder investigation to deal with."

"Oh, no, no." The sheriff wiped his forehead with his hand. "Let's not put the cart in front of the horse."

Cassie straightened. "But, Sheriff Alderman, you don't think what happened to Mr. Gage was intentional? Why else would someone have hidden those nails and gone to all that trouble? There could be a deadly criminal among us, poised to attack other members of the troupe or the community. Why, this very night, before we found those nails, a piece of scenery fell onto the stage right behind me!"

The sheriff sat up. "What? You were hurt?"

"No, it missed."

"But you were an intended target."

"Uh, I don't know that for a fact."

"But you're sure it was done intentionally at least? You saw someone fleeing the scene or something else suggesting a purposeful act?"

Cassie lowered her eyes. "I— Well, no—there wasn't anyone around when I got up to the rigging platform. And looking at the other knots, it's possible the tie-off had been done up incorrectly by accident, making it more likely to fail... But there's no way to know for certain. And overall it's highly unlikely a suspended piece would come down like that all by itself..."

"Better three hours too soon than a minute too late." The lady inmate gathered her skirts in her arms and hugged the fabric to her like a bouquet of flowers.

Cassie blinked. *Did she just quote Shakespeare?*

The sheriff shifted his gaze back to Jake. "Any potential

suspects, then? Anyone who stood to benefit from Mr. Gage's demise?"

"Not yet, sir," said Jake. "But we thought an inquest might—"

"This is what we're going to do." The sheriff used his suspenders to hike his pajama pants over his belly. "Co-*Pro Tem* Deputies Gordon and Hughes, you have brought me no suspect, no motive, no explanation of opportunity, and barely a means." He held up his hand as the two men started to speak. "And, being a wood yard proprietor by trade, a sheriff by election, and a coroner only by very recent default, I haven't the faintest idea how to run a coroner's inquest, select a coroner's jury, or the like. Nor do I have any interest in advertising such to the world at the moment, so I'm not going to do that—"

He lifted his hand higher when the men tried to speak again.

"I'm not going to do that *right now*. However, you all have shown me that there may have been more to Mr. Gage's unfortunate passing than we thought. And it sounds possible that others may be in danger. Whether it's from a curse, a murderer, or an incompetent, I don't know, but the fact remains."

He puffed his cheeks. "So, I want you to look into this, but I am not going call an inquest or launch any sort of official investigation until you bring me much, much more. And I want you to work *quietly*. Understood?"

The only sound in the room for several seconds came from the lady inmate, who was humming to herself as she arranged the pleats on her skirt.

"But how are we supposed to do that?" Jake said finally. "The show's obviously been called off, so the troupe will be on their way out of town as soon as they've packed up the theater. I don't even think it's clear they're going to stay together as a troupe."

Hughes turned his hat over in his hands. "I'd also not underestimate how flighty and suspicious these theater types are. Especially traveler ones."

"You mean superstitious," Jake said.

"Either way. Most tend to be crooks or swindlers of one kind or another—"

"That sounds a bit unfair."

"—so they're bound to get fidgety answering more questions from law enforcement, particularly if they think we might be after one of them. Getting anything useful out of them during the interviews the other day was hard enough... Without a legal mandate to keep them in town, they're sure to scatter at the slightest hint of trouble."

The sheriff took a cookie from the plate the jailor kept on the table for himself. "Well, those are my terms. Figure it out. Perhaps then I'll know who's got what it takes to be my permanent deputy."

He groaned to his feet. "Oh! I almost forgot." He put down his cookie and pulled something out of his coat. "Another one of these came today. I found it on the intake desk when I stopped in this afternoon to pay the jailor."

He held out a pink envelope with a red ribbon on it— exactly like the ones that had fallen out of Hughes's notebook in Mr. Gage's suite the other day—and Hughes quickly tucked it into his own coat, not even bothering to look at it. Who on earth was sending him correspondence like *that*? It wasn't business correspondence, that's for sure...

Stop it, Cassie. She had no right to be jealous.

Cassie brushed the bangs from her face. "I have a thought. What if you convinced the troupe to stay and finish out the show? Then they'd have a reason to stay in town for the next couple of weeks, giving you more time for the investigation."

Hughes and Jake looked at her.

"Not to be a naysayer—" Hughes said.

Jake coughed.

"—but why on earth would they do that? After what's happened?"

Jake jammed a comb into his boot, trying to reach an itch. "Especially if that Mary Rutledge has anything to say about it. She already thought the troupe was cursed."

"And think of the logistics," Hughes said. "Who's going to play Mr. Gage's part?"

Jake stomped and twisted the comb around. "Or perform all his other functions, with the fundraising and everything?"

"Mr. Manning, the stage manager, should be able to sort that out," Cassie said. "Detailing with production contingencies is part of his job. And I get the sense he's more of a detail man than Mr. Gage was anyway. Also, I'd bet Miss Porter could help with the fundraising side. She already knows far more than she should about the personal details of every contributing chorus member."

"That doesn't solve the superstition problem, though," said Jake, giving a final stomp. He put away his comb. "Would Mr. Manning be prepared to replace Miss Rutledge, too? And who knows how many of the others who've been scared off? Also, we still haven't come up with an actual reason for the troupe to stay and continue with the show."

"Money speaks sense in a language all nations understand." The lady inmate again. This time, she'd spouted a far more obscure quote, from a play by seventeenth-century English playwright Aphra Behn, which Cassie only knew because she'd read some of Ms. Behn's work at university.

"I'm sorry, but who is that woman?" Cassie asked.

Hughes sauntered over to the cell and tapped on the bars. "Not sure yet. I picked her up over on Seventh, right before you came over here, for rattling doors on people's houses. She was probably trying to find one she could get into." He leaned in. "Isn't that right, ma'am?"

The woman drew back.

Cassie frowned. The woman didn't strike her as a house thief, or even a vagrant. Her messy hair aside, she was far too gentle, and had eyes like a doe—the precise opposite of street-hardened. "You don't even know her name?"

"I don't know if she even knows her name. Those interjections of hers are the most I've heard her speak."

Cassie glanced at the woman, who gave her another bright smile. There was definitely something unusual about her, but it wasn't a criminal character. "If that's so, I don't think jail's the right place for her. My guess is she's wandered off from a caretaker, and you ought to be finding out where she belongs." As Cassie spoke, the woman leaned forward and grasped the bars. She was wearing gloves, pretty ones with delicate buttons shaped like seahorses. "Here. If you let her out, Flora and I will look after her while you pursue an inquiry."

Hughes smoothed his mustache. "Are you sure that's safe? And how would I even—"

"Aw, I agree with Cassie. She's harmless." Jake looked sidelong at Hughes. "Unless you don't think you'd be able to figure it out."

"Of course I'm *able*."

"Good," said Cassie. "Because she just suggested a solution to your problem. Money."

Jake paused his reach for a cookie. "You mean we should pay the troupe to stay? Where would we get funds for that?"

Hughes mumbled under his breath as he unlocked the jail cell. "M'lady Gwynne's probably got enough to cover it in her pocket right now."

Cassie bit her lip as she helped the woman to a chair. Did Hughes really have a problem with the money she'd inherited from her father? He'd made a few small comments when they first met on the apparent cost of her clothing and hats and things, which she deserved—before coming to the island and meeting Flora for the first time, she'd been worried about making a good impression so had gone a little overboard in that area—but she had interpreted it at the time as a strange way of paying her a compliment. But what he'd just said didn't feel complimentary.

"No," she said. "Well, yes. Prince told me that operating costs are recuperated from the donations before distributing money to the charitable recipients. A fairly routine practice, in my experience with this sort of thing. But the actual donations aren't brought in until the night of the show—only pledges are submitted before that—meaning the actors haven't received anything yet. So if the show goes ahead, they'll get their pay. You just need to remind them of that."

Jake stood. "It's a good plan."

"Ruse, you mean," said Hughes.

Cassie caught and patted the (former) lady inmate's hand as she reached for a flower-shaped button on Cassie's cuff. "Not necessarily a ruse. If we get the chorus members to stay on as well, and still give the money they were planning to donate, they will in fact get paid. And the charity will get its money, too. Everyone benefits."

Hughes hung the jail keys on the hook by the door. "Fine. I'll support it." He glanced at the sheriff, who was checking his pocket watch. "But I'm going to have to get a music score as soon as possible."

"A music score? Why?" asked Jake.

"For when I join the production."

Jake and Cassie laughed, then Cassie paused. "Oh, you're serious. Do you—do that?"

Hughes huffed. "People think I'm all business, but I have an artistic side, too. Tough and manly, but artistic. I sang at university, you know. Yes, I went to university, for a time. Anyway, how else am I to get close enough to the troupe to investigate without them knowing I'm investigating? If I'm part of the cast I can ask questions, watch what people do, and look around, without raising suspicion. Keep the suspects at ease."

"I'm joining, too, then," Jake said.

The sheriff rubbed his temples. "Neither of you are joining the production. The troupe members know you're law enforcement because you were already on the scene in your official capacities. And, as discussed, we don't want them getting jumpy and running off."

Jake and Hughes spoke together. "Then what are we supposed to do?"

"Miss Gwynne will be your eyes and ears."

Cassie choked on a cookie. "Pardon?" So much for delivering the information and returning to minding her own business.

"She's already in the chorus so she can advance the investigation on your behalf, with assistance from Mr. Montgomery. Provided he's willing. Miss Gwynne, you'll speak to him?"

"Uh, I—all right." Had she missed being asked whether *she* was willing?

"Good. And, Hughes and Gordon, you will stay close enough to oversee things and make sure there's no trouble, but not close enough to spark suspicion."

Hughes threw his hat down on the table, sending a couple of the nails skittering. "I'm not working with that man."

"Mr. Montgomery? Why not?"

"He's arrogant, and he talks back, and—I don't like him."

"Not good enough."

"But—"

The sheriff nodded, as did Cassie's new charge, though she may also have been tracking the hamster-sized cockroach strutting across the wall.

"It's settled, then. Team, you have your mission."

7

Cassie dolphin-flopped in her bed and stared at the mantel clock, an annoyingly (at least at the moment) whimsical piece shaped like an oyster shell with a hat and spectacles. It was three in the morning and she was exhausted, but despite the kitten's repeated attempts to curl under her arm and settle in, she couldn't bring herself to lie still. The last couple of days had been tough, but tomorrow would be tougher.

At least her conversation with Miss Porter about the recent developments had gone better than expected. Cassie had worried the information she'd uncovered about the circumstances of Mr. Gage's death might worsen Miss Porter's state, but the news turned out to have the opposite effect. Rather than further devastating Miss Porter, it brought her back to life. As soon as Cassie had told her that her help was needed, she had quickly gone from prostrate to rushing about making preparations, as energetic and chaotic as a punctured party balloon, and in less than half an hour, Cassie had found herself once again puffing to keep up with Miss Porter as she charged down Centre Street.

Having discerned the nightly habits of the troupe through

the ones boarding with her, Miss Porter led the way from Three Star Saloon to Weil's barroom, Hammarby's, and every other such establishment in town until they had located all the required parties and Miss Porter—sometimes using means Cassie herself wouldn't have dared (Miss Porter was not, for example, afraid to pluck a Mile's Pale Ale from a grown man's hand and pour it on the ground)—had extracted their solemn promises that they would be in attendance at a ten o'clock meeting in her library the following morning.

As for the handful of chorus members whose influence, and money, Miss Porter felt would be critical to the cause—which included, Miss Porter begrudgingly admitted, her tea-rival Mrs. Reynolds—Cassie was better equipped to assist. She had expected convincing such individuals to participate to be a significant challenge, especially after Mary Rutledge's renewed cries of "curse" following the incident, but, thanks to the circles she'd been privy to because of her father's clientele, she had spent enough time around society types to know how to leverage her charm.

Miss Porter's suggestion that they hold the meeting at her boarding house was also a good one, as it would increase the likelihood that the promised appearances would be made by at least the troupe members lodging there. In addition, the boarding house was located on the block of Seventh Street between the Lyceum and the Egmont Hotel, where most of the chorus members were staying, and where Hughes and Jake would be stationed, working on their other investigations and waiting to give orders to Cassie and Prince. The Florida House, where the rest of the troupe had taken rooms, was only a short walk away as well.

And Mary Rutledge had declared she would only come to the meeting provided she wouldn't have to set foot in the theater.

We'll have to revisit that last bit at some point. Cassie

started to flop again but reversed course when she encountered a sleepy protest from the kitten. As she sat up to re-fluff her pillow, her gaze fell on the parcel that had arrived that evening from New York, which was still sitting, untouched, on her dressing table.

Was she ready for that? She had been awaiting its arrival for weeks, but she knew that when she opened it, she'd be releasing a whole lot more than the items inside.

Her breath quivered. *No, definitely not ready.* But she probably never would be.

Bracing for the chill about to shoot through her night-dress, she swept back the coverlet and reached for the lamp.

She moved slowly across the room, placing each foot with care to keep the creaking of the floorboards from waking Flora down the hall. By the time she'd picked up the parcel and begun her painstaking return journey back to the bed, however, Esy had awakened and was jumping and clambering up her leg to get at the frills on her nightdress. Letting the kitten bounce off of her and thunk to the floor, she carried the parcel the rest of the way at a normal pace, then, smoothing the coverlet with one hand, laid it on the bed as gently as if it were a sleeping child.

She ran her fingers over the lettering stamped in heavy red ink across the front.

From the Office of the Board of Coroners – Manhattan, New York City

She inhaled, then tugged on the parcel string, her stomach tightening as each bend of the bow drew straight, relaxed, and finally fell away. The brown paper around the box was next, but rather than pulling the whole sheet away at once, she released one fold at a time, smoothing the creases as she went, until the paper lay flat and there was nothing left to do but lift the lid and look inside.

On top was a letter:

New York, December 2, 1883

Dear Miss Gwynne:

We have received your request for the file and other materials relating to your father, Mr. Thomas Gwynne, intake date August 23, 1882, and the funds you enclosed to cover the cost of fulfilling said request. The responsive materials are within.

We apologize for the delay. Your letter was received some time ago, but we could not locate the materials at first, as it turned out they had been removed to the destruction area. According to our records, our office attempted to contact you, the subject's next of kin, with respect to their return upon closure of the file but received no response. In any event, all credit for their retrieval is due to the shrewdness of our able office assistant, Matthew Perahlstrad, who thought to check there and thus saved them from imminent incineration.

Respectfully,

Angus Crawley

Clerk to William L. Keyes, Coroner

Cassie pushed off the kitten, who was trying to lick the paper. She didn't remember anyone from the coroner's office trying to contact her. Mr. Renault had managed her affairs for a time, in addition to her father's, while she was recovering from her injuries. Perhaps the letters had gone to the office and he'd forgotten to forward them to her.

She put the letter down and shooed the kitten when she tried to sit on it.

"Not now, Esy."

Next inside the box was a larger envelope with her father's name written on it alongside a file number. Inside the envelope were two thin packets of paper, one labeled "Coroner's Report" and the other "Physician's Report." She saved those to the side for the moment and reached for what was underneath: a long, blue coat.

Her father's double-breasted summer frock coat, made from dark, indigo-stained cotton, light enough for warm weather but weighty enough to remain smooth and elegant even with handling. It was folded neatly in tissue paper, as though it had just come from the shop, and as Cassie closed her eyes and ran her hand over the lapel, she could almost smell the heliotrope boutonniere her father had always worn in the buttonhole, over his heart.

I miss you, Father. She mouthed the words, afraid they would break if she said them out loud.

She opened her eyes. But the coat hadn't come in from the shop, a place that dealt in fabric and buttons and the business of life. It had come from the coroner's office, a place that dealt only in death.

The coroner's people must have collected it near the scene at the park. Her father had looked as though he'd been running, she remembered—he'd probably pulled it off when he became too warm. And dropped it when he rushed in to save her.

She seized the coat and hugged it.

Peering over the coat back into the box, she saw the clerk had included the shoes her father was wearing that day as well, a pair of still-shiny black boots with the laces threaded through the brass eyelets, but nothing else. No shirt, no trousers, no socks. She squeezed the coat tighter. Nothing else must have been salvageable.

After a few more steadying breaths, she reached for the coroner's report.

Date: August 23, 1882

Name: Thomas Gwynne

Age: 47 y

Occupation: Attorney

Where found: Madison Square Park, evening

Cause of death: Stabbing

Notes: Victim suffered mortal wounds inflicted by unknown masked assailants during a robbery on public property. Female companion also wounded but survives. Value of goods taken: $0.

Fee: $— *(Paid)*

Tears pricked the back of her eyes, and she resisted the urge to ball up the sheet and throw it out the window. The report was so cold, so detached. *Victim. Female companion. Value of goods taken.* An entire life was gone, taken by force, and all that amounted to was a few words on a sheet of paper. She reread the report. It hadn't even been written with care. The way it was composed, one might even think her father was the one who committed a robbery. And was it not worth noting that he had lost his life while rescuing said "female companion," his daughter, legal assistant, and friend of twenty-two years, from the assailants?

Not to mention the details that were plain wrong. *"Value of goods taken:* $0." How could that be correct? What kind of robbers attacked and killed someone and didn't even take anything?

At least the coroner had been sure to mark his fee as paid.

The scar on her neck, a parting gift from the aforementioned assailants, ached under the collar of her nightdress. The wound was long healed, but the ugly, Frankenstein's-monster-esque line of cross-hatched lumps that remained seemed to know when she was remembering and always insisted on having its say, too.

The kitten mewed and stood with a paw on Cassie's arm, trying to bat at the paper.

Cassie shrugged her off. "I said, not now, Esy."

Laying the coat across her lap, she put down the coroner's report and picked up the physician's report. She wasn't sure how much more she could take.

At the top of the first page was a sketch of a man's torso, on which the physician had marked an "x" for each stab wound, along with a notation of the size and depth of the cut. Below that was a list detailing the weights and measurements of various body organs, then a detailed description of the dozens of other bruises, scrapes, cuts, breaks, and tears that had been inflicted on her beloved father.

She had to look away. She knew what had happened to him, of course. But it was a fresh kind of torture to read about it.

The kitten, declining to be ignored, pounced on the coat and gripped one of the buttons in her tiny jaws. Cassie yelled sharply. "No! Esy, no! I told you no!"

Falling back as though struck, the kitten mewed and ran out of the room.

This is too much. Too much, too much, too much. Shaking, Cassie threw the report back into the box and reached for the lid. Why was she doing this to herself?

Then she stopped.

No. Her body tensed as her heart wrestled with her limbs. *No more hiding.*

The whole reason she had written to the coroner's office in the first place was that she needed to face these things. When, during the Peanut murder investigation, someone had accused her of being quick to involve herself in other people's affairs but blind to her own, it had cut her to the bone. Because it was true: within weeks of finding Flora's letters that summer, Cassie had departed New York for the island, a place she didn't know, full of people she didn't know, to visit an aunt she didn't know. And despite the obvious open questions about her father's death that she had never brought herself to acknowledge, much less answer, she had promptly involved herself in a local murder inquiry... relating to a man she didn't know.

She lifted the physician's report back out of the box. This was her opportunity to confront what had happened and give her father the justice he deserved. Law enforcement had been content to put the incident in the "unfortunately, these things happen in big cities" basket and move on, but that wasn't good enough for Cassie anymore. If they weren't going to try to find who had attacked her and her father, she would.

She took a brief mental accounting of the facts. Earlier that day, as she was stepping out to bring her neighbor some cookies she had baked, she'd found a handbill on the doorstep advertising a special book market taking place that evening in Madison Square Park, for one night only. She loved book markets, and this one promised to be especially intriguing, as it was to feature an entire booth dedicated to Asia travelogues, one of her favorite genres. It was a rare specialty, too, and she'd been so engrossed in rereading the details as she walked that she'd plowed straight into a white-haired gentleman on the sidewalk in front of the house, sending the poor man and his walking stick tumbling to the ground. Fortunately, he'd jumped up and gone on his way with hardly even an annoyed word.

In any event, she made up her mind to go, despite the late hour it was to be held and the fact her father would certainly have objected. Truthfully—she was ashamed to admit—the latter may have made her even more determined to attend.

Her heart still squeezed with regret whenever she thought of it. That morning, she and her father had quarreled about that very topic: He'd requested—or demanded, rather—that she start taking their housekeeper, Mrs. Wagner, with her when she went to the food market, citing crime in the city and some nonsense about young women and propriety. But Cassie had done the grocery shopping, not to mention gone to the library, dined out, and even run errands for her father's law practice, on her own for years. And her father had never given a whit about "propriety" before. She simply hadn't understood why he suddenly thought she needed a chaperone, so, she'd fought with him. Then, like a petulant child, ignored what he'd asked.

Unfortunately, when she arrived at the park, she didn't see a market, so she figured she had mixed up the time or gone to the wrong part of the park. She couldn't find the handbill to check, though, and the looming darkness weighed against wandering around searching, so she turned to go home—but found herself face to face with a masked man. He seized her, and, after a brief struggle, he pinned her to the ground with a knife to her neck. She tried to get away but her throat got badly cut, and she was on the verge of losing hope when she saw her father running toward her.

Her father had made short work of that man, but there were more. She didn't know how many, but ultimately they were too much for him, even at the most ferocious she'd ever seen him. The next thing she remembered was sitting beneath that towering statue of a torch-bearing arm, "Liberty Enlightening the World," clinging to his limp body.

Her fingers tightened around the physician's report, as though trying to hold onto him still, and she fought to keep her mind on the task at hand. The coroner's report had called the men "robbers"—she'd made that assumption, too—but they had taken nothing. Upon arrival at the hospital, she still had all her valuables, including the solid silver chatelaine she wore at her waist and everything that had been clipped to it, from her money pouch to a diamond-studded miniature magnifying glass. Nor had the men, now that she was thinking about it more clearly, demanded anything from her. They hadn't said anything at all.

She checked the pockets of her father's coat and found all his usual items there, too: money fold, pipe, and matching gold pocket watch, compass, and vesta match case. She shook out the coat. The one belonging that was missing was both his least valuable and most prized one: his whirligig toy. Though she supposed that could have fallen out if he was running with his coat over his arm.

The final portion of the physician's notes, a section called "Other Comments," stated:

> *While I don't make a habit of including anything but strict scientific observations in these reports, I am compelled to note that the stab wounds sustained by the victim bring to mind a memorandum I submitted to this office earlier this summer regarding several subjects who had come across my table bearing similar injuries. According to information received from a confidential contact in lower Manhattan, those subjects appeared to have been victims of a certain criminal element associated with the Five Points neighborhood—if not by origin, by place of operation—that had recently been making itself a nuisance to local law enforcement.*

Cassie stared at the page. "Nuisance" didn't quite seem the right word.

As mentioned in my memorandum, the common bond of these malefactors is not immediately apparent, as their number appears to include a variety of dissimilar races and nationalities, nor is their motive. In addition, according to my contact, many of their encounters do not end in a fatal result (fortunately—though they are still often violent), and are in fact eclectic in nature, ranging from robbery to simple battery. Having made the following observations with respect to the victims that have come before me personally, however, I do believe this group to be more than an arbitrary assemblage:

One, each victim sustained wounds in a distinctive arrangement nearly identical to the one depicted in the exam notes above.

Two, each attack occurred within a particular area in or near the Five Points neighborhood occupied by Celestials, which some refer to as "China Town."

Three, witnesses to the attacks have noted a consistent insignia borne or displayed by the offending individuals in various ways. I have not seen this insignia myself, but it appears best described as a bastardization of the revered symbol of harmony known as the yin-yang.

While the circumstances surrounding the present subject do not align with all the observations above, the similarities with respect to the first are striking enough, in my opinion, to warrant comment.

Cassie grabbed a bedpost to steady herself. Her skin was prickling all over, and her stomach felt as though it was about to empty itself in her lap.

Was this man suggesting an actual *criminal gang* attacked

them? From Five Points, no less, a neighborhood notorious for its dangerous immigrant slums? And dozens of blocks away from Madison Square Park? Why? As the physician noted, only the manner of the attack seemed to fit the group's known patterns. Though—she looked back down at the report—the similarities there *were* striking. And the physician had admitted that the group's motives were yet unknown.

They hadn't demanded or taken any valuables, so the attack didn't appear to have been a robbery or other such crime of opportunity. Had she been specifically targeted? If so, how had she come within their sights? Surely, she couldn't have done anything that would affront people like that. She'd never even heard of them. Unless it wasn't personal. Could it have had something to do with her father? She couldn't think of what possible interest her father could be to such an organization, either. And how would they have known she or her father would be there? She didn't even know how her father had known she was there.

Cassie considered the mention of the group's insignia. According to the small amount she knew about the yin-yang from a philosophy course at school, the symbol—which was composed of interlocking tailed half-moons, one black and one white, each with a dot of the opposite color in it—essentially represented the Taoist concept, much embraced by the Chinese, that throughout the natural world, equal and opposing forces are interconnected and mutually dependent, and that harmony exists when those opposing forces are combined and in balance with one another.

What would a "bastardization" of the yin-yang look like? She didn't remember seeing anything that would fit that description when they were attacked, but, then again, she hadn't really had a chance to notice much. And what would such a thing represent? What kind of people would want to pervert such a beautiful concept?

Five Points. Cassie sat on the bed with her hands on her head and tried to think of any connection her father might have had with that place. All she could come up with was a single meeting he had taken there once, early that last summer. They had been on their way somewhere else when he'd directed the driver to detour through the neighborhood to a Chinese grocery on Pell Street. As he was getting out, he said he was meeting someone about a case, but he didn't mention what the case was, what the meeting was about, or even whom the meeting was with. And he'd asked her to wait in the carriage, which would have annoyed her if she hadn't been so delighted by the unusual sights, sounds, and smells all around.

Come to think of it, that in and of itself was confusing. He almost always brought her in to assist in meetings like that.

She stood and moved to the writing desk. If she could figure out what case that meeting was about, it might lead to some answers. She'd write the secretary at her father's office and ask him to send her an index of the clients and cases her father had been working on that summer. Then she could narrow it down and have him pull the relevant briefing files for her to review when she got back to New York. While she was at it, she'd ask him to send her father's appointment book as well.

She was preparing her pen when the kitten poked her head around the doorframe, her eyes wide.

"Oh, Esy, I'm sorry. I didn't mean to yell at you. Come here."

Cassie kneeled on the floor and held out her hand, clicking her tongue soothingly, and after a brief hesitation the kitten trotted in and nuzzled her hand. Satisfied with the reconcilia-tion, Cassie was preparing to push herself up when she noticed a square of cardstock on the floor beneath the dressing table chair.

She carried it over to the desk and held it up to the lamp—then nearly dropped it. It was the handbill for the book market.

Where did that come from? She glanced at the coat. It must have fallen from some compartment in there when she was going through it.

That was how her father had known where to find her.

Which begged a follow-up question: How did her father get the handbill? She thought she'd lost it on the way to the park.

She chewed her lip. Well, she could have left it on the foyer table on her way out, even though she'd intended to bring it with her for reference. She did that sort of thing a lot. But Father was supposed to be working late that night. Had he come home early for some reason, found it, then gone to find her? But why had he been running?

And, she realized as she looked at the handbill, she hadn't gotten the details wrong. She'd been in the exact place, at the exact time, specified. In fact, if she hadn't been, her father wouldn't have been able to find her.

The prickling on her skin turned to icy stabs. Had there been any book market, after all?

She rubbed her arms. Hopefully, her father's secretary would answer right away.

Retrieving a sheet of paper from the desk, she sat down and began to write, and with each stroke, she felt calmer and stronger, more empowered. The physician's observations had terrified her, but, as odd as was it was to admit, having a reason, or at least a hint that there *was* a reason, for what had happened was preferable to the worthless "wrong place, wrong time" shrugs that had been all anyone could offer her for over a year. She would get to the bottom of this.

When she finished that letter, she set it aside and wrote another, this one to the coroner's clerk, Mr. Crawley, requesting to see the memorandum the physician had referred to in his report. It wouldn't hurt to have more information about that group he'd described.

The letters completed and sealed on her desk, she carefully

hung her father's coat on a hook by the door and arranged his shoes below it. She stepped back to regard the vignette. When she'd sent the coroner her request, and even when the parcel had arrived in response, she hadn't known whether she'd ever be able to look at anything of his without her heart breaking all over again. But, at least for right now, it was comforting, as though a part of him were there somehow.

Feeling her eyelids droop at last, she removed the kitten from the box, put the papers back inside, and replaced the top. Then she lay down next to it and drew up the coverlet. Esy burrowed under the sheets and nestled into her spot under Cassie's arm, and finally Cassie closed her eyes.

As her consciousness began to slip, her thoughts drifted to the next morning's meeting with Mr. Gage's troupe. She was going to see that matter through, too, with no apologies to anyone for doing what she thought was right. For Mr. Gage, for Miss Porter, and for herself. She was strong enough.

People could call her nosy all they wanted. Father would approve.

8

Several minutes before ten the next morning, the appointed time for the meeting with Mr. Gage's theatrical troupe, Cassie paused inside the picket fence that surrounded Miss Porter's cheerful yellow boarding house and inhaled a lungful of that beautiful scent that she'd grown to associate with the elaborate front gardens the island was known for: a mixture of earth, grass, and so many different flowers at once it was impossible to identify any single one. Miss Porter's garden wasn't as wild and whimsical as Flora's, but with its rows of tidy flowerbeds packed with camellias, snapdragons, and yellow winter jasmine shaded by crape myrtle trees, each of which teemed with tiny wooden birdhouses, it was just as charming.

Cassie stole another greedy sniff. Given the previous evening's exertions—and that, after finally falling asleep, she had sleep-migrated again, this time to a hall closet she hadn't even known was there (it was where Flora evidently stored her summer floorcloths and, as Cassie discovered upon awakening nose to nose with a miniature Santa Claus statue, her seasonal decorations)—this small moment to collect herself was extra precious.

The clouds shifted, setting everything awash in sunlight, and she sneezed so loudly it hurt her own ears.

Another, equally emphatic, sneeze exploded behind her.

"Wow. You weren't exaggerating about your sneezes."

Cassie turned around. It was Prince, clean, sharp, and grinning in a freshly pressed green sack coat. The distracted and largely cheerless man who'd made an appearance last night was, thankfully, gone.

They each sneezed again.

"Neither were you."

Prince handed her a paper bag. "I had to swing by the theater this morning for something and found these things on a chair in the auditorium. Last night you said you'd left some belongings, right?"

"Oh, yes!" Cassie combed through the bag's contents. Inside were her wrap, along with her chatelaine and the gloves and hat that had been with it, and her boots. No scones, though. "Thank you. We ran out so quickly I'd forgotten the point of going there in the first place... I may have to enlarge that tip I promised Paddy."

She tucked the bag under her arm, and they climbed past a succession of trellised tomato plants onto the covered porch, where a motif from the house's pretty bargeboard siding, a repeating sequence of interlocking palm fronds and coconuts, was reprised in cast iron along the railings and in stained glass on the transom window over the door.

They knocked, and, almost immediately, the door swung open, revealing a straight-lipped Mary Rutledge.

"About time you two joined us." She spun on her heel and called down the hall. "Now, will someone please tell me what the dickens is going on?"

Miss Porter's library was Cassie's favorite room in the house, and though she had been there numerous times, when she entered she couldn't help letting out her usual gasp of pleasure at the sight of its dark oak shelves lined with books, which—aside from a few begrudging allowances made for doorways, the bay window facing into the garden, and a mounted display of German cuckoo clocks—covered every wall from floor to ceiling. She also loved the room's collection of antique lamps, and how Miss Porter had placed them about the room at carefully chosen intervals to maximize their cozy glow. Constructed from materials ranging from stained glass and mother of pearl to plush fabric with fringe, and bearing patterns as bizarre as checkerboards inlaid with starfish, each one was absolutely unique and absolutely wonderful.

The size of the group gathered there was unprecedented, though. And, while the room was by most standards a large one, there weren't enough couches and chairs to go around, and many had taken up positions on other available surfaces including the reading desk and a sideboard displaying Miss Porter's collection of Florida curiosities. All of the troupe actors were in attendance—including Mary Rutledge, Marguerite Clifton, Arthur Beath, and Christopher Wilkes, along with a four-member set whom Cassie assumed were the reportedly truant minor players—as were the head stagehand, Harland McGregor; the stage manager, Mr. Manning; and a number of volunteer chorus members, even more than Cassie and Miss Porter had spoken with the night before.

There were two men in Egmont waiter's uniforms circulating with trays of breakfast breads as well. The waitstaff was unexpected, as Miss Porter usually liked to cook and serve herself, but perhaps Miss Porter had felt it extra important to impress today.

Miss Porter seized Cassie's arm as Prince moved a plate of lemon tea cakes to make space for them on the ledge of the bay window.

"I'm so glad you're here," she whispered. "I've been trying

to hold them off, but emotions are running high, as you can imagine."

"Arthur, that was exceptionally rude!" Marguerite, who had been sitting on Arthur's lap in one of the armchairs, leapt up. Both were dressed in elegant mourning clothes trimmed with layers of black bows and lace, and it was difficult to pick whose ensemble was more lovely.

"I said you were hurting my legs. Separately, I suggested you reconsider that pastry you were reaching for. The two were unrelated."

Marguerite huffed prettily.

Lowering his handkerchief, a delicate number crafted from black Spanish lace, Arthur caught her wrist and drew her back. "Come now, beautiful. Don't be cross. You're my dearest friend, so you know I only tell you the truth."

Marguerite pouted but submitted when he brought out a comb and started arranging her long, flowing hair about her shoulders. "I simply don't know how to be around you lately, Arthur. One moment you're sweet as caramel, the next your fangs are in my neck. It comes and goes as suddenly as a cat's claws."

Cassie took a tea cake from the plate next to Prince. *Those two certainly have an unusual relationship.*

Miss Porter leaned closer to Cassie, tugging at the turtle-shaped buttons on her cuffs. "You're going to lead the meeting, right? You know I'm terrible at speaking in front of people, and you're so good with words."

"Me? I'm assure you, I'm far better at eating my words than speaking them."

"See? That's what I mean. You're smart and articulate, whereas most of the time I'm a blubbering, emotional fool." Miss Porter touched her handkerchief to her lips.

"You're no fool," Cassie said, patting her shoulder. "Though blubbering and emotional I might have to take the Fifth on. Either way, I believe you can do it."

"There you go again. So clever." Miss Porter cupped Cassie's cheek. "I'll give it a try."

"Well done, friend," Prince murmured to Cassie as Miss Porter took up a determined stance at the center of the room.

"Ahem. Good morning." Miss Porter clinked a tiny spoon against a teacup. "Thank you all for agreeing to come here this morning even though we've been through so very much. Has everyone had a chance to get something to eat?" She grabbed a platter of potato cakes from one of the waiters and held it up. When that was met by blank stares, she lowered it and cleared her throat. "All right, good... Well, you all know Mr. Gage. And he was... Well, we wanted to ask..."

She threw out her arm and pointed. "Miss Gwynne wishes to speak to you about a matter of importance."

Unfortunately, Cassie, not expecting to be called on, had just shoved her entire tea cake into her mouth. She hadn't intended to eat it all at once, but when she'd tried to bite it, it had started breaking apart, and the only way she could keep the chunks from falling all over the floor was to push the whole thing in. Prince handed her a glass of lemonade as she chewed for several devastating seconds and tried to swallow enough to speak.

"I, uh—" Cassie choked back the rest of her mouthful. "Right. Yes. Miss Porter and I were discussing how important this troupe, and its mission to help hungry children, was to Mr. Gage, and we thought it would be a shame if we didn't see it through."

"See it through?" Harland puffed his cigarillo, and Miss Porter dashed in with an ashtray as he tapped it over a vase of flowers. "You mean go on with the production?"

"Yes, we must!" Mrs. Reynolds, who had commandeered an

entire settee for herself and her skirts, attempted to jump to her feet. But, as the settee was so deep she couldn't touch the floor, and her middle was more perfectly round than even Miss Porter's, all she managed was a slight rock forward. "For poor Mr. Gage." She tried again, and one of her pearl strands flipped up and caught on the upturned portion of her very expensive-looking Gainsborough hat. "And the children. It's our moral duty."

"As has been said." Miss Porter chomped on a potato cake. Apparently hurling barbs at a social rival didn't count as public speaking.

Mrs. Reynolds rearranged herself as though she hadn't heard. "I, for one, am fully prepared to stand by my full original pledge, and I hope my contributing chorus compatriots will do the same. Those fortunate ones among us must not hesitate to share that good fortune with those in need."

Harland watched Mrs. Reynolds make one more attempt to stand, then give up and reach for a piece of cake. "No way. I've already started packing up the sellable items."

"And Ira, Theresa, and I have already booked passage on an ocean steamer to New York." A black-haired woman, one of the minor players, crossed her arms and leaned against the book-shelf with one foot tucked up underneath her. Her hair was gathered in a low plait at the nape of her neck, and she wore a single long earring, fingerless gloves, and a smirk. She played one of the Major-General's bubbly daughters in the show, but, given her overall look and demeanor, Cassie thought she'd have been better suited to the pirate chorus. "So we can start looking for new work."

The man and woman sitting cross-legged on the sideboard next to her—Ira and Theresa, presumably—had foregone glove fingertips and second earrings as well. They had also both mastered the internally contradictory skill of slouching aggressively.

Cassie gulped some more lemonade. If someone had told

her all three of them were real-life pirates, she would have believed it.

"What about me, Vera?" A man with narrow shoulders and a worried nose, the fourth minor player, stood up from the spot he'd taken on the floor by the first woman's feet, accidentally knocking into one of the waiters. The waiter straightened his mustache.

Cassie paused mid-gulp.

"I'm not your mother, Percy. You can make your own arrangements."

"But I don't even know which vessel you've booked."

Prince placed a hand on Cassie's shoulder. "I, for one, vote in favor of going forward with the show. It wouldn't be too big of a project to unpack, if we all pitched in. And steamer tickets can be returned or exchanged."

Cassie shifted her stare from the first waiter to the other one, who abruptly turned and tried to refill a chorus lady's lemonade glass even though she was in the midst of trying to sip it.

No, they wouldn't—

Arthur touched his handkerchief to his cheek, releasing a sigh. "That may be so, Prince, but would you really have us go on with the show here, after what's happened?" He turned to Marguerite. "Hand me the eye cream, would you, darling? I haven't had a moment's sleep in days." Taking the tin she produced from her pouch, he popped off the lid and dabbed some of the white substance inside on the puffy red half-circles under his eyes. "I don't know if our hearts could stand it. I nearly fall to pieces just thinking about how we're all going to have to find new situations."

Mr. Manning hiked the satchel he was carrying up on his shoulder. Cassie could see the multicolored edge of the prompt book inside. "Why does everyone assume the troupe's splitting up? I was actually about to call a meeting myself on the matter before Miss Gwynne and Miss Porter came around. I think we should both finish the show and continue on with the troupe and its important work. It will take some adjusting, but I have everything noted in the prompt book and we could certainly navigate any casting or production issues that arise. It's what Mr. Gage would have wanted."

Arthur slapped the lid back onto the eye cream. "'Some adjusting,' he says. As though we simply need to cover for a singer with a cold. Mr. Gage was our leader, our director, our star. He owned the troupe. No, he *was* the troupe. And what would you know about what Mr. Gage would want?"

Mr. Manning pushed up his eyeglasses. "Quite a lot, I'd think. I've known him for a very long time. Besides, I'm the stage manager, and, with Mr. Gage, that means the everything manager."

"At least you're modest."

"Oh, an *actor* wants to lecture me about modesty?"

"You're not the only one who cared about him, that's all!"

Mr. Manning thumped his satchel onto a table. "Good. You *should* care about him. You all should. And be grateful. Because the way most of your careers were going before Mr. Gage found you and brought you into this troupe—" He stopped, his hands gripping the back of Mrs. Reynolds's settee. "But that's neither here nor there. All I'm trying to say is, in my opinion, we have a good thing going and shouldn't be so quick to give it up."

"I'll show you what you can do with your opinion."

Marguerite flung out her arms as Arthur started to stand, almost dumping her onto the floor. "Gentlemen! There's no need for confrontation."

The waiter with the mysteriously moveable mustache hopped to the side, again narrowly avoiding a blow. This time, his mustache stayed put, but one of his bushy eyebrows tilted. The other waiter—his thick-framed spectacles, Cassie noticed, were missing lenses—tried to gesture something at his colleague from beneath the tray of apple-cinnamon donuts he was carrying.

"I find this whole discussion macabre." Mary fanned herself furiously. "The very idea. With a man *dead*? The head of our troupe, no less? And I'm of half a mind never to set foot in a theater again... To think I climbed on that same mast myself only days before, thoughtlessly putting my life at the mercy of the otherworldly forces that have been unleashing their wrath on us. It makes me long for those simpler childhood times, when I could escape my woes in my little rowboat, paddling around the tidal waters beneath the lighthouse until everything felt better..."

Miss Porter threw Cassie a plaintive look.

"Isn't it true," Cassie burst out, "that all of you troupe members have been here working for weeks but are yet to be paid?"

Mr. Manning brushed a crumb from his short, rigid beard. "Yes. We're normally paid after the show, once the pledged contributions come in." He turned to the others. "She makes a good point. Without the show going forward, and the donations collected, there will be nothing to pay us with. How would you like that, Mr. Beath? All that work and no pay?"

"Not everything's about money," Arthur said. "Mr. Gage told me that."

Prince put out his hands as the two men started to eye each other again. "But if we go ahead with the performance, Arthur, the charity will get the donation we've promised, too. We could sort everything else out afterward, including the larger question of the troupe's future."

"We're in," Vera said. "Percy, too. That is, if he can get his underthings unknotted in time."

Mr. Wilkes, who had been sipping his tea quietly the entire time, put down his cup. "I'll stay if I can take over as the Pirate

King. I know the part already, and it would allow me to stretch my creative wings."

"Aha!" cried Arthur.

Mr. Wilkes stiffened. "'Aha' what?"

"I was wondering how long it would take before you made your grab for that role. Just long enough for Mr. Gage's body to cool, it appears."

"I beg your pardon—"

Arthur tossed his hair. "Please. I know how much you've wanted it. You cornered Mr. Gage about understudying him weekly. And quite rudely at times, if I may say so."

Cassie paused her reach for another tea cake. Mr. Wilkes had crossed swords (or cutlasses, rather) with Mr. Gage over roles?

"Rudeness is different from assertiveness. If one wants to advance his career, he must be willing to go to certain lengths— Wait. How did you know about that?"

"Mr. Gage told me. He also told me that, every time you came to him, he reminded you that he intended to perform the role for the foreseeable future, and, further, that he didn't need or want an understudy. Much less one half his size."

Mr. Wilkes opened and closed his jaw, as though trying to work the rust from a hinge. "I'm not the only one around here with aspirations. You've been wanting to expand your patter repertoire. I've been housed next to you enough times to hear what you rehearse." He blinked slowly. "Perhaps, if I take over the Pirate King, you'd could take a turn at the Major-General. All for Mr. Gage, of course."

Arthur and Mr. Wilkes locked glares, neither moving a muscle. Finally, Arthur turned away and patted his hair. "Fine. For Mr. Gage."

"For Mr. Gage," Marguerite agreed, closing her eyes and folding her hands reverently. Arthur looked at her strangely.

"If Arthur plays the Major-General, I could play the

Sergeant of Police." Percy, the minor player with the worried nose, twisted his gloves in his hands. "And Ira could simply add my pirate crew lines to his."

Vera sneered. "Why not? Any idiot who can keep rhythm and march around like he's swallowed a stick could play the Sergeant of Police. Am I right?"

Theresa sniggered, and this time Arthur, the current Sergeant of Police, got all the way to his feet, spilling Marguerite onto the floor.

"You take that back."

"I will not. It was a joke, and it was hilarious."

"It's not as though your acting abilities are anything to boast about, Vera," Marguerite said, sweeping together the items that had fallen out of her pouch. "Even when you can be bothered to show up."

"Marguerite." Arthur picked a vial out of Marguerite's pile, his mouth tight. "This is Mr. Gage's mustache oil. Why the blazes do *you* have it?"

"He gave to me to hold at some point. What of it?"

Prince clasped his hands together with a loud clap. "So... casting is managed." He turned to Harland. "Harland, I trust we can count on you to take care of the technical side of things?"

Harland withdrew his flask from his teacup and screwed the cap on. "I don't know, Prince. Can you?" His expression was hard, but his fingers tremored slightly as he tucked the flask back into his coat pocket.

Cassie cocked her head. He hadn't struck her as the nervous type.

"Please, Harland. You could use the money, too." Marguerite touched his arm, then drew her hand back.

"I don't..." Harland looked around the room. "You all really want to do this?"

The group returned a hesitant, but affirmative, round of nods.

"Even Mary?"

Mr. Manning, fully collected now, leaned forward so his eyes were level with Mary's. "Remember, Miss Rutledge, if we complete the show, we'll all receive the full pay promised us."

Prince took a knee at Mary's side. "And don't forget the children's charity will get their donation as well. Also, here." He held up a bracelet made from Chinese coins strung on a length of bright red ribbon. Flora's friend Mr. Green had given it to her some time ago during a period of difficulty, and, knowing what Cassie might be up against today, Flora had passed it along. Cassie had handed it off to Prince while the others were arguing.

"This is for you. A good luck charm."

Mary looked at the bracelet. "What does it do?"

"It came from a local Chinese merchant who is very knowledgeable about auspicious articles," Cassie said. "He said the round shape of the coins represents heaven, and the square shape of the holes in the middle represents earth. The number of coins, six, is the number of heavenly luck or energy, and the symbols engraved on the coins work together to provide protection. The mystic knot at the bottom and the red color of the ribbon are also protective."

Mary, clearly intrigued, started to reach for it then paused. "You don't need it, Prince?"

Prince held up the necklace he was wearing, a shark's tooth suspended from a leather cord. "Don't worry. I have my lucky shark's tooth. And I'll be staying close to you, making sure you're safe. Making sure we're all safe."

Lucky shark's tooth? Cassie had never heard of such a thing.

Satisfied with that, Mary accepted the coin amulet with aplomb. "You always were a good boy." She bowed her head regally, the actress in her perhaps invigorated by the attention.

"All right. I will not be one to stand between children and suste-nance. Besides, one is not a true actor if not willing to risk oneself for one's art."

"'One' might say we are a go," a voice murmured to Cassie's right.

"'One' might agree," agreed another, on her left.

Cassie started. The "waiters" had fallen in next to her, one on each side.

For Heaven's sake. Cassie had hoped she was imagining things before, but now that they were so close, there was no mistaking Jake and Hughes. She fixed her gaze on a lampshade across the room—a lovely purple one with embroidered butter-flies—and kept her lips still as she spoke.

"You'll be hearing from me later, Officers."

After the meeting, Prince took Mary on a walk through Old Town, following a suggestion from Miss Porter—having noted Mary's several mentions of her childhood as the daughter of a lighthouse keeper, she'd thought the place might soothe her nerves. Old Town Fernandina, which was located about a mile north of the present town of Fernandina, across a stretch of salt-marsh, was a peaceful riverfront hamlet that had served as the previous site of the city before the trans-peninsular railroad arrived in the fifties. It was a quiet neighborhood filled with quaint, old-fashioned houses, many of which had been around a century or more, and was now occupied chiefly by harbor pilots, mill-men, and others who made their living from the water, including by hiring out rowboats to tourists for pleasure paddles around the harbor—Cassie had enjoyed that activity more than once in the short time she'd been on the island.

To Miss Porter's point, though, one of the most charming features of the neighborhood was how proudly many of the houses embraced the area's maritime history. Cassie particularly liked one on Someruelus Street, near the old Spanish parade grounds that overlooked the water, which used dock pilings strung together with nautical rope as a fence and had a garden filled with gnomes dressed as sailors. But the Gwynnes' former family home, built by Cassie's grandfather Maro, a successful shipping merchant, was her favorite (and would have been, even if she didn't now own it—Flora had passed it on to her as a gift earlier that fall): cleverly built at an angle to the road with a round brick column running up the center and porthole-style windows, it gave a near-perfect impression of a cheerful steamboat chugging up the river.

Cassie, on the other hand, had volunteered to stay behind to help rework plans for the show, and was now banging around Miss Porter's kitchen in search of a kettle, trying to contain her annoyance at the two policemen standing in front of her.

"I can't believe this." She settled for a saucepan and filled it with water from the pitcher on the kitchen table. "The sheriff couldn't have been clearer about your involvement, but here you are, right in the middle of things, at the very first opportunity."

"Aw, no one recognized us. Not even you, until we spoke to you and gave ourselves away." Jake, who normally kept his face cleanshaven aside from a short beard, patted the clump of hair that had been wiggling around above his lip in the other room. It appeared he had fashioned himself a mustache (and new eyebrows, for some reason) from pieces of a ladies' hair switch and children's scrapbooking glue. He'd also made himself an Egmont name tag displaying the name "Jacques." "He did tell us to stay close enough to make sure there wasn't any trouble."

"I agree," Hughes said. "I think we did rather an impressive job with our disguises."

His spectacles had migrated to the tip of his nose, and his Egmont name tag, which read "Francois," was pinned on upside down.

How was it that, as absurd as he looked, Cassie still felt a tingle when she met his eyes?

She watched him run his fingers over his real mustache then blanch when he saw the boot polish he'd put in it come away on his glove.

Miss Porter called from the parlor. "Cassie, be sure to bring more sugar when you come."

"Yes, Miss Porter." Cassie placed the saucepan on the range and adjusted the damper to increase the heat.

Jake handed her the tea tin. "You're not angry, are you?"

"No, not angry. It's just the sheriff was very concerned that you didn't show yourself around—" She paused as voices passed in the hall. "Never mind. At least it's good to see that the two of you are capable of cooperating on something. But going forward it would really be best if— Please don't touch that. It's Prince's."

Hughes paused, his hand hovering over the small box he'd been rifling through, which Prince had set down on the counter after the meeting and forgotten to take with him when he left with Miss Rutledge. Cassie, pursuant to her own gentle perusal earlier, had identified it as the box he had received from the man on the dock the night before. Unfortunately, its contents had confused more than they'd clarified. Inside were two seashells, a carved sea turtle with an acorn in its flippers, and a piece of paper covered in notes she couldn't make any sense of: one side of the page contained the words "Lefty," "fishing from a rail station," "Central Florida woods," and "seaside or island"; and the other contained a list of cities with lines drawn through them, ending with Fernandina.

"Really?" Hughes scoffed. "What kind of a grown man carries around a box of childish trinkets—"

A scream from the back bedroom—man, woman, animal, it was difficult to say—cut off the rest of Hughes's impudent response. A moment later Metta and Paddy burst through the rear entrance to the kitchen.

"There's someone in the back bedroom!"

"He was hiding under the bed but I stepped on his hand and—"

"He screamed like a ghost!"

Hughes grabbed the broomstick. "Where did he go?"

"Out the window. And ran toward the street!"

Hughes and Jake kicked through the door into the dining room and Cassie and the children dashed after them as they careened around Miss Porter's formal dining table and into the library, where the others were gathered in front of the bay window, looking out. Batting their way past them, Jake and Hughes continued into the foyer and out the front door. Unsure what she should be doing to help, Cassie joined the group by the window and watched.

"There! He headed up Seventh!" Jake cried.

Hughes pointed. "No, he went *down* Seventh! This way!"

"I'm telling you, it's that way."

"Come on, we're going to lose— Hey, you're stepping on my—"

"Get out of my—agh!"

Jake and Hughes tripped over each other and fell into a flowerbed, then promptly started grappling.

So much for cooperation.

"I'll credit those waiters for trying, but they didn't give much of a chase," Arthur said, his face pressed against the window. "Though I can't say I'm hating this."

Waiters. Cassie pursed her lips. "Did anyone get a good look at that man running past?"

"Sorry, not me." Mr. Manning sat back down behind the reading desk, where he'd opened up the prompt book, and picked up his pencil. "I'd barely stood up before it was all over."

Arthur shrugged. "It happened too fast."

"We did," Metta adjusted the too-big eyepatch she'd affixed to her face. She must have borrowed that from Flora's friend

Sergeant Denham, a veteran of the United States Colored Troops who'd lost his sight, but, fortunately, not his good nature, in the war. "We were face to face with him in the rear bedroom."

Paddy, who was also wearing one of Sergeant Denham's eye patches, bounced in agreement. "Yes, we were sure to take good mental notes."

"Because we're the Child-Pirate Detectives now!"

That would explain the eye patches. "Is that so. What were you investig—"

Cassie stopped. *Oh no.* Paddy had been with her when they found the nails on the rigging platform so knew there was going to be an investigation into Mr. Gage's death. He must have told Metta. And the two of them, wrapped up in their penny dreadful fascination, had come to eavesdrop on the meeting with the troupe and listen for clues. Cute, but they could compromise the whole thing.

"Haha, that's right!" Cassie forced a laugh and patted Metta on the head, which thankfully confused her. "Your favorite imaginary, made-up game you two are always playing, all the time. What did he look like?"

Paddy blinked for a moment, then shrugged. "He had a very long coat, puffy in the shoulders—"

"And he rubbed his hands together like a mantis. Like this." Metta demonstrated with her own hands. As she spoke, Paddy trotted back into the kitchen.

Arthur gave a double-gasp. "That's exactly what Marguerite said about the peeper! From the theater!"

Cassie scratched her head, trying to dislodge the memory the children's description had loosened. She turned to Marguerite. "Did you see him? Was it him?"

Marguerite, who hadn't spoken yet, drew her black plush shawl around herself. "It was absolutely the same man who peeped into the ladies' dressing room and saw me in my nethers."

"Who hasn't, though?" muttered Mr. Wilkes.

Percy climbed down from the ottoman he'd pulled over so he could see over the others' heads. Without his compatriots around, he seemed stronger and more confident, like a plant that had finally received sun after languishing in the shade of a taller tree. Even his shoulders looked broader. "You know, I wonder if that's not the same man I saw at the theater a few days ago. He was moving quickly, but he looked a lot like him."

"He was *inside* the theater?" Marguerite's hand flew to her chest.

"Same here," Mr. Wilkes said. "Now that we're talking about it. He could definitely be the man I saw wandering around the theater during that last rehearsal."

"What? Where?" Cassie didn't remember seeing any non-chorus audience members in the auditorium.

Mr. Wilkes tented his fingers under his chin. "Backstage, near the east stage door. He was walking around with a leather case under his arm, poking at things and staring at people. I was about to say something unkind to him about touching other people's props, but I figured he was a chorus person and Mr. Gage would want me to be nice. I didn't remember seeing him at rehearsal before, but chorus people kind of all look the same to me. No offense."

"Well, I've participated in every rehearsal, and I've never seen anyone like that." Mrs. Reynolds jutted her chin at Miss Porter.

Miss Porter jutted her own chin back. "I've been at every rehearsal as well, and I haven't, either."

"What was he doing at the theater, then?" Cassie asked.

Percy sifted through a half-empty platter of donuts. "When I saw him, he asked me where Mr. Gage's office was. He sounded English, like Mr. Gage. I told him Mr. Gage doesn't have an office but maybe he could find him at his dressing table. But then Mr. Gage came around the corner, and the man simply walked away. It was all very strange."

"I agree." Cassie tugged on her lip. "Did you notice anything else distinctive about him? What he was wearing, what he looked like, that sort of thing? Other than what the others said?"

"He smoked a churchwarden pipe. And had a billy club at his hip. Actually, it's funny Mr. Wilkes said he assumed he was a chorus member because I had the same thought at first, because of the club. It was similar to the ones we use as props for the chorus of policemen."

That's it! That was the man Cassie had seen hurrying along the fence outside the Lyceum while the coroner was conducting his interviews right after the accident. Not a casual gossip seeker, it seemed, after all.

"He also forgot this!" Paddy announced, coming back into the room with a packet of papers. "In the bedroom, when he jumped out the window."

Arthur took the packet from him and looked at the top sheet. His eyes widened. "This is Mr. Gage's score. The one that went missing the morning of the accident."

Turning back toward the window, Cassie watched Jake and Hughes, who had finally untangled themselves, sprint off in separate directions.

Who was that man?

9

Everything Miss Porter ever baked or cooked was more than delicious: through what could only be explained as some kind of magic, the food she produced possessed a quality that made it impossible to go for more than a few seconds without shoving more of it into one's mouth. So, by the end of a long day spent in Miss Porter's library within arm's reach of an endless supply of freshly made treats, along with a small cow's udder's worth of cheese, as she helped Mr. Manning with plans for the reworked production (the others had lasted precisely an hour before becoming so fidgety Miss Porter sent them for a drive on the beach), Cassie was in serious need of a constitutional.

I shouldn't have bothered getting all those new dresses made before I left New York. Cassie turned onto Centre Street, determined to walk until her stomach stopped feeling like an overfilled party balloon. *None of them will fit in a month, the way I'm going.*

Most businesses were closed for the evening, but Centre Street was anything but dark or desolate. There was a full moon, more brilliant than any lamp ever made, bathing everything in a cool, white light bright enough to make the handsome storefronts squint, and dozens of vendors filled the road, hawking treats like popcorn and tropical fruit to the many well-heeled visitors strolling about in tailcoats and silk velvet wraps. A cold snap up north had sent another wave of winter tourists to the island in recent weeks, and the local entrepreneurs had risen to the occasion.

"Care for a snack, miss?" A man wearing an oyster shell boutonniere shoved a newspaper cone of golden hazelnuts under her nose, forcing her to stop.

A woman with a covered basket hurried toward her from another direction. "I've pretzels and sausages, the best you're ever likely to have. Cheeses, too!"

"How about some ripe, juicy oranges?" called another vendor, a man with curly black muttonchops. He cut off the pretzel woman, waving a fruit above his head. "Or a pome-granate? Grown in the sunshine right on the island!"

Cassie declined politely at first—a suspicious gurgle in her abdomen warned that her body was considering a solution to her fullness problem that wasn't nearly as dignified as an evening stroll—but, as additional vendors converged, a jolt of prey-like panic made her cast around for an escape. Unfortu-nately, her nearest option was the Three Star Saloon, an unapologetically indelicate drinking establishment whose distinctive row of starred windows could be seen pulsing with light and musical revelry most nights until sunrise. It wasn't what she'd had in mind for the evening, but at the moment the chaos within appealed more than the chaos without.

She slipped away from a beak-nosed woman who was trying to put some kind of meat on a stick in her hand and burst through the bar's peeling batwing doors—and knocked right into Hughes.

"Ow! Watch it!" Hughes whirled around. He had been bent over the bar talking to the proprietor, Mr. Marsden, and one of the regulars, Major Drury. "Oh, it's you—"

He flicked his gaze over Cassie's shoulder. Arthur and Mr. Wilkes were at a table behind her, playing dominoes with a group of middle-aged men in blue-gray uniforms—the Nassau Light Artillery must have had an event this evening. Arthur was wearing a different, but no less elaborate, mourning ensemble, which included a shirt with ruffled black lace around the sleeves and collar, and Mr. Wilkes had placed a black ribbon in the buttonhole of his suit coat.

He's right. Better not act too familiar.

"Pardon me, sir. Entirely my fault." As Cassie bobbed, she noticed Hughes slide a medium-sized parcel off the counter and tuck it under a barstool. If he was trying to hide it from her, though, it was too late. She'd already recognized it as a fabric sample box from Mrs. Tanury's store on the next block. Was Hughes shopping for ladies' dresses?

"Evening, Miss Gwynne," Mr. Marsden and Major Drury said, somehow managing to speak in a perfect, slurred unison. As usual, they were three sheets to the wind, maybe four.

Smoothing his mustache (it seemed he had been able to get most of the boot polish out of it), Hughes raised his voice over the piano player, a spindly man with blue suspenders whose jaunty key pounding appeared to have only one volume level this evening. "So, as I was saying, gentlemen, please take a look at this wanted sketch I made of the man I've dubbed 'the Theater Peeper' and let me know if you've seen him or know anything about who he might be." He held up a pencil drawing of the man they had chased earlier that morning.

Cassie's mouth fell open. The drawing was so lifelike she thought the man might take a breath. It perfectly incorporated all the details that had been reported as well, from the insect-like stance and long coat to the churchwarden pipe, billy club, and leather case. When she had suggested that Hughes or Jake make a sketch from the witnesses' descriptions so they could show it around, she hadn't known Hughes himself had any artistic ability.

"No, that's not what you were saying." Major Drury slurped his drink. "You did that earlier. Right then you were asking whether any of the samples in that box would be considered Spanish lace. And the answer is a big fat Heck-If-I-Know."

Hughes slapped the drawing on the counter, his shoulders hunched. Cassie liked the way the tips of his ears had turned pink, though she wondered why he was asking questions about ladies' lace.

"All right, gentlemen, stick a fork in me." Arthur placed his tiles on the table. "Because I'm done." He pushed back his chair and stood.

"Aw, we're just getting started. One more game?" Mr. Wilkes put down his own tiles and scooped everything into a pile as the others threw their hands into the middle. "I'll give you odds."

Arthur slung his coat over his shoulder, assuming a contrapposto stance to rival Michelangelo's *David*. "Nah. I don't want to be here when Miss Pretty Princess Marguerite shows up. No telling what I'll do if I see her right now."

"I don't know what you two are squabbling about, but you ought to kiss and make up." Mr. Wilkes steamed his monocle with his breath and used a glove to rub the glass. "It's uncomfortable."

Arthur shrugged and tipped his hat to the artillery men, then sauntered through the batwing doors, throwing out a salute as he exited.

"Ho there, Miss Gwynne—" Mr. Wilkes waved at her. "I didn't see you come in. How about a game? Throw around some bones?"

"No, thank you. I don't really—"

"Don't worry, little lady. I'll teach you how to play."

Cassie forced a smile. She knew very well how to play

dominoes, but she didn't want to play with *him*. Earlier that afternoon, before she'd sent the group off to the beach, Mr. Wilkes had been getting more familiar with her than she would have liked, touching her back as he passed, leaning too close when he talked, making eye contact with parts of her that weren't her eyes... She certainly hadn't encouraged his attention, but for some men, anything short of a kick in the nether region was an invitation.

She also hated how he called her "little lady," as though that counted as charm. She didn't suppose he'd take kindly to being called "little gentleman."

"Truly," she said, "I only came in for... a quick bite." She winced at her choice of excuse—anyone who had ever taken a meal from Mrs. Marsden's kitchen would have known that was a bald-faced lie—and at the renewed stomach gurgling it had caused.

Why did I eat all that stupid, delicious cheese? She looked around. Where was the privy in this place again?

"I know!" Mr. Wilkes jumped up. "They have a billiards table in the back. I'll buy your meal and teach you to play sixty-one pool while we wait. Once you're comfortable, maybe we can get some proper action going."

He strode over in his Lilliputian boots and took her elbow, the suggestion somehow having turned into a plan of action, and Cassie resisted the urge to look to Hughes for help, even though she knew he was staring after them.

"You know that man?" Mr. Wilkes tipped his head toward Hughes, who immediately began showing the drawing to Mr. Marsden and Major Drury again.

Cassie tried to adjust her arm so his grip wasn't directly in her armpit. "Not really. He just showed me a wanted drawing of the peeper and asked if I'd seen anything."

"Good. I can't stand those town watch types, always sniffing around, telling people what they can and can't do. Makes me both nervous and annoyed— Proprietor!" As they approached the pool table, Mr. Wilkes called across the piano player, who pounded the keys harder in response. "This little lady requires sustenance! Bring her the most toothsome dish you have."

Cassie avoided Mr. Marsden's smirk as he swung through the door to the kitchen (he knew just as well as she that no one had ever used the word "toothsome" to describe his wife's cooking) and worked at the tip of a cue stick with a square of chalk, trying to ignore the rapidly intensifying cramps that had replaced the gurgling in her stomach. She lifted the cue and blew off the excess powder. At least she liked shooting pool. One of the hotels near their house in New York had kept a table, so she and her father had often closed out the evening with a friendly game or two.

"All right, now, little lady." Mr. Wilkes tried to lean in with a hand on her shoulder, but Cassie slid out from under it, feigning concern over a cigar burn in the felt. "The game is simple. You have fifteen object balls, numbered one through fifteen. If you sink one—that means getting a ball into one of the holes at the corners of the table—you get the number of points on that ball. The total value of all the balls is a hundred and twenty, so the first player to reach at least one point over half of that, um..."

"Sixty-one."

"Yes, sixty-one, wins. Very good!" Mr. Wilkes stepped in close to Cassie again and took the cue stick out of her hand. "Now, the catch is, you have to hit this little white ball—" He reached across her and picked up the cue ball. "With the tip of this stick, which is called a 'cue stick,' so it runs into whichever ball you are trying to get in the hole. Does that make sense?"

Cassie had to lock her gaze on the felt to keep her eyes from rolling back in her head. "Yes, thank you."

"And the way you do it is—is—well—" He positioned

himself behind her and tried to reach around with his arms to illustrate, but he couldn't quite reach.

Cassie had a clear shot to his face with her elbow, but she restrained herself and moved away, placing her back against a wall. "Why don't we try playing and see what happens?"

Mr. Wilkes straightened his lapel. "Good idea. You can watch me and see how to do it."

This time, one of Cassie's eyes got in half a roll before she caught it.

"So, what's going on with Mr. Beath and Miss Clifton?" She figured she might as well make the best of the situation and gather some information. "Mr. Beath seemed anxious not to see her here."

Mr. Wilkes snorted and bent over the table with the cue stick, which looked comically long in his hands. "Oh, who could really say, but a lover's quarrel is my guess. They're usually inseparable, but for the last several weeks, almost as long as we've been in this town, Arthur's been acting like a wounded puppy around her. Jealous, sulky, clinging to her like burnt cheese on a griddle. Perhaps she's found a new paramour. Whatever it is, it came to a head this afternoon, I think. They weren't even speaking by the time we reached the beach."

He struck the cue ball with force, hopping up with his hands and feet together like a bunny as he followed through, but he only managed to break out a couple of the balls, neither of which found a pocket. "Or perhaps something from their checkered past has come back to haunt them."

"Their checkered past?"

"Well, I'm sure you heard Mr. Manning reference this morning how several of the troupe were having some—employment challenges before Mr. Gage game along. Marguerite has been expelled from more than one organization for becoming romantically linked to the wrong person. Most recently, I hear, the married impresario of an opera company somewhere in the

Midwest. The impresario's wife, a very influential soprano, did not take kindly to the situation."

Cassie accepted the cue stick from Mr. Wilkes, resisting the urge to jab it in his eye when he purposefully overlapped her fingers in the transfer.

"And Arthur's troubles appear to be in a similar vein," he continued as Cassie bent over her shot, "though I don't know the details. In any event, one could say their hearts get in the way of their careers... Now, you're going to want to choke up on that cue stick a bit. That means move your hand up the shaft like—"

In the midst of her stroke, he placed one of his hands over her grip and the other on her hip, causing her to miss. She fumed at the back of his head as he took back the stick and strutted around the table, evaluating his next shot. Out of the corner of her eye, she saw Hughes stand from his barstool.

"They're not half as annoying as Mary Rutledge, though." Mr. Wilkes potted the four ball, which was hanging over a pocket, and congratulated himself with a swig of beer. "She always has to be the center of attention. And as you've witnessed, she's been an extra-special treasure to be around since she heard 'someone,' we still don't know who, name the Scottish play... When Roland fell off that table, I thought we might have to send her away for a stint in the sanatorium."

Cassie watched him chalk the cue stick. "You're saying she's difficult, and that's what makes it challenging for her to get work."

"Exactly. Everything is about her. Did you know she's halted more than one curtain on account of the temperature not being to her liking? In fact, I wouldn't be surprised if she arranged some of the incidents she ascribes to the curse herself, just for the attention. I don't think she'd hurt anyone, naturally, but the other things, like the props getting moved and lost and such? No, it wouldn't surprise me one bit."

Cassie frowned after him as he circled the table. Even with the caveat, that was a terrible thing to say about a person. But, then again, in Cassie's own short experience with Mary, the woman hadn't exactly come across as reasonable, and she had been pretty furious about Mr. Gage's dismissal of her concerns.

She shook her head. *No, that woman's harmless.*

Right?

"How about the head stagehand, Harland McGregor?"

"Miserable drunk."

"Vera Cook and her band of merry men and woman?"

"Absenteeism, apathy, general unprofessionalism."

"Prince Montgomery?"

"Still trying to figure that out, as he's the newest. He's been a serviceable replacement for Roland in the Frederic role, but I find him, and I think others would agree, particularly Harland, a bit too eager to involve himself in things that aren't his concern. Sure, he was helpful with load-in and all when we arrived here... but the man's been with eight different troupes in the past year, rarely for more than a couple of performances. Something has to be wrong with him if no one wants to keep him."

Eight different troupes? That *was* a lot. Especially for someone who seemed so pleasant and competent, and talented, too. What could possibly make him change employment so often?

Cassie watched Mr. Wilkes put a foot up on the wall to steady himself while he took another shot. "So, what's wrong with you?"

"Absolutely nothing." He missed, then, cursing under his breath, handed the cue stick to Cassie. "Going back to Harland McGregor, though, that's a frustrating case. He used to be one of the best in the business, but, largely due to the effect of drink, he's become essentially unemployable. I wouldn't choose to work with him now myself, if I had my options. Which probably means Mr. Gage got him for cheap. Same with the others, I'm guessing. Discounted talent. For all his love of expensive baubles, Mr. Gage didn't like to spend a dime where he didn't have to."

Taking advantage of the space created by Mr. Wilkes's monologue, Cassie sank the fourteen ball and the twelve ball and, ignoring Mr. Wilkes's gaping, moved around the table to line up on the thirteen.

As she bent over the cue stick once more, she saw Paddy come in and hand a letter to Hughes. Hughes's face reddened when he saw the envelope, then nearly caught fire when he opened it and a dried flower fell out onto the floor.

Cassie dropped her gaze back to the pool table before he saw her looking. It was another one of those pink, red-ribboned letters, and this one had come with a flower token. It was undeniable now: Hughes was corresponding with a woman. He'd never mentioned any such person to her before, though.

But why would he have?

"Ah, almost!" Mr. Wilkes said as the ball Cassie was aiming for rattled out of the pocket. He had leaned over her shoulder, again far too close, right as she took her shot.

Cassie glanced back at Hughes. He shoved the letter in his pocket, then, after another thought, picked up the flower and put that in his pocket, too.

"Well." Cassie moved her hips away from Mr. Wilkes's hand as he slid past her with the cue, facing toward her unnecessarily and moving far too slowly for her liking. "Is there anyone in the troupe who doesn't irritate you?"

Stroking the cue through a part in his beard, Mr. Wilkes made another ball that was hanging over a pocket, the one ball this time, and celebrated by boxing an invisible opponent.

"Vera and Theresa are all right. As long as you're not counting on them to show up for something. They're easy on the eyes, in a might-stab-you-in-your-sleep sort of way. And their friend Ira understands what it's like to be denied opportunities because of one's appearance—He's always getting cast as oafish characters because of his thick physique. The same thing happens to me because of my height... Yes, Mr. Gage wasn't the first director to underestimate my immense talents due to short-sighted biases. I work harder than anyone at my craft, and I get so tired of being ignored."

Cassie thought about the exchange Mr. Wilkes and Arthur had had that morning about the Pirate King role. She was starting to get an inkling as to the source of Mr. Wilkes's own employment challenges.

And to wonder how far he may have been willing to go this time to get what he wanted.

"I'm sure it wasn't anything like that," Cassie offered. "Mr. Gage seemed an open-minded and generous man to me. Perhaps it simply wasn't the right time."

Mr. Wilkes started to aim for the three ball, but the fireplace was too close to the table on that side, and the back of his cue stick hit the mantel. He tried a few contortions, then switched to a short stick but missed anyway.

"Maybe. But it doesn't matter now, does it. I'm finally getting my due."

His eyes widened as Cassie embarked on a three-ball run—thirteen, fifteen, then six—which brought her score to sixty.

He cleared his throat as he took the cue stick back. "You should know, though, Mr. Gage really wasn't all tea and crumpets."

That sounds promising. "What do you mean?"

Mr. Wilkes sidled closer, which Cassie wasn't entirely thrilled about, but she kept her feet steady because she wanted to hear what he had to say. "Well, for all his fancy manners and charm, Lord help you if he was set on something and you disagreed. He had a streak of stubbornness on par with a spoiled child. Why, only a week ago—yes, it was that Friday evening before the accident—I went over to his suite at the Egmont Hotel to see him about—a casting matter and overheard him throwing a fit my three-year-old nephew would be envious of. I was surprised the hotel staff hadn't been alerted."

Cassie straightened. "Do you know what it was about?"

"Oh, no, no. It wouldn't have been gentlemanly to linger."

Cassie coughed.

"Besides, the door is so heavy there you can hardly discern an actual word from the hall when it's closed, no matter how you cup your hand or press your ear. There was another man's voice, shouting as well, but all I could discern was Mr. Gage yelling: 'How dare you, after everything...'"

To Cassie's relief, Mr. Wilkes leaned back to pick up the cue stick chalk, giving her an opportunity to move away.

"Anyway, my guess is that temper of his came from his upbringing... Mr. Manning told us the reason Mr. Gage could maintain such a lifestyle while running the troupe not-for-profit was 'private means,' which must mean family money. I suppose it's easy to be a philanthropist when you're rich, eh? Which is why I could never understand why he was such a terrible miser when it came to the production budget. Mr. Manning would say it was because Mr. Gage wanted to make sure as much money as possible went to charity, but who knows. I never saw those books."

Cassie supposed that answered the question she had had about Mr. Gage's impressive suite at the Egmont, along with his jewelry and clothing. And the state of the wood involved in his demise. Regardless of anything else, that had certainly made things easier for whoever was responsible. But had Mr. Gage really been that devoted to his cause, reserving every excess production dollar for charity? Who was that good?

Mr. Wilkes hiked his trousers and evaluated his next turn. The only reasonable option available to him was far down the table, and, given the length of his arms, he'd need a mechanical bridge to reach it. After a brief attempt in which his foot slipped out from under him, he shrugged and tossed the cue stick on the table.

"What do you say we get out of here? I'm tired of playing games."

Cassie grabbed her stomach, partially out of surprise but also because her food cramps had taken a sudden, more aggressive turn. "Pardon?"

"You and me, leaving. Together." Mr. Wilkes slicked back his hair and sauntered toward her, backing her against the wall beneath a sconce that appeared to be dripping oil.

"Oh, but the food hasn't—" Cassie's stomach clenched again at the idea—of both food and what Mr. Wilkes was suggesting.

"Come on. It's intriguing, right? A night with a dashing actor who travels from town to town, living a life of adventure?" Light and shadow flickered in turn on Mr. Wilkes's face. "I know you rich, sheltered types. You're just dying for an excuse to break out of your 'gilded cage,' to really 'live.' Well, I'm offering you a stellar opportunity here." He winked, and Cassie winced.

"No, I'm— No!" Cassie pulled her arm from his grasp, wishing she could tell him off properly, but the cramps had merged together into pure, urgent pressure, and she was barely able to think. "I—have to—"

Giving Mr. Wilkes a shove that he might have appreciated if he knew about the gastrointestinal mayhem that was about to occur, she broke away and pushed past Hughes—who'd finally started toward them when Mr. Wilkes cornered her—through the batwing doors, and around the side of the building to the grassy square where the outhouse was.

She leapt inside and slammed the slatted door behind her. The saloon-side necessary was the epitome of filth, but, in that moment, no sight had ever been more beautiful to her than that crusty wooden seat with a hole in it.

She had only had enough time to get her skirts up around her waist, however, before she heard a voice outside: Marguerite.

She did whatever the bottom-side equivalent of holding one's breath was and braced an arm against the mildewed wall as the cramps, enraged by her renege, came back with a vengeance.

"I can't believe you're here at a *saloon*, Harland, getting tight again."

"Aw, it's fine."

Cassie squelched a groan. An internal rebellion was imminent.

"I just think you could at least try to cut down the drinking. One day of sobriety here and there doesn't count. Your livelihood is on the line, for Chrissakes—"

"Was." Harland's flask swished.

"What?"

"Was on the line. Gage can't fire me now, can he. The sanctimonious bastard."

So, Mr. McGregor was not among Mr. Gage's admirers, either. Cassie sucked in a silent breath. She didn't know how much longer she was going to be able to hold on.

"That's not funny. And I didn't mean only your job, I meant your career. You have no idea what I've had to— It's just been so much, cleaning up your messes... I don't know how much more I can take."

Same.

"What do you mean 'cleaning up my messes'?"

Marguerite paused. "Harland, I should tell you—"

Nononono...

"Because I'm fully capable of cleaning up my own messes, Marguerite, believe me. I don't need anyone's help. Why is everyone always sticking their damn nose in my—"

Cassie let go.

And what followed was— Well, a lady doesn't discuss such things. Nor would Cassie, with anyone. Ever.

When she was finally able to breathe again (relatively speaking), Cassie realized silence had fallen outside. Harland and Marguerite were gone and, possibly, permanently traumatized. She covered her face. Her only saving grace was they hadn't known who was in here.

She sighed and was about to begin the complex process of getting up without letting her dress touch anything when a tap came at the door.

She froze, still balanced precariously over the disgusting hole.

"Uh, occupied." She tried to disguise her voice by lowering it.

A man cleared his throat. "Sorry for the intrusion, Miss Gwynne, but there's a small crisis happening over at Miss Porter's, and Miss Porter is asking for you specifically."

Hot ice shot through Cassie's veins. It was Hughes.

How long had he been there?

"Um, I'll be out in a moment. I'm just—fixing my hair."

Hughes coughed. "I'll meet you out front."

Horror. Mortification. Death. All the way to Miss Porter's, Cassie—the whole of her face, neck, and chest on fire—kept her eyes on her boots and her mind on a mental accounting of every synonym she could think of for "inestimable embarrassment." *Disgrace. Humiliation. Discomfiture.*

"Cassie, thank heavens you're here." Immediately upon opening the door, Miss Porter grabbed Cassie's hand and pulled her toward the stairs.

"I'll just follow, then," Hughes called after them.

"I don't know what to do." Miss Porter puffed as she climbed, still gripping Cassie's hand. "Miss Rutledge didn't come down to dinner, but I thought perhaps she was napping, since she'd gone out walking with Prince and did look fairly peaked when I saw her in the hallway this afternoon. So, I kept some food warm, in case she came down later, but eventually I thought, I'll bring her a tray, and if she eats it, she eats it, if not, I'll pick it up in the morning." She paused at the top of the staircase to catch her breath, then continued down the hallway. "Only, when I knocked, the door fell open, and—it's this one here—" She gestured into one of the rooms. "She was gone."

Cassie forgot her lingering throbs of humiliation as she stepped inside the shadowy room. Aside from the customary furniture—bed, clothing trunk, a dressing table with a mirror and washbasin—the room was filled with luck and protection talismans of every size, shape, and cultural tradition imaginable.

Cassie touched her finger to a dried bouquet of four-leaf clovers over the dressing mirror, then examined a length of red rope that had been tied into a series of mystic knots.

"There seems to be a theme in the décor here." Hughes bent under the row of rabbit's feet dangling from the door frame like a decorative fringe.

He crossed over to the window, which was covered by a piece of parchment paper painted all over with the numbers seven and eight, and rested his hands on his waist, a pose which, Cassie noticed, emphasized the sculpted lines of his neck and arms from behind. "Interesting. Seven was considered by the ancient Greeks to be the perfect number and therefore auspicious. But the Chinese believe eight to be the luckiest number, and find seven to be unlucky since the seventh month is regarded as the 'ghost month.' She has both on here at once."

He picked up a figurine of a three-legged frog with a coin in its mouth. "Oh, look. A jin chan. Golden Toad... and a Glücksschwein!" He picked up a pig figurine in his other hand. A sudden, childlike excitement had come over him, and Cassie, while astonished by this unexpected knowledge of world culture, adored it.

She tripped over a basket filled with gris-gris bags and bits of wood carved into Italian cornicellos, Swedish dala horses, and Jewish hamsa hands. "How do you know all that?"

The flicker vanished, and Hughes put down the figurines with a shrug. "School." He spun one of the dreamcatchers hanging over the bed.

"Miss Porter, we're here!" Jake rushed into the room, jangling the rabbit's feet over the doorframe with his derby.

Flora appeared behind him, pushing her frizzled bangs out of her eyes. "I'm so sorry, Lottie! Jake and I got caught up in a bit of a—discussion about— Never mind. How can we help?"

"Trouble in Paradise, eh, Gordo?" Hughes said, poking around a pile of old shoes.

Miss Porter stood up a bamboo plant that had gotten knocked over. "Have you seen Prince? I sent Paddy to the Florida House to get him, but he wasn't there and no one had seen him all day. Where could he be?"

"Wasn't he out walking with Miss Rutledge this afternoon?" Flora asked. She had that thoughtful look on her face again.

"Yes, they set out together. But Miss Rutledge was alone when she came back."

Hughes dropped the shoe he'd picked up. "Why do we need him? We have everything under control." He strode to the bed and started lifting throw pillows. "I'm sure there's a perfectly reasonable—Ah! A note!" He picked up a piece of paper that had fallen into a fold in the coverlet and read it aloud. "'Dear friends: The guilt is too much. It was me, all me. I must now face my fate and end this. Please give my gowns to the children. Love, Mary.'" He looked up. "What would children want with a bunch of ladies' gowns?"

Cassie took the note from him and read it over again, biting her lip. *Guilt for what? What was "all her"? She can't possibly mean she was responsible for—*

Miss Porter gasped. "Is she confessing to Mr. Gage's murder? And what does she mean 'face my fate and end this'? You don't think she's going to harm herself?" She started to gasp again but cut herself off with another gasp.

Jake accepted the note from Cassie and angled it toward the wall sconce so both he and Flora could read it. "And she wants us to give her gowns to children?"

"Please! We need to focus!" Miss Porter pressed her hands to her face. "We have to find Miss Rutledge before she does something she'll regret!"

"Yes, right. We'll split up and look for her." Jake handed the note to Flora.

"I'll check the passenger wharf and train depot, then ask around at whatever establishments are still open," Hughes said.

"Miss Porter and I will drive over to the beach and look for her there." Jake turned. "Cassie and Flora—"

"We'll figure something out."

Jake, Hughes, and Miss Porter thundered out of the room and down the stairs, and a moment later the front door slammed.

Arthur's head poked out of one of the other bedrooms down the hall. "What's all the ruckus about?"

"We can't find Miss Rutledge," Cassie answered.

"Oh. Hasn't she come back from her outing with Prince? I suppose I didn't see her at dinner." Arthur gave a luxurious yawn and walked into the room. He looked around. "Holy hatpins. It's like a curiosities museum in here. Or a witch doctor's boudoir."

"She was here this afternoon but is gone now," Flora said. "And Mr. Montgomery can't be found, either. But Miss Rutledge left this note, and we—fear the worst."

Arthur smoothed his eyebrows as he read. "That does sound

bad." After handing the note back, he thought for a moment, then stepped over a line of what looked to be salt and peered under the bed. "Ah. That's something, at least."

"What is?" Cassie asked.

"I don't think she intends to depart this world. Just this place."

"What do you mean?"

"She's taken her valise with her. A beautiful leather piece with maroon cross-stitching—I've always admired it."

"But where would she go? And how is she planning to get off the island this time of night?"

Arthur brushed off his knees. "You'd know better than I."

"If she's trying to leave right now," Flora said, "she's going to need her own means off the island. And, whatever her reason for fleeing, she's clearly distressed. I'd bet she's probably headed somewhere comforting. Where do you think that would be for her?"

Cassie tucked the note into her pouch and looked around the room. She wasn't even sure how she'd answer that question for herself these days.

When her gaze passed over the dressing table, however, she noticed a stereoscope next to a set of viewing cards. The box was labeled "Scenic Views of Monomoy Point Lighthouse." She loaded one of the cards, and when she peered into the eyepiece, it displayed a picture of a cast-iron lighthouse rising above a pair of light-colored outbuildings, one small and one large, on a grassy slope. Two little rowboats were visible in the curve of water at the edge of the image.

She put the viewer down. "I've got it."

"Got what?" Flora asked.

"I think I know where Mary Rutledge is."

10

If Cassie thought the plank walk leading to Old Town was treacherous during the day, it was downright murderous at night. Clouds had moved in, wrapping the moon like a thick woolen blanket, so the only light she had by which to navigate the narrow wooden platform snaking through the marsh ahead of her was a portable lantern, which had a radius of about two feet in each direction. Just enough to assure her that there were no railings or other such impediments to interfere with her entering the murk below in the event of a slip. Confidence is the only way forward in such situations, however, so she pushed on, accompanied by the calls, croaks, and grunts of unseen wildlife close enough to touch.

She sighed with relief when she finally rounded the Harbor Pilots Association's shanty at the Old Town Harbor dock. There was Mary, standing in a rowboat, gesticulating at a droopy-eyed fisherman in a sleeping gown and house slippers. It seemed, as Cassie had deduced, Mary had come to see one of the local residents who offered rowboats for hire. Thankfully, Cassie had caught her before she'd gone anywhere, though.

These rowboats were typically only used for pleasure paddles around the harbor, and, given that Mary had brought her valise along, it was hard to say what her actual plans might be.

When she called out to her, Mary's eyes flashed a warning.

"Stay back, Miss Gwynne." Mary lifted her valise in front of her like a shield. Or a weapon. "My mind is made up. I'm leaving this place tonight, and there's nothing you or anyone else can do to stop me."

The fisherman itched his ear. "Leaving? I thought you said you wanted to go for a little row."

"A little row across the harbor, then on to Cape Cod!"

Cassie bit her lip. *Row all the way to Cape Cod?* It was worse than she'd thought: the woman had lost her mind.

"Uh, ma'am," said the fisherman, "I don't think that's even possible—"

"I'll do what I must do! The fate of others rests on my shoulders!"

Cassie stepped around a coil of rope. "But, Miss Rutledge—"

Mary hopped backward, rocking the rowboat perilously. "I'm warning you, Miss Gwynne. If you don't steer clear of me, you *will* get hurt."

Cassie hadn't entirely agreed with Miss Porter's interpretation of Mary's letter back at the boarding house, but suddenly she felt nervous. Was Mary dangerous, after all?

She looked around for a paddle or something else that might be used for defense. Perhaps she should have gone to get Jake or Hughes first, or even brought Flora, rather than coming on her own.

As she was reaching for a discarded boat hook, however, Mary moaned and pressed the back of her hand to her forehead. "Please. Just let me go. No matter how many talismans I acquire, no matter how many rituals I perform, nothing has been able to rid me of this cosmic stench! Therefore, I must away and bear this foul thing with me!"

Cassie stopped. What exactly was she referring to??

"Let's talk about this," she called, moving slowly so as not to set the woman off again. "For one, how is this gentleman supposed to get his boat back if you row it all that way?"

The fisherman swiveled his head for her response.

"I hadn't considered that."

"Then why not wait until morning? When a train or steamer packet, or even the mail coach, might be available to take you where you wish to go?" Cassie inched forward again.

Mary clutched her valise back to her chest. "No, I cannot wait. I'm a powder keg by the fire, a tea kettle formed from wax, a minefield of dancing fools. Every moment I remain is another moment others are at risk for another strike of supernatural retribution, and it's all because of me."

Good Lord. Cassie held up the note. "Is that what this is about? The curse?"

"Yes!" Mary dumped her valise in the bewildered fisherman's arms so she could properly wring her hands. "It's all my fault! All the accidents, mishaps, misfortunes, whatever you want to call them. From Roland's leg to Mr. Gage's..." She faltered as though to faint, but waved the fisherman off and grasped the edge of the boat. "I really thought if we were careful enough, on our guard, we could make it through this last show... But then this afternoon, I found my hand mirror had cracked! All on its own!

"And no sooner had I seen my fractured reflection than a child, a darling little girl with sausage curls and a red sash, tripped and fell right below my window, spilling her armful of flowers. It was such poetic *horror*. That was when I realized the curse was expanding its reach, growing strength, to who knows what end... The only solution was to renounce the theater and get far enough away it couldn't hurt anyone else."

Cassie cocked her head. She didn't see the connection between a broken hand mirror and a child tripping, even in a curse scenario. But, as for a girl with sausage curls and tripping with an armful of flowers, she might.

"Fortunately, she wasn't terribly hurt," Mary went on. "She stood right up and brushed herself off... But she must have been upset because when she left, she forgot her shoes."

Cassie stifled a smile. "Miss Rutledge, that little girl was my friend Jake Gordon's daughter, Metta. I'd bet if you asked her, she'd say the shoes were to blame for her fall, not you. It happens all the time."

Mary dabbed a tear with her handkerchief. "It does?"

"Yes. She says she can't keep her balance if she can't feel the ground." Cassie tried approaching again, and this time Mary didn't react.

"But that doesn't mean the other things weren't my fault."

Cassie climbed into the boat then, foundering as it swayed below her, sat down, a little harder than she would have liked. "I still don't understand that. Even if a curse were to blame, why would it be your—"

"A curse *is* to blame, and *I* am to blame for the *curse!*" Mary held her handkerchief over her face, the embroidered orange blossom petals on it drooping with shame. "Because I'm the one who named the Scottish play!"

The fisherman gasped and clutched the valise to his chest.

Cassie threw him an annoyed glance. "*You* did that? I thought you heard someone else say it through the wall."

"I lied, lied, lied. Which must have made the curse worse. Evil magnifies evil."

"But if it was such a bad thing, why did you—"

"It was an accident! Roland, the actor who performed the Frederic role before Prince, and I were playing a stupid rhyming game while we were waiting for places to be called one night. We'd made it theater-themed for an extra challenge, and when he said *The Tempest*, I was at a loss for a rebuttal until I thought of— It just slipped out." She covered her mouth, as though reliving the moment and trying to keep it from happening this time. "And, during that very performance, Roland fell off the table and broke his leg. The next day he went home to join his father's mining business. He clearly understood the gravity of the situation better than I... Who, like a fool, stayed on and on, even as more things happened, until..."

She shuddered.

"Which is why I need to go home to Monomoy, where I belong. There's another keeper family at the lighthouse now, Jones, I think the name is, but I hear they're good people. Maybe they'll let me stay with them in exchange for manual labor." She held out her hands and feet and started suggesting to herself various functions she could perform to earn her keep.

Cassie studied her. Even setting aside her apparent plan to take a rowboat a thousand miles up the coast, none of what she was saying had an ounce of logic to it. Someone needed to talk some sense into her, but Cassie was afraid only the truth would be powerful enough.

Cassie turned to the fisherman, who was watching, rapt, as though he'd discovered a free peepshow at the fair. "Sir, if you wait inside for a few minutes, I'll pay you twice what this lady offered you for the use of your boat."

The man hiked the valise over his head and ran off toward the shanty, clicking his heels once before he disappeared through the door.

"Listen." Cassie caught Mary's hands, which appeared to be in the midst of miming her animal-butchering skills. "I can't speak to all of the incidents you're referring to, but I can tell you this: Mr. Gage was murdered. By a flesh-and-blood person, not a curse."

Mary lowered her imaginary cleaver. "He was?"

"I found evidence that what happened to him was indeed

intentional and am working with a couple of the sheriff's men to investigate it. It's the real reason Miss Porter and I suggested the show go forward: we need to keep the troupe here long enough to identify the guilty party. But don't worry. Everyone will be paid their promised wages and the charity will receive a donation, whatever the outcome, even if I have to cover it myself. Only, the sheriff is trying to keep it quiet, obviously, so it's important that you do not share what I've said with anyone, all right? I just thought you should know, now that I understand what's going on with you."

Mary's face was still. Then she leaned forward. "How was it done?"

"Someone switched out the fasteners in the set piece so Mr. Gage would fall when he climbed the mast. Then switched them back to proper ones to cover it up. We found the bad ones wrapped up in a handkerchief hidden up on the rigging platform." She slapped at a mosquito. It was attacking her ankle like a forty-niner with a hot tip.

"Does Prince know?"

"Yes." Cassie slapped at the mosquito again. "He's helping."

Finally, Mary sat back with a sigh. "I'm so glad." She pulled off her hat. "Not glad that Mr. Gage was murdered, of course. That I'm not the one who did it. Sorry, that sounds—You understand. And now I don't have to go to Monomoy."

The mosquito plaguing Cassie still hadn't taken the hint, so Cassie added her second hand and executed a rapid-fire slap attack, then grabbed onto the seat as the boat rocked in response. "I thought you wanted to go home. You spoke so fondly the other day of rowing in the tidal waters around the—"

"Not at all!" Mary brushed back her hair and re-pinned her chignon. "It was cold and desolate there, and even performing basic tasks was a trial. The walls were cracked, the roof leaked... We had to rely on our neighbors, who were not close, for water, since there was no rainwater cistern on site. And the glass panes in the lantern broke and had to be replaced constantly...

"The reason I loved going out in my rowboat so much was that was when I could daydream about getting away to a real city. I loved my family, but life was hard out there— On the days my parents went into Harwich, I was so lonesome I thought my heart would break. So going back now was to be my penance. And exile. In a place like that, a curse would have little power."

"That's—very Shakespearean."

"It is, isn't it?" Mary seemed pleased. "And, as my dear parents are no longer, there wouldn't be a single redeeming point left about the place."

She tugged her necklace out from beneath her cloak. At the end of it was a painted miniature of a windblown family: a serious but kind-looking man and woman, an impish girl, and a fluffy dog, gathered by the base of the lighthouse she had seen in the stereoscope image. Mary pointed. "There's Mama and Papa and yours truly. And Mama's dog, Pliny the Elder." She nodded at the locket on Cassie's chatelaine. "I see you carry a precious picture with you as well."

"Oh, uh, yes." Cassie unclipped the locket and opened it so Mary could see. "This is my mother and father on their wedding day. My father had the original daguerreotype reproduced and set in this locket for me as a gift last year before he— passed. I lost my mother when I was a baby." She swallowed.

Mary leaned across and squeezed Cassie's arm. "So we're orphans together, then, like the rascally Pirates of Penzance." She smiled. "You and me and Prince."

"Prince's parents are—definitely deceased? I thought he said he didn't know where he'd come from."

"No, well, yes—at least, no one knows for sure. But I'm sure the poor dear feels that way. I always look at him during that exchange in *Pirates* when his character, Frederic, points out that the pirate crew is too tenderhearted to make effective pirates, especially when it comes to would-be targets who claim to be orphans, and one pirate replies, 'We are orphans ourselves, and know what it is...' Every time, I think to myself, '*I* know what it is, and so does *he*. I can see it in his eyes.'"

Cassie studied her knees. "It's interesting you mention that line. I didn't use to notice it particularly when I still had my father, but now that he's gone, it cuts through me every time. And all the more since, though it's not the same..." She looked up. "I recently found out I lost my brother as well."

"I'm so sorry to hear that." Mary squeezed her arm again. "How did it happen?"

"He drowned. Swept away in a river during a storm."

"How horrible. When was that?"

"A long time ago, when we were children. Before I could remember."

"Oh! You made it sound like it had just— Never mind. That's very sad. But you've only recently learned of it?"

"I never even knew I had a brother until my Aunt Flora told me what happened a few weeks ago. My father never spoke of it."

"Why wouldn't he have told you?"

"I suppose it was too painful. Which, the older I get and the more I experience, the more I understand."

They sat across from each other in the rowboat for a while longer, soothed by the gentle rocking of the water below.

Finally, Mary slapped her thighs. "So, how can I help? With Mr. Gage's investigation?"

"Help?" Cassie steadied herself with one hand and clipped the locket back onto her chatelaine with the other.

"Certainly. Now that you've let me know what's happening, I mean to make myself useful. Perhaps an interview to start. Yes, I know how this goes. Highwaymen tales are my favorite, but I've been known to enjoy a detective story on occasion. I have Anna Katharine Green's latest in my bag right now, in fact." She tapped a finger against her chin. "Let's see. The first question is, have I seen anything suspicious relating to Mr. Gage, or know of anyone who might have wished him harm? Hm."

She looked thoughtfully at her gloved hands. "Well, I don't know. And I hate to say anything bad about Mr. Gage, as he did hire me when, for reasons that still escape me, I was having difficulty finding new engagements." Her face sharpened. "Come, Mary. This is important." It softened again. "All right, I'll just say it. In my opinion, the way he related to women was awful, and I know I'm not the only one who thought so."

Cassie watched in befuddled fascination. As Mary seemed perfectly content conducting her interview herself, perhaps the best thing to do was listen.

"What do I mean?" Mary continued. "I mean all that carrying on he did, the fanning and the flattering, especially with rich society women, getting them to join his contributing chorus and bring their pocketbooks along with them. No offense intended, Miss Gwynne."

Cassie paused an attempt to reorganize her skirts beneath her. *Oh, that part was to me.* "Offense? No, I'm not—"

"Don't be modest, dear. The money you offered that fisherman is more than he normally makes in a week, and you spoke of the possibility of funding the troupe salaries from your own purse without batting an eye." She flapped her hand. "But that's neither here nor there... Now, I'm not naïve. I realize you must pander to an extent when raising funds and convincing people of the worth of your endeavor, as people are much happier to help those they like. And it was for charity, after all. But it was bound to cause problems. Would you know, some of those dear creatures actually thought he was going to take them away with him?"

Continuing her efforts with her skirts, Cassie tried to lift up but plopped back down when the boat moved, setting off a ripple in the harbor waters below. "I've had similar thoughts on that matter myself. My Aunt Flora's friend, Charlotte Porter, was very taken with him—still is. And I've never seen her act toward anyone the way she does toward that Mrs. Reynolds where Mr. Gage is involved."

"Mrs. Reynolds... the one who looks like a bustle-bottomed cranberry? Her husband made his money in armaments?"

"That's, uh—apt." Cassie straightened her glove. "But were you referring to something specific? Does one of those women left along the way harbor a resentment toward him, perhaps? Or maybe he applied his attentions to someone who wasn't free to accept them, angering a jealous spouse?"

"Well, not *that* specific, I suppose. Prince and I have discussed it a number of times, though—Prince would get absolutely sick about it. Not that he liked much else about the way Mr. Gage ran things... And I've seen Mr. Gage's mail. He received as many hate letters from angry husbands as admiring letters from swooning ladies. Oh! Which reminds me—this may be something—I heard he nearly got himself walloped by one of the chorus husbands in the Egmont Hotel gentlemen's lounge. Last Friday night."

"May" be something? "He did? What was that about?"

"That's all I know. It's just something I heard."

Cassie itched the bite that mosquito from before had left on her ankle. She would have to inquire about that incident at the Egmont tomorrow. Or maybe Hughes and Jake had come across some information about it while looking into their other matters. *Though...*

"Mr. Wilkes mentioned overhearing Mr. Gage arguing with someone in his hotel suite on Friday, too, that same evening," Cassie said. "I wonder if the two incidents were related. It's probably a long shot, but perhaps the man he encountered at the gentlemen's lounge wasn't finished with the—conversation."

"Or Mr. Gage wasn't," Mary answered. "He might have had pretty manners, but he wasn't always a lamb. I overheard him engage in quite the argument myself a week or so after we arrived on the island, in the men's dressing room. I couldn't tell you what it was about—people have such terrible diction when they're shouting—but it was jarring enough to throw me off my vocal exercises. I know Marguerite was in there. Not sure why she was in the men's dressing room, but goodness knows, when a soprano's angry, you hear it. And possibly Harland as well... Or the argument involved Harland. I don't know. All I was really able to pick out was Marguerite saying, 'I'd like to see you try.'" She picked at the beading on the brim of her hat. "Oh, and Prince was there, but that's almost not worth mentioning. Because, well, it's Prince."

Cassie fell still as the ripple she'd created swayed the boat beneath them. *That's new.* Why hadn't Prince told her about being involved in such an argument with Mr. Gage? She thought about his late-night meeting on the Centre Street Wharf and his abrupt mood changes over the past several days, and what Mr. Wilkes had said about his constant movement from troupe to troupe. Not to mention Flora's strange behavior toward him.

She felt around her pouch for her tin of gum. She'd liked Prince from the start, but could she be wrong about him? At the very least, it was clear there was a lot she didn't know about him.

Once she'd managed to pay the fisherman (he'd fallen asleep inside the shanty, so they had to rouse him by poking him with an oar), Cassie walked Mary to Miss Porter's boarding house. Then she waited, trying desperately not to fall asleep on herself, as Mary, after "cleansing" her room of bad spirits, reconstructed a list of locations where the troupe had performed over the past couple of years, along with the associated charities they had been raising money for. Granted, the latter was at Cassie's request, since she figured it would be useful to research the troupe's recent tour path to see if there were any other confrontations or conflicts, or other oddities or problems relating to Mr. Gage or the troupe, that might suggest why someone would hurt Mr. Gage.

By the time she pushed open Flora's front door, she was so tired she could barely lift her feet over the threshold.

And now, the stairs. She missed the hat rack with her bonnet and was trudging through the foyer, swaying numbly as Danger, Luna, and Roger gave her their customary *woof-urmff* greeting, when she heard voices coming from the front parlor, where Flora had her perfume store.

Mustering up what remained of her energy, she stepped through the curtain. Flora and the woman Cassie had brought home from the jail the night before were sitting together on one of the settees by the window, laughing as Kleio hopped back and forth between their heads like a trained circus animal. Esy the kitten was watching from the nearby bookshelf.

"Good evening, Cassie," Flora patted her hair back into place as Kleio hopped from her head onto the guest's, eliciting another joyful laugh from the women.

Cassie stumbled slightly as the dogs and the pig, shoving Cassie aside, rushed in to rejoin the action. "It seems our new friend is enjoying the animals."

"And they, her." Flora patted Luna, who had hopped into the woman's lap and was bathing her chin with her tongue. "Animals can always tell the good ones. Isn't that right, Madame M? That's what I've decided to call her until we find out what her real name is. 'M' for 'Mystery.'"

Madame M leaned her head against the settee to blink upside down at Esy, and the kitten rolled onto her back with her head hanging off the shelf, returning the favor.

"She was a little nervous when she first woke up today, but the animals definitely drew her out. That, and a few readings from Marlowe's *Tamburlaine*, which Austin Hughes suggested."

"He suggested that?"

"Oh, yes. Jake had to go help our friend Mr. Hiller, who injured his foot recently, with something at his house, so he asked Officer—Co-*Pro Tem* Deputy Hughes to walk me home from Lottie's while you finished getting Miss Rutledge settled. Totally unnecessary, but I did enjoy the company. And when I mentioned Madame M, he said that, based on what he had heard from her at the jail earlier, he thought she might be a theater lover, 'like Miss Gwynne.'"

That did make sense. Madame M had spoken only twice at the jail, and each time she'd recited a line from a play, one from Shakespeare's *The Merry Wives of Windsor* and the other from Aphra Behn's *The Rover*. While each of those plays was certainly famous, the lines Madame M had recited weren't the most likely to be known by the casual person.

Yes, a theater lover. "Like Miss Gwynne." Cassie smiled to herself.

Flora studied her, a smile of her own playing on her lips. "He also told me that he once spent a summer as a boy caring for an uncle who was 'similarly afflicted.'"

"Similarly afflicted?"

"He couldn't remember what they called it, but it was explained to him as a sort of confusion that affects some folks in their later years. He said his uncle would have times when you could hardly tell anything was different about him, but also times when he didn't know when it was, where he was, or even who he was, if he spoke at all. And, while in the grips of one of his confused states, he might wander off, usually to a favorite childhood haunt. In any case, Co-*Pro Tem* Deputy Hughes— good gracious, that's a mouthful—remembered his uncle had found it calming when he read to him, so suggested I try it with Madame M."

Dropping down from the shelf with a chirp, Esy rubbed against Madame M's legs, and the woman cooed happily.

"You know, aside being a little dusty, probably from being outside for a time, she seems healthy for her age," Flora said. "And the quality of her clothing is good—the workmanship is extraordinary, in fact. I don't believe she's a vagrant or otherwise typically without a home. She's probably just lost. Hopefully, her clarity will return soon and she can tell us who she is."

"Hopefully." Cassie poured herself a mug of coffee from the tray on the perfume counter and spooned in a little cream and a lot of sugar. "Or Officer Hughes's inquiry yields something. Though his hands are pretty full with other matters at the moment."

"Jake said he'd help. If he's not too busy, as well." Flora, her lips suddenly tight, moved aside a bowl of seashells mixed with scented pinecones and pulled a rose from the vase on the tea table.

Cassie took a gulp of her coffee. "Is something wrong?"

Flora cut the rose's stem and tucked the flower behind Madame M's ear, receiving a grin in return. "I think she may let me wash her hair tomorrow. That'll be nice."

"Aunt Flora?"

"Sorry." Flora nudged a plate with a few bites of food left on it out of reach of Danger's, Luna's, and Roger's inquisitive snouts. "I—Jake and I had a slight difference of opinion earlier." She held up a mirror for Madame M to see herself. "I was carrying some supplies home, and he saw me from across the street. But, instead of waving like a normal person, he dodged through traffic to take my packages for me as though I were about to be crushed. I said I was perfectly fine, but he said it wasn't 'right' for me to be carrying things when he was around to do that for me. Then I asked whether he thought there was something wrong with my arms, and... It didn't go well."

As she spoke, Madame M rose from her seat and, taking Danger's one front paw onto her shoulder, began to dance in place, humming her own accompaniment. It didn't sound like the sort of song one would hear played in a ballroom, though. It had a rollicking, boisterous rhythm, evoking a fife, a ship, and a bouncing knee.

"What exactly upset you about his trying to help you?" Cassie asked, adding more sugar to her coffee. "I'm sure he wasn't trying to suggest you were incapable."

Kleio eyed Danger and Madame M from the counter, then began to bob, whistling along every few notes.

"I know—I know he wouldn't. But this sudden concern with chivalry and pageantry is absurd. He's even tried to suggest we limit the time we spend in a room alone together, 'for appearances' sake'... He'd never once used those words before. It's as though we've gone backward, not forward." Flora reached for a box of chocolates on the side table. Cassie had had it shipped down from New York as a gift for her, and she was glad to see there were only a few left. "It's hard to explain."

"I understand."

Flora bit into a chocolate. "Say, has anyone been able to find Mr. Montgomery yet?"

"Uh— No, I don't think so." Cassie lowered her mug. "But I was only focused on Miss Rutledge."

"Right."

"Why?"

"No reason." She wiped a smudge of chocolate from her lip with her finger and leaned forward. "Anyway, the real question is, how are *you*?"

"Me?" Cassie blinked. "I'm fine. Why—"

"I wasn't sure anyone had asked you that yet." She placed her hand on Cassie's. "And... I noticed the man's coat and shoes laid out in your room. They're your father's, aren't they? From that package you received from New York."

Cassie studied the streaks the coffee had left inside her mug. She hadn't considered what Flora would think when she saw that. "Yes, the coroner's office sent me some of his personal effects from—that day. I know it's strange thing to do, to set them out like that, but..."

"Not at all."

Standing, Flora crossed over to the bookcase and lifted down a swath of pink gossamer fabric that was draped along the top and sides like a stage proscenium curtain. "This is a shoulder wrap that belonged to your mother, my sister, Emma. She used to wear it everywhere, to the market, to the theater, to the beach... Oh, we had the most lovely midnight bonfires at the beach, Emma, Tom, and I. Our favorite spot was on a quiet stretch of sand near the east wall of the old fort—well, in those days it wasn't so old. It was actually in the midst of being built, so you couldn't go up and climb around it like you can now, but there was still something enchanting about gazing up at its ramparts, especially on nights with a full moon.

"And there was a perfect view of the central bastion from where we would go. Tom and I liked to gaze up at it, pretending it was a pirate's hideout and telling stories about the treasures he'd hidden up there, while Emma waded in the ocean nearby, making up songs to go along with them. I'll never forget how she would spin and dance with the waves at her ankles, letting this wrap flutter in the wind from her fingertips. She looked like Titania, the fairy queen."

She held the wrap lightly in her hands, as though expecting that ocean breeze to lift it again.

"For months after she passed, I couldn't even look at it without my breath catching. But one day, I forced myself to take it out and hold it, and suddenly she felt closer, not further away." She sat down on the settee and hugged the wrap close. "I am so very glad for that."

Cassie nodded, her throat tightening. Flora lifted an arm, and Cassie tucked herself under it, meek as a child. She felt the kitten slip into her lap, and, a moment later, Madame M's arms encircled them all.

11

The next morning, Cassie roused herself from the bed she'd apparently assembled in the pantry from a sack of lentils as a pillow and an oversized music score as a blanket (Beethoven's Symphony no. 6, *Pastoral*) and sneezed her way through the brilliant sunshine to the *Florida Mirror*'s newspaper office by the foot of Centre Street, where the editor kept a reference collection of newspapers from around the region. Using the dates and locations on the tour list Mary had made for her, she spent much of the morning searching the pages for coverage relating to Mr. Gage's theatrical troupe. Unfortunately, though she hadn't expected the newspaper collection to be exhaustive (since the troupe only performed one night in each place, the number of different locations was substantial), as she neared the end of the available material, she still hadn't found a single reference to Mr. Gage, his Trip-along Troupe of Altruistic Actors, or any performance by them of *The Pirates of Penzance*.

Why wasn't there any news coverage of the troupe and its mission? She would have expected at least an announcement of an upcoming performance.

Frustrated, she decided to contact some of the charities

Mary had identified to see what they could tell her. That endeavor turned out to be only slightly more fruitful: even after she'd spent a fair amount of money on rush telegrams and the Egmont's telephone exchange, the donation amounts she was able to verify were paltry, and some of the contacts even had to be reminded of who Mr. Gage or the troupe was.

Now she was sure something wasn't right. It shouldn't have been very difficult to find information on the donations the troupe had made. And why had the only amounts she'd been able to verify been so small? Given the level of participation Cassie had witnessed so far on the island, she'd have thought such donations would be major events for the charities.

Was it possible that Mr. Gage, the doggedly devoted, if tantrum-prone and somewhat womanizing, philanthropist, wasn't what he seemed to be? Had he been up to something dishonest? If so, what? Certainly, what Cassie was—or rather, wasn't—finding could simply be a paperwork problem. The information she had been able to access in the short time she'd had was far from complete. But she was starting to have her doubts.

Upon her arrival at the Lyceum later that afternoon for rehearsal, Cassie found matters only a marsh hare's hair short of chaos. Mr. Wilkes was barking instructions to everyone and no one, Harland was stomping around the newly reassembled schooner with a hammer in his hand and a scowl on his face, and the rehearsal pianist was trying to get a half-costumed group of choristers to repeat a sequence of notes back to him while others whirled by, sparring with prop weapons and gibbering diction exercises.

"Listen up, people!" Mr. Wilkes bellowed through a paper-board cone. "Today we're going to start at the tippy, tippy top and go all the way through without stopping. So, in *five minutes*, I want all pirates at places in the 'rocky cavern by the seashore' for 'Pour, o pour the pirate sherry'!" He was wearing Mr. Gage's full Pirate King regalia, which, despite some hastily applied alterations, made him look like a child playing dress-up in his father's clothes. He didn't seem aware of that, however. He was as proud and assured as Cassie had ever seen him. "The performance is coming up, so let's *make this count!*"

Two tall sailor-stagehand types responded by pushing a random piece of set furniture across the stage, though they didn't appear to have any particular destination in mind and they both looked as though they'd accidentally picked up a shorter person's sack at the laundress.

"Who put you in charge, again, Wilkes?" Arthur said, tugging on a boot at one of the pirate's camp tables. His hand slipped, causing his foot to slide and kick a fake turkey leg onto the floor.

"I offered to direct and Mr. Manning accepted."

"And who put *him* in charge of *that*?"

Marguerite glared at Arthur as one of the chorus ladies laced up her bodice on the opposite side of the stage. It was clear they had yet to resolve whatever differences they were having. "Leave it alone, Arthur. Why are you giving everyone such a hard time?"

"I don't recall asking for your opinion, Marguerite."

"Not this again," Mrs. Keene said, testing a fake gold coin with her teeth. Miss Porter shushed her.

"Everyone, listen!" Mr. Wilkes started to climb onto one of the pirate-camp benches to speak, but tipped the satchel he was carrying, sending dozens of leaflets of some kind sliding across the stage. "We have very little time left, and we need to get the show in shape. You never know who's going to be watching!" Each time he bent to pick up one of the leaflets, a few more spilled out.

"What are these?" Arthur grabbed one as it slid by him.

Cassie looked at the one that had landed at her feet. It was a drawing of Mr. Wilkes as the Pirate King, lunging impressively and carrying an oversized Jolly Roger flag, black with white skull and crossbones— Well, almost Mr. Wilkes. The figure had his face, but his height and musculature were much exaggerated. His name and a listing of several productions were printed across the bottom.

Mr. Wilkes put down his bag and started scooping the leaflets into a pile. "Nothing. Just something I had printed a few weeks ago to autograph for my admirers. And in case the critic I invited comes to see the show."

Cassie scratched her elbow. A few weeks ago? That would have been right after the troupe arrived in town. How could Mr. Wilkes have known he would be performing the Pirate King role then?

"You invited a critic?" Mr. Manning sat up from where he'd been lying on his back beneath a bench, hammering at something.

"Yes, I posted a letter yesterday, after I was assigned Mr. Gage's role—"

"That's expressly against the rules. Mr. Gage was adamant about our work not being advertised."

"And I've never understood that." Mr. Wilkes lay his bag on its side and pushed the pile of leaflets into it. "Careers need promoting. How else am I to become a giant in my field?"

Mrs. Keene started to open her mouth, but Miss Porter whacked her in the arm, and both of the sailors, now in the process of carrying a single stool between them, choked on something.

Arthur yanked his other boot on. "If you listened, you'd know it's because Mr. Gage felt publicity was a form of self-aggrandizement, which would take away from the charitable nature of the endeavor. Good deeds shouldn't need recognition."

Marguerite slapped her hand to her forehead. "For Chrissakes, Arthur—"

"Yeah, spare us the moral lecture," said Mr. Wilkes. "I don't think one article featuring me is going to damage the troupe's charitable purposes."

Mrs. Reynolds sauntered out of the wings, resplendently ridiculous in a sea-green aerophane dress trimmed with oversized rosettes (though she was fully fifty, she had embraced her role as one of the Major-General's many daughters more than most), and thrust a sheet of music at the pianist. "If the point of all this is to fulfill William's wishes, we ought to follow through on that fully."

"Oh, it's 'William,' now, is it?" Miss Porter said, fluffing the giant pink bow on the rump of her own dress.

Mrs. Reynolds sipped a glass of iced water. "Absolutely. We'd known each other long enough to become quite good friends, I assure you."

"I hope that doesn't mean you've been neglecting your poor husband."

"Mr. Reynolds is perfectly happy."

"He was thrown out of the Egmont gentlemen's lounge last week for hurling a glass at Mr. Gage's head. Does that sound like a happy husband to you?"

"Of course he's— How dare you! I... At least I have a husband!"

Miss Porter lunged, and as Mrs. Keene grabbed for her and missed, Mr. Wilkes and Mr. Manning rushed in to intervene.

So it was Mrs. Reynolds's husband who had brawled with Mr. Gage last Friday. Cassie had meant to ask about that at the Egmont this morning but had run out of time. Had their conflict gone beyond the gentlemen's lounge?

Guessing it was going to take a moment to sort the two women out, Cassie slipped into the wings and felt her way along behind the backdrop toward the center of the backstage area, where a bar of light glowed below the door to the dressing rooms. She hadn't looked around in there yet.

As she reached for the knob of the dressing room, however, the door flew open so quickly it almost hit her. Mary charged out with an armful of peacock feathers.

"Miss Rutledge!" Cassie grabbed onto a costume mannequin to catch herself. "What's going on?"

Mary heaved the feathers onto a pile of other apparently discarded materials and whirled back toward the doorway. "No time for chatting, dear. I know what we talked about regarding the curse, but there is plenty that remains unexplained, and if I'm going to stick around, I'm going to make sure we've cleansed ourselves of anything untoward."

"Peacock feathers are untoward?"

Mary let the door shut behind her, and Cassie listened as she tossed what sounded like two boxes, a drum, and half a china set onto the floor. After a moment, Mary reemerged with a basket of shiny blue fabric and a three-pronged candelabrum.

"Mr. Gage thought the peacock feathers would add an air of decadence to the pirate camp set dressing." Mary threw the candelabra onto the pile and emptied the basket of fabric on top of it. "But the spiritualist I met with the other day reminded me that peacock feathers should never be brought onstage, owing to the evil eye on the end."

"And the candelabrum?"

"It has three prongs. One must never light a trio of candles onstage because the person standing closest to the shortest candle will die."

Cassie wondered what would happen if the identical short candles on either side of the tall middle one kept relative pace with one another but decided not to pursue it. The answer might be that there would be two deaths instead of one. "What about the fabric?"

"One should never wear blue onstage."

"Why not?"

Mary drew herself up and bore down on Cassie with the full weight of her moral authority. "Because it's *bad luck*, that's why! One should never aggravate the universe if she can help it."

Mr. Wilkes poked his head around the backdrop, a pair of eyeglasses perched on his head and a pencil behind his ear now, though Cassie hadn't been aware he wore eyeglasses, and he wasn't carrying anything to write on. "Mary, there you are. What are you two doing back here?"

It seemed the onstage brawl had concluded.

"Oh, just exchanging recipes and crocheting tips, as we women will," Mary said, giving Cassie a conspiratorial wink. "And clearing out some old props."

"Well, if I could tear you away from your domestic pursuits, I'd like to get started while there's a break in the action." His words were cordial, but his face resembled a teapot on the verge of a whistle.

He turned. "Hey you, sailor-men—"

The sailors popped to attention from where they had been digging around in a costume trunk together for some reason. Their ill-fitting hats were obstructing their faces, and now each was holding up a masquerade mask as well, but the stream of stage light coming through the curtains revealed a drip of boot-black on one man's long, drooping mustache.

Hughes. With Jake. Finally, Cassie was not surprised. Though she did wonder why Hughes decided to use the boot-black again, after seeing the mess it had made last time.

"Who called you in? We're not operating any rigging in today."

"Uh, we were asked to come do some stagehand work, sir. By Mr. McGregor, I believe it was." Jake offered. The "seaman's tattoo" on his forearm, initials with a heart and anchor, was smeared.

"No, wasn't me." Harland strode around the backdrop and pushed past Mr. Wilkes with a measuring tape in his hand. "But we could use a sweep behind the schooner." He paused to shake some sawdust off his boot then strode over to the tool caddy leaning against the wall.

Hughes scratched his nose. "Oh, it must have been George, then."

"Has someone been in my toolbox?" Harland growled.

"Or James. Or maybe a Charles—"

"I asked them to come." Prince, skirting Harland's menacing gaze, walked toward them, his cloak damp from the rain that was now beating on the roof. "I thought we could use a few extra hands on deck, so to speak, so I stopped through the wharf this morning and recruited some help."

Cassie relaxed her shoulders. Prince's quick thinking had saved them. But where had he been all this time? He was over half an hour late.

Harland growled again. "First I find the handsaw on the prop table and now my set drawings are all out of order. How am I supposed to do anything if people keep moving my things?" His frown deepening into a scowl, he pulled out his flask and stalked away.

Mr. Wilkes fluffed his cape. "Well, now that you're here, men, you might as well make yourself useful. Sweep up as Mr. McGregor asked, then take care of this rubbish pile Miss Rutledge has amassed before someone trips on it."

"Much obliged, kind sirs," Mary said, giving another terrible wink. She'd spotted the imposters as well. "But please be sure to use the theater's bin. I know it's all the way around back, but I just got an earful from the neighbor about a troupe member using his receptacle the other day. He insisted we contribute toward the hauler's fee. Which reminds me, Mr. Wilkes, tell Mr. Manning the troupe owes me a dollar."

Cassie caught Jake's elbow as Mary and Mr. Wilkes

returned to the stage. "Don't you two have anything else you should be doing?"

"Gordo doesn't," Hughes said. "Miss Hale won't speak to him."

Jake seemed to startle, but then Cassie realized it was only his glued-on eyebrows sticking to his hat. "Do *you*, Hughes?" he retorted. "Other than fielding frilly little letters from your—"

"Oh, now I remember. I was supposed to put my fist in your face."

Cassie threw out an arm to hold Hughes back. The straining of the buttons on his too-small shirt bordered on ridiculous, but when she looked at his chest pressing against her hand, her breathing became a little strained, too. "I meant, I thought you were supposed to be working on your other cases."

Hughes looked down at Cassie's hand, which she hadn't moved. "Uh, we are. We have spoons stirring in multiple pots. But this is the perfect time to finish searching the theater, while the troupe is busy onstage."

"I guess I can't argue with that." Cassie's eyes met Hughes's for a moment, sending a jolt through her stomach. They both stepped back. "But—God's honest truth—you need to get better disguises if you're going to keep showing up like this. You're lucky everyone else here is in parodic costume right now or else you'd be discovered in an instant."

"Change of plans," Mr. Wilkes said as Cassie rejoined the group onstage. "Given the compressed timeframe and other factors here, I'd like to start with the finale. The entire cast is onstage for that, so I want to be sure everyone knows what they're doing. If we can get it right, it'll make the whole show. As my acting mentor used to say, if you finish strong, people are more likely to forget the carriage wreck that came before. And, don't forget, it's the scene where we'll reveal the highest contributor to the audience, so people will be paying attention."

One of the chorus men raised his hand.

Mr. Wilkes spoke through his cone. "What is it?"

"We're missing some people—Miss Vera and Miss Theresa, Ira and Percy."

"No, I'm here," Percy called out from where he was retying a rope on the schooner mast.

"Where the deuce are the others, then? They're to make call like everyone else."

"They weren't in their rooms when I left Lottie's Cottage," Mary offered, tucking her Chinese coin amulet beneath the sleeve of her piratical nursemaid's dress.

If Mr. Wilkes were a dragon, fire would have come out of his nostrils. "Well, that doesn't exactly answer my question, does it, Miss Rutledge." He swung his glare about him like a medieval mace. "How hard is it to be where one's supposed to be? People have no idea how hard I've—we've had to work for this opportunity, what's at stake."

"Aw, go eat a shoe, Wilkes," Arthur said, somehow managing to make applying rouge hostile. "Being the Pirate King doesn't mean you get to turn everything into a royal decree."

Mr. Wilkes jammed his Pirate King buccaneer's hat on his head with a sniff, but it fell down over his face. "That's it. Mr. Manning, take a note that... that man"—he pointed at the chorus man who had spoken—"will be performing Mr. Hammock's solos, and"—he scanned the sea of chorus women, then shook his head—"Miss Cook's and Miss Crain's solos will be absorbed by the chorus and uttered in unison." He blew his hat feather out of his face. "Harland! Wherever you are! Clear this pirate's camp business and turn things around to Major-General Stanley's estate in Act Two."

As the scene changeover began, he tossed his cape and

swept his arms up, giving an eerily accurate, though miniatur-ized, impression of Mr. Gage. "Stanley daughters, find your pirate partners and go to where you are for the finale, right after I—I mean, Arthur, Major-General Stanley, says, 'And take my daughters, all of whom are beauties.'" He turned to Mary. "Mary, you'll start us off, yes? But I want you to stand here while you deliver your line and move your arms like so." Climbing the step of a statuary fountain someone had rolled on, he shifted his voice to a falsetto and sang her line while flapping his arms like he was conducting a deaf orchestra: "'At length we are provided, with unusual facility, to change piratic crime for dignified respectability...'"

He restored his voice to its regular range. "Got it?" He pointed to the rehearsal pianist, who was in the midst of biting into a sandwich. "Maestro, if you please!"

Cassie took up her position next to the ruined chapel arch that had nearly landed on her head, resisting the urge to look up and see what else could come hurtling down at her.

And on we go.

12

———

The rehearsal was uncomfortable and tense, and Mr. Wilkes's haphazard, largely illogical, and occasionally insulting directing style didn't help. Marguerite even ended up leaving in a huff before they were finished because Mr. Wilkes criticized "the way her face looked" while she sang her coloratura runs. During one of the group numbers, Cassie also realized that she had yet to go through Mr. Gage's hotel room, so, as soon as Mr. Wilkes released the actors, she headed for the Egmont.

Keeping her head low as she ascended the hotel's wide, sparkling steps, she hurried across the breezy veranda and into the lobby. She flicked her gaze across the lush expanse of Brussels carpet to the spot where Mr. Littell, the militantly obsequious proprietor, usually posted himself, ready to foist his hospitality on each visitor that passed. Fortunately, he was busy at the moment scolding a clerk for wearing his hat improperly.

For extra assurance, though, she unclipped her fan from her chatelaine and spread it alongside her face as a screen, then strode toward Mr. Gage's suite as quickly as she could without drawing attention, grateful that she had been there before so wouldn't have to ask for directions. Finding the door unlocked, she congratulated herself on her good luck once again, and thrust it open.

"Ow!" came a man's voice.

Cassie leapt to the side, knocking into a gilded entry table. "Who's there?"

She lifted a porcelain potpourri bowl above her head and shut the door with her foot—revealing Jake, rubbing his nose.

"Jake! You startled the life out of me."

Jake checked his fingers for blood. "My apologies. I didn't expect anyone to throw the door open at my face."

"I'm sorry." Cassie put the bowl back in its place. "I realized during rehearsal that we hadn't come and looked through Mr. Gage's room yet. I didn't know whether the hotel had turned it over already or not, but I figured I'd hurry over and check."

"Same here. Fortunately, we still have some time. I overheard one of the maids saying that Mr. Manning had asked Mr. Littell not to clear the room until the sheriff had contacted Mr. Gage's next of kin, and Mr. Littell agreed. He also waived the fees owed, given the circumstances of Mr. Gage's departure."

"That's generous."

"I'd say, considering what those fees are likely to be for rooms like this. Not bad for a traveling actor, eh?" He started to examine a crystal bowl containing a bunch of grapes, then tucked his hands behind his back as though afraid he would break it.

"I understand he has family wealth, or some other such income," Cassie said.

"He'd have to. I think this is the suite the Carnegies take when they stay on the island." He peered around the window draperies. "But where's all his personal stuff? There's nothing in this sitting room but fancy furniture."

"In the bedroom, I think." Cassie led the way to the adjacent room where she'd found Mr. Gage and Miss Porter the other day and opened the top drawer of the secretary. "This is probably where he'd keep anything of importance."

"You certainly seem to know your way around," Jake said. "Mr. Gage cast the same spell on you as he cast on poor Miss Porter?"

Cassie closed the drawer and opened the next. "That's not funny. We don't know what really transpired between those two. Anyway, you know I was here the other day dropping off an order for Flora."

"Oh, right." Jake pulled a bundle of papers out of one of the bedside tables and began to leaf through them. "If these adoring letters are of any indication, though... There are a lot of lonely women out there."

"You found the letters?" Cassie looked up from the drawer she'd been digging around in. So far, she'd found nothing other than empty boxes, which, based on the markings, had once contained expensive watches and other pieces of jewelry or accessories, along with a pile of similarly impressive shopping receipts. "Mary Rutledge told me Mr. Gage received a lot of letters, both admiring and not. There may be a threatening one or two among them."

"Let's see—" Jake shuffled the pages. "Letter of admiration, letter of admiration, letter of admiration... Ich. It looks as though something sticky was spilled on these." He shook his hand, as though that would dislodge the residue from his fingers. "Oh, here's a bad one. It isn't terribly articulate, but it's definitely angry. This man holds Mr. Gage responsible for his wife being away on her own for hours at a time at chorus rehearsal, excusing herself from social engagements, generally neglecting wifely duties, giving away ghastly sums of money... Hm. That's a lot of gun talk... And here he calls Mr. Gage a 'fraud.' It says he should prepare himself for his 'investible cuppance.' But I think he means 'inevitable comeuppance.'"

Cassie shut the drawer. "Fraud? What kind of fraud?"

"He doesn't give any detail. But he does say, 'I don't believe this angelic character you're playing for one minute. You're a good actor—I'll give you that—but no one is that good, and I intend to prove it.'"

"I wonder if there's anything behind that, or if he was simply upset. Who's it from?"

"It's not signed. Or, rather, there's no signature. No closing either." He handed the stack to Cassie. "You know, we could ask Mrs. Rydell at the post office to take a look and see if there's a way to figure out who might have sent that letter, or at least where it was sent from. If we manage to get a name, we could check the local hotel registers and see if that person was staying in town the night before Mr. Gage's accident."

"That's an idea." Cassie added the letters to the items she'd collected on the secretary. "Though, I do worry about Mrs. Rydell's ability to keep matters to herself."

Cassie was reaching for the next drawer when her gaze landed on a folded square of paper under a paperweight. It was the letter of thanks from that boy, Johnny Varden, Mr. Gage had shown Cassie and the others in the theater.

She read it over. Mr. Gage had held it up for them to see before, but now that she was getting the chance to examine it herself, it seemed distinctly strange. For one, the handwriting was overly messy, even for a young boy, almost as though the childishness of it had been exaggerated. But what would be the point of that? To gather more sympathy? Spur further dona-tions? It was an unlikely dynamic for a seven-year-old to be aware of.

Along the same lines, certain words were misspelled in one place, but spelled correctly in another. One probably ought not demand grammatical perfection from children, but consistency was a reasonable expectation, even in errors. The boy also mentioned "enjoying" the bloater paste and caviar that had been provided as a part of the dinner. Perhaps Cassie, being twenty-three, hadn't the best grasp of what kind of foods appealed to children, but she would have thought a young boy would be more excited about puddings and jams, or even a hearty roasted meat, than cured herring puree and raw fish eggs.

Could the letter have been fabricated? To what end, though?

Jake, who had been poking around the bed pillows, tugged on a small ribbon that was sticking out from behind a fringed cushion. It was attached to a palm-sized notebook.

"What's that?" Cassie asked.

Jake turned a few pages. "Names, addresses... A book of contacts?"

Cassie leaned over his arm so she could see. "Actually—" She reached out and turned another page. "I think it's a little more than that. I'm not sure what you'd call it though—perhaps a prospects book? Mr. Gage was using this to keep notes about people, to record key identifying features like physical characteristics, interests, locations... There's even information about their financial situations. He was probably gathering this information to size up who could contribute what to his projects. It's a little cold, but I suppose it's practical. For what he was trying to do."

"Fascinating. Wait, am I in here? I met him once at a tea at Miss Porter's house." Jake thumbed forward through the book, then backward, then forward again. "Oh, here. 'Jake Gordon: handsome but asymmetric nose, working class/law enforcement, do not pursue.' Hey." He looked in the mirror over the pearl-enameled washbasin. "What's wrong with my nose? Do you—"

He stopped when one of the sitting room windows squeaked open. A pair of thumps sounded—perhaps shoes hitting the floor as their owner hopped over the sill. Then the window squeaked closed. After a brief pause, footsteps began to fall—in the direction of the bedroom.

Exchanging a silent glance, Cassie and Jake each scrambled for a hiding place. Cassie opted for the large white wardrobe by the secretary. Jake, seized by indecision until the last moment, tucked himself behind one of the window draperies as the unknown party entered the bedroom.

Cassie peered through the gap between the doors. It was Arthur, dressed in one of the elaborate black mourning ensembles he had been wearing earlier. His eyeliner, more heavily and more clumsily applied than usual, was running slightly, and his cheeks glistened as though recently dried.

He moved about the room, somehow both reverently and desperately, as though searching for something. He felt around on the floor and along the cracks of the upholstery on the chairs, then lifted the pillows on the bed and the rug by the door—under which he found a bright yellow sock, which he tucked into his jacket pocket—but he didn't open a single drawer in the secretary or go through the clothing trunk or, thankfully, the wardrobe.

As he passed the dressing table, however, he paused, first to check his hair, then to examine the framed tintypes next to the washbasin. One was a portrait of Mr. Gage in his Pirate King attire. The other depicted two young boys at the circus: the taller and more dark-featured of the boys grinned as he held up a triangle of cake like a trophy; the other squinted at the camera as though he were confused.

Cassie tried to decide who the boys in the second tintype might be. Family? No, they didn't look particularly well-off. Based on the state of their clothing, they were more likely to be recipients of the troupe's charitable donations. She thought about the Varden boy's letter and the related suspicions that had begun to take root in her. *Recipients or purported recipients?*

Cassie sucked in a breath. Arthur had turned toward the window where Jake was hiding, seeming to see something, and was now striding across the room with purpose. Instead of throwing back the drapery, though, as Cassie had feared, he dropped to his knees and reached for something underneath the bedside table: a ladies' glove.

"Aha!" He stood, scowling as he held the glove out in front of him. Then he threw it against the wall.

He was still glaring after it when Hughes's voice erupted outside the suite door.

"Excuse me! Maid! What the blazes is this door doing open?"

Arthur scooped up the glove and, almost expertly, as though he'd done it a dozen times, unfastened the latch over the window, dangerously close to where Jake was hiding, and let himself out. Fortunately for him, this suite was on the ground floor, so there would only be a stretch of covered veranda, along with the short, shell-brick wall of a tropical walking garden beyond that, to traverse as he made his exit.

A young woman's voice responded to Hughes. "I—I don't know."

"Does this establishment not consider itself a premier destination for the most discriminating travelers to the South? If so, shouldn't security be a chief concern? Particularly since there have been multiple thefts in the hotel over the last several weeks?"

"I... yes? No. Yes... I only change the linens, sir."

"Who has access to this room?"

"Why, all of us maids do. To all the rooms. That is, there's a wall with keys on hooks we can use when we have to let ourselves in to perform our housekeeping duties. We don't carry all of them around all the time, only what we need."

There was a moment of quiet before Hughes responded— Cassie's best guess, he was trying to contain his outrage at some perceived incompetence. "So, you mean anyone could go into the maids' wing and help himself to a key to any room in this hotel at any time?"

The maid laughed.

Brave girl.

"No, no, sir. Only the maids have a key to the maids' wing. Aside from the proprietor, Mr. Littell, that is. You'd have to ask one of us to get it for you."

"Did someone ask for this key?"

"Not me. Though, I saw one of the other maids walking this way with a young woman a little bit ago. Pretty thing, with a waist so tiny it made me positively ill with jealousy. And there was a good-looking man about the hall a short while after that... But, speaking of security, and good-looking men, who are you, hand-some stranger, asking all these questions? Not that I mind."

Hughes cleared his throat. "Oh, I'm, uh—" He was probably now shifting his hand onto his waist, brushing his coat back to reveal his precious police officer's badge. It had been his preferred show-off stance since the day she'd met him.

"I'm Co-*Pro Tem* Deputy Austin Hughes. I've been investi-gating the thefts occurring around the hotel and—some other matters. Thank you for your assistance, Miss—"

"Curry. Fanny Curry."

"Thank you, Miss Curry." He paused. "Say, while I have you, do you happen to know what kinds of fowl the chef here keeps on hand for private dining? I have a, um, special guest coming to town and was asked to inquire."

"Oh, really anything you want, sir! That is, if you give a few days' notice— Whoops!"

"Here, let me help you with those pillows."

"My, those are strong arms you have, Co-, um, propem Deputy Hughes." The maid laughed again.

Actually, it was more of a titter, Cassie realized. And distinctly annoying.

"Uh, thank you."

"My pleasure. And, if you need anything else—anything *at all*. You come find me, all right?" Titter, titter.

Cassie nearly heaved her lunch all over the inside of that wardrobe.

As Cassie swallowed back her bile, the tittering receded down the hallway and the suite door swung open. Hughes's heels clicked around the front parlor for a few moments, then approached the bedroom.

Realizing that neither she nor Jake had moved from their hiding places yet, and the longer they waited to reveal themselves, the worse it was going to be, Cassie was about to push her way through the velvet garments hanging around her when she heard a thud and a yelp.

She leapt out of the wardrobe, tripping onto the bed, and Hughes whirled around with his fists raised.

"For gripe's sake, Miss Gwynne, you're here, too?" He lowered his fists. "You shouldn't pop out at people like that. I feel like we've discussed this before."

Jake groaned at his feet, clutching his stomach. "You punched me, Hughes. Why?"

"I saw a boot sticking out from beneath the curtain. Am I supposed to assume a man hiding in a murder victim's hotel room merely wanted to shake my hand?"

"But it was *my* boot!" Jake rolled onto his other side.

Hughes turned to Cassie. "What are you doing in here, anyway?"

Cassie rolled back onto her feet and fixed her hair. "We were looking around for information that might help us figure out what happened to Mr. Gage."

"Is that so." Hughes kicked the curtains back into place. "Good of you to include me."

"Don't be a child, Hughes—" Jake started to sit up, but

stopped when he saw Hughes's fists ball up again. "It wasn't planned."

"He's right," Cassie said. "We ran into each other here."

Hughes sniffed.

Jake pulled himself up using the window frame and leaned against the wall, catching his breath. "To be fair, you didn't tell us you were coming, either."

"I was on my way to conduct more interviews about the thefts, and I saw the door open."

"You happened to be passing through the exact hallway where Mr. Gage's suite was?" Jake raised his cherry-red fake eyebrows, which he was still wearing for some reason. "It's one of only three rooms in this wing, none of which were rifled."

"Fine." Hughes brushed something off his sleeve. "But the idea didn't specifically occur to me until I was already at the hotel, speaking to Mr. Littell. There was another theft today, during the rehearsal at the Lyceum, and this time a clerk caught a glimpse of the thief, or thieves, I should say—he claims he saw more than one—but he wasn't able to discern any identifying details. He tried to follow, but he slipped on some coins that the thieves dropped. Again, small change, five-cent pieces. Imagine, after going to all that trouble."

Jake itched his forehead, finally dislodging one of his eyebrows. "Ah. Well, then, in the spirit of things, we should show you what we found." He pulled the prospects book from his coat pocket as he crossed to the secretary and lifted the packet of letters from Cassie's pile. He held both out to Hughes.

"The letters contain both notes from admirers and warnings from their angry husbands, one of which I'm going to look into further," Cassie said. "And we think the notebook is Mr. Gage's record of his fundraising prospects. Names, characteristics, and circumstances for people he's met. That sort of thing."

"Hm. It would make sense for someone trying to raise large sums of money to track such information." Hughes snorted as he turned a page in the prospects book. "You know, I never could identify it before, Gordo, but Mr. Gage is right about your nose."

Cassie crossed her arms. "Is that all you have to contribute?"

"No. I was also going to say that this book might explain some of the items I picked up when I searched Mr. Gage's area in the Lyceum dressing rooms."

"Oh!" Cassie dropped her arms. "I was going to do that earlier when I ran into you backstage but got pulled back into rehearsal."

"Good thing I had some time on my hands after my sweeping and refuse removal duties, then," Hughes said, setting the prospects book aside and emptying a small sack onto the bed.

Was that a smile there, under his mustache?

He sorted through the items as Jake and Cassie fell in next to him. "I found all this mostly in his dressing table drawer, among a variety of perfumes, powers, and paints. I'm not sure how useful it is, but I grabbed it for the file anyway. These are clippings from the *Mirror*'s social column listing the arrivals at the Egmont—"

Jake picked up one of the clippings. "He must have been using this information to see what well-to-do visitors were in town. To supplement his work in the prospects book. See? He's circled some of the names. And crossed out others."

"As I was about to point out, thank you." Hughes took the clipping back. "Now, here's an English newspaper article about some kind of fraud committed on an aged dowager, a few Chinese gambling tokens, news clippings about the play..."

Cassie looked up. "You found coverage about the troupe? I searched the *Mirror*'s collection of regional papers all morning and didn't find a thing." She flipped through the articles Hughes had indicated, but finally leaned back with disappointment. "No, these are older. And they relate to the initial runs in England and New York. No mention of Mr. Gage's troupe."

Jake dropped into the tufted chair next to the bed. "Didn't someone say in rehearsal today that Mr. Gage specifically avoided publicity for his shows? Because he felt it detracted from the charitability or something? Come to think, I haven't seen any announcement made in the *Mirror* about this show yet, either."

"Yes, you're right." Cassie yanked a loose string from her bodice, then clapped a hand to her chest when a button came off with it. "I heard that, too. But based on what else I found this morning, I'm wondering if there might be something more to his desire for privacy."

She more fully described her research at the *Mirror*, along with her efforts to contact the charities on the list. And her gnawing suspicions about whether the beneficence of the troupe's activities might have been overstated.

"If you're correct," Jake said, "and Mr. Gage was up to something underhanded, perhaps something went wrong with whatever scheme he had going on and that's why he was killed."

Hughes pushed his hair out of his eyes, showing off his strong jaw and chin and almost making Cassie forget what they were talking about. "I don't know. Like Miss Gwynne said, the *Mirror* doesn't have every newspaper from every place the troupe has been. And recordkeeping can be a messy business, particularly for a charitable organization unsophisticated in respect of such matters. In other words, the fact she didn't find the information she was looking for doesn't mean it doesn't exist. Or that, even going from there, Mr. Gage was up to nefarious doings that got him murdered."

"But we don't know that it doesn't—or he wasn't—either." Jake picked through the papers again, scratching his head. "And he *was* killed."

"Well, that's true." Hughes stroked his mustache. "By the way, how did you get in here again?"

"The door was open when I arrived," Jake answered.

"And I came in after that," said Cassie.

"Oh. I'd thought maybe it was Miss Gwynne who'd had it opened. According to a housekeeping maid I spoke with, the maids have access to all the room keys, and she saw a—woman heading this way a little bit ago with another maid."

A "pretty" woman with a "waist so tiny" it made her "ill with jealousy." Cassie resisted the urge to preen. It was sort of nice Hughes had thought of her when he heard that.

"She also said she saw a man," Hughes said.

Jake glanced at Cassie. "Mr. Beath came in here looking for something."

"But he came in through the suite's parlor window," Cassie said. "No one would have seen him. She had to be talking about you."

"Right." Jake took out his knife and used it to sharpen his pencil. "That was odd, though, with Mr. Beath. He turned the room over, and all he took was a sock and a ladies' glove. Which he seemed pretty upset about."

"That's why we were hiding when you came in," Cassie explained as Hughes squeezed past her to examine the contents of the wardrobe.

She steeled herself against his masculine, woodsy scent. Why was she trying to explain her actions to him? She didn't have to justify what she'd done.

Hughes closed the wardrobe and turned around to give the room another scan. "I'll have a chat with that maid I mentioned, Miss Curry. Perhaps she can get us some more details."

Cassie picked at her glove. "Perhaps she can." The words tasted bad as they came out.

She wondered if the author of those pink letters Hughes had been receiving had a laugh as irritating as Miss Curry's.

"Though..." Hughes finished his sweep of the room and settled his gaze back on Cassie. "You don't suppose that Prince guy might have been who the maid saw in the hall? Up to something?"

Cassie frowned. "I can't imagine what you mean. Besides, as I said, she was obviously talking about Jake." *Wasn't she?*

"All right." Hughes kicked the curtains again, though they were perfectly in place. "But you ought to be careful around that guy, anyway."

Cassie's frown deepened. "Careful? He's helping us."

"Maybe. But... have you considered the possibility that he's only pretending to help? To stay close so he can keep abreast of what we know?"

"Now, wait a minute. You're not suggesting he had something to do with Mr. Gage's—"

"I'm only suggesting that you not assume he didn't."

Cassie hurled a glance at Jake, but he dodged it. He shrugged. "You can't assume anything about anyone."

"You, too?" Cassie pulled the cover off one of the bed pillows. "I don't even know how to respond to this. It's absurd." She grabbed the prospects book off the bed and stuffed it into the pillowcase, then swept the letters and the other items she'd collected off the secretary on top of it.

"Think about it," Hughes said. "He's been around every step of the way. Right after Mr. Gage fell, who was telling everyone where to go and what to do, before we arrived on the scene? Who was there the whole time we and the sheriff were interrogating the troupe about what had happened, offering his thoughts, unsolicited? Who was it who stuck around the theater for no reason even after that, while we were waiting for the undertaker to come—"

And on the night Cassie came back to the theater with Paddy and found the nails, when that set piece nearly fell on them...

Cassie sputtered. "I don't— None of that requires any conclusion other than that he was trying to be helpful. And I can tell you've had something against him since the moment you met him. I don't know what it is, but it's like you're *looking* for ways to—"

Hughes scoffed. "This isn't about *me*. I can't believe you don't see it! Now, I like you, Miss Gwynne, but sometimes you can be just like all those other girls where you come from, those naïve, pampered girls so sheltered by their money and connections they can't understand the type of evil the world is capable of."

Cassie inhaled for a retort, but Hughes barreled ahead.

"Let me tell you something else about that 'Prince' of yours. There's no record in the town of Yarmouth, Massachusetts, of anyone named Rosalinda Montgomery adopting a child, and not a scrap of paperwork, school, medical, or anything, from the last thirty years relating to a child by the name of 'Prince.' Who is he? Has anything he's told you about himself been true? And why is it that, according to my information, he's worked with a dozen theater companies in the last two years, never staying with any one longer than a couple of months? Is he running from something? What's he hiding?"

I thought it was eight troupes, not twelve. Cassie tried to tie the pillowcase but spilled it instead and kneeled to scoop the items back in. "How do you know all that?"

"We had him looked into," Hughes said.

Cassie stopped. "You did? Why?"

"I wouldn't say 'looked into,' exactly," Jake answered. "We got the report from—"

"Just doing our due diligence. For the investigation."

Cassie remained on the floor, gripping the pillowcase. "Without mentioning anything to me?"

Jake shied slightly. "We're worried you might be—too close

to him. We have to give him the same consideration as everyone else."

Hughes sat against the windowsill with his arms folded. "And it's a good thing, too, because it's obvious now that he's been hiding something. Perhaps we need to rethink the approach we've taken to the Gage situation."

Cassie's knuckles whitened around the pillowcase as she stood, and it took everything she had not to reach in and throw the contents at both of them. "Everyone has things they'd rather not share. But it doesn't make them criminals, or dangerous."

Right?

She was trying to decide how to exit in a manner that would adequately convey her indignation when she noticed something on the floor by her feet. She must have missed an item that fell out of the pillowcase.

When she bent to pick it up, though, she realized what it was: a shark's tooth on a leather cord.

She snatched it up and backed out of the room. "I—have to go do something. And we're done here, I believe."

"What is it?" Jake followed her into the suite parlor.

"Nothing important. I just have to go. I'm sure I'll see you both at the next rehearsal, though. Invited or not."

"Cassie, wait—"

But she was already closing the door behind her.

13

Houses, gardens, stores, and taverns, already in the process of being swallowed up by the hungry shadows of a tropical island at dusk, blurred past Cassie along street after street until finally the Florida House Inn's broad, green-white-and-red porch snapped into focus ahead. She squeezed the shark's tooth in her hand, trying not to think about how Prince had helped put the sets together and knew every detail of how they were constructed. And what Mary had said about the shouting by Mr. Gage's dressing room table at the theater. And how Prince always seemed to be around when they were discussing Mr. Gage, asking questions, commenting—aside from when he was missing for long periods of time or late to rehearsal without explanation, or, as on the night they had found the nails on the rigging platform, poking holes in Cassie's theories, almost as though he was trying to keep her from...

Cassie clapped her hands over her ears. She needed to talk to Prince before her mind went somewhere she didn't want it to go.

"Prince! Are you in there?" She rapped on Prince's door

and turned to peer through the branches of the oak tree that dominated the boarding house's bricked inner courtyard down below. She'd stopped by the other evening, but suddenly she wasn't sure whether she was at the right room. She knocked again. Was this the east wing or the west wing?

She was lifting her hand to try once more when Prince swung the door open, tugging a robe around him.

"Cassie, good evening. Sorry to be so long in answering—I was trying to have a wash and shave. Is anything the matter?"

"I— Can I come in?" Cassie squeezed past him into the room and dropped her pillowcase on the floor.

"But I'm not dr— And you're in."

Closing the door behind her, Prince sat in the chair he'd pulled up to the washbasin and used a hand towel to wipe a dollop of shave cream from his chin. "Well, what is it?"

"What's your name?"

Prince paused. "Uh, Prince?"

"Your full, real name."

"Prince Richard Montgomery?"

"And you're sticking by that." Cassie paced and added a third piece of gum to the two she was already chewing.

"Well, I'm sure I was born with a different name, before I was adopted in Yarmouth, but I can't recall what that was. So, for now, this is the only name I've got. Now, what on earth is going on?"

Cassie considered him. He was so like her, the way he laughed, the way he sneezed at the sun. The way he'd tilted his head the other day when Mr. Gage interrupted his reading, as though it were physically painful to tear his gaze from the book, had even made her think of her dear father. How could he possibly be capable of anything bad? She'd felt comfortable with him before she'd even met him.

He folded his towel over his knee and waited patiently,

though questioningly. He didn't look like someone with a guilty conscience. But, then again, the most dangerous ones never did.

"Why is there no record of your adoption in Yarmouth?" she asked. "Or anything else?"

Prince dropped his towel, then banged his hand on the washstand reaching down to pick it up. "What? Why?" He rubbed his wrist. "Have you been investigating me or something?"

Cassie fiddled with her glove. "No, I wasn't the one— It doesn't matter. I have a little, let's say. But how am I supposed to trust you if I can't even be sure of who you are?"

"Ah." He sat back, still rubbing his wrist. "All right. If it would make you feel better, I suppose I can explain that, even if I don't truly understand it. As I might have mentioned, my mother didn't like to talk about my adoption. What I've been able to gather from other means, though, is I didn't come from an orphanage or other official channel, but rather through a friend who found me.

"And my mother never legally adopted me— I'm not sure why, but I think she was nervous she wouldn't be allowed to keep me for some reason if she put in for the paperwork. That may be why she didn't want me in school, either. Luckily, I like to read, and we had many accomplished and well-educated people move through our circles at the theater, so I ended up with a serviceable education."

Cassie picked at her glove. That much seemed to be true.

"But I do exist, I assure you." Prince winked. "Even on paper. Several years ago, my mother's partner in the theater became desperate for money due to a drinking and gambling problem and he tried to take her ownership interest by deception, then by force. So, I studied every law book I could get my hands on in order to help defend her from his attacks, and eventually we won. In return, I earned several pieces of official paperwork from the proceedings that have my name on them. I could show you, if you'd like."

Cassie looked down at her shoes. "I— That won't be necessary." She was having trouble meeting his eye. This man was smart, loyal, *and* had integrity.

Prince's mouth spread into his usual pleasant smile. "So, now you understand why I feel so comfortable in the theater, even aside from my time as an actor. For all the years before my mother's falling out with her partner, her theater was literally my home. Our apartment was in the attic above the stage, and much of my free time was spent with the company, learning about everything from breath support and set building to sewing costumes. And swinging from the rigging when no one was looking, of course." His eyes twinkled. "Happy as a monkey in a banyan tree."

Prince tried to rearrange his robe, which kept sliding off his knees, then grabbed a pair of trousers from the bed and carried them behind a privacy screen in the corner. "That being said, when Mr. Gage pulled me aside before rehearsal that day and told me he'd changed the blocking for the Pirate King number and was planning to go up the mast—he'd been wanting to add more verticality to the blocking for a while, he said, and had finally decided to do it—I was nervous. I even said so to Marguerite, who was standing next to me when he told me." His head disappeared behind the screen as he bent to pull the trousers on. "And that was without the idea that someone might be trying to harm him."

His head popped up again from behind the screen, and he folded his arms over the top of the frame, resting his chin on his knuckles. "That was part of why I went to sit out in the auditorium with my book for a few minutes before we started, to get my mind off things. Though, I didn't get much reading done, thanks to you." He smiled that smile again.

"I have certainly noticed how much you love the theater. You stayed around after Mr. Gage fell, all through the coroner's inquiry, and were even back there late the next night, when you found Paddy and me up on the rigging platform." She walked over and sat on the bed, tucking a curl behind her ear.

Prince inclined his head. "Yes, but I don't think I would go that far with it. I stayed that first day because, well, I don't know... I suppose I thought I could be of help. A remarkable, terrible thing had happened, and I've never been one simply to stand by and watch. It's not in my nature, I guess."

Cassie shifted. She had been as guilty as he was of that, many times.

"And that next night, I'd only come back to get a pair of shoes I'd left by my dressing table. I wasn't there for the fun of it."

"Right." Now that he mentioned it, he had been holding a pair of shoes when she saw him.

Prince stepped out from behind the privacy screen, buttoning his shirt. "Anything else?"

Cassie flushed. "Oh, I wasn't trying to interrogate you—"

Prince fixed her with his gaze. He knew exactly what she had been doing, and suddenly she felt silly.

But— She unfurled her hand, which still held the shark's tooth necklace from Mr. Gage's suite. Before she could formulate the question, however, Prince plopped next to her on the bed.

"Ah! You have a lucky shark's tooth, too."

"No, I... found it on the floor in Mr. Gage's suite. I don't suppose you—" She stopped. Prince had leaned forward to look into her hand, revealing, right there between the folds of his open collar, his own shark's tooth necklace.

"Oh, no, I really couldn't say who's it might be." He shrugged. "Could be anyone's."

Cassie cleared her throat, glad he'd incorrectly assumed her question. "Anyone?"

"Well, that's an overstatement. I meant it could belong to a number of people in the troupe. A, uh—local merchant was selling them on consignment for his mother-in-law and talked me into buying a bunch, and, as he said they were lucky, I put them out in a basket in the men's dressing room for anyone to take. Quite a few did, I think, aside from Mr. Gage. He said sharks scared him."

Cassie turned the tooth over in her hand. It wasn't the informative item it had seemed at first, then. But the important thing was it wasn't Prince's, since he had his still.

Though, she supposed, that only really meant that he hadn't lost his necklace in Mr. Gage's room, not that he hadn't been there at all.

She put the necklace away in her chatelaine pouch. "I did have one more question... and it's only because I'm trying to figure out who might have wished Mr. Gage harm. Mary Rutledge told me there had been a big argument in the men's dressing room not too long after the troupe arrived on the island, and Marguerite was there, maybe Harland. And... it confused me a little because you hadn't mentioned it before, but... she said you were there, too. So—" She tugged at her skirt. "What were you arguing with Mr. Gage about?"

"Oh, that." Prince folded his hands. "Nothing, actually."

"Nothing?"

"I wasn't arguing with anyone about anything. It was Marguerite and Mr. Gage who were doing the arguing. The only real contribution I had to the conversation was an attempt to extricate myself." He sighed and leaned back slightly, rubbing his knees.

"Right after we arrived on the island and started setting up in the theater, I discovered Harland had made an error assembling one of the set pieces. As I believe I've mentioned, it's a complicated process, taking the set apart and putting it back together each time, and given Harland's experience, I figured it was simply a mistake. It was potentially dangerous, though, so I pointed it out to him—which is when I realized he was so intoxicated he almost didn't understand what I was telling him.

"Still, I gave him the benefit of the doubt. I knew he had a wife back home but was always on the road, so that had to be hard on him. But I started paying attention, and I realized it wasn't a singular occurrence. He reached that state regularly, and I became concerned. Which is why I brought it up with Mr. Gage. I wasn't trying to make any accusations, only remedy a problem, but Mr. Gage was very upset and declared that he was going to put Harland on a probationary watch. He must have said as much to Harland because Harland has been... less than friendly to me ever since."

Cassie's skin prickled. It was hard to miss Harland's hostility toward Prince, but it appeared he had an even stronger quarrel with Mr. Gage. She recalled the scornful way Harland had spoken of Mr. Gage outside Three Star Saloon, when he was with Marguerite. *Speaking of Marguerite.* "What did Miss Clifton have to do with it?"

"Well, not long after, I found Harland and Marguerite sharing a flask of liquor in the men's dressing room. Now, at that point, I would have been happy to turn around and go anywhere else. I'd voiced my concerns and had no interest in being a permanent informant. And I did, in fact, try to leave, but Marguerite, corned as a cow herself, directed that powerful soprano of hers at me and shouted that I'd better not be running off to tell Mr. Gage. Clearly, Harland had told her what had happened. But that's what I get for getting involved in other people's business, I suppose. It's like tidal mud—far easier to step into than out of."

Cassie definitely knew about that.

"Anyway, the commotion brought Mr. Gage and Mr.

Manning in. Harland had managed to run off unnoticed, but Mr. Gage recognized Harland's flask in Marguerite's hand. He was furious, saying Harland was spreading his vices to other troupe members, and announced he would be relieving Harland of his duties. Marguerite, perhaps feeling responsible, drunkenly rose to the occasion once again and reminded Mr. Gage, at volume, that the troupe needed Harland and Mr. Gage was—let's say, lacking in mental faculties?—if he didn't realize that.

"Mr. Gage responded by reminding *her* that, even if the troupe needed Harland, it didn't need her, which really got her going, but then he said something that stopped her as suddenly as if she'd been struck by an errant baseball: 'And no one's forgotten Cincinnati.' She was calm after that. Eerily so. But so was he, and he said would give Harland one last chance."

"Gracious." Clearly, there was no love lost between Marguerite and Mr. Gage, either. Had Mr. Gage been holding something over her? And she'd finally gotten tired of it? "I'm glad you got out of there in one piece."

"Me, too. Hey, is there someone outside?" Prince strode to the window overlooking the walkway. "No, must have been my imagination." As he started to turn back, however, he stopped and stared at the floor by the door. "That wasn't there when you came in."

Cassie craned her neck. There was a large envelope lying on the shoe mat.

"Someone must have dropped it off while we were talking." Prince picked up the envelope and unfolded the sheet inside. "It looks like... a list of directions and a—treasure map? I'm not sure. It appears to be written in some kind of code. But it's addressed to you."

"To me? Who is it from?"

"There's no signature. All I can work out is the sender

wants to give you some kind of information about Mr. Gage, but you have to go somewhere first."

Cassie took the sheet from him, mouthing the words as she read. "And you. See? There's your name, too, but backward."

She held it up to a lamp. Was there something written in heat-activated ink? "How incredibly bizarre."

"Agreed." Prince picked up his coat. "So, shall we go?"

14

Cassie and Prince counted paces, answered riddles, aligned rooftops, and shook palm trees as the evening shadows lengthened into night, following the instructions of the mysterious note they had received. Finally, they arrived at what they hoped was the prescribed meeting point: a stall at Rawling's Livery Stable, a mere two blocks from where they had started at the Florida House Inn.

Prince steadied himself with the edge of a feed trough, his gaze locked with that of a horse who had draped its head over the stall divider, and used a brick to scrape a dung patty from his boot. "Why, on God's good green earth, did whoever wanted to speak with us send us from one end of the island to the other, only to bring us back almost to where we started? But worse?"

"To make sure you weren't followed." Paddy stepped forward out of the shadows, tossing the cape he was wearing over his shoulder—no small feat, given that the cape was far longer as he was and most of it was bunched on the floor around his ankles. He also wore a buccaneer's hat that covered most of his face and a costume mustache that covered the rest.

Cassie shook the papers at him. "This was your doing,

Paddy? This isn't a game! We've just spent who knows how long following these instructions—"

"It was me." Mary emerged behind Paddy and put her hand on his shoulder. "I asked him to help. Though, I didn't think it would take you so long to get here... I was starting to consider whether one of these feed buckets could serve as an emergency chamber pot."

She was costumed as well, in a similarly improbable ensemble consisting of a coarsely woven sweater and vest, rain boots, and fisherman's oilskin trousers, along with a shaggy white wig and sou'wester hat. "Originally, I was just going to have Paddy bring you a note about meeting me, but it turns out Paddy knows more about this clandestine type of operation, and he helped me come up with a secure plan."

"I had lots of clues already written up," Paddy said. "I've been working on a puzzle for Metta."

Cassie blew out a breath. "All right, Miss Rutledge. We're here. What is it you wanted to tell us?"

Mary assumed a crouched stance and hung a corncob pipe from her lip. "Paddy, perimeter check."

"Aye, aye." Giving a quick salute, Paddy took a lap around the stable, hopping up and down to peer into a few of the stalls, much to the consternation of the dozing horses. "Clear!"

Prince coughed into his arm.

"Good." Mary adjusted her hat. "So, I spent the afternoon after rehearsal today searching the theater—dressing tables, costume trunks, prop boxes, and so forth—for suspicious articles. Then, once I knew the troupe had moved out to the saloons around town, as is their daily habit, I went through people's lodgings."

"Now, Mary," Prince started. "I don't know if you ought to have been in—"

"Oh, I didn't mind." Mary pulled the pipe out of her mouth. "I would have had a look at Mr. Gage's room as well, but it was locked when I got there, and the maid I asked to open it couldn't have been more hostile. Apparently, she'd been reprimanded for letting someone else in there earlier without permission and couldn't be convinced again for anything."

She snapped her fingers, and Paddy disappeared for a moment, then staggered back into the stall hauling a crate filled with odds and ends. "I still found plenty of interest, though."

Cassie sifted through the items. "Hammer, quill pen, snuff box, straight razor, bag of coins, a clump of animal hair... What exactly is the theory here?"

Mary puffed her prop pipe. "Oh, that's your job, dear. I'm no deductionist, only a gatherer of information. But all the stories I've read tell me those are suspicious objects."

Cassie tugged a crumpled piece of paper from between two unmarked vials of liquid. It was a letter from a well-known orphan's league in Philadelphia, dated a week ago, thanking the troupe for its "generous" donation. That was somewhat relevant at least, but, unfortunately, the donation amount wasn't indicated.

"Nice, huh? Oh! I found this, too." Mary reached into the waistband of her oilskin trousers and pulled out an envelope marked "Private—Important."

Bending with Prince by the lantern Paddy brought over, Cassie opened the envelope and read it out loud. Inside was a letter from Mr. Gage to Harland McGregor, informing him that he was being terminated from his position with the troupe. As soon as the show wrapped in Fernandina, he was to collect his final pay and make his own way home.

"Oh, my. It seems Mr. Gage changed his mind about Harland." Prince wiped a drip of sweat from his forehead. "Or Harland finally used up his chances—"

"Well, what are we waiting for?" Hughes stepped out from behind a stall door into the hay-lined circle of light. Evidently, Paddy's sweep of the area had been more show than substance.

"Officer Hughes!" Cassie said as Mary and Paddy tried to shrink back into the shadows. "What are you doing here?"

"Yeah," Paddy called from under his cape. "How did you find us?"

Hughes considered Paddy's ensemble, then Mary's, but refrained from comment. Not that he had a right to say anything about such matters, given his own recent performance.

"Co-*Pro Tem* Deputy Hughes. I was at the Florida House, speaking with Mrs. Liddy about searching troupe members' rooms, when I saw Miss Gwynne slip into Mr. Montgomery's for a private rendezvous."

Cassie's cheeks blazed. "That wasn't a rendezvous."

"Oh, so Mr. Montgomery receives all of his guests half-dressed?"

"Listen," Prince said. "I wasn't expecting anyone, and—"

"I don't need the sordid details. Anyway, after I'd finished speaking with Mrs. Liddy, I—happened to pass by the room, and I heard talk of a treasure map, something to do with Mr. Gage. So I waited for them to come out and followed as a small distance."

Prince muttered an oath as he stepped in another horse deposit. "You were behind us the whole time?"

"Why didn't you say something?" Cassie tried to appear more composed than she was. "You might have helped."

"And risk scaring off whoever had sent you the message?"

Cassie lowered her shoulders. "Fine. I guess none of us knew what was— Wait, what did you mean, 'what are we waiting for'?"

"It's obvious, isn't it? Harland McGregor is our man." He looked around at them, then threw up his hands. "Mr. Gage's murderer? I've had my suspicions for some time now, but that letter buttons it up, since it finally gives a motive. And there wasn't anyone in the troupe more equipped to execute this than him. Not to mention that he had access at all times, given his position as head stagehand."

Mary took off her hat, bringing the wig with it (apparently, they were sewn together). "I suppose Harland had mentioned needing money a few times, said he had to save up for something important."

"It makes sense," Prince said. "Maybe when Mr. Gage dismissed him, he felt desperate. And betrayed. He'd been with the troupe for some time, so I can't imagine he would have taken being dismissed well. And, Cassie, I believe he had one of the shark's teeth, too. It's perfect, in fact."

Avoiding Hughes's confused glance (he hadn't been privy to that particular detail and probably wasn't too pleased about it), Cassie touched a finger to her chatelaine pouch, where she could feel the point of the shark's tooth poking through the fabric. They were right. Harland had motive, means, and opportunity, which, together, her father had taught her, were the key to identifying the guilty party.

She turned toward the stall door, scanning the hay for deposits of the sort that had soiled Prince's shoe. "Let's go find Mr. McGregor."

Harland wasn't in his rooms at the Florida House, but his neighbor, a lumber mill foreman with distractingly large teeth, informed them that he'd seen him at the Three Star Saloon earlier, so Cassie, Prince, and Hughes (trailed by Paddy, despite Hughes's repeated attempts to shoo him away), hurried to Centre Street. They were approaching the saloon when a group of men burst from the batwing doors.

"He'll be killed!"

"What do we do?"

"Hey, watch the beer!"

The men staggered toward a crowd gathering by the train tracks in front of the passenger wharf.

"What's happened?" Prince called after them.

"Someone's fallen asleep on the tracks, and the train is coming. Fast!"

Right on cue, a train whistle sounded, close enough for discomfort, and Prince and Hughes dove into the crowd. When Cassie finally elbowed her way through the onlookers, she saw Prince and Hughes bent over a man sprawled across the tracks. Prince shook the man's shoulders and slapped his cheeks, and Hughes hurled epithets at him, trying to wake him. And all the while, the ground rumbled below their feet as the train drew nearer, its whistle desperately blowing at them to Get Out of the Way.

Cassie looked into the light of the approaching headlamps. The train was too close for the engineer to brake in time.

"We'll have to pull him off! Come on!" She threw herself forward and grabbed an ankle as more hands reached in around her. As orderly as a swarm of bumblebees, the volunteers jerked and tugged, and finally they managed to drag the man (and themselves) clear just before the train roared past, throwing them off their feet.

"What—who hit me?" The man, awakened at last by the impact with the ground, groaned and sat up. It was Harland. And, judging by the way he was having trouble keeping his balance even while sitting, he was as drunk as a fly corked in a bottle of whiskey.

He slung his glare at the man to his right. "And why are you holding my hand?" One of the helpers had apparently forgotten to let go.

Prince leaned in as the man scuttled away. "Harland, are you all right?"

Harland snorted. "Of course I'm all right. What are you on about, Prince?"

"You fell asleep on the train tracks. We had to pull you off."

"Train tracks?" Harland swiveled his head to look, almost falling over in the process.

"By the passenger wharf. Thankfully, someone saw you and called for help, or else we might have two of you by now. You are very lucky, sir."

Harland swung his gaze from the tracks to Prince's face, back to the tracks, then into the crowd, who were still murmuring and watching. Finally, about as quickly as water through a used coffee filter, the information started to percolate through his brain.

"Mr. McGregor," Hughes said. "I'm Co-*Pro Tem* Deputy Hughes. I've been investigating William Gage's—fall, and I'm afraid I'm going to need you to come with me to the jail. We have a—"

Harland started to waver again, then bolted straight. He spat on the ground. "Lucky would've been if that train had hit me. Lord knows I deserve it after what I done."

The murmuring stopped, and Hughes stared at Harland. "Pardon?"

Was he *confessing*? Cassie had thought it would be much harder to get that out of him, given his typical orneriness.

Staggering to his feet, Harland pulled a nearly empty bottle of whiskey out of his coat and tipped the last slosh of liquid into his mouth. He regarded the bottle for a long moment, swaying, then abruptly smashed it on the tracks, causing everyone to jump. "That's it, then. No more. You can take me away now."

He held his wrists out to Hughes. "Come now, boy. You said you've come about Mr. Gage, didn't you? Let's go."

"I don't— What?"

"I've already killed one man, and almost just killed another, who happens to be me. Do you want to wait until I kill someone else? This has gone on long enough. Maybe jail is what it's going to take to finally end this."

Prince stepped in front of Hughes and met Harland's eye. "Harland, listen to me carefully. Are you telling us you are responsible for Mr. Gage's death?"

"I am, indeed." Harland lifted one of his hands, which he was still holding out in front of him, to sweep away his gray-streaked hair, then placed it back into position. "Guess you were right, eh, Prince? You did tell Mr. Gage I was going to kill somebody someday."

"Barley tea with a touch of lavender. And orange sugar." Cassie looked up as Flora placed a cup and saucer on the porch step next to her. "I figured coffee would be little too much after the night you've had." Giving Cassie a pat on the head, Flora slipped back under the curtain of mosquito netting over the door and into the glow inside.

Cassie stared at the tealeaf bits at the bottom of the amber liquid, illuminated by the light from the doorway, then turned her eyes onto the wild shadows of Flora's garden in front of her. She flexed her fingers. Only a couple of hours before, she had been at the railroad tracks by the passenger wharf, first saving a man, then sending him off to jail for murder, and her hands were still shaky, making her wary of trusting them with the delicate china.

As though hearing her thoughts, the kitten hopped onto her lap and nuzzled her face into Cassie's palm to reassure her.

Flora reemerged through the mosquito netting with a plate of sandwiches and placed it on a wicker side table next to a vase of cut hydrangeas. Straightening, she turned to where Miss Porter sat in one of the rocking chairs along the wall, gazing out into the darkness. "Charlotte, are you sure I can't get you anything?"

Miss Porter rocked her chair slightly, but didn't respond.

"I'll just keep working then, if no one minds," Flora said.

"That shopping frenzy the other day, when all those actors and chorus ladies came over for music rehearsal, just about cleaned out my stock of perfumed handkerchiefs and gloves, and the peak of tourist season is still ahead of us."

Cassie finally forced herself to reach for the teacup. She curled her hands around it, relishing the warmth as it soaked into her palms and fingertips. It was no New York winter here on the island, but the air could acquire a nip late in the evening.

"Thank you for the tea, Aunt Flora." She took a sip. "It's exactly what I needed."

"You're very welcome. And be sure to have some sandwiches as well, while they're hot." Flora nodded at the plate she'd put out and started back toward the door. "Grilled cheddar cheese topped with sweet pepper jelly. Guaranteed to warm your belly and your heart."

Cassie smiled after her through the fragrant cloud of steam, feeling the curls of her bangs tuck upward from the moisture. She wondered if her mother had said things like that, too.

"By the way—" Flora turned back, her hand resting on the mosquito netting. She raised her voice as the unseen crickets beyond the edge of the porch, either improvising a complex choral number or competing for who could be the loudest, crescendoed. "Remember that new scent I've been trying out? With violet and clove? Well, something was bothering me about it, and I couldn't figure out why it wasn't selling better. So, I took a poll among the ladies from the whist club, and they had a brilliant suggestion—switch the clove for cinnamon! I don't know what I was thinking before. Clove is far too heavy-handed."

Cassie paused mid-sip, her ears perked liked the kitten's (though the kitten, who was watching a fly walk across the floorboards, was occupied differently). *Violet and clove?* The handkerchief with the nails in it up on the rigging platform had definitely had violet in it, and she could have mistaken clove for vanilla. She had a terrible perfumery nose. Which was probably also why she hadn't remembered it was in Flora's new scent.

"Having their input from time to time really is helpful," Flora went on. "The whist club ladies. While I was asking their opinion about the scent, one of them also pointed out that the orange blossom embroidery I'd added to last month's handker-chiefs—I thought I would try it out as a signature of sorts—while pretty, might be too labor-intensive to be sustainable. And they were right. I've decided not to do it anymore. At least not until I find a team of sewers willing to take on the task. Excuse me a moment." Flora slipped inside.

Cassie nodded after her, thinking. The handkerchief she found had had the orange blossom embroidery on it, too, so it was definitely from Flora's store. But why would Harland have had one of Flora's ladies' handkerchiefs on hand? *He* certainly hadn't purchased that from Flora.

Careful, Cassie.

She looked at Miss Porter, who was still rocking quietly, hardly reacting as a puckish sea breeze pulled strand after strand from her careful chignon and fluttered them about her face. She had been happy to hear the news about Harland's arrest at first, but, after the excitement had worn off, she'd been unusually muted. She had also asked if she could stay at Flora's that night rather than go home alone. Perhaps, now that the purpose provided by the investigation was gone, she was being forced to face her loss head-on and feel her heart breaking once again.

Cassie more than understood. It was what she was going to have to do herself, as soon as she returned to New York and opened the door to her father's brownstone.

Carrying her tea with her, Cassie walked up the porch steps and settled into a rocking chair next to Miss Porter, who leaned her head against her shoulder. This is what she should be doing now, comforting her friends and seeking comfort from them, instead of looking for more feathers to ruffle. She sipped her tea, her shoulders relaxing as warmth ran down her throat and bloomed in her stomach.

"So, Cassie—" Flora, laden with an armful of men's neckties, a portable lamp, and a small decorative tree constructed from wire, returned to the porch and sat down in a rocking chair on the other side of Miss Porter. After transferring Kleio, who was perched on her head, to the porch railing, she stood the tree and lamp on another side table and laid the neckties across her lap. "Harland McGregor, the head stagehand, confessed to Mr. Gage's murder. Did he say why he would do such a horrible thing?"

So much for turning her mind onto other matters.

"No one's been able to speak with him further about it yet." Cassie took a sandwich and patted Danger's head as he passed by. "He lost consciousness before they had even tied his cuffs on. He was extremely inebriated— One witness says said that, before he even reached the tracks, he tripped and fell while taking a swing at a passing shadow."

"Gracious."

"The sheriff is going to question him and get the confession on the record after he wakes up, though no one's quite sure when that's going to be. He was unresponsive all the way to the jail."

"That must be why Jake went straight from here to the doctor after he was informed of the arrest."

Cassie pulled a bit of cheese from her sandwich for Esy, who had leapt onto her lap, nosing at her hand, as well as a bit for Luna, who was sitting on her feet, nosing at her knees. "Jake was here visiting this evening? Does that mean matters are improving between you?"

"Not really, unfortunately." Flora started arranging the neckties on the tree, checking the scent of each one first. "We argued again. It was silly, really... He insisted he drive me when

I visit my orange groves down south next month, but I've always driven myself, and—well, the details aren't important. Anyway, I was so worked up I was about to tell him to go on home when Paddy arrived with the message about Mr. McGregor. Thank goodness for that."

"I'm still not sure I understand the problem."

"It comes down to this. Now that we—have an understanding between us, Jake has been acting very differently. Coming by constantly, insisting on meaningless formalities that had never even entered my mind before. Much as I love it when he's around, it's just that... before, when he would do something for me, it felt like a spontaneous kindness, an act of love. Now, it feels like an obligation, on his part to supply it and on mine to accept it." Flora tugged a wrinkle out of one of the neckties. "I don't see why anything had to change just because..." She sighed. "We were happy before, weren't we? We never used to argue about anything, and now we do so constantly."

Cassie chewed her grilled cheese thoughtfully. "Have you tried explaining that to Jake?"

"No." Flora studied the bedecked tree, then pulled all the neckties off and began arranging them again. "I don't suppose I have. I hate to upset him."

Cassie put down her sandwich, fending off a paw-swipe from the kitten. "Aunt Flora, you must. You remember how failing to speak honestly with each other kept you apart for so long."

"Dear Lord." Flora pressed her hand to her cheek. "You're right, as usual. I'll make a point of it the next time we see each other." She started to sit back, then straightened back up. "Oh! Here." She pulled a letter out of her skirts. "This came for you today."

It was from Angus Crawley, the New York coroner's clerk, responding to her request to see the memorandum the examining physician on her father's case had written about that Five

Points criminal group. It seemed, however, the clerk had never heard of the memorandum, and he hadn't been able to find any reference to it when he searched. In addition, the examining physician had left his post shortly after her father's case was closed, so he hadn't been able to ask him about it.

Cassie bit her lip. The physician had been very specific about the memorandum. How had the clerk not even found a record of it? And, though Cassie was not typically one to embrace conspiracy sorts of explanations, she couldn't help finding the timing of the physician's dismissal a little strange. What was going on?

She supposed she would have to count on her inquiry with her father's secretary to yield something useful. Though, she was surprised she hadn't heard back from him yet. If he was having trouble finding the information, she would have at least expected a telegram letting her know.

"Knock-knock," Mr. Manning called over the garden gate, miming the action as he spoke the words. "May we come through?" Mr. Wilkes was standing behind him, his arms folded across his chest.

Cassie stood. "Mr. Manning, Mr. Wilkes. Yes, please do. Is everything all right?"

"Oh, certainly, certainly. Considering, that is." Mr. Manning let Mr. Wilkes through and closed the gate behind them. "Good evening, all."

Kleio eyed each man as they approached but remained on her perch.

"We heard about Mr. McGregor's arrest," Mr. Wilkes said, taking up an official-looking stance with one foot up on a step and his hands on his waist.

"Shocking, isn't it." Mr. Manning shook his head. "But, if I can be frank, not entirely surprising, given the toxic combination of his drinking and his temper. Mr. Gage should have gotten rid of him ages ago... Anyway, Mr. Wilkes and I were talking, and it occurred to us that, now that we know what really happened to Mr. Gage, perhaps there's all the more reason to go forward with the show."

Miss Porter stirred. "Go on with the show? I'd have thought the opposite. Do you think it right?"

Mr. Wilkes slapped at a mosquito and resumed his stance. "There's no question. We've come this far, so we might as well push on. There are still people counting on this show going up."

Mr. Manning nodded. "And we can't let the troupe, and Mr. Gage's memory, be overtaken by this ugly story. More than ever, we ought to ensure Mr. Gage's memory is honored and those children get their money. And all the hard-working troupe members deserve their money, too. So, we're trying to find Mr. Montgomery and come up with a plan for completing the show without Mr. McGregor... We reworked it once already. We can do it again. You agree, don't you, Miss Gwynne?"

Cassie rubbed her cheek. She hadn't really thought about what would happen with the show, now that the murderer had been captured. But Mr. Manning was right—some good could still come out of this.

"I have most everything needed in here." Mr. Manning lifted his ever-present prompt book from under his arm. "If I copy out the scene change instructions, I'm sure a few extra men with ship-rigging experience could be trained in time. But I won't be able to execute everything without help, and Mr. Montgomery is the next most technically knowledgeable individual in the group. Percy Brown was a stagehand himself before becoming an actor, so he'll be useful, but Mr. Montgomery is more of a leader."

"Yes, is he here?" asked Mr. Wilkes. "He wasn't in his room at the Florida House Inn."

"I'm afraid not," Cassie said. "When I last saw him, he was helping transport Mr. McGregor to the local jail."

Flora put aside her neckties. "Would you care for a refreshment, gentlemen?"

"Oh, not for me, thank you," Mr. Manning said.

Mr. Wilkes slapped his hat at what Cassie presumed was another mosquito. "Yeah, we'd really better get— Are you conducting some sort of construction in there?"

A noise was coming through the door from somewhere in the foyer. At first it sounded like buzzing, but as Cassie drew closer she decided it was more like sawing. When she peered around the doorframe, she found Madame M peering back at her. The sound was coming from the woman's mouth.

"Madame M!" Flora fluttered over and took Madame M's arm, lifting the mosquito net so she could come through. "I thought you were asleep."

"Not tired." The woman paused her sawing briefly to respond, then resumed, continuing even as she sat next to Miss Porter in the rocking chair Cassie had been using.

Mr. Manning cocked his head. "I say, that's a rather good mimicry. But is she quite—"

"Our friend is suffering from a health condition." Flora lifted a plaid blanket from one of the chairs and tucked it across Madame M's lap. "So she's staying with us for a little while until we get in touch with her family. On that note, Cassie, I found an empty pill bottle tucked into her dress while I was helping her wash today, along with a sack of buttons. I don't know what to make of the buttons, but the pill bottle has the name of a pharmacy in Jacksonville written on it, so I'm going to send a message over and see if we can't get more information."

"That's great." Cassie looked down as Madame M, finally tiring of her game, grabbed Cassie's hand and hugged it to her cheek. "We could use some good news about now."

15

———

Mr. Wilkes and Mr. Manning, it turned out, were the type of men who did what they set out to do, so soon Cassie found herself once again headed to the Lyceum for rehearsal. Her mind, however, was not on the music, the choreography, or the pirate's pantaloons she'd be wearing in the show (in a directorial choice Cassie could finally get behind, Mr. Wilkes had reassigned some of the women to the men's pirate chorus to even out the gender imbalance Mr. Gage's particular mode of recruitment had created). Instead, she was still thinking about Mr. Gage.

She stopped beneath the shade of a magnificent Japanese plum tree, which was rooted in a house garden but had stretched its spreading branches, heavy with small, orange fruits, over the sidewalk as a courtesy to passing pedestrians, and rested her hands on her knees. She was more tired than she ought to be for such a short walk, but she suspected it was due to all the running her mind had been doing.

She should be happy. Mr. Gage's killer had been caught, and they were about to complete the show, fulfilling the original artistic and charitable mission. But, to her mind, the murder hadn't been solved yet, or at least fully explained, since Jake and Hughes still hadn't been able to take Harland's confession. Upon examining Harland the night he was brought in, Dr. Ames hadn't thought his condition serious, but Harland had then slept for a day and a half in his cell, only to wake up covered in sweat and vomiting. A variety of hallucinations followed, and, according to the jailor's recounting of events, he'd likely experienced a mild seizure as well.

After further examination, Dr. Ames identified the symptoms as alcohol withdrawal. He instructed the jailor to supply him with one beer in the morning and one beer in the evening to ease the symptoms, ply him with as much food and water as he could keep down, and wait until his body stabilized itself. Until then, the questioning would have to wait.

She really hoped the matter would be resolved soon. Her sleep migrations were ranging farther and becoming more bizarre as her uneasiness persisted, and she was afraid if it went on much longer, one morning Flora was going to have to fish her, snoring, out of the marsh.

She believed she understood what had happened: Harland, acting in retaliation to being dismissed by Mr. Gage, had used his knowledge of the set's construction to change out the nails in the schooner set piece so it would fall apart when Gage climbed on it, then covered up what he had done by adding back the appropriate nails and blaming the accident on the wood. However, Cassie still found the imperfect and, in certain instances, entirely wrong, placement of those "cover-up" nails troubling, given his experience. Though, perhaps he'd done a poor job because he was rushing, or he was intoxicated again. It was also unclear why he had hidden the evidence in a ladies' handkerchief from Flora's perfume store.

She straightened up and reached for a piece of gum as a series of carriages began to pass by. Each held two or three young women garbed in the latest tiny-waisted fashions and finery, shaded by ribboned parasols affixed to the vehicles. Judging by the overflowing sacks of swimwear, towels, and trowels they were toting, they were headed for an outing at the beach.

Cassie smoothed her dress. Their conversations were bound to be vapid, and their food too bland and healthful for enjoyment, but, given her own state of mind at the moment, she almost wished she could join them.

Perhaps what was bothering her the most was the Harland narrative hadn't explained the oddities she had begun to uncover about Mr. Gage's business dealings. Neither Harland's drinking, performance, or even his general unpleasantness seemed to have anything to do with that. So, she had spent much of her sleepless nights going back through the contents of the pillowcase she'd taken from Mr. Gage's suite at the Egmont, to which she'd added a few of the items Mary had brought her, searching for a connection. But none had emerged as of yet, and the information before her was as frustrating and unhelpful as ever.

The Varden boy's letter still felt overly crafted, and it continued to annoy her that she couldn't verify the troupe's donation record to her satisfaction. The donation acknowledgment letter Mary had found from the Philadelphia orphan's group helped, but it didn't specify the amount that had been donated, and, in any case, that was only one instance. And there remained the suite, and the clothes, and all the shopping receipts, as well as the (albeit empty) jewelry boxes in Mr. Gage's secretary. Had he really had enough family wealth to keep him in such a state, or was he benefitting from another income stream? If so, why hadn't Hughes and Jake been able to locate any next of kin yet? People of that sort of set were not known for taking the demise of their fellow members lightly.

Then again, information likely flowed more slowly when it had to cross the ocean.

A grapefruit rolled off one of the carriages in the beach-bound Parasol Parade, and a group of children gathered to watch its fate as it tumbled about in the street dust, narrowly missing hoof, then wheel, then foot.

As for the prospects book, after reading her own slightly off-putting, but likely accurate, entry ("young, small with chestnut curls, pretty in a rough-sketch sort of way, only adequate voice but plenty of funds"), she'd noticed that some of the entries had an unusual notation next to them, "XX," which seemed to refer to a person. For example, one entry relating to a potential contributing chorus member read: "Significant funds but little cash, most in trust controlled elsewhere; due to size and lack of mobility, blocking may be issue. Consult XX." Other entries concluded with variations of the same, such as "check with XX," or "ask XX." Who was "XX"? If Mr. Gage had, in fact, been involved in something untoward, he may have had a partner.

Had Harland truly acted the way he had because Mr. Gage dismissed him? And had Mr. Gage really dismissed him because of his drinking? Perhaps there was more to the story. Maybe Harland had found out about Mr. Gage's activities and threatened to expose him. Or, perhaps, they were partners and had a falling out, or Harland wanted it all for himself.

Cassie plucked one of the little orange fruits from the branch closest to her and peeled back its delicate skin, releasing a bright, sweet fragrance. *That doesn't entirely make sense, though.* She used her teeth to pull the flesh from the silky pit inside. Why would Harland have confessed, then? He didn't know they were investigating the matter. He also didn't seem like a money-savvy type. But, Cassie supposed, one never could tell what went on in another's head.

She was about to pass through the Lyceum's gate when

Arthur appeared from behind a particularly large banana tree, his arms and legs protruding far beyond the trouser and jacket cuffs of Mr. Wilkes's former Major-General Stanley costume. He tried to stride haughtily past her, but, given the constraints of his ensemble, was reduced to the uneven swagger of a peg-legged sailor.

"Uh, you know rehearsal's the other way—" she started to say, trying a bit of lighthearted banter. Then she saw his face and realized he looked more like a man set on war than on art.

"I'm off to the jail, to settle something with my *dear* friend Miss Clifton," he replied. "If I can figure out where that is."

"The jail? Why is Miss Clifton there?"

"It seems that, rather than attend rehearsal today, she's decided to pay a visit to Harland McGregor."

Mary, who'd arrived right behind Cassie, her hair pin-curled and tied up in a handkerchief, shifted the clothing sack she was carrying on to her hip. "I've just passed Paddy in the street. Word is the doctor's declared Mr. McGregor fit enough to give his confession. I'm guessing Miss Clifton wants to hear what he has to say."

"But, again, why—" Cassie stopped. *Of course. Marguerite is in love with Harland.* Why else would she have been so startlingly fierce in her defense of Harland to both Prince and Mr. Gage? There had been plenty of other suggestions of the intimacy between Marguerite and Harland as well, including the conversation Cassie had overheard between them outside the Three Star Saloon. And there was the ladies' handkerchief, the violet-and-something-scented handkerchief with Flora's "signature" embroidered orange blossom on it, that was used to hide the nails... And the Egmont maid's description of the woman she'd seen being let into Mr. Gage's suite: *"Pretty thing, with a waist so tiny it made me positively ill with jealousy."* That fitted Marguerite far better than Cassie.

She whispered over her shoulder to Mary. "Miss Rutledge,

where did you find that letter about Mr. McGregor being dismissed?"

"In the ladies' dressing room. Marguerite's dressing table."

Cassie bit her lip. The letter had been found in Marguerite's belongings, not Harland's. Why did she have it? Further, was it possible, in that case, that Harland had never received it? If so, he might not have known that he had been dismissed, which would remove his motive... And potentially pass it onto Marguerite. Had Marguerite intercepted the communication somehow and, having learned of Mr. Gage's intentions, done something desperate in a fit of protective rage? But then why had Harland confessed? Had he figured it out and wanted to protect *her*?

She needed to speak with the both of them.

"I'll show you the way to the jail, Mr. Beath," she said. "It isn't far from here."

"All right, Miss Gwynne." Arthur patted down his plumed officer's hat—at least that fit properly. "Show away."

When they reached the entrance to the jail's rear holding area, Arthur stepped in front of Cassie and threw the door open. "Jailor, where's Marguerite Clifton? I have something to say to that two-bit hussy."

"What is the meaning of this?" The jailor, his legs propped up on the table, glared at the intruders over a pair of small, round reading spectacles. "Officer—Co-*Pro Tem* Deputy Hughes will be back any minute with the sheriff, and I'm already risking his wrath by letting this young lady in here while we have a murder suspect in custody."

He jabbed a crumb-covered thumb at a corner of the room, where Marguerite was perched on a stool by Harland's cell, her arm wrapped around the bars as though they were holding her up. Harland sat up on his cot and rubbed his face. He was softer somehow, his usual bristle relaxed, and there was color in his cheeks that hadn't been there before. Marguerite, on the other hand, looked as fragile and weary as a bird that had been caught in a storm.

"Apologies for the intrusion, Mr. Kriegel," Cassie said. Ordinarily, despite the sobering rifle hanging from his chair, the man's personality matched his rosy cheeks and jelly-ful belly, but it was clear his patience had already been tested today, and their interruption of his plan to tuck into the plate of cookies in front of him likely hadn't earned them any favors. She had to try, though. "If I can vouch for these two, would it be possible to have a few minutes of privacy with the inmate? Just until the sheriff gets here? You know you can trust me. I won't take my eyes off them."

Mr. Kriegel sized up Arthur and Marguerite each in turn, then dropped his feet. "Fine. But if anything goes wrong, you'll be the one doing the explaining." Throwing the group one more look, he grabbed his cookies and lumbered into the hall.

As soon as the door shut behind him, Arthur turned on Marguerite. "Marguerite Clifton, are you not aware that your presence is wanted at rehearsal right now? I thought you were a professional."

Marguerite's lashes fluttered. "I—am. But I heard Harland was up, and I wanted to see him and make sure he was all right."

Arthur snorted. "Ha! Since when do you care about anyone else's welfare? From where I'm sitting, you only care about yourself."

"That's not true! You have no idea what I've been through—"

"I have a pretty good idea." Sneering, Arthur limp-swaggered over to the jailor's table in his too-tight trousers. Then he reached into his jacket with a grunt (Cassie thought she heard a couple of stitches snap as well) and threw out the ladies' glove he'd taken from Mr. Gage's suite.

Marguerite pulled her arm from the bars. "My glove!"

"Aha! So you admit it's yours!" Arthur folded his arms triumphantly.

"Gracious. Must you always be aha-ing? Of course I admit it. It's part of the lovely set, gloves and a handkerchief in a matching scent, that I bought from Miss Hale's store the other day. Miss Hale told me she's decided not to make that particular fragrance anymore, so I've been looking for it quite desperately."

Cassie leaned forward. She had been right. That handkerchief holding the nails, which was infused with Flora's short-lived scent—what was it, violet and clove?—belonged to Marguerite Clifton.

"Where did you find it?" Marguerite asked.

"In Mr. Gage's room at the Egmont Hotel!" Arthur wound up. "Because you were having a secret romance with Mr. Gage!"

"What? I—"

"Before you deny it, you should know I've been on to your furtive philanderings"—he emphasized each initial "f" sound—"for quite some time. All that extra attention to your hair and perfume, the disappearing in the evenings... I knew you were visiting a man, but I didn't know who until after we arrived here, when I noticed you following Mr. Gage around. Speaking with him in dark corners, having private 'meetings'... Oh, yes. You can't hide these things from me!"

He punctuated the pronouncement with a sweep of his arm.

"I fought it for a time. Even during that meeting at the boarding house, when I saw Mr. Gage's mustache oil in your bag, I tried to talk myself into believing I was wrong. But then I found your glove, proof you were in his very bedroom! And now here you are, rushing in to watch his murderer give his confession so you can avenge your heart. It couldn't be clearer. What do you have to say for yourself?"

Marguerite stood, knocking over her stool. "Fine, Arthur! You're right. I've been having a secret romance. But not with Mr. Gage—with Harland!"

Her last word echoed through the ensuing silence, and something flapped its wings in the rafters.

Arthur lowered onto the chair that happened to be next to him. He was lucky it was there because he probably would have sat, either way. "Harland?"

"Yes." Marguerite stuck out her chin. "I love him."

Cassie fidgeted with the miniature magnifying glass clipped to her chatelaine. Her instincts had been right about Marguerite's feelings for Harland. And if she'd been right about that—

"But he's married," Arthur said. "And he's Harland."

Harland stirred. "Hey, what's that supposed to—"

"But he loves *me*, so he's going to get a divorce and we're going get married. As soon as he has enough money for the proceedings." She paused. "Well, he was going to, before—"

Marguerite stopped, then threw herself against the cell door with a despair worthy of Shakespeare's Ophelia. "Oh, just throw me in jail, too! At least then we'll be together!"

Arthur sat up. "Marguerite! What are you—"

"They ought to! I'm guilty of everything he is, for aiding and abetting. See? I even know the words." She pressed her cheek to the bars. "Oh, Harland, why did you confess? I had everything under control, cleaned it all up. I know you didn't mean to!"

Cassie was back to being confused. Was *Marguerite* the one who'd done the covering up? And what did she say, Harland "didn't mean to"?

Harland jumped to his feet, knocking his pillow to the floor.

"Wait just one ever-loving minute, Marguerite." He turned to the others. "She had no part in this."

Cassie's head began to spin—Harland was confused, too. And his confusion was confusing her more.

"Yes, I did! When everyone was outside waiting for the coroner to come, I snuck back in and took the short nails out of the set piece, hid them up on the rigging gallery, and put the long ones in—See? I've learned something from watching you work all this time."

"But—"

"Shh, darling. Then I told the coroner how strong the nails in the boards were, that they were the right and best thing to use, but how Mr. Gage had insisted on getting the wood from a rubbish pile, which was true, and how it must have been so unsound it gave away under the strain. And the coroner agreed."

Cassie stared at Marguerite in astonishment, both because of what she was saying and because she must have discovered a way to inhale while speaking.

"I had to." Marguerite still hadn't taken a breath. "To protect you. I overheard you talking with Mr. Gage during load-in. He said he wanted to add blocking using the mast, and you said there was no way it would hold anyone as it was, it just had the normal little nails in it. He said to make it so it would, and you said, fine, you would have to secure it with longer, thicker ones—the ones you keep in the red compartment of your toolbox for heavy loads."

She sucked in some air finally, but stopped Harland with her hand when he tried to speak again.

"Don't defend me, dearest. I chose this. As I was saying, when the set piece fell apart, I knew you hadn't done what you'd told Mr. Gage you would do. Your drinking had gotten so bad, you were forgetting things, making small mistakes... It was only a matter of time before something big went wrong."

She flashed her eyes at Arthur.

"That, by the way, was the reason I was 'following Mr. Gage around,' as you so condescendingly put it. After that nosy Prince reported Harland for that one little mix-up, Mr. Gage put him on watch. So every time he suspected Harland had taken a sip of something, I had to talk him down so Harland could stay. Because if Harland had been dismissed for drinking again, not only would he be without this job, he wouldn't be hired anywhere else, either. This was his last chance. And you know my career's not something we can count on at the moment, Arthur. Not after Cincinnati. Maestro Rossi's wife has used her connections to blacklist me at every respectable company in the country."

Arthur wavered. "And the glove?"

"I went over there, to Mr. Gage's room, that night before he died, to see him about Harland again because I had found a letter of dismissal while I was snooping in his dressing table, addressed to Harland. After all that time I'd spent trying to show him how important Harland was to the troupe, how he simply needed more time to get himself right."

She wiped a tear away fiercely.

"As it turned out, Mr. Gage had only written that letter to show Harland he was serious. So that Harland knew he had it and could issue it at a moment's notice... Mr. Gage said he'd had lost his own father to the drink so was intent on the matter. But, you know what else? He told me he respected my efforts on Harland's behalf. That he'd guessed we were together and understood what it was like to love someone and not be able to show it."

"He really said that?" Arthur's voice trembled.

"He did. And gave me the letter to hold as a reminder of what was at stake, so I'd make sure Harland kept his promise." She sniffed. "Which is probably why I forgot my gloves when I left. I really loved the scent, though, and I'd already lost the matching handkerchief to the nail fiasco, so when I realized I couldn't replace them, I asked a maid to let me into the suite to retrieve them. But they weren't where I'd left them, and I only found one before I heard someone coming and had to leave."

"Oh, Marguerite." Arthur mopped his eyes with a black silk handkerchief.

Marguerite moved around the table, the ruffles of her white summer dress (her Mabel costume) swishing. She took his head in her hands and stroked the tears off his cheeks with her thumbs. "I wanted to tell you, but it was important no one know about it. We couldn't risk word getting back to Mrs. McGregor before we were ready. Though you needn't have come in here so angry—I know I've gotten myself in trouble being with the wrong person before, but I've learned my lesson."

Cassie looked back and forth between the two. What did Marguerite mean, she wanted to tell him? Were they not a pair? She chewed her gum faster. She thought that was why Arthur was jealous when he thought she was with Mr. Gage. But if she and Arthur weren't a pair, what exactly had Arthur been upset about?

Arthur sniffled and took Marguerite's hand. "Marguerite, dear, I've been keeping something from you, too."

"You have?"

Arthur pressed her hand to his cheek and closed his eyes. "I've also wanted to tell you for so long, but—as you know, some things are—complicated, even if they are joyful. I—" He took a breath. "I don't take notice of women. I mean, I notice them, but... Do you understand what I'm saying to you?"

"Yes, of course." Marguerite blinked calmly. "It makes perfect sense."

Arthur stared at her. "What? Doesn't this surprise you?" His eyes flicked to Harland. "Either of you?"

Harland shrugged disinterestedly.

"I'm not blind, dearest," Marguerite said, patting a stray curl back into place. "And I know you better than anyone. But what was there to talk about, if you were happy? As long as you're happy, I'm happy."

Arthur jumped up and hugged her close, lifting her off her feet. "You have no idea what a relief that is. So you understand why I've been so devastated since Mr. Gage's passing, and so tortured by the idea of his being with you."

Marguerite leaned back and regarded him. "What do you mean?"

"Mr. Gage and I were in love. True love."

Marguerite and Harland gasped together, along with Cassie.

"*That's* what's surprising to you?" Arthur stomped his foot. "What, you don't think someone like him could want someone like me?"

Cassie's mind flashed to the packet of admirer letters they had found in Mr. Gage's drawer, and the letters from angry husbands warning Mr. Gage away from their wives. She was lost again.

"No, no, that's not it." Marguerite echoed Cassie's thoughts. "You're entirely handsome and delightful. It's just that—he was always surrounded by adoring women. And there were *so many* women... It never occurred to me that—"

Arthur crossed his arms. "All of that was strictly professional, for fundraising purposes. He took no personal pleasure from it. He couldn't help that women loved him. But he did need them to contribute to the cause, which was particularly important to me, given my own upbringing without a stable family. We had a long talk about just that shortly before we came to this island. So what was the harm in an attentive word here and there?"

Harland knocked on a cell bar and raised his hand. "Excuse me, Miss Marguerite, may I say something now?"

"Oh, I'm sorry, dearest," Marguerite said. "Certainly."

"Thank you. What I've been trying to tell you all for many minutes now, while you were engaged in your personal revelations is"—it seemed his bristles had pricked back up—"the nails you mentioned didn't have the slightest thing to do with Mr. Gage's death."

16

———

Cassie's hands froze in the midst of retying her bonnet strings. Her mind was trying to race, but it hadn't a clue which direction to go in.

"What did you just say?" Marguerite whispered.

Harland pressed his face to the bars and called out loudly. "Say, jailor-man!"

The door cracked and Mr. Kriegel poked his head in the door. "Yes?"

"Any chance of me getting one of those cigarillos I saw in your pocket? I'll pay you double what it's worth. I've got to do something about this hammering in my head."

"Harland—" Marguerite said as the jailor came back into the room.

"One moment."

Harland put the cigarillo in his mouth and leaned forward so the jailor could light it. He took a long, glowing drag.

"That's better. Well, first off— No, stay. You should hear this." He stopped the jailor as he turned back toward the door. "First off, Marguerite, you clearly didn't hear that entire conversation with Mr. Gage. As my mother used to say, if you're going to eavesdrop, listen to the whole thing or you might miss all of it: After I told him I would put in the longer nails, I changed my mind. Those longer nails would have worked—probably—but when I asked who would be up there, how often, how much weight we were talking, that sort of thing, he said he didn't know yet. So I figured I ought to come up with something that could handle any of it.

"I left the short nails in, and on purpose. As mentioned, they weren't meant for weight-bearing, just holding the pieces together. Since they came out of the wood so easily, see, it made less work breaking down the set and moving it to the next place. Instead of fooling with those, I was going to put in a new type of support system to take on the extra weight. Using leverage and mutual pressures rather relying on than cumulative tensile strength alone."

Cassie nodded along with the others, wondering if they understood what he was saying, because she didn't.

Harland sighed. "I know it's technical. Basically, the boards are cut and arranged with an anchoring piece in the back locking it in. Kind of like the keystone on an arch. It's not an arch, but you get the idea, right? Point is, it's not about what nails you use because the weight is held in other ways."

They all dipped their heads down and up once more.

Harland paced the cell, his gaze fixed on the floor and his hands clasped behind his back as though he were trying to work out a complicated equation. "But I fouled something up. I calculated something wrong, drew something wrong, measured something wrong, cut something wrong, used the wrong piece of wood... I don't know which, though. I wasn't able to investigate what I'd done. Prince rushed everyone out so fast..."

He put his hands over his face and blew a breath out through his fingers.

"I should have double-checked it before Mr. Gage— Well, I mean, I would have if I'd known he was going up there. I'm sure I would have. But it had been weeks since we talked, and, despite his initial enthusiasm, he hadn't changed any of that blocking like he said he was going to, so I'd almost forgotten about it."

He picked up a glass from the tray by his bed and slurped a mouthful of water.

"Later, the coroner asked my opinion on that theory about the old wood and everything—as though any builder worth his salt, even a drunk one, would have thought those little nails could have supported anyone, much less a large man like Mr. Gage, even in a good piece of wood... I didn't know, of course, that Marguerite had changed out the nails... But regardless, I realized they had a theory and were obviously pleased with themselves, so, like a coward, I went along with it."

He resumed his pacing. "Even so, I wanted to know what I'd done wrong. When I finally got back in there to take a look at things, I saw the keystone piece had broken out, but I couldn't find it. It must have gotten thrown away, and the theater's bin had already been emptied by the waste hauler. I then tried to check my calculations, but I couldn't find my drawings. I mean, most of them were where I normally keep them next to my tool-box, if completely out of order, but not the ones I needed. Perhaps I'd decided at some point there was a better spot for those and I no longer knew where that spot was... Anyway, the bottom line is I knew my work failed and Mr. Gage fell. Eventually, I couldn't hold it in anymore."

Arthur smoothed his handkerchief on the table in front of him. "If you'll excuse my ignorance, Harland, I don't see how any of this leads to you being in jail. It all sounds like an accident. You didn't mean to hurt him, did you?"

"Certainly not!" Harland snapped. "But a man has died,

and it was because I didn't do my job properly. That technique I used is one hundred percent reliable when done right. Which means I didn't do it right. There's a legal term, for that, isn't there? When you do something poorly and someone dies as a result?"

"Negligent homicide?" Mr. Kriegel offered. Cassie hadn't realized he was paying that much attention.

"That's it!"

Cassie chewed on her nail. She wasn't sure it was. Negligent homicide was the killing of a person through gross negligence. Such convictions were usually reserved for egregious behavior like speeding one's carriage through a crowded square.

"Mr. McGregor," she said. "Do you really think what you did fell so short of the expected standard of care that—"

"I was drunker than Hell when I built it."

Cassie closed her mouth.

"Yes, very, very drunk. Drunker even than usual. And it was because of my drinking: I was angry Prince had complained to Mr. Gage about it, worried Mr. Gage might fire me because of it, annoyed Marguerite kept telling me to stop doing it... so I drank. No one should be trusted walking home in the state I was in, much less building something people were going to trust with their lives."

He sank down on his cot, running his hand over his hair.

"Christ. That's one problem with sobriety, I guess. When you stop drinking, you start to remember the things you did while you were drinking." He rubbed his temples. "Enough to be ashamed of yourself, at least."

"So, let me get this straight."

They all turned around at the sound of Sheriff Alderman's voice. He was standing by the door with Hughes and Jake, but Cassie had been so focused on what Harland was saying, she hadn't noticed them come in.

"If I'm to interpret what you've said correctly, your confession that night on the railroad tracks was not to murder, but rather to a mistake you don't have any actual evidence you made, which only possibly caused an accident resulting in Mr. Gage's demise?"

Harland spread his hands. "That's correct. 'Negligent homicide,' Or you could go with 'culpable carelessness'—I heard that somewhere once, too. But I think the situation is clear."

"Not exactly the word I would use." Sheriff Alderman turned to Hughes and Jake. "This isn't something you could have ascertained before bringing him in here with all that fanfare?"

Hughes fidgeted with his badge. "Well, he said he was responsible for Mr. Gage's death, which you'd think—"

"And everything else lined up," Jake said, "like how Mr. Gage had just dismissed him—"

"Actually, it turns out he hadn't." Cassie kept her gaze on the floor. "Miss Clifton said Mr. Gage never issued that letter to him. He'd only written it as a warning, to let him know he needed to get himself straight."

Much to the jailor's dismay, the sheriff responded by taking the last cookie and shoving it into his mouth. "What am I going to do with you two? Thank the good Lord I didn't call an inquest. I'd be as mortified as you should be right now."

He glared at them as he chewed angrily for several long seconds, crumbs tumbling down his beard. Finally, he turned back to the jailor.

"Kriegel, release this man. There's no way the state's attorney is going to want to hear from us about this."

"What? No! I'm guilty." Harland grabbed onto the bars and held the door shut as the jailor tried to open it. "And I need the jail time. It'll put cold, hard metal between me and the bottle—"

As Harland continued to resist release and Marguerite and

Arthur joined the effort to extract him from the cell, Hughes's gaze landed on Cassie.

She took an inadvertent step backward. His eyes, those incredible blue eyes that could lift her off her feet, had turned to knives and were cutting her to pieces. She knew the sheriff's words were echoing in his head right now, growing louder and beating him harder each time. And he blamed her.

He turned away toward the window, where a sun-dappled tree branch was tapping against the bars with ignorant gaiety, and Cassie almost fell forward, as though she'd been nailed to a post and suddenly released.

She was, of course, shocked herself at the turn of events and embarrassed by her own mistaken assumptions, but the stakes were far higher for him. And Jake, too. They had been competing for the deputy sheriff position for so long, and now it was possible neither of them would earn it.

Mumbling something about getting home, in case anyone cared, she left. Instead of heading up Third Street toward Centre and Flora's house, however, she started walking east across Cedar. She wandered along the empty street, the normally charming tropical front gardens that lined the road turned to creaking, sawing, hooting wilderness by the darting shadows. In the harbor behind her, hulking steamships lowed like cattle. Far in the distance ahead, the ocean crashed on a lonely shore.

When she came to a turn, she took it. She took the next one, too, then several more, letting her feet mirror the restlessness of her thoughts.

She was glad Mr. Gage hadn't in fact been murdered, but how had they gotten it so wrong? *No.* She kicked up a toeful of shells and dust. How had *she* gotten it all wrong. Hughes and Jake were right to be upset with her. It was her fault, after all, that so many people had been put through so much over the past couple of weeks.

Everyone had been ready and happy to follow Marguerite's explanation. It had been wrong in the details, true, but the ultimate conclusion, that it had been a terrible accident, not a murder, was the same. Would the world have been any worse off if they hadn't gotten the exact story right? And, judging by how adamantly Harland was insisting he be punished for his mistakes, he probably would have "confessed" eventually, anyway.

That was just it. Without her officious intermeddling, her insistence on involving herself and asking questions where no one else had any, everyone would have ended up in the same place, but with a lot less grief.

She tipped her head back to keep a tear from spilling. If it didn't leave the eye, it didn't count.

But still, Harland was *assuming* he had done something wrong, even if he had good reason to think so. What if, by some chance, he was mistaken, and someone else out there had actually interfered? After all, Mary had climbed that mast before Mr. Gage without incident, and if nothing else, Cassie's investigation had shown that Mr. Gage may not have been as perfect as he originally seemed. And it was now evident there were plenty of people who bore him ill-will...

She covered her eyes with her hands. *Oh, Cassie. When will you learn?*

Thankfully (sort of), she was jostled out of her thoughts by the cooked-foot smell of a passing waste-hauler's cart, and when she looked up, she realized she was standing in front of the Lyceum. Why had she come here? To relive her mistakes? To wallow in her shortcomings as some kind of twisted self-punishment?

The waste hauler halted his cart in front of the next house and stood on the driver's bench to peer over the fence. What he saw in there appeared to please him greatly: he punched the air and spun around, waggling his hips in what could only be described as a sort of celebratory dance.

He froze, his rear lifted in the air, when he noticed Cassie watching him. Whistling, he hopped down from his cart and opened the gate.

"It's been weeks since their waste box was full," he explained, unasked, as he lifted a receptacle from behind the gate and emptied it into the back of his cart. "My partner—he's the one in charge of all the money things, keeps the books and such—tells me I'm not allowed to haul anything until a box is full, since we charge by the box, and I don't get paid unless I haul, so... you understand." He finished his task and, brushing his hands on his trousers, climbed up and grabbed the reins. "We all work for money, right?" He clicked his tongue at his mule and headed off.

The waste hauler and his stinky cart made it about a block before Cassie turned around and sprinted after him.

"Wait!" She tripped on her skirts. "I need that garbage!"

Later that evening, Cassie dropped two unpleasantly fragrant pieces of wood on Flora's perfume counter. "These cost me ten dollars, but it was worth every cent." She took out a handkerchief with the vague idea that she'd wipe off the filth on her face from her recent dig through the waste-hauler's cart, but, after a brief survey of the rest of her clothing, she decided it would be about as pointless as polishing the doorknob on a ramshackle house. At least Danger and Luna were addressing her boots with their tongues.

Flora closed the box of beads she'd been seasoning with a dropper of perfume oil. "I'm going to need you to explain that slightly. What is this about?"

"Harland McGregor," Cassie answered and, to the dogs' chagrin, began to pace the room. Flora would probably prefer that to her sitting on the furniture in her current state, she decided, and, besides, her nerves were crackling too much to be still. Kleio watched her from her perch on a wigged mannequin head, her head flipping from side to side each time Cassie passed.

"The stagehand who confessed to killing Mr. Gage? Has he recovered well enough for the sheriff to record his confession?"

"Yes. I mean, he's well enough, though the sheriff didn't— It's a long story. But a couple of the troupe actors and I went to see him this afternoon, and he told us everything. Marguerite Clifton and Arthur Beath had plenty to say as well."

Flora rinsed her dropper in a bowl of water and dried it with a small pink towel. "Did they have something to do with the murder, too?"

"Well, to go back a little, it turned out Mr. McGregor wasn't confessing to murder, per se, but rather to a mistake he believed caused Mr. Gage's fall. Mr. Gage had tasked him with modifying the schooner set piece so that actors could climb it, but Mr. McGregor thinks that, due to his intoxicated state at the time, he did something wrong."

Danger and Luna were still following Cassie back and forth across the room, trying to lick her boots, and Roger the pig, who had decided that whatever was interesting enough for the others was interesting enough for him, was now following behind as well, *urmff*ing as he tried to keep up.

"Oh, my! I suppose that's good? That at least we don't have a murderer in our midst?"

Cassie paused, causing her animal train, which Esy had joined as a fluffy caboose, to jumble together. "Unfortunately, I think we do. And they are still on the loose."

"We—what?"

"Mr. McGregor doesn't *know* he made a mistake," Cassie said. "He *assumes* he did. But he didn't get to examine the piece that broke, the keystone piece that was supposed to hold it all together, because he couldn't find it. It wasn't the nails that were supposed to keep the piece together, by the way, but a different system entirely. Nor could he find his drawings of the set piece to recheck his calculations. Well, I found the broken piece, or pieces, I should say, in the neighbor's refuse, where someone from the troupe had thrown them away, much to the annoyance of that neighbor. I also searched the theater from top to bottom for those drawings, but I couldn't find them, either. Which might in fact support my theory..."

"Your theory?"

"That Mr. McGregor is wrong. He says if he'd done everything correctly, the piece wouldn't have failed like that. But his error isn't the only possibility. Outside intervention is another."

Cassie led the animal train back to the wood pieces and held one up, which Kleio took as an invitation to perch on it. Cassie tipped her onto the counter. "See? The edge is smooth until here, where it's splintered." She put that piece down and picked the other one up. "It's the same on this other piece, but opposite. I believe these are the two halves of the keystone piece, cut to a certain point, then broken the rest of the way. I know it belongs to the set because 'PP,' for 'Pirates of Penzance,' is written on it, along with 'SCHNR-1,' which, based on other markings I've seen, means it goes to the schooner. Prince showed me how Mr. McGregor labels the set pieces to aid in assembly."

"I see." Flora lifted the kitten off the counter so she would stop biting at the splinters sticking out of the wood.

"I also remember there was sawdust on the floor behind the schooner the night I went back to the theater with Paddy to get my money pouch. That must have been from when the piece was cut. Besides—I keep coming back to this—Miss Rutledge climbed up on that schooner mast only a couple of days before Mr. Gage did, with no problem whatsoever. So the cut likely wasn't made until shortly before Mr. Gage went up."

"Meaning—"

Cassie touched a finger to the wood. It was so ordinary, so harmless, lying there in front of them.

"The piece didn't break, Aunt Flora. I mean, it didn't simply break. Someone cut it to weaken it and ensure that it would break when Mr. Gage climbed on it. And that's about as intentional as it gets."

17

Flora gasped. "Who would do such a thing?"

Realizing how loud she'd spoken, she hurried over to close the door to the dining room, which she had propped open so the animals could pass through without ramming their heads into it (as had been their prior method of operation). "Sorry—Madame M is sleeping in the room off the kitchen, and I don't want to wake her."

Cassie leaned over the perfume counter, her fingers pressed to her temples. "That's what I've been trying to work out. It was someone who can read and understand set drawings, for sure. And had access to the set when no one was around... Though it doesn't appear the stage doors are ever locked, so that doesn't narrow it down much. And, of course, someone who wished Mr. Gage ill."

"But Mr. Gage seemed like such a nice man!" Flora picked up the kitten, who was pawing at the back of her arm. "So charming, and so selfless, setting up that charitable troupe—"

"Aunt Flora, there's something you should see. Or things." Cassie retrieved the Egmont pillowcase from her room and, much to the delight of the kitten and the bird, spread the miscellaneous contents out on the counter. Pulling each item in turn from the kitten's teeth or the bird's beak, Cassie explained.

"So you see, there were plenty of other people who were jealous of Mr. Gage and didn't have any tenderness for him to get in the way. And this, the little boy's letter of thanks that Mr. Gage showed us the first day we met him, I wonder if it was made up, in order to trick people into donating more money."

"Oh, no." Flora held up her hand as Cassie picked the prospects book back up and tried to show her one of the pages. "I don't want to know what he has in there about me."

"Most of it's not bad, really. It's just kind of—matter-of-fact. But, read together with my research into the charities, and considering where he stays, what he wears, what he buys... It makes me wonder if he wasn't taking some of the money for himself. Does private family income really fully support him? If so, why haven't we been able to contact anyone from the family yet? If he was doing something underhanded, did he have a partner, and did he perhaps have a falling out with that person? Who is the 'XX' mentioned over and over in the prospects book? It could be whoever that is."

"Might it have been Harland, still?" Flora asked. "Couldn't he have cut the beam himself then come up with another story to cover it up once he was cornered?"

"I suppose that's possible. He's the one who knew the most about the set, and whether or not he was dismissed, he clearly wasn't on good terms with Mr. Gage. But why would he have confessed, then? The first time, I mean."

"Good question." Flora paged absently through the packet of letters. "And you said Arthur was—involved with Mr. Gage? Are you sure nothing bad happened between them?"

"Mr. Beath admitted being jealous of the relationship he suspected between Miss Clifton and Mr. Gage, but he wasn't entirely convinced of it until after Mr. Gage was gone. And even then, it appeared Miss Clifton was the one he was angry with." Cassie chewed her gum thoughtfully. "On another note, I would say Mr. Wilkes hasn't been too broken-hearted about how Mr. Gage's demise has improved his career opportunities."

Flora hmmed. "Have you spoken with Mr. Reynolds?"

"Mrs. Reynolds's husband?" Cassie rubbed her nose. "No, but, right, we should. He and Mr. Gage got into a tussle at the Egmont gentleman's lounge recently about something, not sure what. And Mr. Wilkes mentioned overhearing a row in Mr. Gage's room that same evening." She grabbed at the air behind her arm. There was a loose hair floating around back there, tickling her elbow, but she couldn't seem to get a hold of it.

"Good. Because the letter he wrote Mr. Gage is slightly concerning."

Cassie grabbed at the elusive hair again. "What letter?"

"The letter you just showed me—the 'investible cuppance' one."

"Oh, we don't know who wrote that. The signature page is missing. Which was why I was going to take it to Mrs. Rydell at the post office and—"

"No, it's right here." Flora held up a page. "I think the pages were stuck together by whatever this sticky substance is." She brought the paper to her nose and took an investigatory sniff. "Mulled wine, I believe. With a lot of sugar."

Her annoyance at the hair she was chasing bordering on fury, Cassie lifted her arm over her head and stared under her armpit.

Flora put the letter down. "Is something the matter?"

"No, just a ghost hair." Cassie held the pose for a moment, then shot out her hand like a snake snatching its prey. "Got it."

"Uh, good." Flora washed her fingers in a shallow dish next to her elbow and wiped them off with a towel. "I was going to say, I'm not much for gossip, but, from what I've heard from Miss Porter, Mr. Reynolds's origins are rougher than his present circumstances might indicate. Long before he built his armaments empire, he worked as a building laborer. And apparently his less genteel roots show on occasion... I'd venture this isn't the first time he's been expelled from a club for fighting. Perhaps he was jealous."

Cassie fixed the cap sleeves of her dress. "I'll grant you, his background probably gives him the know-how, but does that mean he would commit murder, necessarily? I could perhaps see him doing something regrettable during a sudden fit of rage, but what happened to Mr. Gage was planned."

"Have you spoken with Jake and Hughes about all this?" Flora asked.

"Not the latest bit. Not yet." Cassie picked at the soiled lace on the front of her dress. "I think I've rather—embarrassed them in front of the sheriff. I want to be certain about this new theory before sharing it with them."

Flora squeezed Cassie's hand. "Just keep going. They'll come around, I know it. They respect you too much to do otherwise. Besides, you sound pretty sure to me. And, for what it's worth, I think for good reason."

Cassie tipped her chin up, never so grateful for anyone in her life. "Maybe once I run it by Harland."

"That's more like it. And you're going to figure this out, I have no doubt. You are your father's daughter, after all. And your mother's!"

Unfortunately, Cassie discovered the next morning that much of what she had planned was going to have to wait. When she arrived at the Florida House after breakfast, she found that Harland, having been unsuccessful at convincing the sheriff to keep him locked in the jail until the state's attorney could (at his insistence) evaluate a criminal negligence case against him, had locked himself into his room and thrown the key out the window. After that, the staff at the Egmont informed her that

Mr. Reynolds had left early for a hunting trip and wasn't expected back until the evening.

She was going to have to pick up the pace somehow, though. Today was the dress rehearsal, and the next day was the performance. After that, the troupe would disperse, and her window to figure out what the Hamlet was going on would quickly slam shut.

The dress rehearsal that afternoon proceeded in a similar manner to the previous rehearsals: chaotically, with plenty of tension and bickering. Miss Porter and Mrs. Reynolds, who had split the chorus into factions, waged a silent war. Mary couldn't stop fidgeting due to the abundance of talismans she was wearing under her costume. Arthur, between complaints about his trousers being too short, kept making up his own blocking. Marguerite was so distracted she missed entrance after entrance, and, by curtain, there were few cast members who hadn't stepped on Mr. Wilkes's Pirate King still-too-long cape, causing him to deliver half of his lines with a murderous undertone.

Throughout it all, Cassie eyed one person after another, trying to decide what a murderer looked like in costume.

Afterward, in an attempt to obtain some peace, Cassie tasked herself with taking Mr. Wilkes's cape and Arthur's trousers to Flora's laundress friend who had a shop kitty-corner to the Egmont, to see if anything more could be done to improve the fit. She was standing outside the laundress's house after dropping the items off, pulling out her tin of chewing gum, when a commotion broke out across the street.

Someone shouted, and a man ran down the Egmont steps, hotly pursued by Hughes.

"Not this time!" Hughes bellowed, twirling a candlestick over his head. He bounded across the hotel's lush front park, the green color of the thick Bermuda grass below his boots deepened by the rich light of dusk, and chased the man through a hedge of orange trees and cabbage palms. He spun to avoid a lamplighter who was trying to pass and leapt over a water trough, then halted at the edge of the shell road, windmilling his arms to avoid an inelegant deposit left by one of the elegant equipages that often waited there to carry guests to the sea beach.

It was an entirely inappropriate thought in the moment, but it occurred to Cassie that he slightly resembled Arthur's rendition of the cartoonish Sergeant of Police.

The fugitive tripped over a downed palm frond and, after a valiant but ultimately unsuccessful effort to right himself in the gravel, fell forward and landed with his arms splayed in front of him, sending a stream of papers shooting out of the case he was carrying. A moment later, Hughes landed on him with the enthusiasm of a professional wrestler.

Hughes flipped the man over.

"Ill-fitting coat! Churchwarden's pipe!" He threw open the man's coat. "Billy club." Tossing aside his candlestick, he stuck the pipe in his vest pocket and the billy club in his belt and held up the drawing he had made the other day. "That's him all right."

He turned to the crowd. "Ladies and gentlemen, I've captured the Theater Peeper!" He swept up a gold chain that had spilled out with the papers. "And, it seems, the Egmont thief as well!"

"I *beg* your pardon." The man, speaking with a ponderous English accent, struggled to sit up. He stiffened when he saw Jake, who'd followed them out, collecting the fallen papers. "You! Don't touch that! Those are private!" He wiggled out from under Hughes and grabbed the sheets from Jake's hands.

Jake glanced at the crowd forming around them. "Perhaps we should take him inside."

Jake and Hughes lifted the man to his feet as he finished stuffing the papers back into his case, his derby perched cock-eyed on his head, and walked him back across the grass and up the hotel steps. Cassie dropped her tin of gum back into her pouch and slipped in after them.

Mindful of her current standing with the officers, she slowed when they reached the lobby and followed the trio at a safe distance until finally, after climbing the hotel's entire four flights of stairs, they came to a heaving stop at the rooftop observatory.

Trying to catch her own breath as quietly as possible, Cassie crouched behind a potted fern in the hallway and peered out. Fortunately, the door was propped open with a statue of a very fat cherub, so through it she watched Jake and Hughes deposit the man at a wrought-iron table with two chairs. The screen of the lantern flickering on the table had a pretty vine-and-grape design that matched the pattern of the furniture, and, paired with the potted palms and magnolias arranged about the rooftop and the now-dark sky twinkling with stars above, it made the scene look more like an evening supper party than an inter-rogation.

"All right." Jake plucked a magnolia bloom and sat down. "Let's have a chat."

"No, no, Gordon. Like this." Hughes strode over until he was standing over the man, his hip even with the man's shoul-der, and smacked the confiscated billy club into his palm a few times. "So, Mr. Theater Peeper Creeper, what do you have to say for yourself?"

"What's happening, Cassie?" a voice whispered into Cassie's ear.

Cassie jumped soundlessly, her shoulder ramming into the chin of whomever had just spoken.

It was Prince. Thankfully, he had noted her clandestine stance and whispered his cry of pain as well.

Cassie held a finger to her lips then mouthed her words. "They have the peeper."

Prince scratched his head. "Tear half the paper?"

Cassie shook her head and repeated the sentence, curling her hands into circles in front of her eyes like binoculars on the final word.

"Oh, the *peeper*!" Prince craned his neck. "Why aren't you over there?"

Cassie gestured at him to wait. That explanation would take far too much haphazard miming to communicate.

"How about we start with what you were doing lurking outside of that woman's room down there," Jake said.

The man glared over at Jake then up at Hughes as he brushed off his hat. "How about we start with what *you* were doing lurking outside of that woman's room?"

Hughes glared back. "It's our job. Your turn."

An owl flapped onto the ledge behind them and sat for a moment, rotating its head and blinking.

"How do you know I wasn't simply walking by?"

"Walking by through the bushes where there's no path? Past a window where a lady happened to be undressing in her boudoir? Please. Besides, I know the difference between walk and a lurk. Especially when the subject matches the description of a known lurker." Hughes showed him the wanted drawing, then put it back in his coat with a righteous tip of the chin.

Next, he pulled out the gold chain he had picked up outside and dangled it in front of the man's nose. "So, whose room did you pilfer this from?" The chain was made from thick, heavy links, and, now that Cassie could see it more clearly, she recognized it as the doubloon pendant Mr. Gage had been wearing with his Pirate King costume the day she'd met him. She leaned forward for a better look. It was engraved "PK."

The man snorted. "I didn't 'pilfer' that from anyone's hotel room. I took it from the theater when I was looking for—" He stopped. "Blast."

Hughes shook the chain triumphantly, bumping a garden statue with his elbow. "So you admit you were lurking at the Lyceum, too. That seals it up: you're the one who was peeping at Marguerite Clifton in the Lyceum dressing rooms."

"That was an accident!" The man slapped his chair. "I'm no peeper. And I'm no thief, for that matter. I'm an investigator. I wasn't trying to see in the ladies' dressing room that day at the Lyceum. I was looking for—"

Before he could finish, Cassie's hand slipped off the door-frame, sending her face-first toward the fat cherub's remarkable belly. Prince had been using her shoulder as his own support, so he tumbled after her, and they let out matching *oof*s as they landed on the mosaiced tile.

Hughes turned and spotted Cassie. "You!" He noted Prince splayed on top of her. "And you!"

The owl flapped off with a declaratory hoot.

"Speaking of lurkers," said the man, folding his arms across his chest.

Hughes slapped the doubloon on the table, jostling the lantern and sending a quiver through the vine-and-grape shapes it was projecting on his chest. "I don't believe it. Or do I? I'm just on the verge of something, and here you are, again—"

Cassie righted the cherub. "I'm sorry. I wasn't trying to—"

"That Peanut case really must have gone to your head. Well, one investigation doesn't make you an expert. Or give you the right to stick your nose into everything else that comes along. Please leave. You, too, Mr. Montgomery."

Cassie's hand flew to her cheek as though she'd been stung. Did he really think of her that way?

"Actually, they should stay." The man leaned forward in his chair. "You're looking for thieves, right?"

"Oh, no," Jake said. "They're not thieves—"

"Yes, they are. Thieves of intellectual property. Just as was William Gage, along with the rest of his plagiarizing players!"

Hughes, his rage derailed by confusion, studied the man, then pointed the billy club at him. "Explain."

Giving a self-satisfied smile, the man plucked his pipe from Hughes's vest pocket and bit down on the stem with a regal chomp. "My name is Frances Dewey. I am a special investigator who has been hired on behalf of Mr. William Schwenck Gilbert and Sir Arthur Seymour Sullivan, and their financial partner Mr. Richard D'Oyly Carte, to track and enforce their dramatic copyrights in the United States."

"Copyright—rights?" Hughes lowered the billy club.

"That's correct." Mr. Dewey lit the pipe. "Perhaps a little background is necessary, however, to convey the weight of the duty which has been impressed upon me. You are no doubt aware of Mr. Gilbert and Sir Sullivan's extraordinarily popular and similarly nautically themed previous work, *H.M.S. Pinafore*, or, *The Lass That Loved a Sailor*? Well, that production, which had been painstakingly written, directed, and staged with the utmost care and detail by its creators, opened in London in May of seventy-eight.

"Over the next year, hundreds of unauthorized performances—many of which were bastardized versions of the masterpiece... burlesques, minstrels, children's shows, even barely understandable foreign-language monstrosities— sprouted like weeds all over the United States, and the men who were responsible for its existence didn't receive a penny. To add further insult, when they attempted to present an authorized American production in New York, they found their audience largely depleted after only a couple of weeks, as many had already seen inferior local performances.

"So, finally understanding the United States' interest, or lack thereof, that is, in preserving the copyrights of foreigners, the gentlemen vowed to protect their investment in their next show, *The Pirates of Penzance*, or, *The Slave of Duty,* by staging the official premiere in New York and thereby securing an American copyright. They went to great and expensive lengths to do so, rehearsing behind locked doors, employing guards to keep away anyone not belonging to the company... They didn't even give the English copyright performance, a small affair in Paignton, Devon, until the very same afternoon as the New York performance, so set were they on maintaining control of their work and preserving the integrity of their creation."

Mr. Dewey's voice shook with conviction.

"And yet here they are, years later, still being forced to wage battle against those attempting to plunder their valuable goods. So, I am tasked with hunting down plagiarist pirates and halting the offending activity. And I am prepared to use all means necessary."

Cassie glanced at the billy club in Hughes's hand. She didn't realize hunting copyright pirates could get as rough as hunting regular pirates.

"Which brings me to the present company." Mr. Dewey drew on his pipe. "If you'll forgive the pun. A few months ago, I was passing through a town in the state of Georgia after concluding another investigation when I heard someone mention having attended a performance of *Pirates* nearby, produced by a Mr. William Gage. It particularly caught my ear because I recognized Mr. Gage's name. He had been one of our own, a member of one of Mr. Carte's touring companies, but departed after that performance in Paignton. His abrupt departure, followed as it was by yet another company member shortly afterward, created rather a headache for the company."

He clicked his tongue.

"Well, you can be sure, he has not come to us for any license. Therefore, I did what I had been sent to do and set about tracking him and his troupe down. Only, he turned out to be savvier than I thought because, while occasionally I was able to arrive at a location following a production, I had trouble catching them the act, so to speak. There was no mention in any newspaper advertising an upcoming production, or even reporting on a past production—believe me, I've scoured months of dailies and weeklies from the region—and he never announced publicly where the troupe would be traveling next.

"I was about to abandon the effort when I found myself at a club one night next to a very drunk, and, soon thereafter, pugnacious, gentleman who provided some useful information. I had to piece it together due to his state, and his frequent and nonsensical use of a certain word, actually, non-word—what was it, 'tupperance'?—but the gist is he was displeased that his wife, who had recently performed in Mr. Gage's *Pirates* chorus, had declared she was going to join the troupe at its next location as well, which she had managed to discover from Mr. Gage himself. And that location was here, on Amelia Island."

Cassie crossed to the edge of the observatory and cast her gaze out over the sleepy houses nestling into their beds of flower gardens and trees below. He had to be referring to Mr. and Mrs. Reynolds.

Not that it's my business.

Prince fell in next to her. "I don't know what to say."

Cassie held her gaze outward. From here, she could see far up Beech Street, its distinctive omnibus tracks lit brightly by the moonlight on their way to the ocean.

She didn't know what to say at the moment, either.

Hughes jabbed the billy club in a planter like the sword in the stone. "I'm still waiting to hear how this justifies peeping at unsuspecting women."

"I told you—" Mr. Dewey sat forward with his pipe, spilling a trickle of ash on his knee. "I wasn't 'peeping' at anyone at the theater. I was trying to locate Mr. Gage's office so I could look for evidence to support our copyright violation claims. Such as that costume jewelry you keep brandishing at me."

Hughes lifted the doubloon necklace. "This is a costume piece?"

"Gracious, yes." Mr. Dewey gestured impatiently, spilling more ash. "I took it from one of the dressing rooms at the theater. The point is, knowing how cunning Mr. Gage was turning out to be, I wanted to be sure the case was as strong as possible, which meant gathering plenty of evidence, before I delivered the cease-and-desist notice so there would be no escaping paying us our due. That's the reason for the secretive manner of my work. You there, hand me my portfolio."

Mr. Dewey anchored his pipe in his teeth and gestured for his case. When Jake brought it over, he snatched it with the impatience of a schoolteacher and flipped it open.

"Mind you, it's private and proprietary, but I can show you my research, if that would make you believe me. In addition to a variety of documents outlining Mr. Gage's history and career in England, I have collected materials relating to his offending activities here in America on the traveling theater circuit—ticket stubs, costume sketches, props lists... Though, unfortunately, I lost one of my key items, which is why I was trying to get into Mr. Gage's hotel room tonight to find something to replace it."

"What item was that?" Hughes asked.

"Mr. Gage's personal *Pirates* score, with his handwritten notes on it."

"Oh!" Jake reached into his coat and pulled out a thick packet of paper. "You mean this music script thing?" He held up the packet Paddy had found in Miss Porter's back bedroom, which she'd given to him after he and Hughes returned from their unsuccessful manhunt. "You left it behind when you trespassed on Charlotte Porter's property."

"Gordon," Hughes said, "you were supposed to put that in the evidence box—"

Mr. Dewey hopped to his feet. "Brilliant! That's it. Return it at once, please."

Jake swung it out of his reach. "But it's not yours."

"Yes, it is. See the mark on the front, in the upper righthand corner? That means it was printed for the performance in Paignton. Below that you'll see the words, 'Proprietary and Confidential Property of DCOC.' It's the score that was issued to Mr. Gage for the performance, which he must have taken with him when he left the company. And used to create copies for his own troupe." He smoothed his lapel. "See? We have violations of performance rights and reproduction rights. And, given Mr. Gage's past with the company, there may even be a good argument for willful infringement—I've done my study of American copyright laws. That's why I was to serve him with this cease-and-desist order once I'd completed my file." He reached back into his case and produced a sheet of paper. He held it out to Prince. "Seeing where matters are now, how about I give it to you instead, Mr. Montgomery?"

Prince put up his hands. "Oh, I'm not in charge. That kind of paperwork goes to the stage manager at this point. He keeps track of everything of importance."

"Can you see that it gets to him, then? Let him know he needs to halt the show."

Biting his lip, Prince walked over and accepted the paper. When he had finished reading it, he held it out to Cassie.

She hesitated—she didn't dare look at Hughes, but she could feel the heat of his glower—then took it. Technically, this was Prince's business and he was asking for her opinion.

"It appears legitimate," she said after she'd examined it. "Based on what Mr. Dewey's told us, they are within their rights to ask this." Girding herself, she tried offering it to Hughes, but he just looked at her. Jake seemed unsure, so she gave it back to Prince.

"And you were in Miss Porter's house, Mr. Dewey, because...?" Hughes asked.

Mr. Dewey blew out a breath. "After Mr. Gage died, I got

wind of the fact that the troupe might be proceeding with the production anyway. I was trying to listen in and find out what was going on."

"How did you know that?" Cassie had tried to catch herself, but she was too slow, and now it was too late. "I mean, that the troupe might carry on with the show. You can't have, unless you were peeping somewhere else when—"

"What is it you Americans say? 'I'll take the Fifth on that.'"

Jake smoothed his coat. "So, all that sneaking around you were doing, stealing things—"

"Once again, I was simply trying to investigate my copyright case. And the only thing I took was the costume necklace. Any paperwork I have I copied then returned. Other than the score, which was ours to begin with."

"Ah." Jake thought for a moment. "How about... Can we see that research you said you had?"

"If you must." Exhaling a labored sigh, Mr. Dewey tipped the portfolio and poured the contents on the table. "The final piece I've been trying to put into place is how much profit is being made so we can calculate the damages for the lawsuit. But I can't find any bookkeeping records about how much money has been going in and out of the troupe. I found the pledge box at the Lyceum and the running list of pledges inside, but that's all prospective until the show is complete and the contributions are collected. And that's only for this performance, anyway. Overall, the financial picture of the troupe remains a mystery."

"Well," Hughes said, "we've been through Mr. Gage's suite and we didn't find anything like that there. There's plenty to indicate that Mr. Gage was an avid spender, but he didn't appear to have a similar enthusiasm for accounting."

Mr. Gage did say "maths" wasn't his strong suit. Cassie itched her arm. But how would one run a business, charitable or otherwise, without tracking that somehow?

As Hughes and Jake bent over the materials, Cassie drifted

to the opposite side of the table, and Prince followed. She let her fingers brush across one of the papers, and when no one objected, she started sifting gently through the heap.

As Mr. Dewey had described, among other things there were several ticket stubs from other performances the troupe had given. Cassie recognized the locations from the list Mary had made for her.

"He's right about these newspapers," Prince murmured. "I'm not seeing any reference to the troupe, are you?"

Cassie shook her head. Even though Mr. Dewey's search appeared to have been more comprehensive than hers, the result was the same: no news about the troupe. She had noticed, however, several mentions of petty thefts similar to the ones reported at the Egmont, all with the same odd mode of operation: The incidents occurred in the hotel rooms of wealthy individuals, but, while plenty of coin purses were missing, no major high-value items were taken. Most of the articles attributed the occurrences to childish pranks, but perhaps the information would still be of some use to Hughes and Jake. That is, if they were of a mind to take any more suggestions from her.

"The omission of references to the troupe is striking, isn't it." She made her voice a little louder. "It can't be that the performances were overshadowed by more interesting news, though, given the number of articles I'm seeing about missing pocket change."

She nudged the relevant sheets toward Jake and Hughes's area of the table with a disinterested shrug. To her surprise and relief, Hughes touched a finger to the pile. She lifted her gaze, and when their eyes met, neither of them looked away.

Jake cracked his knuckles and reached for another sheet of paper. "So it's all about the money, Mr. Dewey? What you do?"

All about the money. An idea started to seep into Cassie's brain, and, like water on a wool rug, it was hard to keep out.

"That's a bit indelicate," Mr. Dewey answered. "Technically, it's about preserving the incentive for artists to create by protecting their right to earn a living from their work, but, I suppose, yes. When you boil it down, it's about the money."

"But the show was for charity, not for personal profit. From what Cassie—Miss Gwynne and Mr. Montgomery have told us, Mr. Gage only used as much money as was needed to meet the company's costs, and even then, he squeezed each penny to its limit. All the rest went to charity. Doesn't that mean anything?"

Hughes grabbed a ticket stub as it cartwheeled away in the breeze. "Yes, isn't there something called 'fair game' or some other such legal term that relates to this?"

Cassie, in the midst of bracing herself against the influx of ideas into her brain—more had followed the first, and now they were piling up like cyclists yet to master the art of braking— tidied the papers in front of her. "Unfortunately, I don't believe the fair use doctrine applies here. A judge might take into account whether there was a commercial motive or not, but charitable intentions aren't an excuse in and of themselves."

Mr. Dewey emptied his pipe and put it away. "That is correct. And, for what it's worth, my personal conviction is that Mr. Gage's charitable claims here are, if you'll excuse my language, horse manure anyway."

"Horse manure?" Cassie heard Jake ask, though it was getting difficult to hear anything over her own thoughts.

"Take the accommodations he's taken here at the Egmont, to start. There are any number of other, far less expensive options, including either of the boarding houses where the rest of the troupe are staying. His choice of accommodations in other locations, as long as I've been tracking him, have been similarly extravagant. And consider his taste in clothing, his jewelry—I'm not talking about his costume pieces—his dining arrangements... He's been living a lavish lifestyle by any measure, so pardon me if I find his 'for charity' rallying cry somewhat challenging to get behind."

Cassie dipped her head. She had long been having the same thoughts.

"But wealthy people are often the most eager to participate in charitable endeavors," Jake said. "They say Mr. Gage had family wealth."

Mr. Dewey blew a raspberry, something Cassie had only ever seen children and goats do before. "That, my friend, couldn't be more wrong. Mr. Gage was orphaned at a young age and brought up in workhouses. I think it's safe to say his family has little to do with anything in his life."

Cassie bolted straight. A train had just run over the heap of cyclists in her brain.

Mr. Dewey dug through the papers on the table until he found what he was looking for. "Here. This is a workhouse record that will allow you a glimpse into Mr. Gage's upbringing in London. It isn't relevant to my case, only something I came across, so you can keep it, if you want. Take those useless newspaper clippings, too, or throw them away. I don't care."

Jake read aloud from the record:

Boy, aged eight, found living in abandoned building near Oxford Street with another boy of approximately same age. Answers to the name William Gage. Strong and possesses unusually large stature for his age, healthy enough to be put to useful work immediately. Requests not to be separated from his friend, but, as the other boy is small-framed and bears a notable squint, the significant differences in physical suitability may prevent placement together.

"So." Mr. Dewey, having collected the rest of the materials as Jake was reading, snapped the portfolio shut. "I'll assume the matter is settled, then." He tucked the billy club back into his belt and started toward the door.

"Mr. Montgomery," he called as he walked, "please inform

Mr. Gage's troupe that we will be sending a demand letter for moneys due once my report has been completed. We will also be requiring the return or destruction of any copies of the music that have been made."

"Wait a moment, Mr. Dewey," Cassie burst out, finally. "What would it take to get permission to perform the show just once more, tomorrow evening?"

"Cassie, what—" Jake started, but Cassie shook her head.

Too slow, too late. And she really had something this time, much more than something.

Mr. Dewey stopped and turned his head. "That would be highly irregular, given the circumstances."

"What if I told you that, if you obtain permission from your employers for us to conduct this one final performance, I'll get you the information regarding the troupe's financials you wanted? You could settle for statutory damages, but, what if, as you appear to suspect, actual damages are higher? Even considering willfulness, which will still require proving?"

Mr. Dewey turned the rest of the way around. "Go on."

Cassie folded her hands in front of her. "Here's my proposal. I'll personally pay whatever licensing fees you require, as well as cover production expenses including troupe salaries, in order to guarantee that every dollar that comes in as a result of the performance will go to feeding starving children. How could your employers say no to that?"

Cassie snuck a glance at Hughes. His expression was as inscrutable as always, but he still hadn't stopped her, which, in Hughes's world, was a lofty gesture—one which, hopefully, meant he was willing to trust her one more time. At least until she had a chance to explain.

"And don't forget," she went on, "regardless of your object, you did, in fact, trespass on private property when you entered Miss Porter's home. However, I believe Miss Porter would be less inclined to press charges if you cooperated with us on this."

Mr. Dewey considered her. "All right, Miss Gwynne. I'll try. Provided we get the appropriate verifications and guarantees."

"There's a telephone exchange in the lobby, and the hotel's telegraph is connected with the city's telegraph."

Cassie let Mr. Dewey into the hall, then shut the door.

"This may be superfluous," came Hughes's voice behind her, "but I trust you're up to something, Miss Gwynne?"

Cassie took a breath and turned to face him. "I believe I am, Co-*Pro Tem* Deputy Hughes."

"And what might that be?"

"If you're willing, I'd like to catch a murderer."

18

At a quarter after six the next evening, Cassie peeked through the proscenium curtains as Flora, who had been asked by the Lyceum Association to manage the front of the house, opened the auditorium doors to an eager audience. Rich velvets and shimmering silks flowed into the room, and the waves of color and texture, crested by brilliant jewels that sparkled in the light from the chandeliers, swirled and crashed against outcroppings of black dress coats and top hats. The swish of taffeta vied with chattering voices raised in greeting and laughter, and a powerful cloud made up of a hundred different perfumes rolled over the stage like a storm on the harbor. Looking around, one might have thought they'd accidentally wandered into the Academy of Music.

If anything, the news of Mr. Gage's accident and how Harland had turned himself in—and subsequently been released—had increased interest in the show. And not only among those currently on the island. According to the clerk at the Egmont, the hotel's bookings, already on the rise due to the usual late winter surge of seasonal visitors as well as the effects of a recent cold snap up north, had doubled over the course of the previous week. That morning, when a large group who had taken the Fernandina Express Train in from Jacksonville specifically to see the performance arrived, the clerk had had to spend the day finding rooms for them in the adjacent cottages because the hotel was fully engaged.

If all went the way Cassie expected it would tonight, they were in for far more of a show than they had bargained for.

She closed the curtain and tugged her pantaloons into place. She was still wearing a corset under her billowy pirate's blouse, but, unencumbered by her stiff bustle frame and the heavy layers of fabric normally draped across it, she felt much nimbler—and, hopefully, ready for anything.

Behind her upstage, the rest of the troupe and chorus were making final preparations. To one side, in the open area beneath the schooner, Mrs. Keene gleefully swished and jabbed her cutlass in a mock battle with some of the other pirate men. She was clearly taking to her new pirate's outfit as well, which wasn't surprising. The woman wore men's trousers and vests almost exclusively in her daily life and had spat out a half-chewed bite of banana when she saw the frock she was to wear as one of Major-General Stanley's giggling daughters. Opposite her, however, Miss Porter skipped by with a gaggle of chorus ladies swinging parasols and sun bonnets while Mrs. Reynolds and her own gaggle of chorus ladies skipped by in the opposing direction, trailing kites and sand buckets—none of them making any effort to avoid bumping shoulders when the groups passed one another.

Cassie felt for the Chinese coin amulet Mary had insisted she take back for herself. She wasn't the superstitious type, but tonight, she wouldn't mind a little luck.

"Good evening, everyone," Mr. Wilkes said as the cast and crew gathered for pre-show announcements. He climbed onto a crate with his amplifier cone. "First off, thank you all for being here, on time, dressed and ready to go, well ahead of curtain. Bravo. Give yourselves a round of applause."

He clapped a hand against the cone with a smile, but, seeing that no one else was joining in, he cleared his throat and raised the cone back to his mouth.

"Secondly, a reminder. Anyone with laces on their shoes, please make sure they're tied before you go onstage. We don't want anyone else tripping and tearing the seat on their pantaloons. Also, recheck your props and make sure they're in good repair. We're lucky that when Mr. Birch's cutlass came apart during the Act Two fight scene the projectile piece didn't injure anyone. What else... Oh. Please, please, *please* watch Mr. Manning for your entrances. He shouldn't have to throw things at people to get their attention when it's time to go on. Be sure to hit those consonants in every word, and, chorus, for the hundredth time, be aware of how you're standing. Always cheat out toward the audience unless you've been specifically directed not to. The audience isn't here to see your rear end."

Prince waved at him.

"Oh, and Prince has an announcement. I don't know what it is, but, apparently, it's important."

Prince, dashing in his Frederic-the-pirate ensemble, stepped forward, holding the cease-and-desist letter Mr. Dewey had given him.

"Thank you, Mr. Wilkes." He ran a hand over his short beard. "I know we agreed to discuss the future of the troupe once this performance was complete, but I thought it important to let you all know that, due to a legal issue that has arisen relating to the copyright for *The Pirates of Penzance*, continuing the troupe beyond this evening will not be an option."

Murmurs of surprise rippled through the group.

"There is the possibility of finding an entirely new show to do, but I understand there may be significant back penalties and liabilities with respect to *Pirates* that would have to be paid by the troupe first, so disbanding will likely be the preferable option."

"How is this the first we're hearing of this?" asked Mr. Manning.

"I was only informed late last evening, via this cease-and-desist we received from Mr. Gilbert and Sir Sullivan's company agent. The agent said a demand for damages would also be forthcoming." He handed him the letter.

Arthur smoothed the pleats on his now properly fitting Major-General Stanley trousers. "A problem with copyrights? I don't understand."

"Does that have something to do with permission from the writers to perform?" Marguerite blinked with worry as she fanned herself with her plumed fan.

"Exactly," Prince said. "We did not obtain the proper permissions to perform the show."

Marguerite pressed her fan to her lips. "That's really the end of it, then, isn't it."

"So what do we do?" Mrs. Reynolds asked. "All those people out there came to see us."

"Cassie Gwynne and I were able to arrange a limited license to allow us to perform this evening. The details are not important, but the bottom line is, for tonight only, we can proceed with the show, everyone will get their pay, and the charity will get its donation. So, let's make it the very best performance we can. For the audience, for the children, and for Mr. Gage."

Miss Porter raised her hand.

"Yes, Miss Porter?"

She shied slightly when everyone turned to look at her, then lifted her chin. "I have a suggestion. To make sure it's special for the contributors, too. Seeing as Mr. Gage won't be able to serenade or 'knight' the highest contributor onstage as promised—"

"Oh, I could still—" Mr. Wilkes started, but Prince stopped him.

"And what's that, Miss Porter?"

"I was thinking... Why don't we write the donations themselves into the finale as well, display the money as a part of the show? Then we can have the highest contributor pose with it while the whole cast sings the closing lines to them."

"That sounds very exciting, dear," Mary said. "How do you propose we do that?"

Miss Porter straightened her dress. "When the contributors come up onstage in a few minutes to deliver their donations, we'll have them drop them in a prop pirate's treasure chest instead of the troupe's usual donation box. Then, in the final scene at the ruined chapel on Major-General Stanley's estate, when Major-General Stanley announces his daughters will marry the reformed pirates, we'll page the drop curtain behind the chapel doorway to reveal the treasure chest heaped with money, along with a banner stating that the money is the 'pirates' bridal dower.'"

The group laughed.

"Then the winning contributor will get the serenade from the happy pirate–civilian couples."

"How delightful!" Mary said. "And very Gilbert and Sullivan."

"My only question is," Prince said, "how are we going to secure the chest during the show while we're all performing, since it'll be full of cash?"

"Oh, that's never been a problem in the past." Mr. Manning was scribbling in the prompt book, no doubt recording the proposed changes. "Normally, I simply keep the donations box next to where I'm calling cues. I have a chain with lock and key I put on it, too."

"Still—"

"And it'll be preset behind the chapel doorway at intermission," Miss Porter said. "Who'd try anything once it's onstage?"

"All right, then. Provided we bring the sheriff in to escort the donations to the bank vault after the show, it should be fine." Prince turned to Mr. Wilkes. "What do you say, director?"

"I say..." Mr. Wilkes hooked his thumbs under the edge of his cape as he looked around, seeming to grow taller to meet the title of "director." "That sounds reasonable to me. Now, let's get this traveling show on the road!"

"Welcome, ladies and gentlemen!"

A few minutes later, Cassie, working at a button of her pirate's blouse that refused to stay closed, watched Mr. Wilkes stride in front of the orchestra pit to address the crowd as they settled into their seats. After a moment, Mr. Wilkes realized that few had heard him, so he grabbed his amplifier cone from the edge of the stage and stood on a chair.

"Ahoy, landlubbers!"

A tinkle of laughter rippled through the audience and the chatter began to subside.

"That's better. On behalf of the Trip-along Troupe of Altruistic Actors and the illustrious guest chorus who will be performing this evening, thank you for coming to this very special performance of *The Pirates of Penzance*. As you hopefully already know, all of the money raised from ticket sales this evening, as well as the generous donations pledged by the chorus members, will go to feeding hungry children, so thank you very much."

He paused for a round of applause.

"Usually, William Gage, the head of the troupe, would be giving this speech. But, as most of you also know, a grievous accident has taken him from us. It was, and continues to be, a shock, but the troupe has unanimously agreed it is our duty to persevere so that we may honor his memory and fulfill the troupe's charitable purpose. Mr. Manning, if you would?"

Mr. Manning dragged a stool and one of the prop pirate's chests onto the stage in front of the curtain. With about as much showmanship as a stable groom forking hay, he propped open the chest, which had been emptied of its fake booty for the occasion, deposited a notebook and a pen on the stool, and walked back into the wings.

"Therefore," Mr. Wilkes continued, "I now invite the contributing chorus onstage to fulfill their pledges by signing the register next to their final contribution amount, in front of all of you witnesses, and depositing the corresponding amount into this pirate's treasure chest. Now, the chest will feature onstage in an exciting spectacle during the show, so keep an eye out! Or, avast ye, I should say!"

Another laugh from the audience.

"Be assured, as soon as the curtain comes in after the show, the chest will be escorted straight to the bank's vault for safe-keeping until an appropriate transfer can be arranged with the chosen charity. Thank you again and enjoy the show! We shall set sail once these swashbuckling scoundrels have finished walking the plank... off the stage!"

The audience cheered and applauded, and the orchestra struck up a nautical jig. The chorus members, dressed for their roles as pirates, policemen, Major-General Stanley's daughters, and other townspeople, paraded across the stage, stopping at the chest to sign the register and deposit their envelopes before moving on, each with a varying amount of theatrical flair. Some even elicited their own applause with spins, cartwheels, and, in one gentleman's case, a mimed bit pretending he had forgotten his money. Cassie gave a little pirate twirl-and-jab herself during her turn and, when the audience clapped in response, she couldn't help basking slightly.

There's nothing in the world like applause just for you.

She looked over her shoulder as she exited. Everyone, chorus and audience alike, seemed to be enjoying themselves, and the performance hadn't even begun yet. Perhaps there was something to this contributing chorus idea.

After the last chorus member had pirouetted past him into the wings, Mr. Manning called out, "Ten minutes, ladies and gentlemen! Ten minutes 'til places!"

"Ten minutes, thank you!" someone responded.

Setting his prompt book at the edge of the curtain, he ran out and dragged the treasure chest into the wings, then carefully locked the chain before picking the prompt book back up.

"Mr. Manning!" Prince leaned out of the dressing room door. "One of the chorus women has broken the handle of her picnic basket."

"Then she'll have to go without—"

"She can't. It's used in an action. Can you help?"

Mr. Manning glanced at the trunk. "Can't someone else—" He sighed. "All right, I'm coming."

He beckoned to Mary, who was nearby doing a vocal warm-up that consisted of singing one of Major-General Stanley's tongue-twisting patter lines in a series of ascending chromatic scales while pounding herself in the abdomen with a fist.

"Miss Rutledge, would you watch this chest while I take care of something? And don't take your eye off it for one second, you hear? It's— Agh!" He tripped over Metta, who was skipping by with a doll in her arms.

"Oops!" Metta's mouth formed a little "o."

"What the— Agh!" He righted himself, only to trip on Paddy, who was passing by in the other direction with a hoop and stick.

"Sorry, sir!"

The children giggled and ran off.

"Who let those children back here?" snapped Mr. Manning.

Cassie straightened the sash that was holding up her pirate's pantaloons. "That would be me. My apologies—Mr. Wilkes thought the villager scene needed more realism and asked whether I knew any children we could add to the crowd."

Mr. Manning wobbled. "Fine. But someone should have told me. Every change needs to be reported to me so I could add it to the prompt book. Everything—"

"Everything goes in the prompt book! *Everything!*" Arthur sauntered by, altering his voice to mimic Mr. Manning's. It was a striking imitation.

Mr. Manning shifted the book. "Uh, exactly. Well, you're responsible for cuing the children for their entrance, then. I'm too busy for another thing. Now, if you'll excuse me." He strode off, snatching up Mr. Wilkes's amplification cone as he went. "Seven minutes, everyone! Seven minutes 'til places!"

"Seven minutes, thank you!" someone responded.

Cassie checked over her costume once more then picked up her cutlass from the props table, mindful of Mr. Wilkes's admonition to ensure it was fitted together securely.

Showtime.

Right on time, the orchestra launched into the overture, and the show proceeded through Act One, set on a rocky seashore on the coast of Cornwall, England. Though many of the audience, according to Mr. Dewey's report, must have seen the production elsewhere before, they all tapped their toes through "Pour, O Pour the Pirate Sherry," sighed at "When Fred'ric Was a Little Lad," danced in their seats then swayed sentimentally at "Climbing Over Rocky Mountain" and "Poor Wand'ring One," and laughed through "I Am the Very Model of a Modern Major-General," reveling in each note and joke as if it were new and the best they'd ever heard. There was, understandably, some apprehension when "Oh, Better Far to Live and Die," the

Pirate King song, began, but Mr. Wilkes had removed all schooner-based blocking, so that quickly dissipated. Overall, Cassie was impressed by the quality of the performance, especially given the checkered set of rehearsals they'd had, and equally enjoyed performing and watching from the wings.

That is, when she wasn't carefully tracking each cast member's entrances and exits, searching for telling behavior.

Act One drew to a close without incident, however, with the pirates dancing, Major-General Stanley and the Pirate King waving their flags, and Ruth kneeling repentantly at Frederic's feet, and the curtain was called in. All had gone off exactly as it was supposed to—not a cue missed, every scene and costume change perfectly executed, and every prop in the right place at the right time.

After a short intermission fueled by hot peanuts from the roaster and orange slices prepared by Flora and other Lyceum Association volunteers, the audience drifted back to their seats for Act Two, and Cassie returned to the wings to watch the final part of the set changeover to Major-General Stanley's estate grounds. The riggers had already brought across the split traveler curtain that served both as a backdrop portraying the night sky and a screen to hide the schooner from Act One, so all that was left to do was lower the arch of the "ruined chapel" doorway. As the ropes began to slide over the pulleys, however, Cassie stepped backward. The sound still made her a little nervous.

Once all was in place, Arthur as Major-General Stanley strode to the bench at the center of the stage, and the women's chorus of girls arranged themselves around him. The orchestra began to play, and, at Mr. Manning's signal, the front curtain opened.

Cassie checked the scene list pinned behind her. There were a good ten musical numbers before she and the pirate chorus would make their next entrance. In fact, they wouldn't appear again until twenty minutes before the end of the show. She pulled a stool over. She would watch from there as she waited.

The show continued on, and Cassie, her face warming in the stage lights, hummed along as Mabel and her sisters sweetly consoled their guilt-ridden father, the Major-General, in "Oh! Dry the Glist'ning Tear," then guffawed along as the police squad prepared itself for battle in the hilarious dance-march "When the Foeman Bares His Steel" (which Cassie had always called "Tarantara," due to the repetition of the nonsensical but onomatopoetic word in the song). She sighed as Mabel and Frederic—upon discovering that Frederic had been born in a leap year so would not reach his twenty-first birthday, when he was to be released from his pirate indentures, for another sixty years—pledged to be faithful "till we are wed, and even after."

Again, for all their faults, she had to admit the troupe was good at what they did. Prince played a dashing yet naïve and earnest Frederic, his clear tenor voice both angelic and as warm as home. Marguerite was the sweetest ingenue Cassie had ever seen. Arthur shone as the quick-tongued Major-General Stanley, Mary handled the challenge of making Ruth both endearing and manipulative with ease, and, all in all, Mr. Wilkes made a compelling, if short-statured, Pirate King.

Cassie stirred from her thoughts when another set of voices began to sing behind her:

"A rollicking band of pirates we,
Who tired of tossing on the sea,
Are trying their hand at a burglaree,
With weapons grim and gory."

The pirate chorus! She leapt off her stool. Their first verses were sung off-stage before the pirates made their entrance, but she was supposed to be with them. She had let herself get caught up in the show, not paying attention to her cue—or anything else she was supposed to be paying attention to.

Patting the item she had tucked into her sash, she slid along the leg curtains to where the others were gathered and fell in next to Mrs. Keene, who, to Cassie's surprise, was singing expressively in a lovely alto tone. At the end of the verse, Mr. Wilkes held up a finger while Percy (as the Sergeant of Police) delivered a line and the chorus of police—softly singing *"Tarantara, tarantara"*—scattered and hid themselves behind various trees and rocks. Then, inhaling as he slowly lifted his hand, he chopped the air and whispered "Go!"

Needing no further encouragement, the pirates leapt, danced, and stomped onto the stage with ostentatious showmanship, singing in ironic contrast:

"With cat-like tread,
Upon our prey we steal;
In silence dread,
Our cautious way we feel!"

Cassie remained in the wings, staring after them. Mr. Wilkes had given the cue. Under normal circumstances she might not have thought much of that, but tonight...

She started backstage, her nerves firing in random but intense bursts all over like tiny fireworks. A few feet away from the wings, however, the light from the stage lamps faded, so she had to grope her way to the wall to grab one of the portable backstage lanterns from under the stairs. Cursing when the match flame bit her finger, she lit the lantern and turned back.

Ice trickled down her spine. Beyond the middling sphere of light from her lantern—designed to provide only the minimum glow needed to make one's way, so as not to interfere with performances—there was only darkness. Darkness that had been merely eerie before but was now heavy and ominous, pressing in from all sides like ocean water when one dives too deep. Onstage, the performance continued, sprightly as ever. Rather than easing her sense of foreboding, however, the contrast between the onstage world and the off-stage world, one filled with light, music, and voices and the other dim and hushed, intensified it instead.

Inhaling, she crept forward, using her free arm and her feet as much as the dull gleam of the lantern to bump her way through the minefield of ropes, costume racks, and set pieces scattered about. She was grateful more than once for the long-sleeved blouse and sturdy boots of her pirate's outfit.

Finally, she reached the edge of the traveler curtain and slipped into the space behind it, in front of the schooner. She slowed her pace even more, wary of tripping over an unlit foot-light, or knocking into the backdrop and causing a ripple in the starry sky.

Onstage, barely audible over the heartbeat throbbing in her ears, the company roared with John Philip Sousa–like enthusiasm:

"Come friends, who plough the sea
Truce to navigation
Take another station!
Let's vary piracy
With a little burglary!"

She rubbed her eyes. The strain from trying to see in the weak light was making what little she could see blur together.

Just a little farther.

She planted one foot, then the next. She hunched forward, her walk becoming a shuffle, and put out a hand in front of her to feel her way—

And grabbed a face.

19

Cassie swung the lantern to meet her hand, and there was Mr. Manning, squinting through her fingers.

She drew back and lifted the lantern higher. The dark clothing he wore as his backstage crew attire made him almost invisible aside from his head—and his hands. One of which was in the treasure chest, which they had preset on a table behind the split in the curtain, wrapped around a fistful of bills.

Mr. Manning dropped the money and straightened up, letting the half-filled carpetbag that was on his shoulder fall to the floor.

"You've missed your entrance, Miss Gwynne. You should be onstage right now with everyone else." His lips tightened, fighting off either a smile or a scowl. Cassie's bet was on the latter.

"I was waiting for my cue."

On the other side of the curtains, Arthur/Major-General Stanley wandered the garden in his sleeping gown, singing:

"The man who finds his conscience ache
No peace at all enjoys;

And as I lay in bed awake,
I thought I heard a noise."

Mr. Manning pursed his lips. "I told Mr. Wilkes to give the pirate chorus their cue. I should have known if you want something done right, you have to do it yourself, especially when it comes to actors—"

"Oh, he gave it. But I was expecting it to come from the stage manager."

"I had to use the necessary."

"Huh." Cassie sniffed the air, keeping her eyes on his. "This doesn't smell like a privy. But what you just said does."

Mr. Manning nudged the carpetbag farther away with his toe. "What exactly is it that you want?"

"I want to know what you're doing back here alone with this trunk full of money."

"I don't have to explain myself to you, but, if you must know, I was getting it ready for its upcoming feature—"

"Stop." Cassie put her lantern on the table. "Mr. Manning, given that we're not in an outhouse and there's a half-filled carpetbag at your feet, we might as well be frank with one another. You were going to run off with that money."

"I beg your—"

"Because now that the troupe can no longer continue its *Pirates* tour, neither can the ruse you've been conducting over these last few years, bilking charitably minded people out of their money."

Mr. Manning, always so articulate, sputtered.

Cassie pressed on. "That's why I brokered that deal with the copyright enforcement agent for the show to go forward tonight, to give the guilty party an opportunity to make a final grab for the money and reveal himself. And whoever was planning to help himself to the contributions was going to have to do so before curtain, since this was the troupe's last performance, and afterward, unlike with previous shows, there would be others shepherding the money along to its proper destination. Because that's what this was all about, right? And why you killed Mr. Gage? The money?"

Mr. Manning backed against the treasure chest. "That's—ludicrous! I didn't kill Mr. Gage, Harland McGregor did, with his shoddy, drunken workmanship. It's an outrage, someone of his experience thinking wood of that condition would hold up with people climbing on it, whatever kind of nail you put in it. Especially after Mr. Gage, who's twice the size of your average man, put in that blocking change for the Pirate King number. Mr. McGregor should have known better. It's worse than negligence."

"By 'wood of that condition,' I assume you mean sawed nearly through." Cassie held one half of the broken support piece to the light, making sure Harland's markings were visible. She'd been carrying it in the belt of her sash since intermission, though the other half was tucked away safely in Hughes and Jake's evidence box. "Because if that's the case, I assure you Mr. McGregor had no idea."

Mr. Manning's face slacked. "I—don't know what that is, or why you're showing it to me." He folded his arms across his chest, turning his head from the block of wood like a baby being force-fed strained peas. But Cassie thought she saw his fingers tremble.

"Unfortunately, I don't believe you." Cassie stuck the block of wood back into her sash and folded her own arms. "In that rant you just gave about Mr. McGregor's so-called negligence, you confirmed something for me about who knew of Mr. Gage's plan to go up that mast. Mr. Gage didn't tell Prince about the blocking change until right before rehearsal that day, and Miss Clifton, who was standing next to Prince, learned about it at the same time. As the backstage was swarming with people by then, there was no opportunity at that point to do any sawing unobserved.

"You, on the other hand, learned about it as early as the day before. When I saw Mr. Gage that afternoon, he mentioned he would be meeting with you later about 'adding a blocking change to the book.' And in any event, as you like to remind us all constantly, the stage manager must know about everything that goes on in the show and record it in the prompt book. I doubt Mr. Gage would have dared change the blocking like that without giving you ample notice.

"For good measure, I'll also point out that Mr. McGregor didn't know about the blocking change at all. He'd modified the set piece some time before so it would be possible, at Mr. Gage's request, but he hadn't been informed of any actual plans to do so. Also, if this wood had been sawed like this when Mary Rutledge was swinging from the mast a couple of days before, she would have fallen, too. It was a trap, set by you, and it was meant for Mr. Gage."

Mr. Manning's eyes flashed with indignation. "But how would I know to do whatever you're saying I did, even if I had wanted to hurt Mr. Gage, which I didn't? And what's all this about sawing a piece of wood? It was the nails—"

"Gracious," Cassie said. "You're still keeping on with that? Fine. We'll talk about who knew about the new support system Mr. McGregor had built for the schooner. This will be quick: Mr. Gage requested it and Mr. McGregor built it, but that's a given and largely irrelevant. Miss Clifton eavesdropped on the meeting where they decided on it, but she missed the relevant part of the conversation—as evidenced by her ill-planned effort to cover up what she thought was Mr. McGregor's mistake regarding the nails.

"But you, as the stage manager and keeper of the prompt book, were certainly a part of that meeting with Mr. McGregor and Mr. Gage, if only to listen and record. Or at least informed of it shortly afterward. Mr. McGregor has confirmed that."

Well, he will, as soon as we get him to come out of his self-imposed bunker at the Florida House.

Cassie's gaze slid over to where she'd spotted the prompt book under the table. He must have put it down to free up his hands so he could load the money in his bag.

"Poor Mr. McGregor," she said. "He was in agony for so long, wondering what he did wrong with the support system. But he couldn't find the broken piece to examine it, or the plans he drew for it to check his calculations and measurements... Because you took them, right? But I found the broken piece, and, fortunately for Mr. McGregor, it clearly shows that someone sabotaged the schooner. If the missing plans, which are normally kept with Mr. McGregor's toolbox, are in your prompt book, I think it'll be pretty clear that you had exactly the information you needed to be that someone."

As she was speaking, Mr. Manning's expression had progressed from surprise to indignation to distress to anger. At the moment, it was hovering close to fuming.

Cassie decided to help things along and see what would happen. "So, why did you kill Mr. Gage? Did you have a falling out over the profits? When I learned Mr. Gage was an orphan and didn't in fact have family wealth, I knew he had to be benefitting from the troupe income. Or, perhaps he was in the dark as much as everyone else, and thought all his blessings, arranged by you to keep him happy, were a result of gifts from wealthy donors, or charitably volunteered—Miss Porter's contribution was free accommodation for troupe members, after all—but he discovered your scheme and insisted you end it..."

She gave an exaggerated nod. "Yes, that makes sense. Oh, dear. Everyone will be so devastated when they learn how you pulled the wool over the eyes of such an admirable man for all that time, causing him to unknowingly defraud hundreds of well-meaning citizens. Perhaps they'll even want to start a memorial fund—"

"It was *Gage's* bloody idea!" The words exploded out of Mr. Manning like the scream of a kettle at boil. It was unlikely anyone else had heard, though, because the outburst coincided with a round of raucous applause and cheering following a musical number.

But Cassie could still hear that he'd lost his American accent. As she'd suspected, he was English, too.

Cassie and Mr. Manning faced each other in the dim lantern light, each seemingly calm on the outside but, on the inside, poised to pounce. Then, as though their gazes were linked, they looked down at the prompt book, which was still under the table.

"Forward, my men, and seize that General there! His life is over!" Mr. Wilkes (as the Pirate King) shouted.

As though heeding the onstage exhortation, Cassie and Mr. Manning both fell on the book, but Mr. Manning tore it from Cassie's grip and clutched it to his chest. And, Cassie noticed, now there was a gun in his hand.

She suspected it was no prop.

She resisted the urge to look over her shoulder. *Where are Jake and Hughes? They should have been here by now.* She had been proceeding as confidently as she could, confirming the identity of the murderer and keeping him from getting away, like she, Jake, and Hughes had planned, but she was running out of things to say.

"As I was saying," Mr. Manning hissed, "Gage is the one who came up with the whole thing. Soon after we joined Carte's touring company, he as a bit player and I as an assistant to the stage manager, he started to gain real notoriety as an actor for the first time... And to notice how effortlessly he could have women, including rich women, eating out of the palm of his hand, willing to do anything he asked in return for a smile and a wink.

"His charm had power. I suppose I'd always known that. It'd been that way since we were children, the lucky bastard. But he'd never really noticed it before. Well, he got a little drunk with it, so to speak, and one day he got word the authorities were thinking of coming after him regarding a scheme he'd run on a lonely dowager. So, after that performance in Paignton —we'd been engaged to do a quick, informal staging of *Pirates*, which had just been written—he suggested we part ways with the company and make our own fortune."

His nose scrunched and unscrunched as he spoke, wiggling his eyeglasses.

"He asked me, 'You ever hear of the "American confidence man"? A brilliant, sophisticated creature who doesn't need to snatch or fight to steal, but rather wins his victims over so thoroughly they simply give him what he wants, willingly? We ought not let our English origins keep us from our true calling. Let's go to America and try our hand at the trade. You wouldn't believe the fortunes growing there. There are people with so much money they compete with each other for the honor of giving it away.'"

He leaned back slightly, but he didn't relax his grip on either the prompt book or the gun.

"Well, it turns out he was right about that. He also figured out that these American society types loved to play and would be even more eager to contribute when presented with the opportunity to be in the limelight themselves. Thus was born the 'contributing chorus.'

"We quickly fell into a natural division of labor as partners. He'd drum up pledges and direct the shows, and I'd handle all the other details. And by that, I mean everything that mattered, like the money. I managed the funds coming in and out and selected the charities we would say we were sending donations to—I was sure to pick real ones, for nodding recognition, but nothing big that people might already be involved with. And, after meeting our expenses, I might donate a little something to get the troupe's name in their records, if they had them, but keep the rest for Gage and me. And it was hard work, too, making sure we spent as little as possible on lesser matters like the production."

Partners.

"So, you kept the financials, then," Cassie said. "I'm guessing, also in that prompt book of yours." That would explain why no one else, including Mr. Dewey, had found any records of the money passing in and out of the troupe.

Mr. Manning pointed at the prompt book with the gun. "Everything goes in the prompt book."

Cassie shifted uncomfortably. *Truly, where are Jake and Hughes?*

"Whose idea was it not to print any publicity for the performances in the local papers?" She'd just have to keep him talking.

"Mine. No need to leave a trail of information for anyone to see and start putting two and two together." Mr. Manning puffed out his chest. "I told you—I handled anything that was more than what a simple actor's brain could handle. I also set the strict one-show limit for each location. And insisted on only hiring troupe members whose careers were in such disarray they were unlikely to leave or speak up, even if they figured anything out."

"Did they? Figure anything out?"

"Of course not." Mr. Manning gave a derisive snort. "I needn't have worried. Actors are reliably self-absorbed and don't notice anything unless it impacts their stage time. Someone did raise a question once about how Gage could afford his lifestyle—Gage did love pretty and expensive things—but all I had to do was throw out some generic story about family money and they were satisfied. Not terribly inquisitive minds, these folks."

"You still haven't told me what happened between you and Mr. Gage, though." Cassie thought about the block of wood in her sash, trying to decide what kind of weapon it would make. "From what I understand, you've been close a long time, starting when you were found together as orphans. A report I saw said Mr. Gage asked that you not be separated. He even kept a photo on his nightstand of himself and another boy—who I assume was you before you were fitted with eyeglasses, based on the squinting. Then you continued on into adulthood together, obtaining employment in the same theatrical companies. What could have made you do what you did?"

Mr. Manning glowered at her. "You know a lot. Perhaps all the time you've been spending with that nosy Mr. Montgomery has rubbed off on you."

Cassie tried to still her fingers as they tapped against her leg. She was really starting to worry that something had gone wrong with Jake and Hughes.

"You didn't answer my question," she said. "About what happened between you and Mr. Gage?"

Mr. Manning listened to the activity onstage. The police and pirate choruses were still chasing each other about in their grand fight scene, accompanied by a jaunty orchestral interlude.

"Fine, I have another minute or two. Well, I blame that vapid Arthur Beath. Apparently, he told Gage a sad story about how he'd been a hungry child himself and that changed Gage's whole view on the matter. Would you believe it? The man finally grew a conscience because some passing person told him it meant something to him."

Cassie sucked in a breath. *He doesn't know about them.* Astonishing.

"A couple of months ago, at our last location, we were having a normal production meeting when Gage told me he wanted to end it. That he wanted to turn us into a legitimate, charitable troupe, donating our proceeds the way we'd been claiming. Starting with the upcoming show in Fernandina. I was aghast! He was the one who had started it all, and now that things were so good, he wanted to stop? Suddenly, there was right and wrong? For the first time in our lives, we had money. And not just a little bit of money. Enough to waste.

"I tried to explain to him it wouldn't work, financially. That we spent everything as quickly as it came in... That once we ended the scheme, we'd be as poor as we'd ever been again in no time. But, like many who suddenly find themselves with money, he either forgot or no longer believed he could ever be otherwise. Instead of listening, he told *me* that if I didn't do as he demanded, he would confess everything, expose us. Expose *me*. For what was all his doing to begin with.

"Not having any other option, I pretended to agree. But there was no way I was going back to the way things were. Not having been through what we'd been through. Do you know what that's like, Miss Gwynne? Being truly poor? Waking up every day knowing you will always be working your way from meal to meal, never able to catch up enough to do anything more than grovel for the next dollar, for the rest of your life?"

He sneered. "What am I saying? Of course you don't. So, you'll have to trust me. In any case, once I had experienced what it was like to be something else, I was never going to live like that again."

He gulped the air, either breathing or choking. "So, my only option was to remove him and take everything on myself. But I still wavered. I loved him, in my way. We were like brothers. Besides, I didn't know how I would accomplish—it.

"When I noticed all that superstitious angst Mary Rutledge was stirring up, though, I had a thought. With a mindset like that, if there were an accident of some kind, minds would be quick to explain it with the curse. So, I fed the story a bit, causing small and harmless, but potentially alarm-inducing incidents like dripping lighting oil onto the stage as though it were leaking, causing special effects to fail, getting costumes taken in or out—"

"And moving and stealing props?"

"Certainly not," said Mr. Manning. "One doesn't fool with other people's props. That's a cardinal sin in theater."

That's where he draws the line. "How about the disembodied singing? And the ruined chapel arch slipping its rigging knot, nearly falling on me—"

"Even if Mr. McGregor's drinking didn't cause Gage's demise, Miss Gwynne, it doesn't mean it was harmless. Mr. Montgomery was right about that. I'd already had to fix those ropes more than once myself, after he'd been up there. But, as for the so-called disembodied singing, who knows? Maybe there is a ghost, after all."

Cassie bit her lip.

"Anyway," Mr. Manning continued, "I was laying the groundwork, but, as I said, I still wasn't sure whether I would go through with it. Until Gage and I had another fight a couple of weeks ago. A big one, in that expensive suite he insisted on despite his grand plans to be a philanthropist without income. I saw that he'd made a sizable donation to a random orphan welfare organization in Philadelphia, nearly all the cash we had left. And large enough to possibly attract some attention. I told him he'd put us at risk, and he said it didn't matter, since we were going to be legitimate now anyway. That's when I knew he'd truly made his mind up—so I made up mine.

"Soon, a golden opportunity presented itself. When he told me he was going to go up on that schooner mast, I remembered the discussion he'd had about it with Mr. McGregor and knew that if I undermined whatever had been done to reinforce it, he would fall. And I'd seen all the fighting going on over Mr.

McGregor's drinking problem. He'd make the perfect scape-goat, if people weren't distracted enough by the curse.

"I went back to the theater, pulled Mr. McGregor's plans from his stack by the toolbox and figured out what needed to be done. I was a stagehand for many years myself, so I knew what I was looking for. And it turned out to be disturbingly easy. All I had to do was cut one piece. After it went over, I planned to leave the piece just long enough so the coroner could see that something had broken—he'd have no idea what he was looking at, only that a drunk man had fouled something up. Then I could 'clean up' and get rid of the pieces in case Mr. McGregor got it in his head to look at them. In his constantly befuddled state, he'd never know for sure what had gone wrong.

"The coroner's conclusion about the nails was unexpected —I believe I have Miss Clifton to thank for that—but it still worked. It was all the better, in fact, as it avoided scrutiny of the real issue entirely. So I played along."

On the other side of the curtains, the pirates sang "Hymn to the Nobility," trying to save themselves by claiming to be noblemen gone astray.

"How did you find that, anyway?' Mr. Manning nodded his head at the wood piece in Cassie's sash. "I threw it away, but not in the theater's bin. Intentionally."

"I dug it out of the neighbor's trash." Cassie tucked her hair behind her ear matter-of-factly.

"Right." Mr. Manning climbed to his feet, picking up the carpetbag. He put down his prompt book and resumed filling the bag from the chest.

"What are you—"

"Don't worry. I'll still answer your questions. But you'll have to be quick about it. I believe the finale is approaching."

Cassie scrambled internally. What did he mean, be quick about it? Did he think he could get away? Well, he might just do that if Jake and Hughes didn't hurry up and—

Oh no. She was supposed to signal Hughes and Jake when it was time by opening one of the stage doors and hanging her Chinese coin amulet on the outside knob—and she had completely forgotten. Either they were going to realize that at some point or she was on her own.

"Did you really have to kill him?" she blurted out, trying desperately to think of what to do next. "Your partner, and friend? You could have done what he asked, given it a try as a legitimate charity, or as a regular traveling theatrical troupe. Or even walked away. How could you have chosen money over the closest thing you had to family?"

Mr. Manning finished filling the carpetbag and threw it over his shoulder. "I told you that already, Miss Gwynne." His eyes glinted, and along with the metal on the gun. "I wasn't going to risk being poor again. Not for anything. And I'm not going to now, either."

Faster than Cassie could blink, he threw the lantern over, shattering the glass chimney and causing a trail of oil and fire to shoot across the floor, then hurtled headfirst through the break in the curtain, through the arch of the ruined chapel doorway, and onto the stage, where the full company was entering the finale.

Two shots rang out, followed by the ping of bullets striking the ceiling—Mr. Manning had fired a gun into the rafters. The choral harmony fell apart into screams.

Yet still Cassie stood frozen, caught between following Mr. Manning and putting out the fire blazing at her feet. That was probably by design, to slow her down. And shooting off his gun was a perfect way to stir up mass chaos—and provide himself an unmolested exit right through the front door.

Cassie didn't suppose one would make it far as a "confidence man" being slow of wit.

Giving herself a massive mental kick in the rear, Cassie tore off her pirate's blouse and threw it over the blazing lantern while she stomped at the fiery oil. Her boots were effective—but her blouse was not. The fabric was too light, and instead of putting out the fire in the broken chimney, it burst into flames itself. She needed something heavier. But what else was there? She threw a glance around, then, gritting her teeth against the pain, scooped up the scalding bundle and heaved it into the empty treasure chest. She slammed the top down, counted, and opened it back up—the lantern was dark, snuffed out like a candle.

Another gunshot sounded onstage.

Taking a diver's inhale, Cassie turned and plunged through the curtain.

"Stop! Murderer!" she yelled into the pandemonium. "Mr. Manning killed William Gage!"

Around her, pirates, (fake) policemen, and middle-aged maids in nightdresses bumped into each other and tripped over set pieces. Mary and Marguerite clung to one other on the edge of the fountain at the center of the stage. Mr. Wilkes slipped on a mess of bills (it seemed Mr. Manning's carpetbag had spilled), then tried to steady himself by grabbing first onto Vera's torso then onto Theresa's. The women responded by shoving him to the ground. In the orchestra pit, instruments clanged as the musicians clambered to get out. Beyond them, the audience was a roiling pot of furs and sparkle.

But where was Mr. Manning?

Then she saw him. He was standing over Prince, who lay by the top of the stairs, blood seeping onto the stage from beneath him. That final shot hadn't gone into the rafters.

Spotting Cassie, Mr. Manning turned and charged down the stairs into the stampeding audience. Cassie raced after him, fat, hot tears nearly blinding her. Her arms roared with pain from where the lantern had burned her, and every few steps, she was knocked back by a panicked patron searching for safety.

She threw and kicked aside anything and anyone that got in

her way, and she'd almost caught up when she saw Flora throw the front doors shut at the back of the house and turn to face the incoming Mr. Manning.

"No, Aunt Flora! He has a gun!" Breathing too hard to shout again, Cassie grabbed a chair and hurled it at Mr. Manning. She hoped to distract him at least, but she missed, badly, and it clattered uselessly to the side without drawing so much as a glance. Then her foot caught an abandoned umbrella and, as he lifted his gun and took aim at Flora, the world slipped upward.

But no shot came.

Instead, right as her chin cracked against the floorboards, she heard a thud, a clang, and a smash, then the tinkle of glass, followed by the thunking of a hundred little somethings hitting the ground all at once. She squeezed her eyes open.

Mr. Manning was sprawled in a pile of peanuts against the wall, unconscious. And over him, next to the mangled remains of the peanut roaster, stood Arthur Beath.

Tears streamed down Arthur's face as he glared down at the motionless man, leaving black battle streaks in their wake. "That was for William." He kicked Mr. Manning's feet into the wall. "And that was for the rest of us. You *fiend.*"

Jake ran toward them down one of the aisles, and Cassie, remembering Prince, hurried in the opposite direction back to the stage. She found Hughes helping him sit up.

"You're alive! Thank God!" Cassie kneeled and threw her arms around Prince's neck.

"Ouch."

"He's lucky," Hughes said, pulling Prince to his feet. "The bullet only struck his shoulder. But I think the impact put him in a pretty good daze." He picked up his hat and gave Prince a sidelong glance. "That was actually... pretty brave of you, Mr. Montgomery. Facing Mr. Manning like that, gun and all. If you hadn't, he might have gotten clean away." He paused, then busied himself with something on his cuff. "I suppose you've got him from here, Miss Gwynne?"

The question caught Cassie off guard. It made her want to deny something, though she didn't know what.

"Oh, I don't—I mean, I'm happy to help, but—"

"Why don't you come with me, Mr. Montgomery," Flora climbed the stairs next to them, smiling broadly at Prince. Which was also confusing. "I'll take you to Dr. Ames and get you cleaned up. There's also something I want to speak to you about."

Cassie watched Flora tuck herself under Prince's good arm and walk him down the stairs, chatting and patting his hand.

What the—

"Miss Gwynne?"

Cassie turned around and found herself facing Hughes's chest. The top two buttons of his shirt had come undone, exposing his collarbone, along with the curve of one of his muscular shoulders underneath.

"I, uh, yes?"

Was he standing unusually close to her? Or did it just feel that way because of the dizzying effect of his cologne? She took a surreptitious inhale.

"You forgot to signal us to come in."

Cassie cringed. She should have known that was coming. "I'm sorry. I got caught up and completely forgot—"

"It's fine."

"It is?" She'd thought he'd be neck-deep in a river of rant by now.

"We each kept a stage door cracked so we could listen for trouble."

"But I thought we decided—"

"*We* decided a good officer always covers his partner. Just in case something goes wrong."

Partner. A smile knocked at Cassie's lips.

"I'm not sure about Jake," Hughes went on, "but I came in when I heard the gun go off the first time. It could have been part of the show, but I didn't want to take any chances. It was so dark, though, and I kept tripping over things—those blamed wing curtains are something evil—it took ages to reach the stage... I arrived just in time to see Mr. Manning shoot at Prince. And you streak after him like a doe being chased by a drunk hunter. I didn't think a human could move that fast."

"Aw, well, I just—"

"But then I saw Mr. Beath haul off. Wow."

Fair.

Hughes tucked his hands behind his back. "What I really wanted to say, though, was, uh..." He looked like he was trying to pass something. "I'm sorry."

Cassie blinked. "Pardon?"

Hughes squirmed and glanced around at the now empty stage. "I'm sorry. For—being cruel. I'll admit, I was angry with you about what happened with Mr. McGregor. But unfairly so. Because if it was anyone's fault, it was mine. I was the one who pushed to go after him."

Cassie regarded him with astonishment. Now that he mentioned it, he was right, technically, but she never thought he'd admit something like that out loud.

"And... I shouldn't have said what I said about the Peanut case. Even with this your—persistent inquisitiveness is the only reason anyone took a harder look at Mr. Gage's death, and I shouldn't have been so quick to dismiss it. Or you."

Cassie's smile finally broke through.

"Hey, now." Perching his hands on his waist, Hughes stepped back and looked down his nose. "I wouldn't take that as an open invitation to—" He stopped, his mouth frozen.

"What?" Cassie looked around. "Is something the..." She trailed off as she followed Hughes's gaze and realized what had caused the train engineer in his head to throw the brake. Her pirate's blouse was in the treasure chest backstage with the burnt lantern, which left her in only her corset. It seemed he'd noticed.

Hopping to, she swept up a fallen Jolly Roger flag and wrapped it around her shoulders.

"Ho, there!" Jake called across the auditorium from where he and Arthur were trying to extract a ragdolling Mr. Manning from the pile of peanuts. "Hughes! Cassie! Anyone want to help us with this guy before he wakes up?"

Hughes's jaw moved in response, but no sound came out. So, Cassie ignored the heat blazing in her own cheeks and re-tossed the edge of the flag over her shoulder like an exquisite wrap. She inclined her head toward the stairs, regal as a pirate queen.

"Shall we?"

20

As waves crashed onto the radiant white beach gleaming in front of her, Cassie scooted to the edge of the blanket she and Flora had laid out at the edge of the island's grassy seaside dunes and stuck her toes in the sand, wiggling them downward until her feet were covered to the ankles. With that accomplished, she leaned back on her elbows to catch the sea breeze passing through and lifted her face toward the sun, tranquil as a lizard.

She sneezed.

"Bless you." Flora winked at her from beneath the long brim of her sunbonnet, an elaborate affair that Metta had trimmed with seashells and trailing twists of violet ribbon. She sprinkled sand over her own buried feet. "I'm glad you're getting the chance to take a breath, finally, after all the bustling around you've been doing the past couple of days, helping get Stuart Manning shipped off to the state prison."

Cassie sneezed again, sending the kitten, who'd just emerged from the picnic basket next to her, scampering toward the water. "Excuse me. Yes, I thought the questions would never end... But I suppose I can't blame them, after our—situation with Mr. McGregor. They wanted to be very certain things were all lined up for the sheriff."

"How are your arms doing? I still can't believe you picked up a flaming lantern like that."

Cassie rubbed her nose. "Surprisingly fine. That salve you gave me must have magic in it."

"You were so daring, facing such a dangerous person alone like that."

"It was worth it. We needed him to confess. And, thankfully, recovering Mr. Manning's prompt book was as helpful as I'd hoped it would be—what he'd said about 'everything' going in there turned out to be very true. Inside were not only Mr. McGregor's missing set drawings, but also many pages of carefully penned accounts showing exactly what money had come into the troupe and where it had gone.

"As we'd feared, very little of it went to charities the way they'd promised it would. Most went straight into Mr. Manning and Mr. Gage's pockets. Then, for the most part, straight back out, to jewelers, clothiers, French restaurants, and gambling halls. It's incredible, given how much they were stealing, how little they managed to save."

She rested her chin on her knees. Down by the water's edge, Jake was showing Metta and Paddy how to drive his sand boat, a wheeled wooden contraption with a sail. They were accompanied by Danger and Roger, who alternated between frolicking in the waves and rolling in the sand in front of the sand boat.

"I see the children have moved on from their pirate-detective inclinations," Cassie said. Neither Metta nor Paddy were wearing an eye patch anymore.

"Yes, they appear to be off the pirate idea for the moment. Which is a relief because even I was getting impatient with Metta for asking for 'cackle fruit' for breakfast then not eating. She hates eggs. But they're still going strong with the detective idea." Flora peeled back the wax paper from a wedge of cheese, then used a knife to shave off a long curl. "Yesterday, they asked Jake if they could come to the jail next week and make 'Bertillon cards' of the inmates."

"What are Bertillon cards?"

"Apparently, there's a man with Sûreté in Paris who claims to have developed a system for classifying criminals based on their body measurements—Mrs. Keene clipped a newspaper article about it. He believes each person's measurements are unique and recommends that police departments keep cards containing such measurements for known criminals, to aid in future identification and apprehension."

Cassie made a face, and Flora shrugged. "At least they're keeping busy."

Jake saw them watching and waved, right before Metta took out his feet with the sand boat. Paddy whooped with laughter.

Flora giggled, too.

"I take it things have improved with Jake?" Cassie asked, tearing off a piece of fresh-baked bread.

Flora intercepted the bread before it reached Cassie's mouth, topped it with marmalade and a curl of cheese, then handed it back. "They have, and thanks to you. You were right. The worst of it came from not speaking frankly with one another, once again. It took a couple of long sessions, but finally he understood I wasn't trying to push him away. It's just that I've worked for everything I have in life, on my own, on my own terms, and I abhor the idea of anyone doing something for me out of obligation, as opposed to care. Especially him. I've seen so many couples robbed of their joy that way."

She studied her hands. "And, as we spoke together, I came to understand about him—and he came to understand about himself, too, perhaps—that he was being so hardheaded because of his wife leaving all those years ago."

Cassie stopped chewing. "His wife *left*? I thought she— passed. I didn't realize."

"That's right. Boarded a train one day with a handsome traveling salesman and left both Jake and Metta behind, without so much as a forwarding address." Flora gazed out at Jake, her eyes soft. "The poor dear. It nearly destroyed him. To this day, he feels it was his fault, that if he had acted differently or better, she might still be here, and Metta might still have her mother... He's wrong, though. I knew them both, and, I assure you, her leaving had everything to do with her, and nothing to do with him. I mean, how could it? Look at him. He's perfect."

Metta took off on the sand boat more suddenly than Jake anticipated, and Jake's hand slipped from the sail, sending him face-first into the sand.

Cassie hid her snort by biting into her snack. "Where are Miss Porter and Mrs. Keene? I'd have thought they would join us today."

"Mrs. Keene had to take care of something but should be here shortly. I doubt we'll see Miss Porter, though. When I stopped in to see her this morning, she was hard at work on ensuring the funds the troupe raised found their way to a proper charity—with Mrs. Reynolds, no less."

"Mrs. Reynolds? I thought they hated each other."

"They've reconciled. Mrs. Reynolds told her she had only been acting the way she had because she'd felt her husband had stopped paying attention to her and she was trying to make him jealous. It turns out Mr. Reynolds thought *she* had stopped paying attention to *him*, hence his own terrible behavior. Including writing Mr. Gage that nasty letter and going after him in the Egmont gentleman's lounge. Well, Mrs. Reynolds was pleased as a peony with that—I think she's planning on having the letter framed—and, declaring herself a new woman, apologized to Miss Porter and offered to help her with the donations.

"It's a good thing, too. It's been a great deal of work. Once Miss Porter selected a charity to receive the donation, she had to visit each of the contributors individually to get their consent, given everything that's come to light about the troupe's problems. Amazingly, though, not a single one asked for their money back.

"And with Prince's help, and Mr. Wilkes's, since he's officially taken over the troupe, she's even managed to negotiate further with Mr. Gilbert and Sir Sullivan's representatives regarding the copyright problem. Given Mr. Gage's demise, Mr. Manning's arrest, and the overall lack of funds associated with either of them or the troupe, they've decided against pursuing a lawsuit, provided the troupe members agree to refrain from the unlicensed use of any of their work going forward."

Cassie clasped her hands together. "How wonderful! About the copyright situation, certainly, but especially about Miss Porter. She did so well with the job we gave her the night of the performance, particularly given her fear of speaking in front of people... Even I believed her enthusiasm when she suggested those changes to the finale. But I was worried that once the show was finally over, she'd be crushed again about Mr. Gage, even knowing what we know about him now."

"She's tougher than you think," Flora said. "When I asked her about it, she was calm. She said, 'I may have been overly hopeful, Flora, but I'm no fool.' She said that when her sweetheart hadn't made it back from the war all those years ago, she'd resigned herself to a different sort of life. So, the attention from Mr. Gage had been 'a nice fantasy, but a fantasy nonetheless.' And she said she'd actually found Mr. Gage's note about her in his prospects book flattering."

"I suppose being referred to as 'a compulsive caretaker' is a pretty high compliment for someone like her. And accurate, too." Cassie tore off another piece of bread and handed it to Flora to dress for her.

"By the way," Flora said as she unscrewed the cap from the marmalade, "she said to thank you for switching out the money in the treasure chest for fake bills. Otherwise, she'd still be in the theater trying to collect the notes that flew out of Mr. Manning's bag when it tore open."

Cassie chuckled. "Paddy and Metta performed disturbingly well for us on that, didn't they, pretending to bump into him backstage and stealing the key, then doing it again to return the key before he realized it was missing. It was a necessary precaution, in case he somehow evaded us. I didn't want to risk those people's money again. Besides, Miss Rutledge insisted we not bring real money onstage. Apparently, that's another gravely unlucky thing to do in the theater. As a matter of fact, I'm surprised Mr. Manning didn't find it suspicious that she didn't object to Miss Porter's suggestion in the first place."

"Yes, it's a good thing he didn't! Oh, here comes Mrs. Keene now, with someone I wanted you to meet."

Cassie unburied her feet and turned around. Mrs. Keene and another woman were walking toward them over the sand dunes, knee-high in fluttering sea oats. The woman, an elegant lady in her later years, wore a dress trimmed by several tiers of extravagant buttons. She looked familiar.

Flora took the woman's hand when they reached the blanket. "Cassie Gwynne, I'd like to introduce Mrs. Angelica Doucet, previously known to you as Madame M."

"Madame M?" Cassie scrambled to her feet. "It's a pleasure to—meet you, Mrs. Doucet. Officially. My goodness, you look well."

The creases around Mrs. Doucet's mouth deepened into a smile. "I realize I seem different to you than before, Miss Gwynne. I'm afraid the privilege of old age has come with its fair share of challenges for me, and I suffer from a condition of the mind that causes me to slip away from myself for periods of time. I've been informed about how you and your aunt took care of me during my latest departure, so thank you."

Flora squeezed the woman's hand. "Thankfully, the pill

bottle I found in her dress led to a special physician in Jacksonville, who was able to tell us who she was and also prepare some medicine that helped bring her back around. Austin Hughes spent an entire day traveling back and forth to retrieve it, as well as tracking down her daughter, who lives in New Orleans. It seems she had run out of her medicine some time ago and wandered out of her home by Egan's Creek, ending up at the Lyceum."

Hughes did all that?

"I spent many of my years as a costumer for theatrical companies, so felt at home there, I think," the woman explained.

"A costumer... Perhaps that explains the button fascination." Cassie recalled their first meeting at the jail.

Mrs. Doucet laughed. The bright, musical peals almost formed a melody. "It's no doubt related. I've always found the variety in buttons intriguing. I collect them."

"What no one's mentioned yet," Mrs. Keene said, "is that Mrs. Doucet also remembers seeing Mr. Manning sawing up that set piece in the theater, even if she didn't fully understand what he was doing at the time. Which is why we were late getting here. She wanted to stop and see the sheriff first. She's also the one who nearly took you out with that backdrop."

Mrs. Doucet pressed a hand to her cheek. "Oh, yes. I am very sorry about that, Miss Gwynne. Usually I simply drift about, singing to myself a bit, but I must have noticed something wrong with the way the ropes were tied—my late husband worked the rigging in a number of productions I was on and taught me a few things—but when I tried to fix it, it slipped."

Cassie jingled the Chinese coin amulet on her wrist. *So, our theater ghost is a sweet old lady. Maybe I don't need this good luck charm anymore.* Then she smiled, remembering one of the lines Mrs. Doucet has recited at the jail: "Better three hours too soon than a minute too late." She had been trying to tell them about her efforts to correct the rigging and prevent an accident.

"I'm so glad you weren't hurt," Mrs. Doucet continued. "I suppose it's a good thing I'll be going to live with my daughter now. Neither of us realized matters had progressed so."

"Where's Lottie, Flora?" Mrs. Keene squatted down and rummaged through the picnic basket. Pushing aside the kitten, who was trying to climb in on top of her hands, she selected a mushroom croquette and took a huge bite.

Cassie picked up the kitten as she prepared to try again. "She's working on the troupe donations with Mrs. Reynolds."

Mrs. Keene spat out her croquette. "Mrs. Reynolds? What a bore. Did you know, she once told me she eats string beans with a spoon 'for the challenge'?"

"Ahoy, maties!" Prince strolled over the dunes. He probably would have waved, or perhaps saluted, but one of his arms was wrapped in a sling, and the other was occupied by the parasol he was holding over Mary Rutledge.

"Good, there they are," Flora said, shaking the sand off her feet. "There was someone else I wanted to introduce you to, too, Cassie."

Cassie looked back at Prince and Mary. There wasn't anyone else with them.

As they stepped off the dunes, Flora ran across the blanket and gave Prince a long hug, making him drop the parasol. Finally, she turned back to Cassie, holding him close.

"Cassie, I'd like you to meet Burt Gwynne. Your brother."

Cassie dropped the cat. Thankfully, kittens are made of rubber, so she bounced off the ground and, releasing mew-tinous complaint, ran off toward where Jake and the children were playing with the sand boat.

"My..."

Brother. It was such a simple word, but she couldn't manage to form it.

Burt, her brother who'd been lost during a storm and presumed dead for twenty years, was alive? And here? And he was *Prince*? Willing her head not to float away over the ocean, she moved her lips a few more times, even getting her jaw to join in once, but she couldn't get any sound to come out. And she couldn't stop looking at Prince. Or Burt, rather.

Burt/Prince looked at her back, his expression neither light-hearted nor serious. "I would have shared this with you earlier, and it wasn't exactly a secret, but it was—not the kind of thing usually brought up in casual conversation. I've been searching for my birth family, in somewhat of an unconventional way.

"It hasn't been great for my career, but, for the last couple of years, I've been taking roles with traveling theatrical troupes purely based on where they're going to perform. Because— Actually, let me back up." He ran a hand through his curls. "After the trial I told you about, for the theater, my mother decided, after all that, to sell the whole thing and retire to Paris. Between the increase in property value and the useful assets the company had acquired over the years, it was worth quite a lot by then, and she felt she could finally live in style.

"While I was packing up our apartment and deciding whether to join her or to take the money she'd given me and start my own venture, I discovered an old letter, dated in the mid-sixties, from a soldier asking about a child he called 'Lefty.' Lefty, it turns out, was me. And that soldier, a former paramour of my mother's, was the one who found me, eventually handing me over to my mother to raise.

"So, I tracked him down. But, due to the effects of injuries he'd sustained in the war, his recollection was poor, and he had little detail for me beyond the fact that he'd found me wandering in the woods of central Florida in the height of wartime. He couldn't remember exactly where, either, and as many people were displaced by the conflict, there was really no telling where I'd come from anyway. Also, though I was older than a toddler, I was injured, and was so disoriented and upset I would hardly speak.

"He said I mentioned something about going to a rail station to fish, which didn't make much sense, but I had seashells and a carved sea animal toy in my pockets, and that made him think I'd come from some seaside place. The problem is, there are many locations around the South that fit that description... So, I started using engagements with traveling theatrical troupes to advance my search. Each place I went, I hired someone to help me review local records and figure out if anyone had reported a child missing who matched my circumstances. I knew it was a long shot. But I wanted to know what had happened to my family, to know, once and for all, whether I really was an orphan or if there was hope for a reunion."

Cassie suddenly understood the list she had found in the box he'd left in Miss Porter's kitchen. And was ashamed. She might as well have broken into his bedroom and read his diary.

"I usually tried to keep my search quiet, if I could. Doing what I do, and being on the road for as long as I have, I've seen, met, and dealt with all types, witnessed the best and worst of humanity. I wondered what I would do if, when I found my family, they turned out to be a bad sort... And, to be completely candid, I have a little bit of money now, from my mother—I didn't want to be taken advantage of."

He placed his hand over Flora's. She was having trouble keeping back her tears. "But I don't have to worry about that anymore." He handed her his handkerchief.

"When I got to Fernandina, I had high hopes. Everything seemed to line up, but my researcher's initial findings were disappointing. Once he started in on things, he told me it was unlikely the city would have kept many records of that type, missing children and such, particularly given that the war was going on at the time and most people had evacuated the island. There were ups and downs as the process continued, in addition to what was going on with Mr. Gage, and the whole process made me feel like a child's bandalore. I'm afraid I wasn't able to control my emotions very well."

That explained the ranging moods.

"Fortunately," Burt said, "the man I'd hired to help with the search for my family had been hired to look into *me* by Miss Hale. A Mr. Charles Hiller. Your friend Mrs. Keene's son-in-law, I'm told."

"So I'm told, too," Mrs. Keene said, picking up another mushroom croquette.

Cassie scraped together the shreds of her ruptured brain. Mr. Hiller must have been the man she'd seen Burt meeting at the Centre Street passenger wharf that night after Mr. Gage's fall. And all those other times he'd been dashing off to secret meetings and couldn't be found. But Flora had been the one who had had Burt "looked into"? That must have been why she'd acted so strangely toward Prince when they first met. Deep down, she had felt something about him and wanted to know why.

"Mr. Hiller has moved on from his work in insurance," Flora said. "He was convinced that each time he sold a fire insurance policy, he was ensuring the structure would burn down. And after helping with the Peanut matter, he realized he was good at finding documents and information, so he thought he'd see if he could make a living from it. I'd say he's off to a wonderful start, even with all the limping around he's been doing with that injured foot... When he looked at everything he was working on, he noticed that his first two clients might in fact be each other's answer. That we might be the family Prince was looking for, and Prince might be the boy our family lost. But it was Miss Rutledge who filled in the final missing pieces."

Mary planted the parasol back in Burt's hand. "When I stopped by Miss Hale's to see you about something before the performance, you were out, but we ladies got to chatting and I noticed a family portrait behind the perfume counter. I said, why, Miss Hale, that little boy with the pretty curls looks just like Prince when he first came to us."

"Miss Rutledge has known Burt for a good long time," Flora said. "Before he joined Mr. Gage's troupe."

"Oh, yes. In fact, I'm the reason he joined. After Roland left, we needed a strong tenor to replace him in the Frederic role, and I thought of Prince. Or Burt, rather. We were still in touch, and I remembered his voice was magnificent. So I asked him. He was reluctant at first, but when I described where we would be performing, he signed on right away."

She tilted the parasol in Burt's hand to reposition it against the sun. "I belonged to the same troupe as his mother, Rosalinda, and was there when she brought him home, you see." Mary leaned her head against Burt's shoulder. "He was very sweet, but so quiet at first. He slept all the time and didn't even speak for several months. We could tell he had been through a great trial, but we didn't know what. Not even Rosalinda, I think.

"She didn't much like to talk about his adoption, though, and to strangers she introduced him as her natural-born son. She worried constantly that, her being unmarried and an actress, too, some mythical 'more proper lady' would come along and take him away from her. But I can't say I entirely blame her. Even today society doesn't think people like us have much of a place in domestic life. That is, unless maybe we marry someone respectable and leave the profession behind... But I digress."

She patted Burt's good arm. "Anyway, when he opened up, goodness did he open up. He was so bright, so curious. Smart as they come—you needed only tell him something once and he'd remember it better than you."

Burt dipped his head shyly, but as he did so, his face passed beyond the edge of the parasol, into the sun. He sneezed thunderously, and Mary and Flora fell back as though from a blast.

"Pardon me," Burt said as they fixed their hats. "Apparently, I get that from my father." He grinned.

Mary blinked. "Anyway, when I told Miss Hale about the belongings Prince—Burt had in his pockets when he was found, she identified the carved turtle as something her brother-in-law might have made for his son, before he was lost."

"It was holding an acorn in its flippers," Flora said. "The sea turtle. Who else would have carved such a thing? Tom used to say that acorns were magical, that if you carried one in your pocket, it would protect you from harm. So, he often incorporated acorns into his figurines, even when it didn't make any sense."

"Acorns are very lucky!" Mary said.

Flora looked up at Burt. "And sea turtles are known for their homing instincts, too. I guess it was good thing to be carrying."

Cassie still hadn't spoken. Her whole body was tingling, and there was something rising in her throat. It wasn't that old, familiar lump of sadness, though, she realized.

It was a bubble of joy.

"I knew I liked you for a reason!" she burst out. Releasing that bubble into the cloudless sky, shimmering and sparkling more brilliantly than any gem, she threw herself into her brother's arms and squeezed him as hard as she dared.

She leaned back. "Say, why did the man who rescued you call you 'Lefty'? You're not left-handed, are you?"

"I have a theory," Flora said. "The shoe we found after he disappeared was the right-footed one. So, when he was rescued, he probably preferred his left foot because that was the shoe he still had on!"

They all laughed.

"Great Juggling Jesus!" came a shout from the beach.

Cassie turned around, her eyes wet with mirth. She gasped.

"Hold on! I'm coming!" Hughes was tearing off his hat and his shirt as he charged into the water, his gaze fixed on something small and white bobbing in the waves. He dove in and after a few strokes, he scooped up whatever it was and held it above his head while he slogged back to shore. Rather than stopping at the waterline, however, he lowered the object, which appeared to be wriggling now, to his chest, grabbed his clothing off the ground, and strode toward Cassie and the others.

He hulked at the edge of the beach blanket, dripping, and held out what he had been carrying.

"I believe this is yours, Miss Gwynne."

The kitten mewed pitifully, her legs dangling from his hands.

"Esy!" Cassie clutched the kitten to her. "What happened? She was just here—"

"Best I could tell, she was stalking a fiddler crab when a wave knocked her over and carried her out. She has a bit to learn about self-preservation."

"I, uh— Thank you. Really." Cassie pulled a towel from her beach bag and wrapped up the kitten, trying not to stare at Hughes's bare chest, shiny and wet from his dip in the ocean.

Hughes dried his face with his shirt. "That's all right. Though, I came out here to monitor the crowds for beach-use violations, not mind pets." He cast a glance by his feet, where Luna the puppy was gazing up at him through the hair flopped over her eyes. "I can't get this one to stop following me."

"Ah, I was wondering where she'd gotten off to." Flora petted Luna's head, but Luna stayed fixed on Hughes.

"I found her up the beach," Hughes said. "She looked so sad —she must have chased after something and lost track of where she was—I gave her some of my sandwich and carried her for a little while so she'd stop crying. Now she won't leave me alone."

"It sounds to me like she's simply a good judge of character," Burt said.

"Sure. Whatever you say." Hughes flashed his eyes at Burt,

then at Cassie, who definitely hadn't been tracing the musculature of Hughes's arms with her eyes.

"By the way," Burt continued, "congratulations on your promotion to deputy sheriff. Well deserved, I might add. Only hours after delivering the murderer-confidence man to the sheriff, you took down a multi-state theft ring. That was good thinking, putting up a bounty to the Egmont staff."

Cassie countered Hughes's frown with a smile, begging her heart to stop pounding. "I agree with my brother. That promotion was a long time in coming. And with Jake putting in his bid for the open coroner position, I think this community will be in great hands."

Hughes's face slacked. "Mr. Montgomery is your—"

"The name is Burt Gwynne, actually. Or also." Burt stuck out his hand. "Pleased to meet you, officially."

Cassie felt her face flush when she saw Hughes pause, the sharpness in his blue eyes suddenly—briefly—soft and bright.

"Uh, yes." Hughes picked up the puppy to get her to stop pawing at his foot and assumed his normal haughty contrapposto. But Cassie knew what she'd seen.

"About the thefts, I thought there had to be someone at the Egmont who knew something—nothing goes totally unnoticed anymore—but there was probably a reason they hadn't come forward. So, I brokered a deal with Mr. Littell to provide a reward, and job immunity, for any staff member who brought me information. And, right away, one of the maids told me that she had been using the hot bath in one of the guest rooms while she knew the guests were out a couple of weeks ago, obviously a firing offense, when she saw someone rifling the bedroom. Once she was sure she wasn't going to lose her job for speaking up, she provided an identification. It turned out to be Percy Brown, one of the bit players in the theatrical troupe."

As he talked, Hughes's accustomed bravado flowed back through him. "Mr. Brown immediately confessed when I confronted him, and turned in his confederates, too—three other troupe actors, by the names of Vera Cook, Theresa Crain, and Ira Hammock. He said he was relieved he'd been caught. The others had always abused him, apparently, and he was glad to serve his time so he could move on from them and pursue an actual acting career.

"The whole thing was Miss Cook's idea, he explained. Since they knew when the chorus members would be in rehearsal, they had a much easier time getting into their hotel rooms undetected. They were after five-cent pieces—certain ones have a Roman numeral 'V' on them not followed by the word 'cents,' meaning they can, with a little plating work, be passed off as five-dollar pieces... They'd been pulling the same scheme all over the South, wherever the troupe went. As I realized from a review of certain newspaper articles." He tipped his head in Cassie's direction.

"It was pretty smart, really, what they were doing. A few missing change purses usually won't attract too much attention from the local authorities. But, unlucky for them, the law enforcement here doesn't let things slide by. And it's a good thing, too, because a couple of them were starting to get greedy, taking more than change purses. They had been stealing and selling off some of the troupe's props, and they even went through Mr. Gage's room after he died and took his valuable watches and jewels, which were worth a small fortune. Mr. Brown showed me where they'd hidden it all."

"I'll bet that shark's tooth you found in Mr. Gage's room was Percy or Ira's, then," Burt said to Cassie.

Hughes frowned. "Again, what's this shark's tooth business?"

"Excuse me." Paddy tugged on Burt's arm. "I think Mr. Jake needs help with the sand boat."

Metta, who was right on his heels, pointed. Jake had somehow managed to get a leg caught in the ropes of the sail, and, despite Danger's determined tugging at his shirttails, he didn't look as though he'd be free of them any time soon.

"Oh, I see." Burt slapped a hand on Hughes's shoulder. "Don't worry, Deputy Hughes and I are on it."

"Speaking of boats, Gwynne," Hughes said as they turned to follow Metta. "I've been meaning to ask. Everyone has been calling that ship in the play a 'schooner,' but it only has one mast. Wouldn't that make it a 'sloop'?"

Burt slapped his thigh. "You're absolutely right! Single mast, single deck. It's scripted as a schooner, but I suppose that detail was overlooked in the design."

"Jibs and spankers!" Metta scrambled along next to them. "Is there still a poop deck?"

Hughes pushed his hair out of his eyes. "And another thing. Isn't Penzance a genteel sort of place? What kind of pirates would come from there? And what's with all the nonsense words and lines? 'He's no orphan and never was', 'She'll be faithful until her wedding day, and even after'..."

"Well, it's meant to be a comical—"

"And what does 'tarantara' mean? Are they belittling the police force? And why..."

The wind carried away their voices.

"It looks like someone's found a new friend," Flora said.

Cassie nodded. "Or more than one." They watched Luna try to climb back into Hughes's arms as he set her down to help Jake.

Flora drew her wrap around herself contentedly. "I'm glad. I've been looking for just the right home for Luna for a while now—I can't keep saving animals unless I let some go on to their new lives. And I think she could help him better survive his mother's upcoming visit."

Cassie abandoned the croquette she'd been about to lift out of the picnic basket. "His mother is coming here?"

"Oh, yes. And she's a very difficult woman. She's been

sending him letters of instructions for weeks. Dress orders, hotel demands, floral inquires... One wouldn't have thought a little pink envelope could have such an effect on a grown man."

A little pink envelope. Cassie laughed out loud, both relieved, she had to admit, and amused. Those letters Hughes had been getting weren't from a sweetheart. They were from his mother. She wondered whether his redoubled intensity about the deputy sheriff promotion lately had to do with her impending visit.

"Jake, too," Flora continued. "She's Jake's aunt. That family relocated to Connecticut during the war, but I remember she used to terrorize them as children, turning the smallest of matters into a competition and pitting them against each other. I think it probably explains something about their relationship to this day."

"I'd say." Cassie was reaching for the picnic basket again, chuckling to herself, when she realized Paddy was still standing next to them. His hands were in the pockets of his sailor suit, and his gaze was on the toes of his little black boots.

"What's the matter, Paddy?"

Paddy slowly pulled a telegram from his pocket but held onto it. "Baba says not to give bad news in the middle of the day. Only at night, when there's time to reflect, or in the morning, when something can be done."

"Paddy, you're speaking in riddles—"

"I'm sorry, Miss Cassie. I peeked when Mrs. Rydell wrote out the message at the post office. That's why I was trying to wait until later, but—" He held out the telegram. "You don't have to tip me."

Not at all comforted by Paddy's dramatic preface and his unprecedented tip forbearance, Cassie accepted the envelope.

"Oh, dear," she said as she started to open it. "It's from my housekeeper, Mrs. Wagner. I told Mr. Renault of my delayed return, but I forgot to tell her. She'll have already started opening up the house—"

She stared at the paper. Mrs. Wagner had indeed gone to the house to start getting things ready for her return—and walked in on a group of rough-looking men tearing it apart. Whether they were stealing or searching, or simply vandalizing, the woman didn't know because one had promptly knocked her unconscious. Thankfully, she hadn't been very hurt, but she'd woken up with a "peculiar" bruise on her face from whatever had been used to strike her—"shaped like two half-moons with tails impaling each other."

Two half-moons with tails impaling each other. That sounded almost like a yin-yang, but wrong. Or, one less delicate might say, bastardized.

The paper slipped from Cassie's fingers.

So much for taking a breath.

A LETTER FROM GENEVIEVE

Dearest reader,

Thank you so much for choosing to read *A Plot Most Perilous*. If my story made you smile, gasp, cry, aw, aha, or laugh out loud at least once, I've done my solemn duty as a writer, and hopefully you'll want to keep up to date with my latest releases—which you can do by simply signing up at the following link:

www.bookouture.com/genevieve-essig

Please be assured, your email address will never be shared, and you can unsubscribe anytime.

As you have already begun to discover, 1880s Fernandina on Amelia Island, Florida, was a special, fascinating place, one far less traveled in literature than the larger Victorian-era American cities so often written about—which is why I wanted to set this series there and bring readers by for a visit. Dubbed the "Newport of the South" and "the Island City" by contemporary travel publications, Fernandina enjoyed its own short but significant Golden Age during these years as not only an important rail and shipping crossroads but also a popular retreat for well-heeled tourists, including members of the Carnegie, Du Pont, and Vanderbilt families. At the same time, Florida, which has always been a bit of an outsider state, and, therefore, a haven for outsiders as well—including at various points in history persecuted monks, British settlers fleeing the Revolutionary War, pirates, escaped slaves, consumptives, and itinerant "cracker cowboys"—still had a touch of the wild about it. And late nineteenth-century Fernandina, a place where the glittering social elite and patrons of rough-and-tumble saloons shared the shade of the same palm trees, was no different.

Therefore, I have invested hundreds of hours into historical research so I could share this place with readers as accurately and authentically as possible. Many characters in the book are inspired by real residents, and the book is filled with places and events inspired by real places and events. There really was a Lyceum building on Centre Street, which could be configured to serve whatever function the community needed at the time, including, but not limited to, theater, ballroom, lecture hall, courthouse, and roller skating rink. It was no stranger to the musical stylings of Mr. Gilbert and Sir Sullivan, either (note that Sullivan was knighted by Queen Victoria in 1883, but Gilbert was not knighted until 1907, by King Edward VII): The hall hosted visiting productions of *H.M.S. Pinafore* in February 1880 and *The Sorcerer* in May 1881 (the latter also being complemented by a juvenile troupe's matinee performance of *Pinafore*). In the summer of 1881, it almost saw a local amateur production of *The Pirates of Penzance* go up as well. But, alas, according to a local news outlet, that production was "indefinitely postponed...on account of the absence of several principal characters."

The Three Star Saloon, the Egmont Hotel, and the Florida House Inn were real places as well—you can stay in the Florida House Inn to this day, and, while the Egmont Hotel and the Three Star Saloon are no longer, you can still view Three Star's three-star façade on Centre Street. There is also a series of cottages displaying woodwork salvaged from the Egmont on Seventh Street. Just head down from Centre and look right as you approach Beech.

In any case, I hope you loved reading *A Plot Most Perilous* as much as I loved creating it. If so, I'd appreciate your writing a review. It's invaluable for me to hear what you think, and it will help new readers discover the book.

I'd also love hearing directly from you. It is one of my greatest joys in life to discuss nerdy things like my books and research, so feel free to reach out and nerd out with me! You can get in touch on my Facebook page, through Twitter, Instagram, or Goodreads, or via my website.

Happy reading, and thank you.

Humbly yours,

Genevieve Essig

genevieveessig.com

facebook.com/essigauthor
twitter.com/essigauthor
instagram.com/essigauthor

A BONUS FOR FOOD LOVERS

If the kitchen creations in this book sent you rummaging for a snack, you'll love this recipe for Miss Porter's Lemon Tea Cakes. Miss Porter serves them to Mr. Gage's theatrical troupe as they gather in her library for an important meeting, and they smell as good as they taste! But take a lesson from Cassie—don't shove an entire one in your mouth at once, unless you're sure no one's about to ask you to speak...

Miss Porter's Lemon Tea Cakes

Makes 15 tea cakes.

Tips:

These American southern-style tea cakes have a soft, cakey texture, unlike English tea cakes, which are typically a yeasted sweet bun. Just as tasty, but very different!

Ingredients:

1 cup unsalted butter, softened
1 tablespoon lemon zest
2 tablespoons lemon juice
1 cup brown sugar
2 eggs + 1 egg yolk
1 teaspoon vanilla
2 teaspoons ground cinnamon
1 teaspoon ground ginger
1/2 teaspoon ground cloves
1/2 teaspoon ground nutmeg
2 teaspoons baking powder
1/2 cup shredded coconut
1/2 teaspoon salt
2 3/4 cups flour
Powdered sugar for dusting

Instructions:

1. These tea cakes take what nineteenth-century bakers like Miss Porter would call a "brisk oven," so preheat your oven to 350°F/180°C.
2. Whisk together the butter, lemon zest, and lemon juice in a large bowl.
3. Whisk the brown sugar into the butter mix until well combined.
4. Whisk in the eggs, egg yolk, vanilla, cinnamon, ginger, cloves, nutmeg, baking powder, coconut, and salt.
5. Stir in the flour until the dough comes together.
6. Form the dough into balls the size of small eggs and arrange on a baking sheet.

7. Bake for 12–14 minutes until the bottoms are golden and the cakes start to firm up.
8. Transfer to a cooling rack.
9. Dust with powdered sugar and enjoy!

Still hungry? See *A Deception Most Deadly*, A Cassie Gwynne Mystery Book 1, for Aunt Flora's Special Stuffed Potatoes recipe featuring asparagus, caramelized onions, oven-roasted garlic, and cheese.

ACKNOWLEDGMENTS

I am grateful every day for the incredible amount of enthusiasm and support I have received, and continue to receive, from family, friends, co-workers, and others during this authorship adventure. Particular thanks go to:

My parents, Fred and Yau-Ping Essig, and my brother, Justin Essig, for loving me unconditionally and for supporting me in my choices and endeavors, even when they fear for me.

My partner, Daniel Alfredson, for being my greatest advocate, and for always having an inspirational rant at the ready to lasso me out of my occasional slips into existential panic.

E. Lynn Grayson, my mentor in law and role model in all things, for making it possible for me to pursue my many different dreams.

Gage Burke of PGB Creative, for lending me his artistic eye and my fictional murder victim his name.

Esy the kitten, my missing piece, my missing peace, who is with Cassie and Flora now.

Musette the kitten, the new fur-keeper of my heart, for sitting on my keyboard whenever it's been too long since I last took a break.

My agent, Dawn Dowdle, for picking me out of the crowd.

My brave Bookouture editor, Kelsie Marsden, for jumping onto this speeding train and taking hold of the controls without batting an eye. Even Cassie would be impressed.

CPSIA information can be obtained
at www.ICGtesting.com
Printed in the USA
JSHW031727220522
26114JS00003B/15